THE ROSEWATER REDEMPTION

PRAISE FOR *ROSEWATER*

"A magnificent tour de force, skilfully written and full of original and disturbing ideas"
Adrian Tchaikovsky, author of *Children of Time*

"A sharply satirical, ingenious thriller about an alien invasion that's disturbingly familiar. Tade Thompson has built a fascinating world that will suck you in and keep you guessing. This book will eat you alive, and you'll like it"
Annalee Newitz

By Tade Thompson

Rosewater
The Rosewater Insurrection
The Rosewater Redemption

TADE THOMPSON

THE ROSEWATER REDEMPTION

www.orbitbooks.net

ORBIT

First published in Great Britain in 2019 by Orbit

1 3 5 7 9 10 8 6 4 2

Copyright © 2019 by Tade Thompson

Excerpt from *Red Moon* by Kim Stanley Robinson
Copyright © 2018 by Kim Stanley Robinson

The moral right of the author has been asserted.

A CIP catalogue record for this book
is available from the British Library.

ISBN 978-0-356-51139-9

Typeset in Sabon by M Rules
Printed and bound in Great Britain by Clays Ltd, Elcograf S.p.A.

Papers used by Orbit are from well-managed forests
and other responsible sources.

Orbit
An imprint of
Little, Brown Book Group
Carmelite House
50 Victoria Embankment
London EC4Y 0DZ

An Hachette UK Company
www.hachette.co.uk

www.orbitbooks.net

To Hunter.
Middle children are the bestest!

Man has no Body distinct from his Soul; for that call'd Body is a portion of Soul discern'd by the five senses.

William Blake,
The Marriage of Heaven and Hell

Prelude to Redemption

Last Days

I am the wrong person to tell this story, but nobody else is willing. The few who have all the facts, or at least more facts than I, have no interest in reliving it. I have no interest in reliving it, but I do want to tell the story, so I will. Some say information, like energy, can never truly be destroyed. I don't know about that, I'm not omniscient. I do know that the edges of my reality are blurring, so I'd better tell this quick.

I am the wrong person to tell this story because I am too close to it and not at all objective. I may even change some facts to make myself more relatable. If you can accept those caveats, then listen: my name is Oyin Da, and I'm here to tell you the beginning and the end.

I've been chased about for most of my adolescence and all of my adult life. The government says I'm dangerous, and I am, if you think ideas are dangerous. A bullet is an idea.

So is a shotgun. At times I wear a djellaba so people can't know what time I am from.

There is a problem with my time travel. Not that it isn't working; it is. What's problematic is the how. The guy who

1

originated the machine, Conrad, he was ... intelligent, but, from what I saw of his writing, deeply psychotic – I mean, what the hell does "hucfarlobes" mean? All Conrad's papers are full of such nonsense words, neologisms and metonyms. No extrapolations by me, my father or the professor could change it into the Lijad. Not to mention the kind of miniaturisation required for my cyborg parts.

We should start. There is no time to waste. And yet I'm wasting time right now. It's not knowing where to start. So much has happened; so much is happening and so much is yet to happen. Rosewater is on the world stage, with the African Union debating what to do with it. It won't be hard – they absorbed all of the Caribbean islands recently. Rosewater will be easy. Except nothing about Rosewater is easy or predictable. Yes, it has free icing sugar, but you pay for the cake. You do.

I am Oyin Da, the improbable, the Bicycle Girl. I am an artist; history is my clay. Follow me closely. There will be turns, sudden shifts of perspective, hurricanes without warning.

I am Oyin Da, the improbable, and these are the last days of Rosewater.

Killing in Rosewater

In 2068, because healing happens all the time now, instead of once a year, it is nigh-on impossible to kill anybody within Rosewater city limits, and my crew of four has been shooting this man for fifteen minutes, reloading, firing right into his brain, trying to destroy it so completely that when it regenerates, the person he was will no longer be, and the aliens can't use the body as a container.

"Wait," I say. "Try a chem charge."

The skull is open, the face obliterated, but even so, it is growing back. Tolu places a charge in the middle cranial fossa and runs for cover. "Fire in the hole."

The blast is muted, but a chemical fire flows everywhere, and I know his brain cannot possibly survive that. We already have his ID chip.

"Come on, before the constables arrive," I say.

They escape their way, and I fade into the xenosphere.

Koriko means Grass

She likes the mornings. She likes to hear the earthworms gently turning in the soil and the birds trying out their songs, and to feel the moistness of morning dew. The sun is just over the horizon and the new brightness causes a surge in all the life forms that surround Alyssa, including the humans and her people, the Homians. She has slept outside again, and from the crystals on her body, tendrils have grown into the soil and branched, covering her with a burst of delicate, branching stems. She yawns and breaks it all off by stretching, then stands.

From here she can see the Yemaja Valley, and the city growing out centrally and the sprawl on the periphery. The boundaries with Nigeria enforced by robot sentries and the tech-jacketed humans of the night shift.

Where the biodome used to be, there is an airport. Adjacent to that, the Honeycomb, where Homians are managed.

This is what she has always wanted – not the human part; her Homian self – a world unblighted by toxins and unbridled industry. There are no foreign drones in the air. The Nigerians have learned to stop sending them, too expensive to keep replacing after the numerous ganglia kept shooting them down.

She is the city and the city is her. Wormwood's nerves run up the walls of every structure, reticulated under the topsoil, in the river. Everything is hers, everything is her.

Thus, she both feels and hears the bang of an explosion. Too far away from her body, but her consciousness moves into thoughtspace – into what the humans call xenosphere.

What do they call me? Koriko, which means grass. They must call me something in order to worship me. I don't know why. I never answer their prayers and I attend only to Homian business, but I hear them all the time. Some of them think of me as the city and call me Rosewater. There is some truth to that, although Wormwood is the reason the city exists in the first place. As I think this, Wormwood stirs, warming thoughts, affirmation of affection, but not for me. It is dreaming of my predecessor, Anthony, of its old, dead avatar. It preferred him, I think. For me there is silence.

It's a playground. Or was. A bomb crater, new, contains dead and damaged human children. Unexploded ordnance from the insurrection bombings, no doubt. The metal of the swings and slides is twisted, hot, smouldering. Sixteen children are wounded, and Alyssa heals them within minutes, before the distressed parents come around.

Alyssa hears prayers, but she does not falter, her resolve untouched. She gives the instructions, and deep beneath the city, Wormwood stirs. The ground shifts and rumbles for the second time, and tendrils break free of the soil. They coil around the five dead children and take them inward, embracing Wormwood's bosom, amid fierce, futile supplications from parents.

Do they not know? Why do they ask? Why do they keep asking? Billions still wait on the Homian moon for an Earth host, and Alyssa-Koriko is their psychopomp.

4

"Look to your own gods," she says to those praying.
She leaves her place of slumber to tend to the five.

Limits

Oyin Da watches Koriko walk away. She has to remind herself
that every problem has a solution, to ward off hopelessness. She
senses the same attitude from Tolu Eleja, who lurks beside her.
Since she and Kaaro rescued him back in '66, Tolu has taken
to the resistance with gusto, untiring, effective against government agents, focused on the main objective, a good soldier.
Unfortunately, Koriko presents a different situation from what
anybody anticipated, and Tolu's skills are not so impressive for
the task at hand.

Tolu says, "She is too powerful and unapologetic."

"I know," says Oyin Da.

"How will we—"

"I don't know," says Oyin Da. "But I want us to test the
limits of her ability. Let's go."

Mafe

The witness tells Aminat that the dead man was always going
to die young.

"His name was Jackson Mafe and he was a fool. I don't care
how patient you are, Jackson could piss you off. He was a bit ...
you know?" The witness points an index finger at his own
temple, then circles the tip while raising his eyebrows. Aminat
nods. Jackson was learning-impaired in some way. *Go on.*

"Six a.m. on Lumumba Road, I'm setting up. I see Mafe
march past, I say hello, he doesn't. I shrug. A few minutes later,

he walks by in the other direction, only he's not walking. He's marching, but not regular marching. What do you call it when you raise a boot really high? When you don't bend the knee?"

Goose-step.

"Yeah, that's right. He was goose-stepping."

Whatever the case, Mafe is stiff and cold now, frozen in the position he fell, wet from the sweet Rosewater morning dew, wearing the clothes people saw him in the day before, face somewhat peaceful, unlined and expressionless. He can't have been dead long. The ghouls haven't claimed him yet, and while stuck there he's become a reanimate. You don't see many of those any more. The Homians are fast to colonise any available body, sometimes mere moments after death. By the time Aminat has finished reviewing witness statements Mafe is a mass of uncoordinated twitching and his eyes are open. It seems to Aminat that his gaze is on her, accusing.

She takes a contingent of detectives aside and orders them to arrest the suspects.

"Why?" says one.

Because that is your job, says Aminat, which provokes laughter in all. This dies when they see her stony face.

Four arrested, one in the middle of a meal of abula, a handful of which he insists on bringing along because "prison food is rot". Despite being handcuffed, he bites off a piece and smiles.

Their ID scan shows multiple errors, as Aminat expects. They have government-issue civilian tags, but also military upgrades due to the war, and ghosted IDs, which the entire criminal class has. Aminat herself has a ghost ID, which she used when she was a fugitive during the insurrection.

Before Aminat arrives at her office, the mayor calls.

"Let 'em go," he says.

Let who go? Aminat plays stupid.

"You know who I'm talking about. I have a lot to do today, and so do you. Stop wasting your time on war heroes."

War heroes? They bullied a vulnerable man to death. They made him—

"Did they shoot a person in cold blood? Stab? Bayonet? Beat?"

No.

"Then release them, Aminat. Jesus."

This was not in the service of a ... business enterprise.

"Good bye, Aminat."

Aminat gives the necessary order, but authorises arthro-drone surveillance off the books, and has the data streamed to her subdermal. She follows all four intermittently all day. The pathologists say Mafe has walked away, not repossessed, just standard reanimate. Koriko must be too busy.

Later, she steals out of her house using the ghost ID Bad Fish made for her. She feels apart from her lover, but in some way thinks there is time to fix the relationship, while also feeling the emotional equivalent of rolling down the side of a mountain just ahead of an avalanche.

Not Really Asleep

Kaaro wakes as soon as Aminat leaves the house, torn from a dream about scraping his cheek against rough-textured adobe plaster, forced conscious by the severing of their psychic link. He does not get up, does not even stir. He knows what comes next. She will be gone for a couple of hours and return sore and bruised, but will not speak of it, and Kaaro will not look inside her mind for the answer.

His phone glows, and at first he thinks it's a message from Aminat, but it's a software update notification for his sub-dermal phone, which he accepts and switches to night mode.

He turns over and goes back to sleep.

Fishy Business

An important part of Bad Fish's world disappears, and he stops his research into non-contiguous network connections to investigate.

He takes off the connection helm and blinks, adjusting his eyes to the light of his workroom. Three Yahoo-yahoos are asleep on the floor in various poses, one with his mouth open. Hanging on the wall is a connection suit Bad Fish is working on – almost finished. He slides to one of his five workstations, missing a leg by inches, then calls up the details in hologram.

Bad Fish has a map of all the ID chips, with people of interest highlighted.

Kaaro is one of the top five; Bad Fish checks him assiduously every day.

Kaaro's ID just disappeared.

This could mean many things. Software error, entering a hardened facility, or even death.

Bad Fish refreshes his system, brings hard focus on Rosewater, but Kaaro does not reappear. He looks for Aminat, and finds her in ghost form. He calls up surveillance and other footage around her ghost, no mean feat since she is cyber-invisible in that form, and there are other crude ghosts around her. The Yahoo-yahoo closest to him farts, and Bad Fish kicks him.

He rubs his chin. Aminat looks to be in the middle of some kind of operation, and to contact her now might compromise things. He could call Kaaro, but the asshole might be part of the operation, even though he is "retired". Bad Fish runs a minute check on his hardware instead, battling unease the whole time.

Bad Smell

I know something is wrong, but I'm not sure what. I sit staring at the wall with pinned information on all the players. My last trip to 2067 felt odd, mostly because I have been to that exact moment before, and I remember it differently from what I saw this time. Is that a problem of memory, or is the machine drifting into other, alternate dimensions?

My eyes ache, and I rub them, then take in the board again. Kaaro. Aminat. Jack Jacques. Hannah Jacques. Alyssa, or Koriko. Taiwo. Femi Alaagomeji. Bad Fish. Wormwood. Rosewater.

A vortex swirls around all of them, the future of humankind in the balance. Perhaps I am the only person who can make sense of what needs to be done and when. I hope.

I rip off all the papers and throw them up in the air, then I gather them, stack them together at random and pin them up in a new order, hoping this will jog something loose, triggering new inspiration.

I bang on the wall twice. My room is like the inside of a water tank, which it probably was at some point. All screens dark; the emanations distract my thinking. A port opens and a hand holds a cup of steaming coffee, my fifth in the last hour alone. I burn my tongue, but barely notice. Something acid churns in my belly – apparently man cannot live on coffee alone. Neither can woman.

I play I. K. Dairo, starting with "Salome", sing along, nod my head.

I think.

Finding You in the Hole You Crawled Into

Dahun, unlike most people, is content.

His house is in Niger, on the Sahara side of the Great Green Wall, where the air is fragrant and the heat is pleasant. The nights are mystical and the ambient voices are in variants of Arabic. On a clear night, he can hear throbbing music from the one dance club, The Disco Inferno. He sits on his veranda, toasts the full moon and reads about the stock market. He doesn't know anything about it, but he aims to become an expert, seeing as he has the cash from the last job. He wonders if he has retired from the contracting business, because he cannot feel any will to put himself behind a machine gun or in harm's way for whatever sum.

He drinks his gin in one swig, pours himself another.

He is unsteady by the time he finishes the bottle, and makes his way to his bedroom. He gets an impulse and decides to take a walk instead, clear his head. It's still early; maybe he'll walk all the way to the village, talk to actual human beings who are not on the other end of electronic media. He puts on a hood – it's weird how cold the desert can be at night. As soon as he's two feet away from his home, the security protocols activate.

He walks down the drive and turns left on the dusty, shrub-lined road. He feels an oddness two seconds before something twists over his mouth, around his throat, and pins his arms to his sides. It's like a python or boa constrictor, organic, muscular, unyielding. Dahun tries to bite, to no avail. He falls to the ground, cursing himself for getting soft, and notices the man who seems to control the snake.

"Caleb Fadahunsi," says the man. "Keep calm. I'm taking you into custody."

The man's outline is odd, even in shadow. He's wearing some kind of hooded jumper and tight dark trousers, but the thing that holds Dahun down seems to extend from the man's right arm, like it's a part of him. He knows Dahun's first name, which means they've done their homework, whoever he works for. Dahun is sensitive about being called Caleb. A car approaches, too convenient to be a coincidence. It's a blacked-out jeep, vaguely military, closing fast. It starts to slow twenty yards away, which is when Dahun's pursuit drone drops a mini missile on it. The man starts, as Dahun does when he realises the car is intact, armoured most likely.

"Do not engage," says the man.

This is unwise, because the drone will start firing in a few seconds. It's keyed to Dahun's ID and will hit everything but him. It has just cleared the roof and races towards them. The man is calm.

"The bullets are armour-piercing," says Dahun. "Just walk away and we'll call it a night." But his words do not make it out unmuffled because of the snake.

The drone is chased by two shadows, and in the full moon Dahun can see that they are flapping. Owls. Cyborg observation owls. They close on the drone, which tries, too late, to compensate and change target. Between them, the owls bring the drone down without making a sound.

The tentacle – and it is a tentacle, not a snake – loosens. The car bounds forward and stops by Dahun's side.

"Get in," says the man.

Dahun stands. "You only caught me because I decided to go for a walk."

The man places his hand over Dahun's head as he steps into the car. "And who do you think put that thought in your head?"

The car is driverless, electric, probably government-issue. The man applies handcuffs and straps Dahun in. Fair-skinned and some kind of grotesque, definitely from Rosewater, which is confusing because the Nigerian government controls the COBs, the Cyborg Observation Beasts, and there's the military car. Dahun parted on good terms with Mayor Jack Jacques at the tail end of the war. Jacques paid generously, and on time. Why would . . .

"Who are you?" asks Dahun.

The man's face remains within the darkness of the hood. The tentacle curls and slaps the seat like Satan's tongue.

"Who do you work for?"

More silence.

"Are you from Rosewater? Are you reconstructed?"

The car hits a bump, and the man rolls against the seat belt. "Stupid."

"What?"

The man inclines his head forward, but the gap in the hoodie makes it seem like a yawning abyss. "You are stupid. But don't worry, it's not just you."

"I don't think—"

"My mother was a lawyer and she used to tell me that every single person arrested in a free, or nominally free, country has the right to remain silent. But do they exercise that right? No. Every fucking time, they have to open their mouths, hey? Like the police are your confessors. I mean, they'd like to be, but they aren't. Everyone wants to tell their story, but in the telling

12

is incrimination. Caleb, shut the fuck up. You have no idea who I am or why I've taken you. Anything you say could help me."

He sounds South African, that weird not-Dutch thing they do with their English.

"Am I under arrest then?"

But the man from South Africa takes his own advice and does not speak.

While You Slept

Kaaro's phone wakes him, unknown number. Aminat's side of the bed is cold.

"You need to come to the prison, Mr Kaaro." It is the voice of a stranger.

"I'm not allowed in government buildings any more. And it's just Kaaro."

"Your restrictions have been lifted for this occasion, and precautions will be taken."

"Yeah, but I don't have to do what you say. I don't work for the government," says Kaaro. "I'm retired."

"Femi Alaagomeji has asked for you, sir."

Kaaro glances at the absence of Aminat, then says, "I'll be there in an hour."

That Bastard Locke

"I'd like to go to Hannah Jacques for a response to that," says the host.

Hannah does not hesitate. "To explain this, I'll give an example that's universal, whether you're in Rosewater or Ojuelegba, Lagos. Take a person, a woman of forty years,

Shakespeare's forty winters. She has a car accident or falls from a height. Either way, she gets a brain injury, a severe one, but she does not die. After a period of intense medical and surgical intervention, she lives, but she is no longer herself. Her personality has changed. Take this same woman, no accident this time, but forty years later, she has Alzheimer's disease. She is no longer the person she was at forty or even fourteen. Now, same person, no accident, no dementia, but she has a stroke and has problems understanding and expressing words. Not like she used to be. I could go on. Schizophrenia? Post-traumatic stress? Dissociative amnesia?"

"You have to answer the question, Ms Jacques," says the host.

"Personhood cannot be limited to a person's memories. We are to believe that in death the reanimates lose their selves, and when resurrected by Wormwood, they are just bodies, biological vessels waiting to be filled by alien presences. It's like a nightmare built by the ghost of John Locke. You've got these stupid but technologically advanced aliens who stored the memories of their people and then *murdered them*. Locke would of course say the memories *are* the people, so each one, stored on a server trillions of light years away, is still alive in that sense. He would also say the reanimates are not alive as they appear to have no memory of their previous lives. The use of reanimate bodies as hosts for Homian dead would be as easy and ethically challenging as putting on clothes from a charity shop. In actual fact, using reanimates is salting the wounds of the bereaved."

The host raises his hand. "I'm afraid I'll have to interrupt you and direct you to the question: do you consider Homian reanimates people?"

"I consider the bodies into which these memories are

inserted to be people. Humanity is not just about memories. Selfhood is embodied, and a reanimated Hannah Jacques is still Hannah Jacques, just like a Hannah Jacques with dementia is still Hannah Jacques."

"Who, then, is a Homian?" asks the host.

"The Homians are all dead from an act of auto-genocide disguised as a desperate gambit for survival. Here's a question for you: when they download their selves into the human vessels, does a copy remain on the server? Then which is the Homian, the copy on the server or the one inside the human body?"

"That's all we have time for. Ladies and gentlemen, Hannah Jacques."

When the applause dies down, and the mics are no longer hot, the host whispers to Hannah, "Your husband isn't going to like this."

"Your eyebrows are inexpertly plucked," she says, and walks away.

Soledad Sister

Femi squints when they come for her. She is usually in darkness for twenty-three hours, solitary, on bread and water, a bucket in the corner being the whole extent of her facilities, with the added humiliation of knowing she is watched from the infrared camera in the ceiling. She stopped counting the days, but she knows she has been in detention without trial for eighteen months or thereabouts. Her periods stopped after the first six months: malnutrition. Every month she gets a physical from an indifferent medic. Every day, in her one hour of sunlight, she checks the state of her sores, her nails, the colour of her skin, just to see how far the vitamin and micronutrient deficiency has

15

progressed. The bread is often mouldy, and she hopes the penicillium species produces low levels of antibiotics and perhaps some useful minerals.

Her mind.

At one point, Femi was sure she had lost her mind, but she has since revised that opinion.

She has not been interrogated, she has not been tortured, she has not been molested. Technically, this kind of detention is seen as torture by the United Nations, but who listens to them any more? The UN descended into infighting once the US left and the UK wasn't strong enough to hold China or Russia in check.

Are you afraid?

No. Sure, they have control over my body, but my mind is stronger than all of theirs put together. I won't break, if that's what you mean.

What about death?

If I die today, I die no more, as the song goes.

I need you to live.

My dear, I do enjoy our talks, but I cannot guarantee my own life right now. Maybe they'll see me talking to thin air and take me to a mental hospital.

I still have a lot to tell you …

If she has to, Femi can take solitary confinement. Not that it would be easy, but she can do it. She has the advantage of knowing exactly what her strengths and weaknesses are, and this bothers other people, because she cannot be flattered and is rarely uncertain or embarrassed. The truth is that she has had an unexpected visitor in the cell, a regular one, and this has made the months more bearable. But her captors do not know that and she imagines them confounded by her calm.

It's not time for her one hour of exercise and fresh air, so she's confused when they come for her. The light is also brighter than she's used to, because this is mid-morning. Usually her hour is in the evening. Perhaps Jack Jacques has grown the stones to order a summary execution? Femi isn't ready to die, but there are many things she has not been ready for, and done when they presented themselves.

They put her in front of a meaningless bureaucrat with pretensions of grandeur, who tells her she is to be freed the next day, but not why. It is an exaggeration to call it freedom, as she is to be in permanent exile from Rosewater.

"I want to speak to Kaaro," she says. "Not on the phone; in the same room. Today."

Taking_Exception

The query is for her name.

"Lora Asiko."

They want to know her age. Options: factual/flippant. Flippant.

"A lady never tells."

Laughter.

Query for her occupation.

"I'm executive assistant to Mayor Jack Jacques."

Query for her favourite food.

"Chocolate ice cream, no sprinkles."

Query for where she was born.

Retrieval error.

"I'm sorry. I didn't quite get that."

Query repeated.

Retrieval error.

#Risk_of_recursive_loop

Guess/lie.

"I was born in Lagos, like the mayor."

Query about why she is anxious.

"I've been away from the mayor too long. He needs me to run his office and his life. I am keen to get back."

Query: square root of 8936.

"94.53."

Query about the meaning of "Mo beru agba".

"Yoruba phrase, literally means 'I fear my elders', but really speaks to a fear of supernatural entities like wizards, wise men and witches. It's also a back-door wish for respect or fear when one grows old, or an entreaty towards good behaviour while one is young so as to have a quiet senescence. I think."

Query about—

#Interrupt.

#There_is_no_further_need_to_answer_queries.

#They_know_you_are_functional_and_operational.

"I no longer wish to answer questions. I wish to leave."

Query—

#Interrupt.

"I'm leaving. Goodbye."

She Knows

I know what Eric is doing. I know the exact strategic value of the mercenary Dahun as a bargaining chip. I had known how much time I would have with Femi, but it still wasn't enough.

"I know too much," I say to the hollow space. My voice seems to leave my mouth and stop a few centimetres in front of my face. "Oooooooohhh! Awwwwwww!"

No echo.
"*The Woman Who Knew Too Much!*"
I get serious and update my board.

Attire

Bad Fish finds Kaaro again. Software update was the problem.
He confirms visually, using the nearest cameras.
What the fuck is he wearing?

Spaceman

Rather than take precautions to isolate him in space, the
prison asks Kaaro to wear a body suit with a visor that lends
the world a faint green tinge. He looks like an astronaut, but
thinks that apart from isolating him from the microbes that
constitute the xenosphere, the suit is meant to disguise him.
It's hot and uncomfortable, especially in the armpits, elbows
and crotch, where the material bunches. He is also sure the
air tank attached to it is old or depleted, because breathing is
an effort and what makes its way into his lungs is not fresh.
He probably should have used the loo before putting it on,
because now he wants to piss. He wonders where they got the
suit from.

Two armed guards lead him through the bowels of the facility, hands at his elbows to keep him steady as the suit makes
him clumsy. At least it means he cannot smell the grime.

He does not see any other prisoners, although at intervals a
guard or two comes out of his peripheral vision to startle him.
There may actually no longer be any prisoners, some used as
vessels for the aliens upon death, some freed after serving as

soldiers in the War of Insurrection. Kaaro was forced to fight in that war, lost friends, learned new abilities, and experimented with homicide.

They finally deposit him in a room, ten feet by ten, single naked unlit bulb hanging from the middle of the ceiling, spider's webs in the corners, wall gecko chilling at a forty-five-degree angle to the horizontal. Yoruba people won't kill a wall gecko because it is believed to protect the integrity of a structure, and if it dies indoors the building may collapse. Two wooden chairs, dusty, arranged side by side, yearning for a table. Kaaro drags one into a face-to-face position and sits. It creaks under his weight.

He doesn't have to wait long for Femi to appear.

She's gaunt, blue jumpsuit hanging off her frame like curtains, short hair, sunken eyes, thong slippers on her feet, not the person he knew eighteen months ago. The guard stays by the door while Femi slouches and sits in the empty chair. No jewellery, no make-up; the beautiful woman she is lies hidden under months of deprivation. She is undefeated, though. The iron in her eyes, the hard gaze, the determination undiminished. Was she tortured?

"What did they ... do?" asks Kaaro.

"Not important. Kaaro ... it's good to see you, albeit through a space suit. How's Aminat? You were my favourite agent, you know that?"

"You don't have to flatter me, Femi."

"I'm not. I wanted more for you, but you were focused on your penis."

"Do you need a lawyer? I can—"

"I do not. Listen, I need you to take that helmet off."

"What? If I do, the xenoforms on my skin will—"

"Form a network in nanoseconds and you'll be in the brains of me and that moron by the door. Yes."

"And that's what you want?"

"I don't remember you being this slow or daft. Pay attention because I don't know how long I'll be free to speak to you. Read my mind, and do it fast. Read everything, or everything you have time for. Go."

Kaaro begins to work off the helmet, counting the seconds before the guard will realise what is happening and either raise the alarm or attempt to stop him. In Kaaro's head –

The earliest hangings were from trees, especially if Jesus came down from the cross and accused you of insubordination when your team loses the last seven finals. The hanged may defecate, and their legs might be smeared by faeces. Dynamic Rosewater athletes dying on rail tracks while trying to outrun trains as training. Geddit? Training? Read the attached paper every day for five years, and watch as your hair turns white and your brain goes to mush. People will come to view your hair. The line will back up out of your garden, down the street, where it will finally cause a traffic jam. An upright neighbour, an acolyte and sycophant-in-chief to the prime minister, will snap and machine-gun them all till they are dead. The neighbour will herself be executed by bouncy castle after due process for defacing number plates on cars parked outside zoos.

– Which does not matter. By the time Kaaro can adjust to his new mindset, he is lying on the floor, handcuffed and held down by shouting people, his cheek losing heat to the floor, dust in his nose, staring at Femi, who is likewise cuffed and staring back at him.

"Don't worry," says Femi.

Kaaro can feel his eyes become heavy with tears.

"It's all right," says Femi.

All this time, this is what has been on her mind? This is what she carries?

"I love you," he says. It's not a romantic gesture or feeling. It's what happens when you fully understand another human being, when you have complete empathy, like with him and Nike Onyemaihe, the only other person he shared brainspace this completely with. It's knowing her history, her flaws, why her flaws exist, her pain, her suffering, her shrunken and hidden heart. It's the love you feel for a sibling or an aunt, the kind that endures and survives adversity bruised but intact.

"I am going to be fine, Kaaro," she says. Yells, really, to be heard above the panicking guards.

"I know," he says.

They drag her out of the room. "I'll be in touch."

I know.

There, Now

Prayers to Koriko offered, borderbots stood down, opposing contingents from Nigeria and Rosewater meet at the north of the city-state boundary. Eric stands above on a gentle rise, providing oversight and overwatch. It's evening, with a blood-red sky in the dwindling light. The tentacle idly loops around his neck and unloops. They are almost fully integrated, he and it, although at times Eric detaches from it, to feel human again, albeit for a few minutes. It scares people off, makes them think he's alien, doesn't matter that the tentacle was crafted by a human.

A van arrives on the Rosewater side, rolls to a stop,

headlights die. The security personnel open the back and a thin Femi Alaagomeji is led out. The tentacle jerks, probably from Eric's surge of anger, and he calms himself. This woman, this resolute, beautiful woman who saved his life, has been incarcerated and he has not been able to get her free until now. Look at what they've done to her. He signals his people to take Dahun to the swap. Some in the agency worried about Eric's plan; after all, Dahun was a mercenary and the mayor has no loyalty to him. Eric thought differently, and was right. It boiled down to the kind of person the mayor values, and how he treats his people, whether they are contractors or not.

Eric has some disquiet this close to Rosewater because he knows Kaaro is in there: Kaaro the gryphon, Kaaro who warned him off the city, and who casually took control of his brain without straining himself. Too powerful to fight, even though the two of them are the last surviving sensitives and should be working together.

Eric stays this distance away from the exchange out of respect. He does not wish to accidentally read Femi's mind.

Six hours later, outside her suite at the Hilton, wearing a bulbous, oversized hoodie to cover his tentacle, he hears the call to enter. Femi is in a purple bathrobe, hair cut even shorter and left natural. She is still bone-thin, but some tension has gone out of her. It should have, with what the government is paying for the place. A colleague of Eric's who has been to prison says it leaves a stink that never quite goes away. That may be true for everybody but Femi. He is also aware that she has a layer of antifungals all over her skin. Nobody trusts sensitives.

"I'm ready to debrief you and catch you up, ma'am," says Eric.

"Not necessary," she says. "Nothing happened except they kept me in a box with no human contact. I don't need support, and I've already caught myself up while I was in the bath. Do you have my orders?"

Eric taps his wrist on hers. By orders she means S45 authorisations and bona fides that were deactivated when she got captured.

"Thank you for coming to get me, Eric," she says. "I won't forget it."

"Yes, ma'am." He almost wonders if he should hug her. Almost. "What are your instructions for me, ma'am?"

"Our goal, Eric, is to save the world from Rosewater. As of now, we must consider the city a beachhead for extraterrestrial invaders. We're the opposing force."

"Do we have the resources?"

"The President has assured me all the resources I need will be coming my way, and the African Union and Association of Caribbean States are hearing closed-session depositions so that a coalition might be formed. But for now, it's just Nigeria."

"Yes, ma'am."

"We also have bedfellows."

"Bedfellows?"

One of the bedroom doors opens and a woman walks out. In contrast to Femi, she is tall, but fleshy, and she has Afro puffs. She raises her hand to shoulder height and gives Eric a weak wave.

"Eric, meet the fugitive Oyin Da."

Chapter One

My earliest memory is of a neighbour's naming ceremony in the village of Arodan. I go with my father and hold his hand all the way through.

You don't just slap a name on a Yoruba child the moment they are born. Names have significance in terms of the destiny of the individual and the alignment with the will of the ancestors. My full name is Oyindamola, although I only go by Oyin Da. It means "sweetness/honey mixed with wealth or well-being"; a good name, one that the Ifa priest said my ancestors favoured. I am not nor have I ever been sweet, but that never bothered my parents.

The ceremony takes place in the courtyard of the baby's parents. There is a dais on which a decorated high table dominates. The parents and the baby sit, while the chairperson, a stout, intense woman called Doyin, holds forth on a microphone. My father points out a stranger just to the left of the dais with a briefcase chained to his left hand. This is a man from the government, the registrar, who has to attend all births and naming ceremonies. In the past people took children to birth registration, but things are different now.

I watch Doyin start things off with an opening prayer. Back in time, this would be an exhortation to ancestors, but with the advent of missionaries, colonialism and American-style fundamentalism, Christian prayers came to dominate in the twentieth and early twenty-first century. The Yoruba recently reverted to the ancestral theme, when the role of fundamentalists in the near-destruction of the world became clear. When stoking apocalyptic events did not lead to Armageddon or the Rapture, Immanentising the Eschaton fell out of fashion, and Christianity became either nominal or fringe.

Doyin pours out spirits to the ancestors, and the naming begins. The child has four names, agreed by everyone to be fortuitous and strong. It is given a taste of the seven flavours of life: water, salt, honey, palm oil, kola nut, bitter nut and pepper. These are just rubbed against the lips of the child, and each comes with a prayer for a long and prosperous life, using puns on the names of the flavours.

After the pepper, the registrar steps forward and opens his briefcase. He takes out a smaller case, like the kind of box you'd have an engagement ring in, and breaks a seal in full view. He hands the box to Doyin who examines it and turns to the crowd.

"I attest that this is not an Ariyo chip." She is referring to the brand of chips so infamous in Nigeria for their dangerous malfunctions that this proclamation has become an accepted part of the ceremony.

She hands it back to the registrar, who has a jet injector ready. He picks out a chip from the box, charges the injector and places it on the neck of the baby. He fires, with that truncated hissing sound, and the crowd bursts into song and laughter. The registrar does not stick around. The baby cries and the mother whips out an engorged breast to feed him.

"Did I have one of those, Daddy?" I ask.

"Yes."

The earliest effort of the Nigerian government to tag all citizens with ID implants was a disaster because the pilot group got toxic chips that poisoned them, first driving them mad with heavy metal, then killing them. Not all, of course, but about seventy per cent, a PR disaster since not everyone was convinced that they wanted to be chipped in the first place. It became a rallying cry for privacy advocates and delayed the ID programme by decades. Now it is a slick machine, with chipping at birth, then repositioning at ten and nineteen.

While my father drops an envelope for the new couple, I examine the baby's neck and spot the red dot where the chip was applied.

"Come on," says my father. "Let's go to the forest."

My father is not typical of Yoruba or Nigerian men. He will die young, but while he is alive, each day is a surprise. For one thing, he has no trade, and that separates him out from the other village men, but when I say he has no trade, I don't mean he is without occupation, I mean he has not settled on any one thing. He has a multitude of skills and from each day to the next he does whatever he wants. He can hunt, butcher, do carpentry, lay bricks, and his natural curiosity leads him to tinker with machines.

After checking the integrity of the traps, we head for the cashew tree and pick up the fallen nuts, piling them into a two-litre tin can. Father digs a hole and sets a fire in it, then we suspend the tin over it, allowing the flames to make contact with the can. In a few moments we both hear the hiss-pop! of the cashews roasting. The fleshy bits we gather in a bucket – it can be caustic in these amounts. Outer casing crisp and black, we crack the nuts free and I do not burn myself once. My father's face is calm, like a pond surface. When I do something with particular verve, he breaks into a smile, but remains quiet.

Later, when we check the traps again, we have two grass-cutters and a bush rat. Father lifts me up, and places me on the bamboo bench. I giggle as he washes my feet. He cuts down fresh bamboo stems, then opens them lengthwise. He skins the animals, then chops them into bite-sized pieces, which he lays into the concavity of a portion of the bamboo stems. He squeezes out the cashew juice into the meat, then adds the nuts and whole wild chillies we picked on the way. He seals the concavity with green bamboo leaves, and repeats the whole process a second time on a different stem. He restarts the fire from before, then places the two bespoke bamboo pots inside.

"What do you want to be when you grow up?" he asks.

"Always right," I say.

He cracks a smile, and may have chuckled briefly. "I don't think your mother could stand being sandwiched between two know-it-alls."

We eat the stewed meat in the bamboo grove out of bamboo bowls, sitting in the bamboo shelter he built. Shadows are longer now, and I sit in the shade of my father's. I smell his sweat and hear his mastication and brief burps. I'm dozing when he lifts me up, and the gentle rocking of his gait on the way home sends me off to sleep.

I wake and turn, realising that we are not at home, but in the workshop, where my father tinkers on a monstrosity. I sleep off before he notices that I am awake.

My mother writes a single sentence of four hundred words in Yoruba and explains to me why it is meaningless. She teaches me that this is the essence of politics: to say much, but mean nothing. My mother is warm-hearted and soft of feature, all curves and roundness, sharp contrast to her incisive brain. She does not have an ID chip. A census-taker tried to berate her for it once and she beat him to death with verbal hypotaxis. Metaphorically, of course.

I don't learn English until I am ten years old. By this time, my father is gone.

I have never seen my parents kiss, although for some reason, for many years I think I have. Later, when I revisit, I realise I have not. Is it just me? Is this the fiction that children who lose their parents create? Or is the past changing in subtle ways?

Arodan, our village, has a single claim to fame: proximity to twelve wind tunnels built to support the abortive Nigerian space programme. When the resources dried up, the workers simply downed tools and walked away. One day the place was a thriving anthill of activity; the next, abandoned. I have been to see the tunnels, screeched inside them, fearful of my own echo. I have been dwarfed by the giant fans, each blade five times my height. I imagine them moving, first slow, then faster than the eye can follow. The tunnels fill with imaginary air and blow my mental self away as though I am a leaf. The spaces look like the belly of a concrete leviathan, dilated from putrefying gases. I am an undigested morsel, standing alone among waste.

"Daddy, tell me about aliens," I say.
"They are green-skinned, and they come from Mars."

"Daddy . . . "

"They have spaceships made of corn husks and superglue. They have to eat a lot of beans."

"Daddy . . . "

"Because theirs is a spaceflight powered by—"

"I'm going to tell Mother that you won't tell me."

"Aliens . . . aliens are only a problem in London, my little heart."

"Have you been to London?"

"I've been to Birmingham, but I know what London is like."

"What is it like?"

"London is like Lagos. It is built on the blood of others and is home to bandits and freebooters."

"And aliens!"

"And aliens."

My father is very strict with discipline in that I don't get away with anything, but immediately after my punishment he is very warm and affectionate.

I deliberately transgress because of this sometimes.

Arodan as a village clutches a gentle hill, then spills down the west side to the plains, stopping at the banks of a river, a nameless tributary of the larger Yemaja. That description makes it seem large, but there is a lot of space between dwellings. This place has been resettled twice, once after a British punitive expedition razed it to the ground for some infraction lost to time, and the other time in 1956 or so, when all the inhabitants were found dead, mauled by carnivorous animals.

There has always been internal pressure to maintain a rural feel. We know each other's families at least. Yes, we all have

ID chips, but there is only a dirt road that links the motorways with Arodan, and though there are a multitude of footpaths, only one road down the hill through the middle of the village. We have some electricity, potable water from boreholes, sewerage, a post office, but that's it. The cinema is a ninety-minute drive away, and nobody ever visits.

Which is why a stranger in town is always news.

Which is why the woman staring at me, a visitor, is both memorable and strange. My first impression of her is of a person completely at peace with herself. You get that sense even before you take in her physical presence, her lean frame, her fair skin, her light-brown eyes, her blue tie-and-dye wrap, which stops just above her breasts, her bare arms and feet. I can't say how old she is. To me, at my level of maturity, there are only four ages: baby, child, adult and old person. She is an adult.

"Oh. You're revising," she says. I may have misheard. It doesn't matter, because she disappears after that. Without drama, no sparkles, no dissolution, just there, then not-there.

I argue the memory with myself sometimes, and even consider that I may have imagined her. Nobody else saw her on that day, and even though I had never seen her before, I could not shake a feeling of familiarity.

This is one of the few things I never told my father.

Priests in red fussing around the smoking ruins of a home destroyed overnight during the thunderstorm; my father and I in the crowd that gathers to watch. It is the quietest crowd you've ever seen; not a soul speaks. I do. I ask who the people in red are.

"Sango priests," says my father. "Lightning struck the

house last night. Sango is the god of thunder, and any dwelling that has been brought down like this must be purified before repair."

"They don't seem to be purifying. They seem to be looking for something."

My father nods. "The thunderstone, the thunderbolt calculus. The process can't begin until they find the lithic manifestation of the lightning."

"I don't understand."

"They're going to find a pretty stone they'll call the thunderstone, then they're going to begin purification rites."

And so they did.

Later that evening, while working on the engine, he tells me they aren't really going to find the thunderstone. They will find an interesting pebble and decide it is the thunderstone. I ask why they still go through the motions. He says there is community cohesion in the old ways. Think of the poor character who has just lost their home and in addition suffers some injury or has a deceased family member. A visit from the god makes them feel special. It makes whoever has to live in the property feel safer. I say, it's fake safety.

"Never underestimate the effect of neurotransmitters," says my father.

A month later he winks as he hands me a thunderstone necklace.

We should talk about the engine.

Chapter Two

I hate to bring the British into this, but it's unavoidable. To understand the future, we need to understand the past, not just as context, but as the seeds of catastrophe.

During the British Empire's halcyon days in Nigeria, a document created from the delirious ramblings of a priest with malaria wound its way to Whitehall. It had two hundred and fifty-six pages.

The writings first found their way into the hands of the Lander brothers, John and Richard, while they were charting the course of the River Niger, and they brought them back to the UK with them in 1831. John took them to the Custom House in Liverpool without reading them. When he joined the patronage of Lord Goderich of the Royal Geographical Society, he brought the papers with him to London and read them one evening when he was sad of heart, missing his brother Richard, who in 1832 had returned to Nigeria, where he would contract the lung inflammation that would ultimately kill him. After reading a third of the papers, John immediately called on Goderich to report what he had found. Goderich took them to Whitehall the next day.

It is unclear what happened exactly, but copies were made. One was sent to the British Museum in Bloomsbury under seal, and this is, sadly, the only extant copy.

The priest's name was Marinementus, and he is a character to whom we shall return, but he died in a rainforest somewhere in the west of Nigeria. This was his first death, I believe. The document was a rather accurate set of prophecies. It predicted the sinking of the steamship *Lexington*, the Opium War, the death of American president William Harrison, the brilliant work of Ada Lovelace on the first computer program – it is said that faint shadows of code are replicated in the prophecy – and the blueprints of a machine that Babbage worked on at some point, the cannibalism of the Donner party, the Irish famine, the cholera outbreak in London, vaccination, air flight, various eclipses, lunar and solar, the two world wars, the loss of colonial power in Africa, and the descent of a meteorite called Wormwood in 2012, after which the prophecies stopped abruptly.

After a year or two of predictions better than Nostradamus' Delphic shit, the British government hired a tight-knit staff to see how the Lander document might benefit the Empire. This tradition led to dire consequences for the village of Arodan, which was mentioned by name in the prophecies.

The writings contained the blueprint for a machine, an engine that ... well, didn't seem to do anything, according to the scientists who pored over it, but there remained the possibility that some context was missing. In 1956, they shipped over a scientist called Conrad, along with soldiers and assorted security types. They spent the first weeks on their bunks with amoebic dysentery, shitting their bowels out. When they recovered from this, they got malaria and several of them died. It's one of the reasons the whites did not wish to visit the interior. They were the first Caucasians my ancestors had seen close up, and they were amused to find that their shit also stank. Literally and metaphorically.

It took two months for Conrad to get healthy enough to start work. He was a tall, skinny, dark-haired, intelligent man with sunken eyes and no appetite for food or wine. He also had no other carnal appetites that anyone could discern, but white men were known to be insane, so this was not commented on as much as it would have been if he were black.

He built prototypes and scribbled notes and built others. He had dynamos set up from various bicycles and had the wheels elevated. Vehicles that went nowhere. Did I mention that white men are insane? The women were more sensible. They often stayed indoors, avoiding the sun that burned and peeled their skin. Conrad fiddled, tinkered and adjusted, to no avail. The machine grew to the size of a house, parts for which he had brought in on rails by box car.

If Whitehall had known what the machine was, they'd have sent a whole battalion of scientists. As it turned out, Conrad really was insane. He was sent home in 1960, when Nigeria became independent from Britain. He was committed to the Hanwell Asylum on Uxbridge Road, released in the 1970s, and subsequently died by suicide.

The machine languished and decayed from neglect for decades, until one day my father came upon the box car that housed it. He never knew Conrad's history and I didn't find out until much later. There was a photograph of Conrad with the boys who rode the dynamo bicycles to nowhere, with "bicycle boys" written in cursive on the back.

Throughout my childhood, until I was eleven, my father

worked on this strange engine. At times we would go to Ilesha or Ibadan to buy spare parts or electronic components. Understand that Rosewater did not exist at this time. Wormwood had obliterated Hyde Park and was hibernating, growing, thriving, but it had not decided to travel in the Earth's crust to Nigeria. None of us in Arodan cared that a meteorite had landed in the heart of London, because it was so far away.

I would come in and sit near my father, "helping". I did my homework, set for me by my father or mother. I could not go to regular schools. For one thing, I was smarter than everybody else, and this kept me apart from my peers. I did not think they were stupid; just unfocused and ... childish. I knew too much to endear me to my teachers, and while I understood the difference between slippers and court shoes, grooming was not my priority.

"She will not marry if she keeps this up," said an elder to my father one day.

"I won't marry," I said. "I'll never leave home; I'll live with my parents for ever."

The elder was scandalised but my father shook with laughter.

I read books, for my father did not trust the electronic words. He said you remembered less when you read off a screen, something to do with using multiple senses like tactile and olfactory when you handled a book. I never got to test his theory.

My father corrected the blueprint of the Great Engine, but when he activated it, nothing happened. Except once. Whenever he failed, we'd go looking for new spark plugs or resistors or brand-new cables. It made no difference. My mother saw it as his hobby and did nothing except check my sestinas and my essays.

I was learning something from my father's work, but I didn't know what.

Anyway. He activated it one day, one time I wasn't there.

Boom.

Explosion.

His body completely obliterated. Nothing to bury.

I refused to believe it. I still do not. I did not attend his funeral and refuse to speak of him to anyone even now.

...

...

What's important is that I inherited his obsession. I had to learn English first, which I did using an English–Yoruba dictionary and a Yoruba bible, both written by Bishop Samuel Ajai Crowther in the 1880s. As you can imagine, it lent my speech a certain archaic affectation. I don't mind, although I think interactions with others have cured me of this.

I figured out what the machine was meant to be, although I had to get a professor of theoretical physics to confirm my ideas before I acted on them.

It was a time–space machine, of course.

Chapter Three

This is Kaaro, the very best of an almost extinct breed of human that can manipulate the alien planet-wide network of linked microorganisms called the xenosphere by some. You know him. He is one of the last sensitives.

Recently, he has been suffering from nosebleeds, and his lover, Aminat, has said she wakes up with the sheets looking like he was murdered in the night. As Rosewater's top cop, she may have murder on the mind. He counters by grasping his morning wood and saying that when he's dead she'll know it because this will be gone. He is unaware that corpses also have erections, and this is not the only thing he is wrong about.

Kaaro is retired. He imagined that he would not have to get out of bed before eleven o'clock, but he can only sleep for four hours on his best days. Some nights, since absorbing the surface memories of his old boss Femi Alaagomeji, he cannot sleep at all. He does not know how she can sleep at night, but he knows why she does the things that make it hard.

He feeds his dog Yaro from a box that is almost empty and scratches the back of the mutt's neck absently.

For the aliens, the xenosphere is the most important

infrastructure. Homians engineered fungus-like organisms, *Ascomycetes xenosphericus*, or xenoforms, and released them into the atmosphere over thousands of years, forming a network. The xenoforms connect to each other and to human nerve endings, from which they can thread their way to the brain, extract information and share it with all the other xenoforms, creating a field of historical and real-time information. The data goes both ways: whoever controls the xenosphere controls thoughts, and thoughts create reality. Through a genetic quirk, some humans can access this field, and even manipulate it. We end up with a universe that is a construct, part sensory information, part memory, part imagination.

The kitchen fades and Kaaro slips into the xenosphere. His guardian, the giant Bolo, scarred from the insurrection, thumps about as he paces the yawning fields of Kaaro's mind. He should heal Bolo. Do the scars represent some aspect of his own mind wounded in the conflict? Jesus, once he was a carefree thief bent on drinking and fucking himself to death. Now he has actual battle scars from a war of conscience.

He has not told Aminat what he is here to do. For one thing, he is not entirely sure he can, or wants to. He is only convinced that he should try.

First he commands Bolo to stand over him. The long braids hang on either side of him and he is now in shadow despite there being no sun in this place. There is no real light and only a cursory adherence to the laws of physics. He doesn't think about it too much.

He expands his awareness to the drop-off, the free xenosphere where the new god, Koriko, gnashes her teeth, seeking the dead to devour into her Homian–Earth pipeline. The floating consciousnesses are still there, representing the people in

Rosewater and beyond, blissfully unaware of their role in the communal dream of humankind. There is no sign of the god, and Kaaro feels safe to attempt what he came for.

Back in the boundaries of his own mind, in a grassy field, he kneels, and, with his bare hands, begins to dig. The soil is soft, loamy, easy to grab to start with, but the silt-clay composition begins to increase. He digs faster, and finds himself in a hole two feet, three feet deep, in a fraction of the time it would have taken if he were in the real world. He digs. The sand he throws out forms a dust cloud that swirls in air currents that do not exist. The hole begins to excavate itself, and Kaaro is caught in a dust devil that swirls faster and faster until he is in a sandstorm. The force lifts him off his feet and flings him out of the hole into the air. Bolo catches hold of his leg and drags him down to the ground.

A hand grasps the lip of the hole, a second hand, and a head emerges.

A woman pulls herself out and stands in front of him, looking up at the giant, to her left, right, then finally at Kaaro. She wears the nightgown he last saw her in.

"Kaaro," she says.

"Welcome back, Nike," says Kaaro.

She examines her hand. "Back to what? I'm dead."

"Yes," says Kaaro. "And you're probably not even you."

Nike Onyemaihe was an older, dying sensitive who Kaaro met in his twenties. At the point of death she emptied all her memories into Kaaro, changing his entire view of life over three days. This was the end of his misspent youth. Well, the beginning of the end.

"Why am I here?"

"Because ... well, good news, Nike. Really good news.

I've ... I'm more experienced than ever. I've honed my ... our gift beyond my previous imaginings. I ... Last year I realised I could possess multiple people as long as they were mindless reanimates. You know what reanimates are?"

"I do not."

"It doesn't matter. You will. The point is, because of a situation we have with some aliens, I know how to bring you back to life. I can take this manifestation of you, of your memories, and load it into a body. You can walk the Earth again, new body, new chances, just like the aliens do."

Nike is silent.

"Errr ... what do you think?"

Her appearance is in the process of changing. She started as an elderly, gaunt woman, but her self-image is transforming to a time when she had no aches and pains, and a straighter back, longer hair. It's not that she's made herself younger, but healthier at her own age.

"It's certainly a noble thought, a noble thing to do. One wonders if you have become altruistic or soft in your old age."

"You should see my belly. Wobbles like jelly."

"I have no doubt. Thank you, but I shall have to pass on your ghoulish offer. I have no wish to live in the body of another."

"Wait, what?"

"I was ready to die when I passed on, Kaaro. It was my time. I lived a full life, not perfect, but full of pleasure and pain. I'm content with what I had. Besides, you forget yourself. I know where we are. There's a reason you shouldn't let people in your mind and have a giant Rasta patrolling. I'm aware, for example, that even you don't know the reason you resurrected me. Would you like me to tell you?"

41

"I—"

"You think it's because there are no more sensitives, and that there should be. The only other survivor, Eric, is the one you drove away. You regret that now, even though it was done in the heat or aftermath of battle. This is what you think."

"I—"

"But the real, deeper reason is that you want another ally in the fight against the Homians because of what you took from Femi Alaagomeji. You are scared, like you've always been. But there is one good thing I see in all of this."

"What's that?"

Her clothes change into a flowing dark gown, and her hair plaits itself into cornrows flat on her scalp. She begins to float in the direction of the drop-off.

"For once, you are not just afraid for yourself, or for your lover. You are actually concerned for the whole of humanity, and that's an improvement in your character that almost makes me want to stay and fight for you. With you. Almost."

She picks up speed, her gown billowing about her, granting her a wraith-like quality, and then she is gone.

Somewhat unsatisfactory.

At least he got some insights into his own motivation. He stands looking out of the kitchen window, the tap-tap-tap of Yaro's wagging tail hitting the floor providing a metronome for the song of pain in his heart. The encounter with Nike twists at the core of him, stirring everything else that isn't working in his life. He is lonely. And afraid.

Outside the property the verdant greens and browns of Koriko's vegetation flow over the walls of other buildings. The wind is fragrant from the flowering plants that surf the static waves of creeper vines. He resolves to pick some for Aminat, hoping that wild flowers will soften her, or at least distract her from her mission, though he knows this is futile.

His palm vibrates; it's Layi, Aminat's brother.

"Big brother! How now?" Layi is perpetually of good cheer. In anyone else his unaffected benevolence would repel Kaaro, but Layi is the real deal and nobody hates him. He channels the xenosphere in a unique way, being a firestarter. Kaaro has been helping him focus and control his abilities, important since certain mishaps have led to houses being burned down.

"Ready for your session?"

43

Chapter Four

Lora stands outside Jack Jacques' door, waiting with the first two of his contingent of bodyguards. They are arguing, the mayor and his wife, an occurrence that is becoming more and more common with each passing week. Lora has a short internal conflict about how to react when the mayor comes out, but he takes this away from her. He emerges too fast, and is already wheeling down the hallway by the time she can move. She falls in behind him, as do the bodyguards, power-walking because the mayor seems to have set the chair speed faster than expected. Lora wishes he had stuck with the prosthesis, but it's his choice. He was the one who got his leg shot off.

"Mr Mayor . . . "

"Welcome back, Lora. How was your vacation?"

"Diverting, sir."

"Excellent, excellent. Is that a new dress?"

Lora has on a summer dress instead of her usual suit. "It's a hot day. I'm trying something out."

She hands him his bracelet, which synchronises with his phone implant after recognising his ID chip. He never takes work home, but the engine of state does not stop running for his family life. The bracelet has eight hours of new information too sensitive to entrust to the air.

"What have I got?" asks the mayor.

"Your head of security is waiting outside your office."

"Aminat? Does she have an appointment?"

"No."

"Why didn't anybody stop her?"

"She's the head of security."

Jacques sighs. "What else?"

"You have to inspect the Homian Resettlement Institute and—"

"Jack!"

Aminat has lost patience and strides towards them. The bodyguards bunch protectively, but the mayor waves his hands. "It's Aminat. Come on. What's the matter with you? She's not here to kill me."

"Don't be too sure," says Aminat.

"You need to call me Mr Mayor in public, Aminat."

"You gave Femi Alaagomeji back to the Nigerians."

"I prefer to think of it as gaining Dahun."

"Why the fuck do we need Dahun?"

"We don't. I just like him." The mayor smiles. Lora has seen him do this before, where he is not amused but uses the smile against an opponent. He wheels past Aminat, to the statues of Orisha that precede his office. All bar one are made of rock. The final one before his door is gleaming metal, a robotic sentry that acts as the final defence for the mayor. It had to activate during the War of Insurrection, but the artist who provided the camouflage is in Nigeria now, so it hasn't been covered in clay.

"What do you want me to do with him?" asks Aminat,

jogging to keep up with the mayor, who deliberately uses the maximum speed on his chair.

"You don't have to do anything with him, Aminat." He sheds his bodyguards outside the office, then transfers to his chair behind the desk. "Maybe use him in the police. Crime is up by thirty per cent this quarter."

"Thirty-two per cent," says Lora.

"Thirty-two per cent," says the mayor.

"But that's your fault," says Aminat.

"How is that?"

"Don't play games with me, Jack. Don't play stupid."

"What?"

"Why didn't you tell me you were going to trade Femi?"

"Didn't Kaaro tell you?" Lora says. "From what I hear, he interrogated her the day before."

"You what?" Aminat looks surprised.

"You need to work on those communication skills, abi?" Jack says.

Aminat seems to square up and Lora feels a self-defence subroutine pushing against her protocols.

"How can I ease your pain?" says the mayor. Again, this is a thing he does, making fun of a person's issue then becoming all reasonable and serious.

Aminat points to Lora. "Ask her to leave. I want to talk to you in private."

"Not a chance. This woman knows more about me than my wife. She stays."

"Fine. I quit."

"No, you don't. Come on, Aminat. You're being petulant. You were never like that. At least sit down."

Aminat sucks her teeth and sits in the chair opposite the

mayor, desk between them. "You asked me to do a job. I cannot do it if you keep interfering, and if you keep information from me."

"The crime rate isn't on you."

"I know. It's on you. You have to let me prosecute your war buddies. I know what they did for us, but they get one free pass for that. They have all used their passes. Now you bring Dahun into the mix, their leader."

"No," says Lora. "Dahun trained them for us. He had his own men. He has no loyalty to—"

"Please stop talking. He said you could listen, but that doesn't mean you have to speak." Aminat swings back to the mayor. "We did not win a war. Instead of freedom from Nigeria, we got taken over by the Homians on one hand and criminal organisations on the other. I need carte blanche."

"Aminat—"

"Carta blanca!"

"All right, Jesus. Fine."

"No more executive pardons?"

"And you have to use Dahun."

"I—"

"Package deal. Take it or leave it."

Aminat seems to think for a second, then she leaves the room.

"That's what you wanted all along," says Lora.

"Yes. She's not wrong about the crime thing. It is my fault, and I do have to stop interfering."

"She didn't know about Kaaro meeting Femi," says Lora.

"No, which is interesting. And you say there's no recording of what transpired between them?"

"None."

"Is it a romantic thing?"

47

"Intelligence suggests he hates her, sir."

"Hmm. Love and hate can be sides of the same coin, and like a coin, they can flip."

"I don't understand."

"Give it time." The mayor checks his correspondence. "What's this church thing?"

"The primate of the Anglican Church in Nigeria says we can't have a bishop in Rosewater after the breakaway, so she instructed the archbishop of the Ibadan province. The archbishop of the Ibadan province, to which Rosewater belongs, is who instructed the bishop of Rosewater cathedral to return to headquarters. Except our bishop refused to leave. *This* letter is asking you to set the bishop free."

"What? But I didn't—"

"I know. The bishop doesn't want to leave his flock."

"He's free to fuck off if he wants to. He knows that, right?"

"Yes. This is propaganda. I'll draft a response stating simply that the bishop is free to leave. I'll leak it to the press as well."

"See if I can attend his service on Sunday. That'll make a good photo op."

"Done."

He squints at the next thing. "I must be ... This has to be a mistake."

"It's not."

"Lora, there's a think tank asking that Rosewater establish a navy."

"Yes."

"We're landlocked."

"I know."

"Is it for our river? Are we to patrol the Yemaja River, first east, then west?"

"There's a report that comes with the letter, sir."

"I'm not reading that. It has a hundred and thirty pages. Did you read it?"

"Yes, and you should read it too, but the bottom line is our imports are coming in on vessels that are being harried by Nigerian troops or customs, or Nigerian-sponsored pirate ships, and that's even before the cargo makes its way in-country to our borders. We'd have a merchant navy and a few gunboats in international waters capable of keeping the vessels safe up to Nigerian ports."

"We're landlocked. It's the appearance of stupidity that bothers me."

"There's precedent. We wouldn't even be the first land-locked African nation to have one. Uganda holds that honour, although you could argue that it is Ethiopia."

"Fine. Turf it to the cabinet. Let them debate it while I read the report, then we'll decide what to do."

"Done."

He reads a few more letters, discarding some, generally whisking through the pile. "Okay, can we go now?"

"There's one more thing not on the pile, but I had no time."

"What?"

"We have a floater problem."

"How so?"

"When … the new god removed the dome and spread the boundary all over the city, she inadvertently released the sur-viving floaters, so they're now in the wild. There have been some attacks on people."

"So we need a special detachment?"

"That would breach the protocol we established with the Homians. We'll have to talk to the god about it."

"That'll be fun."

"I think a useful entry point would be that the floaters have eaten all the raptors. Coat it in environmentalist language, and she might listen."

"*Have* they eaten all the raptors?"

"Yes."

"Wow. Okay, I'll ruminate on what to tell Alyssa."

"They call her Koriko now."

"Noted. Shall we go?"

Before the war, the centre of Rosewater used to be home to a two-hundred-foot-tall biodome, which grew over the giant alien Wormwood. The city grew around the alien, and the old god favoured a dome to keep his domain separate. The new god had no such ideas and made the entire city her domain. The site of the old dome retains its power in human and Homian imagination. There are markers for those who died, the hundreds of people chosen to live with the god in the dome. There is a new airport, and a shopping complex. It turns out many corporations like winners of rebellions and competed to redevelop the bombed-out city.

One of the new structures is not of human origin. The Honeycomb is a complex of hexagonal column cells between sheets of a material the Homians developed. It is the centre of alien existence and the unofficial embassy, which is why it is perpetually picketed.

The mayor's outriders make a path and the main vehicle sails through. In the sealed environment the voices of the protesters cannot be heard, but the placards speak with great eloquence. If you discount the fringe groups, there are two main factions: humans who protest the alien occupation, and humans who want to be aliens. It's a strange thing that the Honeycomb does not accept volunteer humans as Homian hosts.

The car comes to rest outside a reception area where two figures wait. The doors open, disgorging Lora, the two bodyguards and the mayor. The wheelchair transfer is automated. To Lora's mind, the mayor seems to revel in this wheelchair whenever he is with the Homians.

By all standards there should be no difference, physically, between humans and Homians. The bodies are human; the only difference is the mind, the driving software, from Lora's perspective. Yet the two sent to greet the mayor exemplify their otherness. There is a constant, fine tremor to the hands, not marked enough to affect their motor skills or dexterity, but Lora has seen it in all of them. If you talk to a Homian for longer than five minutes, the eyes seem to lose synchrony and drift apart, only to rapidly correct themselves as if they are aware of it. Every last one of them has a mild green tinge to the whites of the eyes, like jaundice. Lora finds it interesting that these changes are not seen in reanimates. Either way, it would not be difficult for any of them to pass as human.

"Mr Mayor," says the second oldest Homian in Rosewater: Lua, the scientist charged with keeping all the billions of Homian minds safe on a moon too many light years away.

"Lua."

They shake hands and go into the closest of the honeycomb cells, which is a cavernous hall with sparse furnishings. The floor is soundless, and even the mayor's wheels are silent. The ceiling is high and there are hangings on the wall, geometric patterns that Lora does not know whether to consider art or a kind of coat of arms. She inhales, but the space is odourless.

They go through a pair of doors and the temperature drops noticeably.

"The first thing that happens, Mr Mayor, is we receive the deceased, whether they are quiescent or in the reanimated state. To the left, you'll see our refrigerators, what you call a morgue. To the right, the antechamber of the reanimates."

"We used to keep them in prison," says the mayor. "How long since you finished this place?"

Lua squints. "It's not finished. The structure is modular. We will continue to expand according to need, and, of course, dependent on your generous donation of land."

Flattery. That's new.

The first transfer of mind patterns from the Homian moon took place in Rosewater prison just after the war, as an act of faith between the mayor and the new god. Lua was part of that batch. Humans took care of the orientation at that time, but the whole operation is Homian-run now.

The contiguous space is vaulted, walls curving to the ceiling, and while there is no stained glass, there is a religious aura. Lua has lowered her voice.

"The intermediary is here. She takes the bodies or reanimates one at a time into the temple."

"You call it that?" asks Lora.

"It's not a religious thing, but some of what happens is akin to worship, I admit. Why?"

"Just curious. You are aware that she is considered a god?"

"And why not? Does she not have power over life and death here?" Lua's voice holds a hint of sarcasm.

"So the brains are just ... downloaded?" The mayor is trying to avoid any incidents. He wants the aliens compliant, in the space that he makes for them, so that they won't create a flashpoint for the humans.

"In a manner of speaking. Each Homian mind is encoded on a server. The constructs that maintain the integrity of data get a signal, then prepare to entangle the mind with a few billion xenocytes. Once that is ready, the transfer occurs in what you call the xenosphere. The uppermost xenocytes of the sphere are in inner space and the intermediary escorts the reborn individual within that psychic space into the body. Then the body wakes. Through here."

They do not get to see much of the temple, or the work the god does, or even the god herself. Instead they are ushered to a recovery area, which is full of beds and a recording of surf. The sound of waves crashing and breaking, with the occasional seagull, is meant to be soothing. Lora doesn't get it, but she learns.

Lua stops and turns. "The rest of the complex is for orientation and education. Physiotherapy, getting them used to their new bodies, language acquisition, social studies, setting them up with a place to stay, that sort of thing."

"And where are the failures?" asks the mayor.

"I don't understand."

The mayor has tented his hands, elbows on the armrests of his chair. "These are largely biological processes. I'm guessing this process works ... ninety-seven per cent of the time? In a bell-curve distribution, if ranked? That means some failures, the ones outside two standard deviations, the transfers that did not go well. Where do you keep them?"

Lua says, "I'll need to consult."

"And that's how I know you're lying."

"No, I need to be sure that I know everything that is going on. Not everything is a conspiracy."

"Oh, everything is, Chief Scientist Lua. There are those who know, those who guess, and those who are oblivious. Go consult. We'll wait."

Sotto voce, Lora says, "This is the real reason we're here."

The mayor nods.

"You knew?"

"I suspected. It's not the fact of it that bothers me. It's the fact that they tried to hide it. I don't like allies who don't come clean."

"Are they?"

"Are they what?"

"Allies?"

Lua returns. "Mr Mayor, there is such a place for failed transfers, but I'm informed it is too dangerous for humans to enter."

"Why? Is it toxic?"

"No, but there's a risk of compromised mental integrity."

"My mental integrity has always been suspect, but I take your point. My executive assistant, Lora Asiko, will go. She's a lot more stable than I."

Lora bends at the waist to speak in the mayor's ear. "Sir, I'm not leaving your side."

"They won't harm me in here, Lora. Don't worry. Just inspect the facility."

"Don't speak to anyone," says Lora.

"I'm not a child," he says, but Lora detects the tone in his voice that suggests a joke.

Lua does not speak, but leads Lora down a side corridor into a room that requires some kind of verification. She is so fast that Lora is sure she was being deceptive before when she feigned ignorance.

There are sixteen people on cots, some strapped down, all attempting to scream at demons unseen. There are staff members trying to comfort the wretches, to no avail. Lora takes a step into the room, but an arm whips around her head and sprays a mist into her nostrils.

"I'm sorry," says Lua's voice. "I can't allow you to remember this."

A self-defence protocol activates, and Lora seizes the arm and throws Lua over her left hip. The chief scientist does not resist, so Lora simply steps on the alien's chest. She looks around to see if anyone else is coming to assault her, but the only noise is from the suffering rejects.

"You think whatever pharmaceutical you sprayed into my nose will kick in soon, and that's why you're relaxed lying on the floor," says Lora. "I know it will not kick in at any time, and that's why I'm relaxed standing on you."

"I don't understand. You should be hallucinating," says Lua, now fidgeting, but the frame of her body is slight, not built for physical conflict, and Lora controls her easily.

"How do we resolve this? Your intention was to deceive me and maybe harm me. Do I kill you now? Do I have you tortured to find out why? You can see how this makes you inherently untrustworthy."

"I underestimated you, Miss Asiko," says Lua.

"No, you didn't estimate me at all," says Lora. She stamps on Lua's head twice, hard, until she is sure the alien is unconscious, then takes her time assessing the room.

Later, after she has briefed the mayor, he decides the patients are Homian business, but resolves to have armed cover the next time he comes into the Honeycomb.

Chapter Five

It's not hard to remember, I don't think; it's just ... well, it's not the same. The past is somehow not what it was when I experienced it, when I lived it. It's like watching a movie ten years later and having a different experience because the you is different. But, no. No, the facts are slightly different, slightly modified, slightly simpler.

At the age of eleven, I am even more isolated from my peers. They think I'm some weird savant who knows everything. I do know a lot, but I am lonely. I don't have playtime because I have no one to play with. My mother, perplexed at my father's obliteration, and never that close to me to begin with, does not know what to do, so she indulges me. She lets me.

My mother is one of those people, the ones you meet and you just know they have steel instead of calcium phosphate in their spine. You don't know of any exploits and you've never heard anything, but there is a look to the eye, an edge to the words, a clarity to the body language. She teaches me how to shoot using my father's rifle. A part of me remembers this as a shotgun, sometimes single-barrelled, sometimes double. She scrapes out targets on the trunk of the iroko tree and I shoot at it. I have the knack. Bisi's father spends a lot of time telling us the tree is sacred, and I think my mother says, "So is my poop," or that may be new past. I spend a lot of my afternoons targeting raptors and I pretty much kill all the ones over Rosewater. Over Arodan, I mean. Rosewater comes later.

I start rebuilding the machine from boredom. I wasn't born smart, but I was socialised to love knowledge and my curiosity is unfettered.

When I am almost done with putting the engine together I lose my nerve and check Nimbus at the post office. I look for professors of theoretical physics and engineers. My English is not good enough to be understood by emails. No. It's good enough for basic conversation, but I have not mastered enough for scientific discourse and I come across like a Yahoo-yahoo boy on cough syrup. I have to go there to physically convince them (no pun) by showing them the plans for the engine.

I find Professor Aloysius Ogene at the University of Lagos, languishing at the Akoka campus. His work on alternate dimensions, quantum realities, wormholes and black holes is competent, although lacking in any real imagination or oomph. He breaks no new ground, but he plods along, abiding, being, an academic determined and destined to be unobtrusive.

I change his destiny; I turn him into a mass murderer.

When he sees the blueprints, he thinks them an artefact in and of themselves, the layers of writing from Conrad to my father to me. I cannot communicate easily, so I coax him away from his comfortable, non-homicidal chair to Arodan, to see the engine. He gasps in its presence, but not because of the complexity of the thing. He sees the pillbox building, the dozens of bicycles embedded in the concrete – from which Oyin Da gets her nickname – the Frankenstein's monster of

Tade Thompson

an engine, the layers of age all as an artefact just like the blueprints.

He makes some notes adjacent to the blueprint – he will not sully such a thing with his handwriting. He has an almost religious reverence for it. He works for hours in the dark, dank building while I take pot shots at cyborg observation hawks. Back then there were no arthro-drones. Miniaturisation keeps improving.

My mother drags Professor Ogene away when it gets dark, and I follow. I am so hungry, I don't even taste the food my mother lays out. I cannot, to this day, remember what it was. Every time I visit there's a different thing on the table.

I sneak out when everyone is asleep and hyenas cry and laugh. I apply all of Professor Ogene's modifications by gaslight. When I activate it ...

One thousand, one hundred and seventy-five. 1,175. The population of Arodan village. In a single moment they are translated into light, and so am I.

We are in the pillbox building, looking out, looking at what I cannot describe. I can tell you that at that moment, I see myself, and I see versions of myself, ghosts, detaching from the main me and floating off into alternate futures. This keeps happening until the original, all used up, begins to fade and is consumed by the divisions.

When you don't look at the passing lights, the colours, the shapes, you can almost forget you are moving through time and space. Almost.

We begin work immediately, budding out from the back of the pillbox and building a new village that is in the perpetual motion of potential existence/non-existence. The first men who try to build in the unlight of eternity all go mad. We start again, slower, because we are blindfolded, and because the best builders went first.

Professor Ogene is blamed for the killing of my entire village, but the Lijad, as we now call it, has different plans. We swing back into the time stream and pick him up. That was when I needed the entire village to travel with. The prof named it the Lijad. I didn't want to call it anything.

I should tell you about one of my selves that separated at the explosion. I follow her, and see the alien, Wormwood, and I see Rosewater, and the biodome it calls home. The biodome is diseased, and being eaten by cherubim. The city itself smokes, its high-rises broken and burning, the people scattered. Arthrodrones swarm like their insect lookalikes, and COBS bob from structure to structure, carrion birds that lase targets for higher-altitude autonomous drones. The smell ... burning crude oil and singed flesh. This is the future.

Even then I knew it was not fixed, not the way I know it now, or the way it is untethered, but I knew I could interfere, make a better future. At twelve I knew this. I still know it now.

I tell my vision to Ogene and he writes it all out, asking questions and clarifying it even more for me. Living in the Lijad is timeless, but Ogene and I find that we cannot go into the future beyond burning Rosewater.

"Maybe we will die there?" I say.

"No. Your mind is fixed. There's more to it than we're seeing."

"We don't even know what this city is. You see no landmarks that you recognise. It's not on Nimbus, I checked. What if it's alien? Not even on Earth at all."

"Then why are you there, Oyin Da?"

I shrug and turn my back on him. That's not the real question. The real question is, where is Ogene in the vision? Where is Arodan? Where are its people? Are they all dead, and do I wander creation alone looking for other life?

When we pick up supplies, we attract desperate people and we take them in.

One day, on a food run, we pick up Kaaro Goodhead. Okay, that's unfair. I should call him what he wishes to be called, which is Kaaro. No surname.

I am in my early twenties and I've never had a boyfriend. There is something lost about him, his nature struggling against himself, or so I thought at the time. He is ... not intelligent. Not hard to look at, and possessed of the charm of borderline bad boys who stay just this side of being delinquent. I do not know whose side he is on, and I am prepared to shoot him with my shotgun.

I don't. I ... fall for him a little bit. Not so much. I mean, I only masturbate to his face a few hundred times, that's all. That stupid face with the feigned ignorance and the ... and ... yes. That face. Once you look past the face, the whole of him falls apart. He loves these stupid designer clothes, pays the mark-up and advertises for the person who made the clothes.

Okay, I fall for him a lot, but I never tell him. He would be insufferable. And, at the time, he was discovering his powers, his ability to read minds. I was with him when the alien came to Nigeria.

Kaaro and I are sent in by the government to make contact with the alien in the hope that we'll win it over to our side, although the meaning of "side" is somewhat ambiguous. Kaaro goes because he is coerced in some way; I go because I'm looking for a place for my people. Understand that this is after the Nigerian government has sent in attack helicopters to kill the alien without success.

The main alien is underground, what we call Wormwood. I know. Biblical. Wormwood has a humanoid proxy, Anthony, a body built from the blueprints of a real human long ago. He interacts with the people scattered around the forest where we found him, healing them, talking to them, generally being benevolent until the second government attack. It had become a settlement with vagrants, malcontents, religious refugees, exiles, women fleeing matrimonial violence, run-aways, and mainstream society's detritus who had found peace around Anthony.

There is a second attack, which starts with a sniper shot, aimed at Anthony. Kaaro, in the most selfless act I have ever seen, dives in the path and takes the bullets.

At that moment I feel stupid. I should have told this boy about my feelings and done something to keep him safe. I have no experience with such things, and now he will die. The settlement's militia return fire around me, but I'm in a fog. Kaaro is on the ground, still breathing, froth bubbling out of his chest wounds and his nostrils. Anthony stares at him, an expression of confusion on his face. The alien seems unconcerned by the gun battle around him, or the flashes of light from within the darkness. There's a keening from the homunculi, smaller pilot-fish aliens who inhabit the woods and are a hivemind.

I am holding Kaaro's hand and trying not to notice the breathing slowing and the skin cooling.

"Did he just sacrifice himself?" asks Anthony. "To save me?"

My cheeks are wet and I cannot bring up words.

"Why would he do that?"

"Does it matter?" I say.

"No." Anthony looks around and takes in the battle around him. "I'm tired of humans running around, trying to exterminate me with their tiny weapons and, as usual, ending up hurting each other. This happened in London too. That's why I left."

I stuff fabric in Kaaro's wounds, trying and failing to keep the blood on the inside. "I need medical attention for this man."

"Oh, right. Step back, please." Anthony crouches, and touches Kaaro. "And try to hold on to something. I'm going to make some changes."

"What do you mean?"

I soon find out. Kaaro's wounds expel their bullets, then close. He starts to breathe, then cough, and the warmth returns. At the same time the ground starts to change: rocks push out, organic tentacles uproot trees and clear space all around us. The settlement gathers closer and a wave of soil, wood and rock radiates outward, stopping the gun blasts short.

"You should leave," says Anthony.

"No, I'm staying, and I'm bringing people with me."

"And him?"

Kaaro is stirring, but not awake.

"I'll talk to him."

Kaaro is tempted, I can tell, but he elects not to stay. It feels like a stone dropping into my heart, which is absurd, but I forgive myself because it was my first crush. I watch the dome form around the settlement, organic sheets that form a wall, the meeting of the walls, first translucent, then opaque. For me it is watching Kaaro disappear. I see him with burned black helicopters behind him, framed in smoke, looking lost.

I signal Professor Ogene and the Lijad takes its final journey into the biodome where we live while the town, then city called Rosewater grows around us.

Chapter Six

ID error. ID error.

Aminat still has the ghost ID activated. She switches her palm implant back on.

ID confirmed.

Welcome, Aminat. Plug into Rosewater Drive?

"Yes, thanks."

Where would you like to go today?

"I've queued the address on the phone. Take it from there."

Thank you.

While the car pulls out of the drive, Aminat ties her hair into a bun, holds it together with one hand, then takes the clip from her lips and secures it. She has a brief sense of déjà vu: herself as a child watching her mother perform the same manoeuvre from the back seat of the family car, Father driving, Layi chained at home. She ruffles her collar, and stares in the mirror, raising her eyebrows and hating her lashes. She has always wanted longer lashes. The car is in the stream of traffic now, turning, modulating its own speed at just under the limit. Aminat keeps an eye out for Kaaro; stupid man went jogging. Not a good idea in Rosewater with the level of street crime.

Why does he think she had treadmills installed? Still, maybe a good thing that she doesn't see him. Kaaro should know better, know that keeping things from her – like his meeting with Femi – will remind her of his indiscretions with Molara in the xenosphere a few years ago.

Would you like commentary on locations?

"Deactivate feature."

Thank you.

The weeders are out, meaning traffic is slow. Ever since the war, the ground has a tendency to be covered with a layer of moss, more like felt, or baize, only alive and quick-growing. Weeders have to scrape the layer off the roads twice a day. They went on strike for two days one time. Rosewater looked like a lost city in an old film.

While the car cuts through traffic – the police, fire and ambulance vehicles are tagged and given preferential treatment by the software – Aminat rehearses what she will say between getting updates by text from her subordinates. She cannot concentrate so she shuts down notifications. A quick sweep of radio yields nothing she would rather listen to. Laps. That's what she should be doing – always makes her head clearer. The car slows into a narrow street.

We have arrived, Aminat. Would you like me to idle or park?

"Idle."

Thank you.

The address is some kind of split-level house. Intelligence that Aminat has seen suggests that this is a step down for the occupant. The door swings ajar just as she is about to knock. Dahun stands three feet into the house, hands in both pockets, barefoot. A wiry, short man, he wears a white shirt, open at the top two buttons, and white casual trousers. Fleshier than when

Aminat knew him. His teeth are almost as white as his apparel. Last year, Kaaro told Aminat that Dahun dreamt every night that his teeth became liquid, like mercury, and flowed out of his mouth, pooling on his bed. For this reason, he scrupulously attended dentists and oral hygienists, paying generously, avoiding sugar, cleaning his teeth with great care before bed.

"You just open your door for anyone?" says Aminat.

"I knew it was you. Kaaro's woman."

"You have it wrong. He is my man."

Dahun nods several times, but in a way that suggests he does not believe her.

Aminat says, "I remember you from the bunker. You left when it got hot."

"The mayor released me." Dahun doesn't bat an eyelid.

"And now you're back because the president won't let you live in Nigeria."

"I'm back because you people kept that witch, Femi. I do not wish to be here, Aminat."

Behind Dahun Aminat spots art on the walls. New, and newly commissioned, from the faint smell of oil. Even before the insurrection, one of the problems of Rosewater has been a lack of history. It has no age. It is new. There are no tales of plucky escaped slaves or invading Arabs. No old art, or monasteries, or Portuguese missions. One of the walls displays a 2D animated children's programme, an action cartoon with lots of laser blasts and shouting heroes.

He sees her watching and smiles. "I like them. They always announce what they're doing. Listen: *Action Hero Activate!* Splendid. Splendid, no?"

"What now? The mayor wants us to get along. I'm to put you to work."

"You can't afford me," says Dahun.

"Then I'll have to take you to the border and drop you off in Nigeria. Is that what you want?" She cannot do this, but Dahun's body language suggests he would rather not be left to the tender mercies of the Nigerian secret police.

"What do you want me to do?" he asks.

"What do you want to do? Because I don't even want you here. On the other hand, the people causing me the most trouble were trained by you."

"I warned the sahib that this would happen," says Dahun. "I hold no responsibility."

Aminat's phone vibrates. "Excuse me," she says, and turns her back on the contractor. It's the car.

Aminat, your police channel reports a gun battle between street thugs and the Rastafarians less than a mile away. I thought you should know.

"Thank you." She looks over her shoulder. "Go put some shoes on. You're coming with me."

The car comes to rest under the gaze of Ras Kimono, patron saint of Nigerian Rastas, staring from twenty feet up, painted on the south wall of the community centre. The chorus of automatic weapons has begun, the conversation oddly courteous, with call and response, the phut-phut-phut of the Rastas' preferred suppressed weapons alternating with the clanging, boastful firepower of the street gang.

The two factions fire at each other across Majek Fashek Road, which has been the Rastas' quarter since the insurrection. There is a police cordon to keep civilians out of harm's way, but as far as Aminat can see, there is no actual incursion planned. Two cars and one van are on fire and pumping black smoke into the sky, one on its side. Incongruously, it is a nice day, clear, cloudless, with a breeze that takes the edge off the midday sun. The buildings on each side are pockmarked with bullet holes, and have windows missing glass. Old-style quadcopter drones hum about, only to be shot down by both sides. Aminat wonders how far down the road the firefight rages; Majek Fashek is a mile, end to end.

Aminat, would you like me to idle or park?

"Park, out of harm's way." Aminat leaves the car, but returns when she notices Dahun hasn't moved. "Come on."

"Why? What do you—"

"I want you to see the mess you created, and to help if possible. If I'm stuck with you, then you're stuck with me. Come on."

"I'm wearing white. Any one of these bloodclaarts will shoot me just for the fun of it, because I'm like a beacon. And I have no armour."

Amina mimics crying. "'I have no armour, I have no armour.' Now you know what it feels like to be a non-combatant with bullets flying around you. Get out of the car and come with me, or I'll shoot you and say it was a ricochet."

There is music blasting from the Rastas' side, percussion- and guitar-heavy unpolished raga from their dance halls.

The officer in charge has no plan yet. He assures Aminat that everything is under control because nobody is dead yet and no RPGs have been fired.

Aminat activates her armour, and the skin-tight fabric changes configuration. One of the constables has gone to search out something for Dahun. "What are they fighting about?"

The Rastas have their own supply of cannabis, pure herb, no adulterants allowed. Skunk is strictly forbidden. Nobody in law enforcement cares about this because they never supply outside their community and it's for religious purposes and therefore protected. According to eyewitnesses, a group of men arrived and talked to a group of Rastas about alternative sources of weed. Altercation ensued. Guns were drawn.

"The word is the visitors are Taiwo's men," says the constable. "So we didn't bother."

"Didn't bother what?"

The constable shrugs. "They ... You can't prosecute Taiwo's men."

"You will apprehend and arrest as your duty requires, Officer."

"Yes, ma'am."

"You have a PA system up?"

"Just about." He hands Aminat an ear-clip mic.

She walks slowly down the middle of the road just outside the line of fire, within quick-sprint distance of the trees. The chorus slows and stops. The drones have picked her up and they can see her badge.

"This ends now," she says. She can hear the reverb, an odd way to hear her own voice. "You drop your weapons now, both sides."

A voice rings out from the Rasta side. "What you want, Babylon?"

Amina recognises the person. She is sad that life has come to this for the Rastas. They are peaceful, although always ready to defend themselves. *We brought violence to them, we brought war and bullets and explosives. And now there are shootouts a few feet from their children's bedrooms.*

"I wan speak to Ras Fanta," says Aminat. "Say im lickle pikiny from las year wan chat to am."

After the insurrection, when Aminat first took the job, she had to come to the Rastas' quarter to either convince them to disarm, or come to an understanding about what would and would not be tolerated. Ras Fanta gave assurances as one who could speak for the community. An elderly greybeard with a youthful glitter in his eye, he was easy to negotiate with and reasonable. He invited Aminat to have a spliff with him. She did.

Now, after a couple of minutes, his voice rings out. "Aminat, is that you?"

"It is, sir," says Aminat.

"Come up, little girl."

"I have an assistant with me," she says.

"Im Babylon?"

"Yes. Like me."

"Nobody like you, lickle girl." He laughs to himself. "No. Just you, Miss Policewoman."

She is in Fanta's front room, without backup. There are two youngsters with twentieth-century shotguns on either side of him, male and female. Aminat spots a resemblance and wonders if they are twins. Fanta is in a commodious robe made of Ankara print, but his protruding hands and forearms are skeletal.

"Grandchildren," he says, waving at the guards. "You want some herb, girl?"

"No thank you, sir. Can we stop the shooting?"

Fanta cups his hand over his left ear. "You hear any shooting? Me no hear no shooting."

"Your people returned fire after being provoked. That's fair. What I am here to ask is that you let me and my officers take them into custody without any ... incidents."

Fanta nods slowly. "You want to arrest Taiwo's men, go right ahead. They'll be out in less than a day, of course. But you tell them this from us: if they come back around here, they will leave in coffins."

"Leave Taiwo to me." Aminat gets up to leave.

"Wait."

"What?"

He nods to his grandson, who leaves the room. He returns with two bound and gagged Rastas.

"Take these with you. They wandered in yesterday, must be lost from the Honeycomb."

Passers. Homians trying to pass for human. Finding themselves in new bodies is a strange experience for the alien mind, and each reacts individually. Some try to act like humans and even convince themselves that they are now human. Strangely, the passers are the worst at mimicking human semiotics, and these two are caricatures of Rastas. Since everyone in the community pretty much knows everyone else, having grown up together, passers who decide to come here are particularly daft.

"I'll make sure they get home," says Aminat.

Downstairs, with the uniforms carting Taiwo's men to holding, Dahun leans against the car, which continually warns him not to, and stares at Aminat throughout the bureaucracy of arrest.

"What?" she asks.

"Nothing," says Dahun. "Is this your job then?"

"This is the job. What? You're too good for it?"

"I work for pay. I've killed people for pay. Believe me when I say there's nothing I'm too good for."

"Fine. Get in the car."

"Where are we—"
"We're going to see Taiwo."

Taiwo Sanni lives in a castle of his own devising, which is to say it looks expensive, but terrible. It's about thirty feet tall, sprawling in that Nigerian I-have-money way, but with no symmetry, and designed by an architect constantly changing their mind. It is an odd assortment of spires, ramparts, cupolas, loopholes and truncated crenellations. Some gables have relief renderings of Taiwo's profile, others are blank. A ten-foot wall encloses the entire abomination, with drones criss-crossing the airspace night and day.

What did he tell Aminat about himself at the end of the war? *It's going to be interesting living in Rosewater from now. I mean, look at me, a free man, all sins forgiven, and a war hero.*

"What is this thing?" asks Dahun. His mouth is open and Aminat has to suppress laughter.

"This is Taiwo's house."

Aminat, would you like me to idle or park?

"Idle, yellow alert, counter-measures on standby." Aminat unclips the seat belt.

"I am coming with you," says Dahun. "I know Taiwo well."

"You mean you used to know him. Before all this." She points in the general direction of the castle. "Don't say anything you don't want him to know. Assume he is listening and recording at all times. Do not start a fight. This is not the time."

"Yes, ma'am."

"I mean it, Dahun."

Drones descend to inspect them and the car, insect-like

71

designs that swarm and buzz like real arthropods. The larger drones stay up high, fifteen feet, and Aminat figures they bear weapons. Dahun tries to wave them away or clap, but they easily avoid his hand.

At the gate, a three-foot-high quadruped construct reads their ID tags. After a minute, a voice comes from its speakers. "Miss Arigbede! The chief of police! It's so nice to see you again."

"My actual title is head of security," says Aminat.

"Of course. Of course. Come in. The construct will show you the way. For your own protection do not draw a weapon. You know how glitchy this old US technology can be."

Aminat's attempts to memorise aspects of the place are thwarted by the winding, descending and ascending corridors, the darkness of the hermetically sealed interior coupled with disorienting blinking from the construct. The central climate control is so cold that she shivers. She checks her phone implant and confirms what she suspected: no signal. The place is obviously shielded.

Taiwo Sanni has changed since Aminat last saw him. He is significantly larger, with a lot of the weight concentrated in his belly. He sits on a broad sofa, seeming to occupy all of it. He smiles like a satisfied god, which he kind of is.

He is also like a museum exhibit. The smart glass has blocked out all the light from the sun, and a single source illuminates him. He takes the paranoia seriously.

"How can I help the fine officers of this fair city?" he asks.

"You have enough business in Rosewater," says Aminat. "Leave the Rastas be. Abo oro." *Half-word.* Good people only need to be told half of good advice; it becomes whole inside them.

"I have no business with or close to the Rastas," says Taiwo.

"That isn't true," says Dahun.

Taiwo slowly turns his head, leaden with meaning. "Yes, Sargy, I do notice you."

"His name isn't—"

"We used to call him Sargy, short for drill sergeant, during the war. He shot some of my soldiers."

Dahun shakes his head. "Those weren't soldiers."

"Okay, I don't care what grudges you both have. Don't fuck with the Rastas, Taiwo. There are children there."

"I don't know anything, but rest assured, Madam Head of Security, if this *were* something done by my employees, there would be discipline. It's not. But if it were . . . "

"Don't make me come back here," says Aminat.

"The construct will see you out, my dear. Give my love to Kaaro. Tell him I'll see him soon."

On the drive back, they are silent for a while, as if each is thinking of what Taiwo means to them.

"How is Kaaro?" asks Dahun.

"Retired," says Aminat.

"Yeah, I haven't heard that before."

"Forget about Kaaro. What I need to know is if you think you can work with us to keep Rosewater safe."

"I don't know."

"You don't know?"

"I have to assess the risks before taking an assignment. I can handle Taiwo's men, but I don't know anything about your aliens."

"Go on Nimbus."

"Too much information. Too much disinformation."

Aminat sighs. "All right. Crash course. There are five basic types you need to know about. They're all from a planet whose name means 'home' in their languages, so we call them Homians. I know, shut up. Homians. Squatters are your basic Homians in a human reanimate body. They tend to stay in the Honeycomb or live quiet if eccentric lives. Passers you've met already. They try to pass as human and integrate. They're not harmful, just irritating. There are sleepers, who are Homians who just seem overwhelmed by it all and spend their time catatonic or asleep, also in the Honeycomb. Synners are the ones you need to be careful of. They love to transgress and they treat humans like they're not real."

"So you arrest them?"

"Sometimes, I guess. I generally have a shoot-first policy with them. They can and do cause harm."

"How do you identify them?"

"You follow the carnage."

"Understood."

"One final bunch you have to know about. The norms. They're actually human."

"What!"

"They're humans pretending to be Homians in human skin. Like Homian wannabes. You'll find them outside the Honeycomb, protesting some motherfucking thing or the other."

Dahun laughs in a way that rings false. "And this is your job? Chasing extraterrestrials and breaking the back of Taiwo's gang?"

"The mayor wants me chasing subversives, seditionists and spies. I'm not allowed to touch Taiwo or his people."

"But you do it anyway?"

"Make up your mind what you want to do, Dahun. I like to know what pieces I have on the board."

She tells the self-drive to take them to headquarters.

Later that night, ID swapped, disguised physically, after she has visited retribution on Taiwo's released men, she thinks she sees a shadow that looks like Dahun. It is nothing when she looks again, so she continues home to Kaaro.

She finds his side of the bed cold these days, and she spoons him.

Chapter Seven

"Hannah," says Jack Jacques.

She holds up her hand, one finger extended, still reading.

"Hannah, I'm going to be late."

"I'm not finished," she says. She adjusts her glasses.

Jack rolls to the bar, takes a shot of whiskey, then pours a half-pint of beer.

"Take out all the statutes. This is not for your cabinet or for a courtroom, this is for lay people. And it makes you seem like you're bloviating."

"I'm not—"

"I know that, but your audience won't." She frowns. "Cut out all the 'I's and change them to 'we's, otherwise it looks like you're trying to profit from it. Your message is that this is not political capital. This is a necessary righting of wrongs."

"All right. Anything else?" asks Jack.

"No. It's ready. Don't perform it, don't sell it. The news is momentous enough on its own. Don't wait for applause or do any kind of victory lap."

Jack drains his tankard and drops it on the counter. "Got it. Kiss for luck?"

Hannah comes over and kisses him on the lips, then rubs off the lipstick.

"Are you going in the chair?" she asks.

"Yes."

"You still don't want a new leg?"

Jack shrugs. "Maybe a prosthesis?"

"Your choice. Koriko can grow you one just as quickly."

"Pass."

"As long as you know what you're doing. You're sure you don't want me by your side?"

"No, we said we wouldn't do that shit, right?"

There is a lot they agreed they would not do, and it hangs heavy in the room, unsaid for now.

Outside the living quarters, Jack is joined by his bodyguards and Lora. It is a short walk to the courtyard, where the press corps awaits. He goes down to them, even though in the past he has spoken from the first-floor walkway. The reconstructed mayor's mansion is less ornate than the original, which was partially destroyed in the insurrection. The administration lived and worked largely underground.

The press do not need to be at the mansion in person, but they come out of some sense of respect or fealty to the history of state press conferences. The approved camera drones hover around each reporter. Some are still chewing the snacks provided by catering, as though they were taken by surprise.

"Thank you for being here today. This will be brief, and we will not take questions. After months of negotiations, debates and hearing from affected individuals and groups, the administration has come to a decision. It shall be the policy of this administration to support the rights of every individual, regardless of declared or undeclared sexuality or gender. Specifically, this will abolish any previous prohibitions of same-sex marriage and adoption, homosexual acts, transvestism, fertility treatment and others not mentioned. An information pack on the new legislation will be sent to your approved phone implants within the next sixty seconds. Let me say here today that homophobia is un-African. We have pantheons of gods of ambiguous gender, and this was not a problem. Let us return to the tolerance that is our tradition."

He closes the folder and removes it from the podium as the courtyard erupts into a hail of simultaneous barked questions. One in particular pierces the din: "Sir, do you have a plan for those who will seek refuge here?"

Jack stops, turns, returns to the podium. "This changes nothing. Rosewater will continue to accept anyone who crosses our borders in good faith. In other words, if you're not a spy, you're welcome here."

Lora tugs at his arm, and they leave.

On the way to his office, Lora keeps up a stream of information about how the announcement tracks on Nimbus. It is an explosion, radiating along fibre optics and wireless pathways around the connected world in minutes. A series of notifications arrive at Jack's phone, which he both anticipated and ignores.

"Sir, the president of Nigeria is trying to reach you," says Lora.

"Is he trying to send me another dick pic?"

"His people say they want a summit."

Of course they do. "Set it up."

One of the bodyguards pushes him to the wall. "Sir, stay behind me."

Mottled, frantic shadows and gasps from the gathered press.

The sky is full of movement, but it is not random. Jack tries to look, but one of the bodyguards encircles him in a bear hug.

"Leave me alone," says Jack.

"Sir—"

"Move or lose a foot." Jack rolls close to the balcony and raises himself up so he can see the sky. Up there, massed, flying in a clockwise circle, is the largest number of floaters he has ever seen. There must be over a hundred of them, swirling, diving, then rejoining the group. The circle sometimes becomes a lemniscate, then an ever-widening spiral, before returning to clockwise motion. It's like a murmuration, like the swallows do.

There are objects hitting the ground, sounding like hail. Floaters are known to shit while in flight, or drop prey they have no further use for, but these are ... machines. These are damaged drones. The skies of Rosewater can be a fierce battleground for ownership. The raptors have already lost and either died or moved to the periphery of the city. The drones usually avoid capture, although there is an acceptable loss rate in single digits every month. Each hits the ground bleeding cash from government coffers, and Jack winces. He settles back into his chair.

"Lora, set up a meeting between me and Koriko," he says.

"Yes, sir," says Lora.

"Have you ever seen anything like this before?" he asks.

"No, sir."

Jack turns to his bodyguard, who shakes his head.

The first meeting of the day is with a solicitor called Emeka Owa. Everything about him screams proper, with his three-piece grey suit, his Malcolm X glasses, his short, tight haircut, his shiny court shoes and his simple wedding band. Jack is seated behind his desk when Owa comes in. Lora stands to the left, still, silent as usual.

"What can I do for you, Mr Owa?" asks Jack.

"Oh, I'm sorry, Mr Mayor, I think there has been some mistake. You see, it is Ms Asiko who I'm primarily here to see. I asked you to be present as you are registered as her next of kin."

Jack turns to Lora, who seems surprised.

"I don't understand. Why would you need to see me?"

Owa turns to her. "You were affiliated with a Mr Walter Oluwole Tanmola. The writer. Is that correct?"

"Yes, we were lovers. What of it?"

"Well, Mr Tanmola is deceased."

"I know this." Lora looks to Jack for guidance, but he shrugs.

"I'll get to the point. You, Ms Lora Asiko, are the sole bene-factor of Mr Tanmola's estate," says Owa.

"He left all his money to her?" says Jack. "He left all his money to you. Huh. That's ... interesting."

"Why would he do this? Does he not have family?" asks Lora.

"No." Owa produces a single sheet of paper from his brief-case and slides it on the table towards Lora. "I will need your bank account details."

"How much will she get?" asks Jack.

Owa hands him a copy of the letter. "This is a preliminary figure. Mr Tanmola's royalties arrive twice a year, so that will be ongoing."

"Sir?" says Lora.

"Lora, you're rich," says Jack. "That scribe bastard. Who

80

would have known that he had this much in him? This calls for bubbly wine."

There is a lot of paperwork to do, and Owa scans Lora's ID chip and checks credentials, but finally he transfers funds and makes an appointment to contact her later. Lora is silent through all of this. When Owa is gone, she stares at Jack.

"What does this mean?" she asks.

Jack laughs. "For one thing, it means I can no longer afford you."

"You're firing me?"

"Lord, no. I just ... You no longer have to work for me."

"Did you think I was working for you because of the money?"

"Of course not. But you have more options now."

"So you thought I was working for you because I had no options?"

"Lora, can we just be happy that you have financial independence? You will probably live for centuries. This means that long after I'm dead, you'll be able to afford whatever life you want."

"I don't want you to be dead."

"Me neither, but it is going to happen, and on that day, you're going to look like this. Go. Visit space. Do something wild."

"But not today."

"But not today. Who's next?"

Chapter Eight

I bang on the metal wall, needing more coffee. The port opens and I reach out for the mug, but nothing happens, so I push my hand further, eyes still on my board. I encounter skin, soft, and whoever it is recoils from unexpected contact, as do I.

I look. Framed in the metal gap is a little girl. She screws up her face because I have poked her in the eye. She has unruly natural hair in a black cloud around her head, no earrings, big eyes that remind me of my own. She could be my sister. She's about ten.

What?

"Who are you?" I say.

"You don't recognise me?" she asks, but looking unconcerned.

"No. Where's my coffee?"

The girl turns her face to the side and yells, "MUM! Mum, she can't remember me any more, and she's asking for more coffee."

"What's going on here?" I ask, but she just shakes her head and puts a finger to her lips. She doesn't even look at me. A hand pushes her head away and a woman takes her place.

"I know you," I say. "You're the woman who visited Arodan that time. You disappeared."

"Oh dear. Is that all you remember?" She seems amused and serious at the same time.

I am awash with a feeling of unfamiliarity. The room, the chart on the wall, the empty mugs of coffee, some on their sides, even my own body, all seem ... contaminated and unreal.

The voice of the girl punches in. "Let me see, Mummy."

"Shush! This is not a game." To me, gently, the woman says, "Where do you think you are?"

"I ... This is my workspace."

"Yes, but where is that workspace? And when do you think this is?"

I don't know the answers to any of those questions, and it's as if I never thought to ask myself before.

"Oyin Da, do you remember going in there?" asks the woman.

"I don't." I'm feeling some anxiety and it affects the pitch of my voice.

"All right, farabale. I want you to come out of there." She speaks in a calm, reasonable voice, and I do find her comforting, but.

There is no door here. I'm in a metal container with a single port, and frame bars travelling up to a ceiling. There are screens and key holograms and devices that I thought made sense but that now seem nonsensical conglomerations of wires.

Why would I seal myself in here? Did someone else do this? Is it to protect me or lock me away from others? I probably should not be too hasty about coming out, even if I knew how.

"I can't come out," I say, but it sounds weak, like a lie.

"Oh, for the love of ... Stand back," says the woman. She looks behind her. "You too, darling."

Four fingers appear against the lip of the port and she pulls.

The metal screams and rends. I press myself into the far wall. What manner of woman is this? The tear extends downwards and sunlight pushes into my workroom. She bends the flap outwards, then pulls the other side, tearing a crude opening for me. Beyond her, I see the kid. They are standing on black volcanic rock.

"Come on. Ma'a bo. Jade n'beyen." Come out of there.

"Who are you people?" I ask, not budging from the safe place.

"I'm Nike. This is Junior."

Junior waves.

"Are we ... are we related?" I ask.

Nike and Junior exchange glances. "Yes, you might say that," says Nike.

"Come out," says Junior.

Because she looks like me, I trust her and I step out.

We're on a plateau, maybe in Jos? I look back at the structure I've been ensconced in; what looks like an eight-foot-high metallic bubble constructed from scrap. Plates, strips of street lamps, car doors, gold ingots, ball bearings, a chain-link fence and other bits I cannot recognise. The sky is cloudy in a dense, uniform way, and it is windy, but not cold. There are mountains here and there, close and distant, but not snow-capped.

"Before you ask, this was your choice. You chose to be here," says Nike. She and Junior are holding hands. "Do you want to go home?"

"How can you tear metal, Nike? Who are we to each other?"

The two of them step towards me. "That was not metal, honey, and this is your daughter. As for me, I am your wife."

*

Walking through the rocky landscape, I think that this family thing, this has happened before. A wife forgets her husband and daughter because she is no longer the thing they think she is. She is a god. Alyssa to Koriko. I remember this, but have somehow forgotten to anchor myself when travelling in time.

"Don't worry," says Nike. "This has happened before."

"Many times," says Junior. "It's boring now."

"Junior."

"It is."

Nike, at the front, shakes her head. "She takes after you, you know?"

"We're going home. Whenever you get infused with this heroism, you brood for a while, and then you isolate yourself, and then ... well, you build a big metal nest and wall yourself in."

"What heroism thing?"

"You're trying to save the world," says Junior. She is casual in her speech and her footing.

There is a descent to the footpath, and a drop-off to the right, a sheer wall of rock leading up into heaven on the left. We have no climbing gear or breathing apparatus. Given the clouds ...

"This is impossible. We should have equipment for this climb at this altitude," I say.

"We're not at altitude," says Nike.

"If we take you home too quickly, you get ... funny," says Junior. "Funny mummy."

"We're here," says Nike. Her voice changes in timbre. It's subtle, but I pick it up.

We have stopped at a metal door set in the rock face. No hinges, no handle, just a rusted surface. I touch it. Warm.

"You have to go in there," says Junior. She actually yawns as she squats, her back against the rock.

"We'll be with you," says Nike. "But you have to go first, my love."

She kisses me on the head and lifts my right hand and pushes against the door, which gives slightly. I complete the push and the door falls into black space. I follow.

The blackness turns into Arodan at night. I know when I am too. This is just after the engine exploded.

I am in the centre of death. The air is full of ozone and the smoke smells like burned rubber. Bodies surround me, some charred, some untouched. In the periphery, dozens of COBs: hawks mostly, but pigeons too. They are dead and inactive. I start when Nike touches me. She points. I see the body of a young girl, Junior's age, burned, but with an unmistakable necklace, a thunderstone set in a gold pendant. I finger my own neck, and the necklace is there with an identical stone, identical setting, identical chain.

"Am I ... dead?" I look to Nike.

She has a pained expression on her face. "No. She is dead. As for you ... It's more like you have never really been alive."

"Are you saying I'm some kind of mimic? A doppelgänger?"

"No. You, me, Junior, none of us have ever been alive. We are ghosts in the xenosphere, repetitive information patterns."

"How can that be? I have ... I took these people in ... What about the Lijad? I have touched people. I have smelled things. I can still smell them right now."

Government vehicles arrive and troops begin to take bodies away, and bury others.

I begin to remember, though.

"This is the point, the time of your birth. From what I can

tell, you have a powerful will to exist. You are the most powerful xenosphere ghost I have ever seen. You being oblivious added an extra dimension. Did you know that solid objects are mostly empty space? Through the xenosphere you can manipulate people's perceptions and make them sense you — hear, touch, taste, smell and see. You, Oyin Da, do it without thinking."

I don't know why I'm hyperventilating. If what Nike says is true, I don't have lungs, I'm just echoing the idea of overbreathing. "I'm not real."

"I didn't say you weren't real. I said you weren't alive. There's a difference."

I know her at that moment. "You are what I was seeing in Kaaro, aren't you?"

"Oh, honey."

When we kiss, my entire body remembers hers. My mouth and tongue respond from muscle memory.

Circling us playfully, Junior gags. "Can we go home now?"

It all comes back to me.

The xenosphere is a thoughtspace connecting all humans to each other by way of alien bioengineered neurones in the atmosphere. The aliens use it to store the entire history of mankind, including the biological history, with contextual feelings, everything. Some alien consciousnesses are in there as well as some copies of personalities of dead humans. Ghosts. Like me.

The problem of the data is the problem of memory. Things remembered are revised. Memory is changed by the living, and without regular error correction, events drift. The general shape may seem to be the same, but the details shift. False memories can be implanted and disseminated. And this is why travelling back in time is so hazardous. That same autocorrection facility can and does erase my memories. Well, no, it erases my recall. Not the same thing.

All that time when I thought I was in a craft called the Lijad, I was swimming in the xenosphere, travelling back and forth in time, seeing companions which were quasi-ghosts, having conversations with my memories of the people of Arodan. I was in supreme denial. Maybe the pain was too much for me.

Human consciousness time-travels all the time, albeit at a low level. Sensory input that arrives in the brain can have multiple interpretations, and the brain has to choose a "reality", which takes about half a second. Once it has chosen, it does a temporal shift of awareness back to the moment of sensory perception. I do this same thing on a larger scale in the xenosphere, which, among other things, is a vast data storage of human sensations.

Home is a house made of bamboo, alone in a clearing surrounded by palm trees. I am sitting on the veranda watching Junior leap from rock to rock. She is nimble and fearless, like a goat. The light is from everywhere, and bright. There is no sun. The sky is violet and cloudless. We lack for nothing because we do not need anything.

"What's the actual year, like now?" I ask Nike, who is beside me.

"2068."

"And the aliens are still embedded?"

"Yes."

"Can we do the future?"

"The future hasn't happened. To go there is extrapolation. You have done this, and it sent you scurrying back to the past to give warnings to your favoured humans."

"Kaaro?"

"Yes. And Jack Jacques."

"I remember some of that. I didn't do anything. I told Jacques to wait. I don't remember what I did with Kaaro."

"Do you remember what you saw that made you tell him to wait?"

A vision of Rosewater in flames, razed by Nigerian automatons, children, elderly, infirm, all liquidated, the biodome pulsing with the dark energy of its death throes as it is choked by an extraterrestrial vine. Wormwood dead, the dream of a city of the future gone.

"Surrender didn't go well for Jacques," I say. "Or for the rest of the city."

Nike looks out at Junior. I see a smile form around her mouth. "You intervened with Kaaro. You said if the mercenaries entered his house he would have died in a friendly-fire incident."

"Really? I don't remember that," I lie. "But it turned out all right?"

"He killed six innocents."

"Mercenaries aren't innocent."

"They were innocent of trying to kill Kaaro."

"Have we had this argument before?" I ask. "Because it feels like we have."

Nike waves to Junior, who waves back. "Are you going to continue this crusade?"

"I don't think the aliens are good for humanity, Nike."

"But we're not human, honey. We are human patterns, but we're stored in and maintained by an alien organic infrastructure. Among other things, the xenosphere is a data server, in which we live, and where we can interact with human consciousnesses if we choose to. I suppose it's normal to be loyal to your origins, but you have a particular difficulty letting go, which is why we have this recursive argument every time you go gallivanting."

"You think I'm wrong to do this, to help free Earth."

"I don't care about that. I have perspectives on life. I was a sex worker. We're pragmatic. You have not thought of everything. You only think you have."

I lean forward. "What have I not thought of?"

"That destroying the aliens might mean destroying the xenosphere. Which means Junior and me and the love that we have will be gone if you succeed."

I have no answer to that, but this is just another problem to solve. How to save the world from aliens, yet keep their infrastructure.

"You know, after the British left, we kept the trains," I say, mischief in my voice.

"You always say that." Nike rises and walks into the house, but I don't hear her footsteps. I do hear her yell at Junior to come in if she doesn't want monsters to get her.

I stay outside and yearn for my metal nest.

Chapter Nine

Mufutau Ogbe lives with four other people in a single room so tiny they can't afford to have furniture because it takes up too much space. It goes without saying that they don't have any money.

Mufutau came to Rosewater in '66 with unbridled Burkitt lymphoma. One of his eyes was twice the size of the other. His face was asymmetrical, with a swelling from his cheek bulging out. Mucus dribbled from his nostrils incessantly and people shunned him. He got no education, and no training for a vocation. As a burden on his parents, he was abandoned with a herbalist who said he could cure him where chemotherapy had failed. After the Opening of '67, Mufutau saw his own face undistorted for the first time in his adult life. It cost him every kobo he could save to get to Rosewater.

At ten past midnight, his phone wakes him. He stands, stretches and dresses in all black, careful not to wake his roommates. He checks his pockets for any identifying mark. He opens his palm and the plasma display glows in the darkness. He touches the ID hack and his chip is deactivated. He leaves the room and makes his way down the stairs. Outside the hostel, a car waits. A drunk pukes against a street light. On the night air a flowery fragrance dominates, as if Rosewater is trying to live up to its name.

The car door opens and Mufutau gets in the back.

It starts to move as soon as the door is shut. There are four other occupants. The light in the car is dim, but all are dressed the same, in lightweight material, with dark hats. One is Mufutau's friend Segun, who is a weeder by day, and who got him this gig. Most of the others are unremarkable, but one has the glowing green where the whites of his eyes should be. An alien. Ogberi.

"I'm Laark. The last of you is here and in a few minutes we will arrive at our destination, a government facility. If anyone wishes to back out now, please speak. You can keep the deposit I gave you. I don't care if you snitch or not, because it won't matter. Anybody? No? All right then."

Mufutau tries to avoid eye contact. Everyone knows they can jump into your body if you stare too long.

"I'm going to give you each twenty devices. I'll tell you what to do with them when we arrive. Once you have done this, I will pay you in full. Twenty thousand dollars, as agreed."

Mufutau looks forward to the pay. With that kind of bank balance he can leave Rosewater and return to Nigeria. It is odd to think of the city as a different country, but that's the new reality.

"Shouldn't we be armed?" asks someone.

"No need. The facility is forgotten, left behind in the rash of government infrastructure works and self-congratulatory war memorials." Laark yawns, but not like one tired. He seems to Mufutau like a lioness doing that thing they do.

The car halts and they all spill out. The door shuts and

the car drives away, programmed to return in an hour. Laark hands out backpacks to everyone, then leads the way to the gates of a building in the middle of nowhere. There's a chain-link fence, rusted, covered in creeper plants, flowers and thorns. About ten feet high, though it's difficult to tell through the dense leaves. A raw ganglion discharges close by, sending lightning up into the sky with a green glow.

"Drones?" Mufutau whispers to Segun.

"That thing with the floaters yesterday took care of them," Segun says.

Mufutau doesn't know what "thing". He pulled a night shift at a restaurant and slept all day.

Old as the gates and fence are, there's a keypad keeping everything inaccessible. Laark knows the code, and the gates spring open. There are no lights, but some of the men have torches. The creaking of unoiled hinges leaks away into the night, but Lark doesn't care, so Mufutau doesn't. They are in a concrete space with vines that criss-cross the ground and crunch underfoot. There is a flat main building that Laark trots to, garlanded with six-foot biohazard symbols and warnings to back the fuck away in English, Yoruba, Igbo, Hausa, Arabic, Mandarin and weird writing that might be Russian. The warnings seem to be stuck on with stickers. Mufutau notices a sheen of dust on every surface and dirt on the air, competing with the flowers.

Nobody else seems worried about the symbols, so Mufutau keeps quiet.

The building and the door appear to be made of reinforced nuplastic. Laark ignores the door, sprays something foamy on the wall in a vague circle, and waits. A foul stench fills the air and the nuplastic flows like liquid into a puddle. They have an entrance. The entire block is a large, wide auditorium that could perhaps contain forty people. In the centre, the floor is open to a sub-level. Mufutau and the rest walk up to the edge, kicking up dust from the floor.

Even before they see what's down there, they begin to cough from a chemical smell, and Mufutau thinks again about the biohazard signs. Laark has one of those glow orbs that are activated by contact, and he tosses it in.

At first glance it looks like someone has driven large trucks and eighteen-wheelers and trailers into a hole in the ground. The gap in the floor is itself a hundred metres square. The vehicles seem to draw the eye, before their load takes over. There are hundreds of variously sized drums in the space, on their sides, upright, intact, broken, all covered in bio- and chem-hazard symbols, and the obvious source of the vile smell. But Mufutau is from Rosewater now, and he reasons that whatever harm they come to will be healed by Wormwood or the god Koriko. They no longer need to wait for the Opening, which is a thing of the past since the dome disintegrated.

He cannot see the how deep the hole in the ground goes. That's a lot of barrels and a lot of toxic waste.

Laark gestures towards the hole. "Get in. Leave one charge on each vehicle."

"I'm not going in there," says Segun. This makes the others hesitate, although they fan out around the hole. Laark materialises a handgun. He moves so fast that Mufutau has no idea where his holster could be. It's one of those models with inbuilt silencers.

"I thought you said we wouldn't need guns," Mufutau says.

"The job doesn't require guns, but it seems I need to motivate at least one of you. Now get in there." Laark waves the gun in an arc that covers all the hired men. "It's twenty large, my human friends. Did you think you would be planting cocoyam and singing *Ipi Tombi*?" His eyes are even greener in the dim light.

"We should have hazmat suits," says one of the others.

"You don't need them," says Laark. "Believe me."

Mufutau is closest to Laark and the alien pushes him. He pinwheels, but manages to land awkwardly on something slippery. He ends up hanging on to a drive shaft with his feet trying to get purchase on the body of a barrel. It's a short fall, maybe six feet, so he isn't injured. He hears other impact thuds as the others jump in, but he has already started to lay charges, a driver's cabin here, a petrol tank there, a hole in a barrel elsewhere. The stench is unbearable and he wonders how much oxygen is down there. At times an air bubble bursts lazily on the surface of the black goo in which the barrels and cars rest.

Mufutau half fears Laark will leave them all down in the hole to rot, and is pleasantly surprised when a rope ladder unfurls into the hole, and they are all helped out, soaking wet and perhaps burning because the liquids are maybe low-grade corrosive as well as toxic.

Laark pokes an app on his plasma phone and Mufutau feels a reassuring vibration, notification that the funds have been transferred. He plans to have a long bath in an expensive hotel and to locate the most expensive sex worker he can find.

"Thank you, gentlemen. You have performed exemplarily. Now. Run." Laark's hand hovers over a control grid on his phone. A button blinks amber.

Mufutau and the others slouch towards the exit.

"You're going to need to run a bit faster than that, my

friends. But as you wish . . . " He pushes the amber button, and it turns red.

The reports from the explosions are different, as well as the shock waves. Some just pop, others are ear-shattering, while many just go "whumpf". The hired men start to run, but waves of heat and kinetic energy bowl them over before they reach the door. Mufutau looks back and sees flames reaching out of the hole as if it is a doorway to hell. The fire is in strange, thin columns, deep yellow, blue and red. There is a cloud, grey, almost black, rising.

Laark just stands there laughing like a fucking hyena while the exhalations of the hole burn and dissolve his body.

Mufutau thinks the alien collapses in a fit of coughing before the smoke makes it impossible to see anything.

Or breathe.

Chapter Ten

The cloud comes from the west, protected from dispersal by the hills that surround Rosewater. It comes overnight, so most of the dead are taken in their sleep. Maybe one or two here and there wake up, only to find their skin sloughing off and their lungs boiling within their chests and their eyeballs exploding. Many call to the god of Rosewater, but Koriko is silent. Or she is too busy collecting the dead to save the living. Maybe she intervened, but those saved do not know it, therefore are not grateful. Maybe the disaster would have been much worse without her.

The scientists determine that there are at least two forms of the cloud, one being toxic vapour, while the other is a mixture of smoke and dust. Within the first hour the vapour takes half of the total casualties. The dust cloud and the smoke persist and cause slower death. Not as many floaters die as one would expect.

The mayor authorises sodium chloride cloud seeding, and within half an hour there is rain over the city. People are warned not to drink or shower in the rain. The dust and smoke dissolve and flow down the streets, into the sewers, but also into the respiratory holes that Wormwood uses.

It is unknown if the toxins can harm the alien.

At the facility from which the cloud originates, the fire service manages to put the blaze out by encasing the entire building in foam, which finally starves the flames. There are six corpses, all badly corroded. The police soon find out that one is Homian.

The information lands on the desk of Aminat Arigbede and she takes it straight to the mayor's mansion.

"It's a synner," she says to Jack Jacques.

"You're sure?" says the mayor.

"Hundred per cent."

Not every road in Rosewater is on the map. The same probably applies to the city you live in. There are narrow roads and streets that no window or door opens on to, where surveillance is forbidden, where there are devices that distort electromagnetic waves to stymie satellites. These are the byways that Jack travels through when he leaves the mansion. Rosewater now has a standing army, and the Engineer Corps has the unenviable task of keeping the mossy alien growth off, like the civilian weeders, only more efficient.

Mile 18 is an area in the north-west of Rosewater. Sparsely populated, and therefore almost returning to verdant bush, it is the designated meeting place when Jack wishes to speak with Koriko. The spot is at the root of the ninety-fifth ganglion, which is naked, meaning without an Ocampo inverter, and shuddering with power. While just as powerful as the old ganglia, Koriko's versions are more conical, with broad bases tapering upwards to a point. Every leaf and flower in Mile 18 is wet from the rain. Jack hopes the puddles on the ground will not conduct electricity from the ganglion through his chair. The car idles three yards away, driverless. Lora stands beside him.

Koriko emerges from their left. Her gaze does not seem as focused as Jack is used to from previous conversations. She is wearing a wrapper with gele.

"Are you well?" asks Jack.

"I am busy," says Koriko. "What do you want?"

"The chemical cloud that killed thousands. You know about that?"

"Yes, I have been busy gathering the bodies of the dead for occupation."

"It was synner activity," says Jack. "Someone called Laark."

"If you say so. It is all one to me. More hosts for Homians."

"This was an atrocity, Koriko. Mass murder. You have to curb the synners at least."

"This sounds like something you should take up with the Honeycomb, Jack. Like enforcement or something. Apprehend the culprit and punish accordingly."

"They died. It was a suicide run."

"So why are you talking to me about—"

"Because Laark will just come back on the next boat from Home."

"At which point he may kill again," says Lora.

"What do you want me to do?" asks Koriko.

"I want you to heal people affected by the cloud, instead of waiting for their corpses. And I want you to stop Laark from recycling," says Jack. "Please."

"I am healing the injured, as agreed. I am taking the dead, also as agreed. You know I have no influence over who goes into what body."

"They worship you," says Jack. "We worship you."

"That's under the control of the people doing the worshipping, because I'm sure I didn't ask for it. Now, I am busy. I will leave now."

"Wait. The floaters are affecting the local biomass. And they're destroying all our surveillance drones."

"You don't need drones, Jack. You have me." With this, she walks away.

Lora starts back to the car. "Was she even listening?"

"She was listening. She heard us about the floaters at least. I'm not sure what she'll do about the synners, but maybe we can work something out with Aminat."

"Sir, I think we need a clause in the agreement with the Homians."

"What kind of clause?"

"Finite lives. If all they do is come back in a new body after death, synners won't need to learn any lessons. Death has to mean death, otherwise Rosewater, Nigeria, heck, the world will just be a video game for them where they will just respawn and humans will be non-player characters."

Jack knows she is right, but does not see himself as being able to negotiate at the present time. There are 204 active court cases against his government, from the victims of rape during the insurrection to trade unions who say their contracts were affected by the schism with Nigeria. And you can only suspend due process so many times before you become a banana republic. Not a good look.

"Tell me, Lora, should we invite Kaaro to the mansion? He knows the alien mind and I need someone like that." He transfers into the car, and notes that his forearms ache, though he doesn't know why. His chair is mechanised.

"No, sir. If you would rather not transmit by phone, I could be your envoy. He can't read my mind. There is information in your mind that should not be known to Kaaro Goodhead. Besides, he hates you."

On the drive back, Jack tries different permutations of what assets he has, and there is nothing he can bring to bear on the aliens.

He does not like it.

Chapter Eleven

A person is talking, but I have missed the words because I am distracted by the fight I had with Nike. It seems like the words were directed at me because everyone is looking in my direction, expectant.

"What?" I ask.

"Are you feeling okay?" asks Femi Alaagomeji. "You don't seem your usual sharp self, and I can't use you if you're distracted."

I am not okay. I have just found out that I am some kind of data ghost in an alien information network, a copy of a dead person's brainwaves.

"I'm fine. Repeat the question."

It's a meeting. Femi does not have an office yet, so she has adopted the Hilton suite as a temporary base of operations as long as the FG continues to pay, which it does, although the guilt must be finite and come to an end one day. Invited and present: me, Femi Alaagomeji, Eric Sunmola, my rebel scum compatriot, Tolu Eleja, and, holographically, Kaaro. I have to keep reminding myself that this is 2068, and it is real time for the people around me.

Eric sits by himself on a sofa, with his tentacle coiled around his trunk, smelling of honey. He seems sullen, and I notice he stares at Kaaro a lot, while the latter ignores him. Kaaro is different, a lot more serious, and a lot more scared. The signal is not great, and he fades out at times. He and I are the only ones not physically present, although nobody knows about me. They think I teleport with machinery worked into my forearms and thighs. They think I time-travel. I used to think this too, but now that I focus on it, it's impossible. Power supply considerations alone make it implausible.

Femi stands in the middle of an ornate circular Persian rug and slowly turns when she speaks to each person. Tolu is to my left. Behind him is a buffet. The insurgency must be well funded if there's a buffet.

"Let's start again," says Femi. "Pay attention this time. For our purposes, Rosewater is not a breakaway nation in the middle of Nigeria. Rosewater is a beachhead, and we are being invaded by Homians. From the perspective of my paymasters, our mission is to destabilise the government, to soften it up for a future attempt to bring Rosewater back into Nigeria, but it can't be done in the open, so this is off the books. I see my mission differently. We are Earth's defence, people. We are it. We have to stop the Homians here or billions of them will replace the billions of us.

"You each have your own abilities and some of you have already engaged in the fight, but at this point, we need suggestions. Nothing is too stupid, just go for it. This is where I turn to you, Oyin Da."

I clear my throat to buy time. "I can tell you how to think about the problem, but I have no ideas right now. There are four sources of the problem. Wormwood, the reanimate–Homian hybrids, the xenosphere and the home world. We can attack one or more of these four, or we can take the fifth solution."

"Which is?" asks Femi.

"Avoidance. Evacuate the Earth."

Everybody groans at this.

"I've only just got a sofa that I like," says Kaaro. "I'm not moving."

"I'm just putting all the options on the table. Let's start with Wormwood. It has a different strain of xenoforms than the ones that make up the xenosphere. We can't bomb it, because that's been tried before and it didn't work. It's bigger now, and if we were to try a more powerful bomb, it would kill everybody in Rosewater."

"Millions versus billions, Oyin Da," says Femi.

"It won't work. Even something with a nuclear payload won't work because it's resistant to radiation. And it's not the only one of its kind, even if we did kill it."

"Poison it? Infect it with something?" says Eric.

"Wormwood literally heals all diseases. There is nothing we can throw at it by way of pestilence that it can't handle." I want to say that's a stupid suggestion, but I hold my tongue. This is why I don't work in groups. It takes too long. "Wormwood is not the answer, people."

Tolu pipes up. "Can we nuke their home world?"

"We don't know where their home world is," says Eric.

"Besides, interstellar travel is unproven and takes too long. Ships have gone out, but we won't know for decades if it worked or not. And think of this: not even the Homians used any kind of space vehicle to reach us. Think of how far it must be, how many millions of light years." Femi sucks her teeth. "But I like how you're thinking. Destroy the reservoir of aliens, then mop up here. Good, good. But we need something else."

"Someone just took out two thousand six hundred people with a toxic waste dump and a few bombs," says Kaaro. "It's thought to be alien action. Synners. They might be stepping up their own transfer rate by killing humans."

"I'm not hearing a suggestion." I turn to him, though. I know what he's about to say. Slow, slow, slow.

"Attrition. Kill them with guns, fire, bad breath, whatever we have," says Kaaro.

"One at a time, if we have to," says Tolu. "They are hard to kill, though. The ammo required would be phenomenal. The healing is in the way. Perhaps if we directly targeted Koriko."

Femi shakes her head. "No, that would become open war. Once we move, we have to do it fast, or one or more of us will fall, and the scheme will become known."

"Besides, it would not work. We don't have enough information," I say. "We need to understand the enemy better. We need to know the past and the present. Surveillance of some kind."

"I can keep tabs on them in the xenosphere," says Kaaro.

"No, we can't use the xenosphere for this," says Femi. "They're watching you watching them."

"Hack the drones?" says Tolu.

"Eighty per cent of them went down when the floaters had their murmuration. We'll be noticed by Jack's people," says Kaaro.

"Don't you mean Aminat's people?" says Eric.

Kaaro gives him the finger. "Fuck you."

"Let's be civil," says Femi.

"I'm serious, ma'am. Kaaro is in bed with the chief of security. How do we know he's not pillow-talking us into failure?"

"Because he said he would not and I believe him," says Femi. "We are of one mind."

"I don't trust him," says Eric.

"No, you don't like him. It's not the same thing," says Femi. "Do you trust me?"

"Yes, ma'am."

"Good. Surveillance of the aliens. Workable ideas? Anyone?"

"I may know a guy working on a thing," says Kaaro. "Leave this to me to research."

"Then that's your job." Femi looks at me. "You mentioned the past. You're a time-traveller. I need you to find out if there are weaknesses we can exploit."

"I can do that."

"I'm not finished. You once told me you could go anywhere."

"I can."

"I want you to go to America."

Interesting. In the silence that follows I start to think of the real question: can I cross the Drawbridge protocol?

I say, "I guess I have my homework."

"You do."

Tolu raises his hand in honest-to-God schoolchild fashion. "There's something else."

"Go."

"My cousin in the University of Lagos is working on something that might be useful. A way of screening people from the xenosphere that doesn't require thick layers of antifungals, but might also be able to expel aliens from human minds. I don't fully understand the work, but I'd like to go check on him."

It makes sense. At this point in history there are no more pristine brains, brains without xenoform contamination. An artificial brain can be created clean and tested under different conditions of exposure and proposed cures. Instead of screening a contaminated brain, you start from a different direction.

I wonder at Tolu. I saw him in my extrapolations and excursions into the future. This is the reason I went to save him from detention with S45 in the first place. But I didn't know why exactly; just that he was important to the resistance. Since that time he has been ... adequate, but nothing Earth-shaking. He obeys instructions, he goes on raids, he monitors Koriko. He works as expected, a good soldier. I confess to some disappointment. What if he's here not because of himself, but because of his cousin? But if his cousin's device works, why haven't I seen it?

Femi turns to Eric. "Go with him. I'll get you both checkpoint passes."

There are more words, more suggestions, but I have tuned out. I can tell even before the speaker finishes that the ideas will not work. My mind is on that great big barrier that keeps the US unknowable to the rest of the world, and how I'm going to get past it. I have thought about the problem before, of course, but that was before I knew what I was.

"Someone has to keep the pressure on Rosewater while I'm away," says Tolu. "The resistance factions have to keep going otherwise they'll know something's up. They're quasi-autonomous, but they need direction."

"I'll coordinate and provide hardware and support," says Femi. "But I won't kill people. I'll degrade infrastructure and sabotage things like power."

I say, "It wouldn't matter if you did want to kill. We've found that killing people is no longer easy in Rosewater. The healing field is formidable."

"I'm formidable too," says Femi.

*

After the meeting I go back in time to check on details and I find something that wasn't there before, or rather, that I hadn't noticed. I travel three times in the data stream to be sure it isn't some psychological projection of one of us present. That does happen sometimes, and causes the alteration of memories.

Femi says, "I'm formidable too." The meeting breaks up soon after that when basic logistics are decided. I see myself depart and I see Femi drink red wine from the bottle and fiddle with the in-house entertainment. I hear a knock at the door, and a man comes in without being invited. At first I think it's a sex worker and I don't want to see that, but this man is not beautiful or even vaguely attractive. He looks both brutal and brutalised and he has a permanent frown etched into his features. He also looks familiar to me.

"Are you ready?" asks Femi.

The man nods.

"Did you get the funds and equipment?"

The man nods.

"Good. Go and show him who's the older brother."

"I'm the second twin," says the man.

"It's a shame that people have forgotten our traditions. Your name, Kehinde, is a short form. It's meant to be Omokehindelegbon, which means 'the second twin is older'. You sent your brother out to taste the world because he recognised your authority as elder. I've reminded you. Go and remind him."

Oh, shit.

If this is the twin I think it is, Rosewater is about to have deeper problems.

And Femi is even more devious than I thought.

Chapter Twelve

Bea lifts up a house plant and, after looking left and right, spits into it. "This, my darling, is piss-poor champagne," she says, wiping her mouth with the back of her hand.

Aminat does not disagree. Efe would not have approved. "I think we should leave."

They were not invited, at least not in the first round. The memorial for Efe was organised by her mother-in-law, who she hated, and who blamed Aminat for everything. Bea heard about it and dragged Aminat along and they crashed in mo-gbo, mo-ya fashion: I heard and I dropped by. Bea is such a bitch in that she can eat ice cream, cake, frosting, full-fat Fanta, anything she can throw in her gob, without putting on weight.

Attending was a mistake. Everyone, including Efe's husband, ignores them, although Aminat supposes that is better than outright melodramatic hatred. She still blames herself for her friend's death.

Having no activities on the programme, Aminat and Bea wander through the house, admiring the table with Corinthian-style columns for legs and gilded edges as the height of strange decor. They take drinks from every floating waiter – Aminat thinks their host has tried to save money on liquor – and comment on each painting they find in the hallway. There is an outlaw feel to their actions and Aminat gets lost in it, relaxing for the first time in ... she doesn't know how long.

A little boy in the middle of the next corridor stops them. Efe's little boy Ofor.

"Are you running away?" he says. He is six and sounds both innocent and wise.

Bea crouches so she is nearer his height. "Yes." She nods as she speaks.

"Take me with you," Ofor says.

Bea looks back at Aminat.

"Have you ever been in a police car?" asks Aminat.

This is unwise, Aminat.

"Shut the fuck up. Speed-limit override. Speed seventy miles per hour," says Aminat.

Destination?

"Pending. Go east."

The city speeds past them and Bea has her hands up while she screams. The kid has never gone this fast. The AI smoothly avoids obstacles, and obstacles avoid the car, corrections and adjustments made with the central AI preferring the police car in its routing algorithms. Bea and Ofor marvel while Aminat, calm, watches the city. The new verdant reality means each structure has become a vertical garden of sorts, bursting out in flowers or crops with no rhyme or reason. Landscapers have become scarce and charge quadruple their previous rates to keep windows clear of vegetation. Neither does it matter how tall the high-rise is. Rosewater's plants don't respect gravity.

When the car slows to corner, there is more to see. On the walls that are bare, graffiti reigns. Commonly, *Rev. 8:10* can be seen, without context: the verse in the Bible where Wormwood is mentioned. Jacques' name accompanied by inventive profanity. Your basic tagging. Declarations of love. Declarations of hate.

There are details of cherubs on some corners, carved into gables and as gargoyles on religious buildings, the artistic subconscious reacting to the trauma of the insurrection. After all, they did see aliens versus angels play out in front of them, degrading the dome just when they needed Wormwood most.

But fuck you, cherubs, we killed you, thinks Aminat.

But barely.

And she isn't sure she's happy with the outcome.

Her phone vibrates and she sees Ofor senior's number, the boy's father, obviously looking for the child.

"Hello, Ofor," says Aminat.

He sounds angry. "Are you out of your—"

"Sorry, I can't hear you. I'll call you back."

The buildings they pass are shorter, flatter, more residential. They are approaching the periphery of the city, the border with Nigeria.

The boy is lucky to see one of the border patrols, two mechanised humans, looking more like robots than cyborgs. Aminat had wanted full constructs, but the Ethiopians had gifted Jack with a squadron as a gesture of goodwill and he had to use them somewhere. When they have gone past, she notices—

"Stop. Hard stop. Now."

Negative.

Minor in vehicle. Possibility of harm. Slowing … slowing … stopped.

Idle or park?

111

"Idle. And unlock the fucking door," Aminat says.

"Language," says Bea. She covers Ofor's ears.

"Shilekun," says Aminat.

Just outside the border, there is a vertical pipe reaching forty feet high and seven wide, surrounded by bamboo scaffolding. The machinery about it, and the fact that there seems to be an inner pipe pistoning, makes Aminat think it might be some kind of mining rig. But what the fuck are they mining? She films it on her phone.

"Ki lo n'yaka fun?" asks Bea. *What are you cursing?*

Aminat notices her again. Her arm stretched, palm outwards, fingers splayed does look like a curse position. "Darling, I will call you later. The car will take you back. Mwah, mwah! Bye, Ofor."

She instructs the car, and keeps filming.

Aminat finds Dahun at his dining table, though not eating. He has goggles on with magnifying lenses, and he is working on some device.

"What are you doing?" she asks.

"Hello to you too," says Dahun. He doesn't look up. "I make my own weapons. When they snatched me from my home, they didn't allow me time to pack."

"Can't you buy weapons? I thought contractors had sources for this kind of thing. Besides, if you go to Ona Oko at night, people will sidle up to you and try to sell you 'my father'. They're talking about guns."

This idiom started in the days of muzzle-loading weapons. Handguns were called "my father who eats with his bottom and voids with his mouth", and over time got shortened to "my father".

"If I create a weapon, nobody knows what it is, and therefore they cannot devise counter-measures. What do you want?" He pushes the goggles to his hairline, looks up now and sees her in her gown.

"I went to a memorial," says Aminat.

"Fine, but why are you here?"

"There are . . . towers or pipes . . . oil-well-type things being built just outside the city limits," she says.

Dahun says nothing.

"You knew about them."

"They aren't hidden, Aminat. They were built in plain sight."

"You know what they are for."

He inclines his head to one side, then the other. "I don't know. I suspect. I heard something when I was on the other side of the border. It's shit."

"I don't care if it's shit, Dahun, I want to know."

"I mean it's actual shit. It's Wormwood's waste products." *What?*

"Okay, I never even . . . I've never contemplated that such a being would have waste, but why would they mine it?"

"I don't know. What I do know is that S45 took a report to the president. A source told me. I never saw the report and I was out of Rosewater, so I was only half interested at the time."

"A report on Wormwood's waste?"

"No, a report on the spoor." Dahun turns back to his work.

"Stop. What spoor?"

"Wormwood is moving, Aminat, and so is Rosewater. Slowly, but definitely moving southwards in the direction of the sea. Some S45 scientists examined the track and found what they postulate to be the waste products. You didn't know this?"

"I did not. I thought Wormwood stopped moving once it arrived here from England."

"It did, but apparently it started again sometime after the insurrection."

"Why do they want its waste?"

"I don't know, Aminat, and I don't care. Look, it's space alien waste. Maybe it's radioactive. Fissionable waste would be a great resource. Are you done? I'd really like to finish this before Taiwo comes for me."

"Taiwo isn't coming for you."

Dahun laughs. "It's like we were in a different conversation. Trust me, he's coming for me. And he's coming for Kaaro."

Aminat thinks he's finding this a bit too funny, but she leaves him to his weapons creation. They say he killed the people who took Jack's leg with tiny arthrodrones of his own creation. Aminat hates people who are self-contained and don't seem to need anything or anyone. She rises abruptly.

"I'll see you at work tomorrow."

"Yes, ma'am."

She can still hear the last laughs coming from him.

Chapter Thirteen

Hannah Jacques takes a sip of water, and sets the glass down on the lawyer's table, then she begins.

"Olubi Inuro was a husband, a father to two daughters, and a farmer. His plot was a mile from his house and he walked there and back every day. One day, he walked his daughters to the school bus, then continued to his plot. He had been working for fifteen minutes when an AI error took a lorry off the road and right into Olubi's farm, where it killed him. Two hours later, Olubi returns home, sits down at the dining table and makes eating motions even though he has no food, no dishes, no cutlery. There's blood everywhere, but Olubi's wounds are healed. He's a re-animate, functioning body, lost mind. At least that's what they tell us.

"After an hour or two, Mrs Inuro is trying to process what has happened, when some people knock at the door, some officers. They've seen the accident and they want to take Olubi in for processing at the Honeycomb.

"My client contends that there is no habeas corpus here, that the government has no right to take Olubi Inuro, and

115

we contest the idea that Mr Inuro might be dead. We sought and received a temporary restraining order from the court, and we wish—"

"Objection, my lord," says Blessing Boderin, the tall, bearded defence lawyer, who suffers from albinism.

"It's an opening statement," says the judge.

"May we approach the bench?"

The judge beckons and both lawyers huddle.

"My lord, we are concerned about a conflict of interest. Mrs Jacques is the wife of Mayor Jacques."

Hannah says, "I am not here as the wife of anybody, my lord, I am here as an attorney-at-law representing my client. There is no conflict."

"The vagaries of this case may affect the marriage, my lord, and when the government wins—"

"If."

"When the government wins, it may cause irreparable damage to the holy union."

Judge Lafe holds an indulgent smile in place. "Get back to your seat, Boderin. Don't interrupt my court with nonsense just because there are feed cameras."

Hannah's first witness is the police officer who came to take Olubi away. As the officer is sworn in, she notices Boderin pass a message to a paralegal, who leaves the court.

Meetings all day.

There is a lancing pain deep within Jack's forehead and he hasn't had the time to take analgesia or a break. He is also on a caffeine buzz. He needs sleep. He takes another pull of coffee. Cleaning up a chemical spill, even with Koriko and Wormwood helping, was a nightmare. Getting relatives to understand that the bodies were too toxic to embalm. Some were so badly contaminated that even Koriko did not want them for Honeycomb.

He had known about the toxic waste dump. Femi Alaagomeji told him about it during the war, but he had not thought about it since. Until the phone call that woke him and announced the tragedy.

Lora signals to him, and he wraps the meeting up.

"What?"

She hands him a note.

"What's a Boderin?" asks Jack. "Am I meant to know who this is?"

"He's one of your lawyers, sir," says Lora.

"The government has many." Jack squints at the paper. While he knows there are numerous court cases going on, he never has to give them direct attention.

I am sorry but I could not prevent the trial from going ahead. This one can hurt you, the scribbled note says.

"What case is this?" asks Jack.

"Olubi, Rosewater high court, family suing your government for the body of their patriarch. Your wife is lawyer for the plaintiff."

"Oh. Okay. But we've been sued before." Hannah did not mention this, but then they had a half-rule not to discuss work. Jack didn't even know she was licensed to practise law, or if she had ever tried a case.

"Not by your wife, sir, and not with international media covering the trial live."

"Not Gone Charity ... they don't get involved in legislation usually."

"All indications are that this is a test case."

117

It doesn't seem possible, but his headache worsens, kicks the pain up a notch.

"Sir, judging by minute changes in your breathing, a slight narrowing of your eyes, a furrowing of your brow, I'd guess you are in pain. Are you?"

"It's just a headache."

"Diagnostics," says Lora.

Yes, Ms Asiko.

"Health check on the mayor."

Affirmative.

"It's just a headache," Jack says again.

Three thin metal rods emerge from the floor of the office up to six feet, and scan Jack, triangulating findings.

"Test case, you were saying."

"Yes, sir. If only one person is able to avoid going to the Homians, a precedent would have been set."

Lora doesn't know the half of it. Or she knows and is not saying, which is a thing she does sometimes. If the hosts don't all go to Honeycomb, the deal with the Homians is in jeopardy, which means Koriko might not defend Rosewater, which means Nigeria could invade again. How good a trial lawyer is Hannah?

"Please clear my schedule for an hour," says Jack. "And bring up the feed."

"Aminat Arigbede is expected in twenty-five minutes."

"What does she want?"

"She said, and I quote, 'The city is moving and shit.' End quote."

What the hell?

"I don't have time for her."

"Yes, sir."

The lights dim automatically and the feed rises from the desk. A flat version of the scene remains on the surface.

"Zoom," says Jack, and the images become larger. He loves Hannah's hair all severe, under a wig, which she doesn't have to wear.

Ah, shit. This is going to hurt.

" . . . say that you have expertise on the topic of so-called reanimates, Dr Soko?"

The witness nods. "That would be a fair assumption, yes."

"How long have you studied them?"

"Since 2056. More than ten years."

"How many reanimates have you personally examined?"

"Six hundred and fourteen."

"Exactly?"

"I keep meticulous records."

"Isn't this dangerous?"

"Not most of the time. There are many myths about reanimates, but the truth is they reflect their environment. I have found that a peaceful, gentle environment gives a peaceful, gentle reanimate. The rates of violence from and among reanimates is comparable percentage-wise to any human population."

"Could you tell the court how you examine them."

"Basic anthropometry, physiology, blood chemistry, ultrasound scans, encephalograms, electromyograms, brain imaging, like that."

"Doctor, would you say so-called reanimates are alive?"

"Objection," says Boderin.

"Overruled. The witness will answer," says the judge.

Soko says, "They are certainly alive in that their hearts are beating, their lungs oxygenate their blood, they have brain activity, their eyes are open, and they have goal-directed activity. They suffer pain. They require nutrition or they die. Isolated from water, they die within a week like any human."

Hannah clasps her hands together in a gesture that seems to imply supplication. "Doctor, how do reanimates differ from you and me?"

Soko exhales. "I should preface this by saying we use re-animates as an umbrella term. They are actually quite a heterogeneous group, so what I'm about to say will contain generalisations.

"In the early stages of reanimation, cortisol ... that is, stress hormone levels are quite high, but within a week this returns to normal. EEGs of most reanimates show disorganised background activity, generalised slow-wave activity and a lack of response to opening or closing the eyes. Functional MRIs show reduced blood flow to the frontal lobes. There are other minor changes, but these can be found in regular humans on either side of the bell curve."

"Bell curve?"

"Normal distribution."

"I see. And what about their memories of themselves?"

"That's difficult to answer."

"How so?"

"On the one hand, it's very clear that they are not functioning like their previous selves. They are not verbal, for example, and their complex abilities seem to have gone. Certainly their frontal lobe functions are impaired. But that doesn't mean the self is gone. It may be locked in, trying and failing to communicate."

"Objection, speculative."

The judge turns to Hannah with a raised eyebrow. She looks down, and takes a minute to think.

"Doctor, could you tell us what the self is?"

"Self, mind, consciousness, these are terms that are difficult to define due to their subjectivity. It is about an entity existing as distinct from the environment and being aware of this. One of the problems is that existence is subjective."

Hannah laughs. "I'm sure many of us here, myself included, would be shocked to be told reality is subjective."

Soko says, "What we perceive to be reality is information brought to our brains by our senses. But there are multiple representations in the brain for each perception. The brain has to make a choice about which representation to use. The choice is based on the environment in which that brain developed, and current context, which can be rather individual. The brain then reconciles that representation into the whole of reality of that moment. We each create our own reality. The self, or the mind, can be conceptualised as the observer of and interactor with that reality."

Hannah says, "And is that mind separate from the body in the Cartesian manner?"

"No, that's been debunked and is, at best, an intellectual curiosity."

"Objection."

"Most investigators do not believe there is any such thing as Cartesian duality any more."

Hannah says, "So you are saying the mind and body are linked."

"I am saying the mind and body are one, irreversibly linked. I am saying the self is embodied."

"Objection." Boderin stands.

The judge, benevolent uncle, inclines his head. "What's your objection?"

"This is a nice digression, my lord, but what does it have to do with Mr Olubi?"

Hannah turns to the judge. "My lord, the government contends that Mr Olubi Inuro lost his mind and selfhood at the time of his accident. The government would have us believe that Mr Inuro's body is an empty vessel to be bartered away to alien overlords and filled with an alien interloper."

"My lord, this bashing of René Descartes is all well and good, but I wasn't aware that it was time for summation."

"Objection overruled, but Mrs Jacques, get to the point, hmm?"

"Objection, prejudicial."

"It's prejudicial for her to get to the point?" asks the judge.

"It's prejudicial to call her Mrs Jacques. She is the wife of the mayor."

"Don't irritate me, Mr Boderin." The judge gestures for Hannah to continue.

"Dr Soko, you've examined Mr Inuro."

"Yes."

"Would you agree with the government that his body is empty of any mind?"

"I would not."

"But the government has a whole policy based on giving quote unquote empty bodies to aliens. What is your evidence for this?"

"Mr Inuro went home immediately after the accident. He performed several ritualistic actions relating to his life. He acted like someone severely brain-damaged, but he was himself. As of when I last saw him, he would go about the motions of driving a tractor. This is consistent with what I've found when studying other reanimates."

"So would it be fair to say that there is no factual basis in the government's claims that there is no human left in reanimates?"

"It would. I consider the reanimate to be in a state of diminished function, but not dehumanised. This is the same consideration for people with catastrophic strokes or severe advanced dementias."

"Some commentators say that people with advanced dementia have lost their personhood."

"I am not one of those."

"Thank you, Doctor. Nothing further, my lord."

The judge nods, then turns to Boderin. "Would the defence like a recess before cross-examining?"

Boderin stands. "No, my lord. I only have one question for this witness."

"Proceed."

"Dr Soke, thank you for informative and helpful testimony. You are obviously a man of great probity and compassion. It's an honour to be here with you. Please tell the court, if you will, would Mr Olubi be alive and performing all these wonders of neuroscience and philosophy without the presence of the alien to reanimate him?"

"No."

"Thank you, Dr Soke. I have nothing further, my lord."

"Well shit," says Jack.

Lora says nothing.

"At least Boderin isn't a complete fucking idiot."

"What do you want to do, sir?" asks Lora.

"I do not know."

Jack's phone beeps. It's a text from the president.

Remind me to send your wife a lovely bouquet of flowers. You know, a man who can't keep his house in order has no business being a leader. You would have been better off marrying your assistant.

He seems almost cheerful. Bastard.

Fuck, fuck, fuck.

Hannah cannot be allowed to win the case.

"Do we know the judge?"

"Conservative, harmless, family man, two children, husband is a dentist."

"Background?"

"Pristine."

Fuck.

"Sir," says Lora. "Isn't it time you had a word with your wife?"

Jack has no answer. She's right, of course, but she doesn't know Hannah or the arrangement they have.

Maybe the president is right. For all the time Jack spends with Lora, he should have married her, and at least she is always on his side.

Hannah leaves the court escorted by the bodyguards. She is stoic in the face of the reporters, encouraging to the Inuro family before they leave, and allows the driver to lead her into the car. She activates the tint on the glass, including the barrier.

"Clear all transmissions."

Yes, Mrs Jacques.

Finally alone, shaking with adrenaline, Hannah weeps.

Chapter Fourteen

Someone, maybe the giant, shoots Aminat in the face.

It hurts, although the armour absorbs most of the impact, and the rest of the force flings her to the floor of the flat. She blinks to clear her vision. She hears another shot, but it misses her entirely because she feels no impact. Three regulars and one giant. As she recovers, she removes the ankle piece.

Get up, get up, get up; can't die here.

She shoots first, not aiming at anyone, just causing disorder. Some dummy is trying to get out of the door that she locked in full view of all of them. She flips up and the giant comes for her, his Afro scraping the ceiling. She hates fighting giants, so tall, their limbs seem to be all over the place. She kicks him in the chest, the highest she has ever kicked, and as he recoils, she leaps and slams her knee into his midsection. She shoots the guy on her left in the foot, then again in the arm. The giant is still in the fight, swinging, although he hits his compatriot by mistake.

Aminat stamps on the giant's knee and feels it go. At close range, she shoots his thigh, then what she thinks is his liver. While he screams and writhes she shoots the third guy in the back.

She pulls the giant up by the sweatshirt and punches his face. Again. And a third time. Fucking hard skull. He starts to laugh through his bleeding nose.

"What the fuck is funny?"

"You are ... you are so funny," says the giant in that resonating voice they all have. "You think we don't know who you are. We have always known. This ... being targeted by you ... we use it as an initiation. The more you beat me, the more you shoot me, the higher my status. Hit me more. Go on."

Aminat drops him and the thud vibrates through the flat.

They had kidnapped six people, not rich ones, and extorted money from the desperate families. Released without charge.

"Come on. Don't you want to arrest me?" says the giant. "I might go and commit another crime."

Aminat walks out.

At home she retracts the armour and showers away the sweat and blood. She uses a shampoo that Jack Jacques presented to her a few months back, crafted specifically for him. The mongrel is awake, but not excited at Aminat's presence, though he follows her with his eyes and wags his tail desultorily. At least he's not in their room.

She sits in the living room, feeling sorry for herself, contemplating some mindless broadcast, flipping through feeds. She is yet to select anything when she hears Kaaro's slouch. He stands there and yawns while scratching his lower belly.

"Are you hungry?" he says. "I can make food happen."

"I'm not hungry," says Aminat. "Take me to bed and fuck me till I'm raw."

"Yeah, I can make that happen too."

*

126

Later, in the xenosphere, Kaaro and Aminat watch a waterfall of mercury while sitting on an outcrop. She tells him her pain, her confusion. He listens in silence, batting away stray globules of silvered liquid that have broken free of the flow.

"Kaaro," says Aminat. "Why would Wormwood be moving?"

"I don't know."

"Can't you ask it?"

"I could, but I don't want to."

"Why?"

"I don't have the same relationship with it. Anthony was my guy, and he's dead. Koriko is a different kind of god."

"Did you always need Anthony to talk to Wormwood?"

"Yes. I tried talking direct once and I was catatonic for three days. I tried getting into the mind of a floater and it was like trying to swim in broken glass. These entities are alien to us."

"Could you ask Koriko?"

"I don't think so. She is single-minded in her pursuit of bodies to contain their people." He throws a rock into the pool beneath the waterfall. "Besides, has it occurred to you that Wormwood might be acting autonomously? That it doesn't want Koriko to know? If I tell her, she becomes alert to it."

"Do we benefit from a schism between Koriko and Wormwood?"

"We as in humanity, or Rosewater, or the government of Rosewater?"

"Any of the above."

"I don't know. It all depends on why Wormwood is moving."

"Why don't you ask her about the waste? She can see the mines herself."

"I ... Sure. But she's already seen the mines and doesn't care."

"Ask."

"Yes, ma'am."

"Am I using my police voice?"

"You are."

"Sorry."

"I can think of where your police voice might be handy ... "

"I'm going to need some time," says Aminat.

"You have five minutes."

"I feel like I don't know what's going on with you."

"You've been busy," says Kaaro. "But don't worry. We'll get to it."

"You should have told me about Femi, about meeting her."

"Yes."

"God, she gets me ... Grrrrr."

"She's under a lot of pressure."

"Are you defending her?"

"No, I'm just saying she has responsibilities that make what she's doing seem odd and callous. If you knew what she knows—"

Aminat draws away. "You *are* defending her. Do *you* know what she knows?"

"Do I ... Yes."

"You read her thoughts, didn't you?"

"She told me to."

"Did you sleep with her too? I know you've always wanted to."

"Aminat, Jesus, that was ages ago. I was a kid."

"You've never read my mind."

"What's going on here? You seem to be looking for a fight."

"Oh, this is my fault for being an irrational, emotional female? Get me the fuck out of this place. And two things: one, nobody wants a fucking mercury waterfall. Mercury is toxic. Two, when I'm looking for a fight, you will absolutely know it from the sound your face makes hitting my knuckles."

Stroking the mongrel, Aminat catches the highlights of Hannah Jacques' day in court. No wonder nobody wanted to talk to her about the mines or the moving Wormwood. Aminat had thought of Hannah as decorative and distant. She knew the woman had a law degree, but this is ... was Nigeria. You can buy degrees. You can buy people to take exams for you. Anyone with enough money can become a lawyer. It looks like Mrs Jacques is the real deal. There are scores of people suing the government and trying to get their deceased loved ones back before alien implantation, but this is getting attention because of who Hannah is. Aminat has seen Boderin before, in the mayor's mansion. Bit of a hunk in spite of his albinism, quiet, which is strange for a lawyer. He seems to know what he is doing in the video footage, but he can't possibly be as confident as he seems. Jacques must be shitting himself.

Just before falling asleep, Aminat starts to contemplate resignation. She can start a new life with Kaaro in Lagos. Rekindle. Reignite the passion in a crowded, dirty, desperate city with no automatic healing. Yeah. Sounds romantic already.

Chapter Fifteen

I've hemmed and hawed enough. I have to go to America. Once I have agreed to do so, what remains is the method. I have no idea how to get there. It was easier when I thought I was a person using a time machine and teleportation device. I could go anywhere by just programming and punching a button. But now that I think back, and have been back, I see that the details blur like staring through gauze. There is no detail, just the effect. I have experimented. I have visited the past without pretending to use a machine. I just concentrate. The problem with America is I have no referent.

In this house of thought, in this bed of imagination, I stroke my lover's belly, going over the soft folds as she recovers from our exercise, following the lanes laid out between stretch marks. The bed has a canopy, and a filmy netting covers all sides, blurring everything outside. Violins mix with talking drums, coming from memory rather than a hi-fi system. Is this real? As real as it needs to be, I think.

"Nike?"

"Hmm."

"How do I get to the US?"

Nike groans. "You're still going?"

"Yes."

"Where's the child?"

"Junior? She's with friends." It still shocks me that Junior found people to play with, but it seems on her own explorations she met children in reverie or some other REM sleep often enough to form relationships.

Nike opens her eyes and simultaneously the lighting of the room increases, though still soft and filtered. "I wouldn't know how to get there. I've never been."

"That isn't true. You went to Disneyland as a child."

"Ahh, so you were listening."

"I'm always listening," I say.

"Well, girl, that was a long time ago. I don't remember enough of it to serve as a pathway through the xenosphere for you."

"Who built this place?" I ask.

"We both did. We both are. It is constantly being rebuilt within our agreement."

"Show me what the xenosphere actually looks like. Can you do that?"

Nike sits up. "Yes. You can do that too, you know. At least, you will when you remember."

"Show me."

The bed, the fabric, the music all dissolve, and both of us are standing in the dark surrounded by thin strands of organic matter forming a network around us. One is beneath our feet. Each connects with every other one along its length. Some are white, some grey, and, looking closely, they don't actually make full contact with each other. There is a space across which puffs of either gas or liquid drift. There is some kind of script on each, but it is not readable.

The dark lights up with electricity and the strands break off from each other, only to re-form the links seconds later, not always in the same position as before. Protean cells push pseudopodia into the spaces and correct the lost positions. After this they seem to disappear.

Nike holds my hand and begins to run down the xenoform. The motion does not seem adequate to cover the distance and I suspect Nike is moving the landscape as well as herself.

The xenoform leads us to a convergence point, where a being rests at a nexus, receiving information from all. It is arachnoid, but no spider ever had this number of legs.

In this house of thought, in this bed of imagination, I stroke my lover's belly, going over the soft folds as she recovers from our exercise, following the lanes laid out between stretch marks. The bed has a canopy, and a mosquito netting covers all sides, filming everything outside. Violins mix with talking drums, building to a crescendo, coming from memory rather than a hi-fi system. Is this real? As real as it needs to be, I think.

Something seems familiar ...

In this house of thought, in this bed of imagination, I stroke my lover's breasts, going over the soft folds of the skin as she recovers from our exercise, following the planes laid out between stretch marks. There is no sweat, but between her legs tastes like pomegranate. The bed has a canopy, and a filmy netting covers all sides, blurring everything outside. Violas mix with talking drums, coming from memory rather than a hi-fi system. Is this real? As real as it needs to be, I think.

I'm not sure if ...

In this house of thought, in this bed of imagination, I stroke my lover's belly, going over the soft folds as she recovers from our exercise, following the lanes laid out between stretch marks. The bed—

"There you are. Don't worry; I'm here." Nike takes my hand, and we are looking at the spider again.

"What happened?"

"Thought parasite. Don't worry about it. You got caught in a recursive loop and would have been stuck there or ultimately consumed."

"Are they alive?"

Nike squints. "Hard to tell if they have any self-awareness, honey." She points to the spider. "She knows everything. You can ask her."

"You're not coming with me?"

Nike puts a hand on both of my cheeks and kisses me. "Girl, someone needs to bring you back when you get lost. And you will get lost."

"Won't the spider tell me how to get back?"

"Your self, honey. You will lose your self, dissipate it in the data stream. And I will collate you and bring you back, me and Junior, like we always do."

"How long have I—"

"Years. Too long. Go. I'll be here when you're done."

I kiss her. "I will not get lost this time."

There is a twinkle in her eyes and her mouth twitches as if she is about to say something, but she doesn't. She turns to leave.

I turn around.

No spider, no strands of xenoforms. I'm standing in front of a naked woman, dark skin, short hair, six-foot butterfly wings extending up and out behind her.

"Bicycle Girl," says the woman. She has a large mouth

with a toothy smile, like she is about to eat prey. "It's not time yet."

"Time? Who are you?"

"I'm ... Call me Molara. I'm the data harvester. My work here is all but done, but I have to wait for the transfers to be complete before I die. Do you want to amuse me while I wait, Bicycle Girl?" She thrusts her hips forward then, lascivious.

Gross.

"I need to get to America."

"Maybe I wipe your memory and kill your wife and child, Bicycle Girl. I could do that. Then maybe I amuse myself, whether you like it or not."

I am afraid, but I see something in her, an emptiness, a lack of substance that tells me this is all posturing.

"Send me to America, Molara. I know you're weak or dying."

"Still strong enough to eat you."

"But you won't. I have a mission."

"To help the humans." She laughs. "Do you remember helping that dissident escape? Tolu Eleja? Remember that?"

"Vaguely. I saw him recently."

Molara touches my forehead. "Remember."

And I do.

I had been gazing at possible futures with Junior. Nike. Nike junior. Extrapolating, we had seen Tolu Eleja in ... the same meeting with me, Kaaro, Femi, Eric. He seemed important. When I checked in 2066 he was in captivity with S45, but I didn't know where. I enlisted Kaaro, the only finder left alive, and we ... rescued him. Kaaro used a decoy body from Wormwood. I was incorporeal, so it was of no significance. The xenoforms. They affect organic matter, it's how they heal.

They broke Tolu down and absorbed him into the xenosphere, reconstituting him where I instructed, with the resistance groups. So I *can* teleport. Of course I can. That's what I did to Ogene when I sprung him from jail, except I never re-formed him. I did it to Kaaro, bringing him to the Lijad back when I thought it was an object of science, not imagination.

But then I see even more. The plant that nearly destroyed Wormwood and had to be destroyed physically and in the xenosphere.

With Molara's help.

"You've helped the humans. You fought with them." Just being close to her brings a lot more back. We are part of the same system of data. She is, like me, a creature of the xenosphere.

"For our survival, not for theirs," says Molara. "But what does it matter? Amuse yourself if you must. The humans have already lost this world. The flow of Homians has started and cannot be stopped."

"So you'll help me?"

"If you call it that. You're going to London. In 2012."

"Wait! I said America. The United States."

"There's an electromagnetic cordon around the US, the Drawbridge. You know that. There are xenoforms in there, though. You'll be fine, Bicycle Girl."

Molara pushes me and I fall down a tunnel. I know it's a neural pathway, but it feels like gravity has me, rather than neurotransmitters. I form my metal cocoon with pewter cups and old televisions and gold from mines in Ilesha and tin from Enugu and the roof of an abandoned tractor we used to have in Arodan. Inside, though I am still falling, I feel safe.

Chapter Sixteen

The tinny sound of Tolu Eleja's music bounces around inside the army transport, irritating Eric. The tentacle, sensing discomfort, casts about looking for danger, settling after not finding any, then rising again to search. Tolu's music can be piped straight to his brain by directly stimulating the vestibulocochlear nerve, like all modern phones, but obviously he wants Eric to hear the repetitive concussion. Which has been going on for an hour now.

"What are you listening to?" asks Eric. Might as well.

"Samples of background drums for a track I'm mixing. I'm trying to decide which one to use." Tolu sounds uncertain.

"You obviously want me to ask if you're a musician, to which you'll answer ... " Eric points an open palm at Tolu.

"Trying to be. It's very competitive."

"How do you find the time?"

"I do it in between, like now, driving to Lagos."

Eric nods. "Okay."

"Can I ask you something?"

"Go ahead."

"Do you drink a lot of honey?"

"Why do you ask?"

"You smell of it. All the time."

"Is it unpleasant?"

"No. Just an odd thing to be smelling."

Eric has grown so used to it that he does not think about it any more. "It's the tentacle."

"You got it from Rosewater, right? You were there?"

Eric nods. "I don't really want to talk about it."

"I was tortured there."

"I'm sorry to hear that."

"By a sensitive like you. Kaaro."

"Kaaro's not like me." More of an edge in the voice than Eric intended. "Kaaro's not like anybody."

"He also came to rescue me. He and Oyin Da."

"He tortured you, then rescued you?"

"It was S45. Not personal. He worked for them."

Twenty minutes to Lagos, Agent Sunmola. Credentials checked seventeenth time. Light rain at destination. Synchronise with Lagos AI?

"Affirmative, but maintain military override on orange."

Yes, Agent. Will you be needing light arms or umbrellas?

The tentacle samples the air again. "We have enough arms, and umbrellas are for those limp-dick army boys. We're the real thing."

Tolu deactivates his phone and the music dies.

"Listen," says Eric. "You're here because Mrs Alaagomeji wants you to be. You escaped because she wanted you to. If Kaaro and Bicycle Girl came for you, it's because Mrs Alaagomeji orchestrated it in some way. That woman thinks so far ahead of most people that her actions seem insane, illogical, random, even. She is loyal to the people of Nigeria first and will always act in their best interest, and you better believe that if anyone is going to purge those aliens successfully, it will be her."

Tolu shrugs. "That's the most I've heard you talk since I met you. Why don't you like Kaaro? I saw how you look at him."

"He saved my life and humiliated me all at the same time. I don't want to talk about it."

"Okay."

"He threatened to kill me."

"Before or after he saved your life? Because I'm confused."

"It was after the ... I had an assignment in Rosewater and ... It doesn't matter. Let's focus on the mission at hand."

The light rain turns out to be heavier than anticipated, but not a thunderstorm. It gives Eric the chance to hide his tentacle under a coat, but it likes moisture and it struggles against his will, trying to be in the rain. Tolu has no coat, but does not seem to be bothered. His cousin is in the Akoka campus of the University of Lagos. Walking to the agreed academic department, they have to wade through students, young flesh-flaunting bodies. Eric is reminded that he has not been with someone in more than a year.

Tolu is familiar with the campus. He says this is where they recruit dissidents, and that before Rosewater he protested the Nigerian government. "I was arrested here, you know."

Tolu's cousin has deadline warnings aimed at students on the door of his office. Just before knocking, Tolu says, "Don't mention his hair."

"What?"

The door swings open.

"Ey, Baba Isale!" says Gregory Eleja.

"Oga at the top! Ewo l'ewo?" says Tolu.

Gregory's hair is ... implausible. Though dry, it glistens as if wet. The curls churn over his scalp, dropping down over each ear. His skin has been treated with lightener, giving him that false yellow complexion except around the eyes, ears, lips and knuckles, which appear darker than the rest of him. He looks like a parody of a black man in a Dutch parade.

After going through the greeting ritual with Tolu, his eyes settle on Eric.

"Awo abi ogberi?" he says.

"Partial awo," says Tolu, smiling.

"Ewo tuni partial awo?" Gregory seems confused.

They seem to genuinely like each other, which amuses Eric and contradicts his relationship with his own cousins.

Gregory offers a handshake, but Eric keeps his arms in his coat.

"What do you have for us, Professor?" he says. "Every minute I spend here is a minute away from my boss."

"What's under the coat?" asks Gregory.

Eric shows him.

"Extraordinary." Gregory immediately moves close to the tentacle, unlike most people, who recoil. The tentacle does not respond, remains inert. "And this is artificial?"

"Entirely."

"The person who made it?"

"Deceased." Eric has a flash of Nuru blown into calamari by miniature explosives in Rosewater.

"A shame. I would love to have discussed it with them."

"About your project ... ?" says Eric.

"Yes, yes. Please lock the door."

Gregory goes behind his desk and emerges with one of those sealed, refrigerated boxes used to transport organs in dry ice. This one is a foot square, give or take.

"I'm not going to open the box," he says. He passes his palm over a sensor and a hologram appears above the box.

Eric sees four fleshy lumps of grey and white, each roughly ovoid, suspended in fluid with numerous strands projecting from each one to every other one, then outwards in every direction.

"What am I looking at?" says Eric.

"It's an organoid."

"You say that like I should know what that is. I'm not a scientist."

"It's part of an organ grown entirely in a lab. This is a cerebral organoid, a brainoid, if you will. It's not terribly new. Cerebral organoids have existed since about 2013. Each one of these is basically a hippocampus-amygdala-caudate nucleus complex."

"What does that mean?"

Tolu says, "They're the brain's apparatus for storing memories."

Gregory says, "Simplification, but yes."

Eric strokes his chin. "Can we put data in there?"

"We've detected neurotransmission between them. They're talking to each other. Theoretically, yes, I can introduce data."

"What do they say to each other?"

Gregory shrugs. "You ... We can't know that. They don't have any sense organs, so there's no input from surroundings."

"I need to make a phone call," says Eric. "Where can I get some privacy?"

Femi listens quietly to everything Eric says, and studies the 3D photographs he has sent. When he finishes, she is silent, and if he could not hear her breathing, he would wonder if the secure connection got cut. He turns, but is careful to avoid the walls. Students' toilets are not hygienic.

"What tactical advantage do you think these organoids will confer?" asks Femi.

"If we can download one of the Homian brains into these, perhaps we can study them, find weaknesses, like Bicycle Girl says. Perhaps we can replace someone's brain at the point of death and gain control over them. I don't know, ma'am. I'm your soldier. Strategy is not really my thing, but on the face of it, this seems to be something we should maintain control of."

"Eric, can he build a whole brain?"

"I read his mind, ma'am. He has never done it before, and there is widespread condemnation amongst the scientific community of even attempting it, but Gregory is convinced that he can do it. He even has some outlines of steps involving a bio reactor, pseudo stem cells and other stuff I can't understand."

"Why condemnation?"

"Ethical. Philosophical. If it works and the brain develops a mind, have we created life? A mind so generated would be artificial. What responsibilities would we have towards it? Would it have rights? Would destroying the brain become murder? Shit like that."

"Okay." Femi goes silent again. "Okay. Here's what you're going to do ... "

No sightseeing, no shopping; the military escort takes Eric, Tolu and Gregory out of Lagos without fanfare. The box, all Gregory's papers and a smattering of equipment ride with them, bolted down. The hard drives of all devices are either brought along or formatted and placed in a magnetic field for full erasure.

Tolu is playing his music, and his cousin nods in sync. Eric tunes out.

Chapter Seventeen

The Tired Ones do not exist in any manner that something as simple as a Nimbus search will reveal them. There is no word of mouth. A network of African leaders and potential leaders, the organisation exists to remove the despotic-style leadership that most African countries end up saddled with. Their main thrust is education, support and resources for candidates they back. It is strictly by invitation, and leaks are unheard of, though there are always rumours. The candidates, Tired Men and Tired Women, usually know of and support each other in elections, logistics and other ways. Their resources are considerable. The Tired Ones took the young Jack Jacques out of an abusive situation, trained him and expected him to take his place in their new African order at a time of their choosing. Instead, he saw and chose Rosewater before anyone else could see the potential.

To Jack's surprise, the president, against whom Rosewater fought the insurrection, is also a Tired Man, but this does not help their relationship as it would for any other two people.

Now they meet, not on neutral ground, but in Nigeria, in full view of other Tired leaders of the African Union. Junior members are allowed to observe because lessons are to be learned by all. There is a slight preponderance of women, mainly because the balance of power in the continent has always leaned towards men. The Tired Women see the time as ripe for a course correction, and the Tired Ones have adopted this as an agenda. In fact, Jack has heard a rumour already that the next president of Nigeria will be a woman, a Tired Woman that he knows from the day of his induction.

They walk in together. A weird coincidence lines Jack up with the president. He looks down on Jack's wheelchair.

"So you have sympathy for the gays now," says the president.

"The fact that you call them 'the gays' tells me everything. And they don't need sympathy, sir, they need equality."

"I have no problem with them. But my constituents do, and so, to get re-elected, I perform. On re-election I can serve the greater good, as a Tired Man."

"I—"

A voice speaks over them. "Will you both keep quiet? You know you can't do that here." She sucks her teeth loudly.

The room is circular and dark, a diameter that Jack thinks might be thirty feet, with modular tables arranged in a circle as well. People he knows have affinity for one another sit close, even though placement is meant to be random. An exception is Jack's mentor, who sits so far around the circle that they are almost opposite each other; not a good sign. He is considerably thinner. Last summer he picked what he thought was a pimple off his face, but it was a skin tag. The spot bled for days and a test finally showed he had some kind of blood cancer. He won't come to Rosewater on principle, despite Jack imploring him. He thinks what Jack did in the insurrection was wrong, and people like that believe hard, even unto death. So be it.

He has come in a kaftan, not agbada like everybody else, including Jack.

The proceedings are led by the secretary, a promising Tired Woman from Gabon.

"Welcome. We're here for a follow-up session to the previous negotiations between the Federal Republic of Nigeria and the city state Rosewater, as both heads of state are Tired Men. I'll start with what's settled.

"There will be no hard border, but credentials will be checked and either side reserves the right to deny entry. No visa will be required, but a form can be filled outlining purpose of visit at or on approach to the border.

"Food export from Rosewater to Nigeria will continue, as will international imports to Rosewater.

"Health tourists to Rosewater will be taxed and all the revenue shall be ascribed to the government there, minus a twenty-five per cent administration fee.

"There shall be no attempts by either country to undermine the other, including, but not limited to, espionage, overt military action, inducement of dissidents or other extra-natural means as is abundantly available in Rosewater.

"There shall be no allowance for so-called Homians or any other extraterrestrial to enter Nigeria. Should they break bounds, Nigeria may take any steps necessary to protect the populace, including destroying such extraterrestrials. Rosewater will take reasonable precautions to prevent this from happening.

"Gentlemen, does this summary meet your mutual approval?"

Grunts, glares and nods from both parties.

"You'll have to speak for the record, please."

"Yes."

"Yes."

"Right," says the secretary. "We'll start by repair of—"

"He legalised gay marriage!" The president's eyes are bulging. His right index finger pokes at Jack, and it trembles. If it were a weapon, Jack is sure, he would be dead.

"Shock. Horror," says Jack.

"I will show you shock and horror," says the president. He nods on each word.

"Gentlemen, please."

The president gestures, and a graphic appears in the centre of the circle. "These are the active and suspected gays we are monitoring."

Jack cannot believe what he is seeing. "You're monitoring ... Never mind."

"Since Jacques' stupid announcement, they have been steadily moving to Rosewater. Look at the graph."

The time lapse does show a net influx to Rosewater, and with alacrity, which Jack does not regret. Every single one of them would vote for him in an election.

"These would be criminals in Nigeria, no? So you are glad to be rid of them?" asks Jack. "You're welcome."

"You are disrupting the social order, my friend."

"How is that? What exactly is vexing you in this thing, Mr President? That they are homosexuals, or that they are escaping your grasp?"

"It is an abomination and unnatural. And un-African."

Jack sighs. "Un-African isn't a real word. And we've always had people attracted to the same sex. In antiquity we may not have had the concept of being gay as an identity or identifier, but, haba, are you going to sit there and argue that men have not loved men? Women have not loved women?"

"You sound like you are a gay yourself," says the president. "You and your supporters." He waves his hand generally to a section of the crowd.

"Are you talking to me?" says one of the Tired Women, rising in her seat. One of the president's men rises in response. Angry words. More people stand.

Jack doesn't see who throws the first punch, and it doesn't matter because pretty much everybody joins in. He backs his chair up to the wall and watches as noses are broken, ears are bitten, unfit people slip and fall, and the din of rage rises higher and higher. There is one incident of projectile vomiting. The president punches and swings, missing half the time, and nobody hits him back because it's a felony. Jack remembers that when the man was a young senator, there were many fist fights in the House of Assemblies.

His mentor walks towards him and leans against the wall beside Jack.

"Looks like we'll be needing a visiting dentist," says the mentor.

"At least. Some of these will have to visit Casualty. That lady over there's unconscious," says Jack.

"No, she's not. She's waiting for ... There you go."

"Oh, yeah. Wow. That was effective."

"Jack?"

"Sir?"

"Do you know what you're doing?"

"Not a clue, sir. I have a general idea about what I want, but I'm formulating my plan as I go along."

"Do you think you might be deliberately provoking the president?"

"He sends me dick pics, sir."

146

"So? Let him be juvenile."

A tumbler sails across the room and shatters against someone's head.

"Sir, if I may say so, you seem sanguine about this ija igboro."

The mentor looks at Jack with the sad eyes of a dying man. *"Disgraceful if, in this life where your body does not fail, your soul should fail you first."*

He quotes Marcus Aurelius, but he is talking about Jack.

"Sir, please come and spend a weekend with me in Rosewater."

He shakes his head.

"You are going to die," says Jack. He feels crushed by the sorrow and certainty of it.

"I surely am. You know, when the British colonisers wrote about our pacification, they put it about that we did not resist. They killed our brave men and women, silenced our griots, destroyed our records. They made us out to be cowards and collaborators. Granted, seeing a Sikh redcoat with a drawn sword issuing a battle cry is a terrifying thing to behold, but that doesn't mean we gave them a pass. Jack, you are giving these Homians a pass, and that goes against everything I taught you. That is a failure of the soul. That is disgraceful. Life doesn't always put individuals in a position to affect history. You are in such a position. Why become what our entire belief abhors? 'Self-rule or death' is the motto. No foreign powers, no global corporations, no vested interests. We rule ourselves."

"I'm sharing the wealth, protecting the disenfranchised—"

"Stop dissembling."

"I'm not. I'm trying to bring about the kind of society we

always wanted, that you dream of, with representation. You have to see the aliens as a resource."

"A resource that's killing you slowly."

"And what national resource doesn't? Oil? Coal? Nuclear power? Even solar power requires storage in batteries that we have to detoxify. This is how resources work, sir. We use them, they kill us, until we find the next one, or completely fuck up the environment and all die."

"Boy—"

"Come to Rosewater, sir. Get healing, live. You can berate me when you're alive enough to do so."

Jack wheels out of the melee to where Lora awaits.

Later, in the hotel bar, while he drinks watered-down Johnnie Walker, a woman sidles up to him. He knows her from his time in Lagos.

"Jack," she says, "will you work with me when I am president?"

"Yes, ma'am. As long as you don't send me pictures of your genitals."

She turns, then looks back with a ghostly smile. "You never know. The sight might tempt you away from your skinny wife. Give me a call when you want to try ampleness for a change."

And, of course, she is only half joking. He is not sure if she is talking about being president of the Tired Ones or of the country.

He pays his bill over the protestations of the bar staff, and wheels to his room.

Chapter Eighteen

A man walks through the avenue dressed in a long white robe and wearing a white headscarf, barefoot, dark brown skin glistening in the sun, whether with sweat or anointing oil is anyone's guess. He has a handbell that he rings just before he speaks of doom and destruction.

Koriko watches from the shade of an almond tree. If the prophet of doom sees her, he does not indicate, although he continues to list the sins of Rosewater without pausing for breath. His feet and the hem of his robe are both dirty, mud from the rain no doubt. He is unaware, but he is walking along the path that directly overlies one of Wormwood's pseudopodia. Humans aggregate over the tendrils like iron filings on magnets, which makes Koriko wonder at their potential, their ability to subconsciously discern the alien's presence.

They see you, she thinks to Wormwood.

There is no response. She sighs, because there has been no communication since the day she took over from Anthony, the previous avatar. Wormwood obeys her whims, does what she directs without hesitation. But they have no intercourse, no communion, no relationship other than master–slave, and Koriko does not know why. Is it mourning Anthony? It almost died during the insurrection. Could it be suffering some post-traumatic reaction?

The chemical explosion created many bodies, which took days to transport to the Honeycomb, and so she is tired, but more than that she is lonely. There is nobody like her and nobody she can talk to about anything. She starts to walk down the road, along the same pseudopodium, querying Wormwood as she goes. She eats the flesh of an almond fruit, discarding the nut. A small knot of humans follow her casually, some just to see if she will do something entertaining, like find a dead body, others with prayer cards and supplications, regardless of how often she sends them away.

She breaks off one of the stone organelles on her skin and drops it. A wall of dense woven vines grows between her and the people, blocking the road entirely. On a whim Koriko goes to the residence of Alyssa Sutcliffe.

It is both different and the same. The house has been remodelled and the grounds landscaped. Koriko wonders what the residents' association feels about the palm trees in the yard. She makes herself invisible by removing awareness from the visual cortices of people nearby. They will edit her out of their own visual fields, although cameras and electronic devices will still pick her image up.

The family seem to have just received a grocery delivery. Pat, the child, grown taller now, stacks items into a pyramid. Mark, Alyssa's husband, is loading the fridge with cellulose water bottles. Alyssa is putting other items away. Not Alyssa, but the being she constructed and imbued with Alyssa Sutcliffe's memories. Alyssa is dead.

Koriko stands unseen, unheard, unperceived in their kitchen, feeling the unspoken bond between them, casting her own aloneness into relief. She lurks in their house all day, moving out of their way when they come close, shifting into different rooms with them, watching old movies, tasting their food, all the while ignoring indications of the dead from the rest of Rosewater. They will rise as reanimates and she will find them and bring them to the Honeycomb without fail.

She watches ersatz Alyssa make love to Mark in the dark, though she can see multiple wavelengths and darkness is a meaningless concept to her. Alyssa straddles Mark and rocks, still with her nightgown on, breathing heavily. Mark strokes her arms and cheeks. His eyes are open. The room itself is thick with sweat and passion. Koriko tries to leave. In a sudden, sharp motion the Alyssa construct stops moving and turns in Koriko's direction, frowning, squinting, sensing something, but seeing nothing.

"What's wrong?" asks Mark.

"Nothing, I . . . Nothing."

Koriko makes her way to the garden and calls Wormwood. It responds, takes her into the soil and transports her to the toxic waste-contaminated zone. The buildings here are stripped of the vegetation that climbs over the rest of the city. When she emerges, a moray accosts her.

"This area is toxic. Leave," it says.

Morays are serpentine robots used in disaster areas to hunt for life signs of survivors, or to root out pockets of hazards to warn rescue teams. They have a limited AI capability outside those functions.

"This area is toxic. Leave." The moray will continue to repeat the injunction until it gets some kind of response.

"I acknowledge your message," says Koriko. "Will you follow me around, little creature? Will you keep me company?"

"Do you need assistance?" asks the moray. "Are you in pain?"

"Yes."

"How may I assist you?"

"Follow me around," says Koriko.

The robot slithers alongside Koriko, and she in turn asks the kind of inane questions that it is capable of answering. At intervals it defaults back to asking about toxicity, but on the whole, she finds it a useful companion.

Some of the buildings have been reduced to rubble, but Koriko moves through them, the bitter residue of a chemical fire in her nose and the back of her mouth.

"How many people did you save this week?" she asks the moray.

"Sixty-eight. Twelve of those died in the hospital."

Nothing grows here any more. The soil is poisoned, and it will take Wormwood some time to repair. Humans cannot live here. It reminds Koriko of where she was, back on Home, the last person to leave the planet, cataloguing, dilly-dallying because she did not wish to live in space.

The moray scrunches up, shortens itself to six inches, then springs up to bound across a gap between islands of dry surfaces. Some of the toxins are corrosive, and while the robots are resistant, this feature is not absolute. At times they meet other serpentines: eels, centipedes, boomslangs, worms; all synchronise data before moving on. The moray is one of the better designs, working with air cells as bellows, and able to pitch, yaw and roll smoothly.

As the hours pass, lights come on in the moray's segments,

and soon they run into a search party of sorts, humans in hazmat suits who stop when they see Koriko.

She tells them she wants the moray, and reverently they rush to accept. They make tweaks to the AI and leave.

They continue together, the moray and Koriko, it after the living, she after the dead.

At the Honeycomb, Koriko delivers the last of the day's dead into the electrolyte baths. Organic neural computers grow on the walls looking like fungus, but made of the same durable material that constitutes the alien headquarters. This is secreted according to plans stored in the xenosphere, directed by Chief Scientist Lua.

The computers keep track of all the transfers and alert when anything goes wrong, which, according to Lua, it frequently does. One of the assistants asks Koriko to follow her; says the chief scientist would like a word.

The moray coils around her ankle, uncharacteristically silent. Koriko thinks it is recording where it is, because not many humans or human constructs are allowed into the Honeycomb.

Each chamber leads into another, which may be larger or smaller, on the same horizontal plane, lower or higher. Koriko slows when they pass the holding room for the passers, those Homians who either think they are human or pretend that they are. They lie in neat rows, their heads covered in mucoid sludge while they are being re-educated. The humans bring them in, usually protesting and under restraint, and Lua's people smear them with neuro-active bio-material. Then they hope for the best. If it doesn't work, they are held in the Honeycomb indefinitely.

Koriko meets Lua in a chamber of quiet music where a woman struggles against leather straps in a chair. There is no greeting exchanged – they do not have that kind of relationship – but there is the faintest impression of a nod.

"Is that ... human technology wrapped around your ankle?" asks Lua.

"It's my pet," says Koriko.

"I ... Never mind. This person is, used to be, Manpreet Kaur."

Koriko notices the green sclera, and the fact that the moray does not react to her. "She's not human."

"No, she's Homian. She's a re-host."

"I don't know what that is. I thought if the transfer didn't go well, we just sent them to the west wing?"

"The problem here isn't the transfer. This person has already been hosted, but destroyed her body deliberately. The algorithm just queued her data back to the front and the process transferred into Manpreet."

"Are you saying she committed suicide?" asks Koriko.

"No. Or maybe a suicidal act of terrorism. This is Laark. He created the toxic spill and died in the process."

Koriko knows of Laark, knows him of old. Instead of the gentle takeover of indigenous populations, Laark advocated large-scale murder to hasten the coming world for Homians. He and his ilk were purveyors of a particular brand of eschatology that required Homian intervention, bloody intervention if necessary.

"The spill gave us a lot of hosts," says Koriko.

"But the tactics—"

"I'm only doing what you want to do but can't. Or won't," says Laark. "There are no laws against it."

Lua raises her eyebrows. "Human laws—"

"I do not recognise human laws. You might as well say insect laws or bacteria laws. All are the same to me."

Koriko turns to Lua. "Why are you showing me this person? What is my role here?"

"What shall I do with him?" asks Lua. "Previous synners only killed one or two, but this is systematised."

"Set him loose," says Koriko. "And the next time he dies, re-host him. This makes my work faster."

Lua's mouth drops open. "You mean . . . "

"Yes," says Koriko. "And don't bother me with this again."

Laark nods, giggling, unable to contain his glee.

Koriko and the serpentine return to the edge of the toxic zone, and she waits while it explores. Before long, Laark drifts from her mind.

Chapter Nineteen

Taiwo bets on the hyena and loses.

He spits and watches the celebrations of those who won. Bastards. How could a dog beat a hyena? It boggles the mind. They carry the limp animal away, but the night is young. Hyena men, despite their name, have always walked with other animals. Usually monkeys, snakes and other small mammals. The men and boys come to gatherings like this, nomadic, with their womenfolk and children a few miles away in a camp, although the whole family unit takes part in the domestication of the animals.

Dark night, but clear, and only a whiff of a chemical smell on the wind. Taiwo is at a table, one of those round ones old men sit at to gossip. He is the only one sitting. His crew, about twenty men and women, are scattered around a pit dug through what used to be a basketball court. The lights that would have been illuminating night games are now focused on the animal fights. There are four hyena men, wiry, of good cheer, wearing animal skins, charms hanging off them, high on mushrooms and khat, which they picked up from the Somalis on their travels. The pit is four feet at its deepest point and the bottom is smooth, swept clean so that the animal footpads can gain the best traction.

The dog bout was unplanned. One of Taiwo's men had an Alsatian that he swore could take the hyena. Turns out he was right. Doesn't matter. Ten per cent of his winnings will automatically go to Taiwo, no matter the source. Every drug transaction, every extortion, every murder-for-hire, every kidnapping, all of them send ten per cent to Taiwo if it happens in the Rosewater area. If a villain crosses the border from Nigeria seeking criminal asylum, it is twenty per cent.

The ones Taiwo hasn't found a way to plug into are the organ traffickers, and the problem vexes him. He gestures and a boy pours him more whiskey in a shot glass.

The next bout is a snake versus a mongoose. Everyone knows the outcome of this, so it's more of an entertainment bout with no bets. Uncanny how the furry, super-fast little mammal goes straight for the snake, a predator with no idea that its time has come.

The problem with the organ trafficking is that it's not done by professionals. Anybody with minimal pain tolerance can have a conspirator cut out, say, the liver or a kidney. Wormwood grows a new one, then the old organ can be reinserted in the abdomen, where the alien will again reattach it to something and heal the wound. The carrier now has an extra kidney or liver plus a brand-new pot belly. They cross the border into Nigeria, get a surgeon to cut it out of them into a dry ice box, get paid, then hop back into Rosewater. The entire process can be over in forty-eight hours.

Taiwo is contemplating killing the traffickers on the return leg as a lesson when he sees himself approaching on foot. There are three layers of bodyguards between Taiwo and the outside world, but they do not stop this man. They do, at least, search him, which goes without incident.

Kehinde. His identical twin brother.

Taiwo turns to the boy holding the whiskey. "Get another chair."

Kehinde looks as though the shadows stick to him. His eyes glow and he smiles, showing the gap in his front teeth, eji, that Taiwo sees in the mirror. Eji is a sign of beauty among the Yoruba, but Taiwo doesn't deceive himself. He and his brother look too brutal to be handsome. Kehinde is trim, walks with a grace and muscularity that Taiwo hasn't had in a couple of years. He can't think of anyone he hates more than his twin brother.

God, I hope I don't have to fight him again. The last time took months to recover from. For both of us.

Kehinde takes the chair from the boy and sits down beside his brother so that he is facing the pit where the mongoose is playing with the serpent. Taiwo stares at the whites of Kehinde's eyes, checking for the telltale green tinge that would mark him as an alien, but it isn't there. He scoops up some sand with his hand and throws it on Kehinde's leg, standard check for ghosts in Yoruba folklore if a person who hasn't been seen for a long time turns up. Kehinde isn't an extraterrestrial and he isn't one of the dead.

"Where have you been?" asks Taiwo.

"Enugu prison. Some bullshit charge, but I was detained without trial, then they lost the arrest paperwork or something. I walked away during a riot." Kehinde's voice is relaxed, unhurried. "You're fat. You're not looking after my body."

"Oh fuck you. And talk to me with respect. I'm twenty minutes older than you."

158

"Omokehindelegbon. I am the older twin who comes out second. I sent you into the world like an outrider, or have you forgotten our traditions as well?"

"What do you want? You want your share of the city back? Because things are different now."

"So I see."

"Are you here to fight?"

"No. But I will tell you this: I'm going to kill your people. I'm not going to accept their surrender. I am going to kill them, your entire operation."

Taiwo laughs. "You're going to kill me?"

"I can't kill you. Omo iya ni wa. You're family. No, I'll just kill everyone around you. Then I'll take what's mine."

"Brother, my men aren't the lot they were before you left. They are seasoned soldiers, trained by a special forces guy. They are decorated war heroes like me."

Kehinde places his elbows on the table and picks up the shot glass that Taiwo has forgotten about. He drains it and throws it into the pit. The mongoose has the snake's head in his mouth, in a death grip. It is startled, but does not let its prey go. The spectators look up, puzzled.

Kehinde says, "Given enough time, all honours become meaningless. What is meaningful is the one thing that you want, that you've always wanted."

"And what's that?" asks Taiwo.

"To be better than me." Kehinde rises and wipes his mouth against his right palm. He raises the arm and spreads the fingers out. Then he makes a fist.

There is a brief whistle, and the pit explodes in light and flame. The shock wave knocks Taiwo over and sets his ears ringing. Windows in selected buildings shatter, which, to

Taiwo, means their snipers are killing his snipers. He sees Kehinde walk away, black-clad armed men gravitating towards him and buzzing about like hornets, accepting nods from him. They shoot survivors and stragglers before disappearing into the night. In the pit, the flames from the rocket attack have subsided and there are only the dead, no wounded.

Taiwo stands, surveys the scene. He is irritated to find his heart racing and his breathing fast.

He summons reinforcements, then he calls the mayor's direct line.

Chapter Twenty

My cocoon crashes into the tarmac in London in 2012, weeks after Wormwood has established itself. I break out of it and I'm on what looks like it should be a busy road. I have never been to London, but the xenosphere tells me what I need to know. The cocoon dissipates within seconds, followed shortly after by a healing of the crack in the asphalt. I am not really here. I can have limited interactions with people, but I cannot change history; this has already happened. This is a collective and collected memory. If I do something at a critical point, I may affect how people remember, which can have consequences for the present, my present, especially if it affects their decision-making. None of my actions are part of that.

So why is this road empty in the middle of the afternoon? There are cars, but they are vandalised: no tyres, no windows, even the doors of many have been ripped off and taken away. It's quieter than any metropolitan area I've ever seen.

I start walking. A road sign tells me it's Tottenham Court Road. There are rows of shops advertising electronics, home goods, food, and other things that are too obscure to understand. There is a theatre at the end of the road, the Dominion, advertising *We Will Rock You* with a cut-out of a man. Here is some kind of intersection with traffic lights, but long dead. In fact, I see no sign of electricity at all. There's an Underground station, which I wonder if I should explore.

Whatever happened here must have happened a while back, because there are plants growing and dirt on the roads. There are no people, dead or alive, that I can see. Other than these structures, it's like the humans have gone. If I didn't know I can't be harmed, I would be worried.

This is freaky to me, because I am not alive at this time. I was born in 2033. I have to keep telling myself that I am walking in archives, exploring information. It's like being in a really interactive library, or a game, except that I am a non-player character, which is absurd.

I walk into a megastore called HMV. I sing a few notes, which echo back to me. There are rows of shelves, discs of media on the floor, broken or empty. I do not recognise any of the formats.

Oyin Da, what are you doing here? How is this going to help you get to America? Why have you come?

This is the most studied period in recent Western history, with tendrils of popular thought winding out into conspiracy theory. Strange that when it was truly aliens to blame, fringe folk wouldn't believe it, and blamed the government. London was evacuated, but not everybody left. There is dirt everywhere, dust, plus whatever the wind carries in from the outside. The doors are stuck in the open position. It's windowless and dark inside because none of the lights work. The refuse is mostly food wrappers, bits of paper and dried-up vegetation. I imagine the latter blowing around like urban tumbleweed.

I climb up the escalator. I am brazen because I'm not in

danger here if all I'm doing is mining information. It all feels real, though. And old. My usual instinct is to scavenge electronics, back when I thought ... back when I was alive. When I thought I was alive. It's confusing. Anyway, this shit is so old that none of it is useful. Or it would have been useful if I used real technology.

This level is for film in DVD format. None of the shelves are stacked, so I don't know what that means, but it must be in physical media, like the music. They have digital music and films, but it won't be here. I'm turning back down when I hear a sound, like a box falling over.

"Hello," I say. I know I've been heard because there's that echo effect that you get in a large room without soft furnishings.

Nothing. No other sounds. I stay where I am because it's dark and the light from downstairs doesn't penetrate any further.

"Hello, hello?" One last time, then I go down the escalator.

Outside the store I think I see the flap of a coat go round a corner into an alleyway. I sprint, and there he is, my first human of 2012. He is pissing on the wall, his back to me, long dirty coat, collapsing shoes, and very, very dirty. He whistles to himself as he urinates and I take two steps back to give him some privacy. He finishes and turns around, song dying as he notices me.

"Hi," he says.

I can't answer because I'm stunned. It is Anthony.

"Anthony?" I say. "Anthony Salermo?"

"Do I owe you money?" he says. I can smell booze on him.

It *is* him. Him before Wormwood. He looks the same, but with a harder edge than the Anthony I knew. The angles of his mouth turned downwards, lines between the eyebrows permanently etched. His hands shake so violently he is finding it difficult to put his manhood away.

"You don't owe me money," I say.

"Good. Because you ain't gonna get it, see." His speech is slurred, there is a tangle of thin blood vessels at the tip of his nose, and his watery eyes are yellow-green. Liver disease. "I'm leaving."

"Where are you going, Anthony?"

"How do you know my name?"

"We've met. A long time ago, for me, at least, and not in this place."

"Did we fuck?"

"Eww. No. Besides, I like women."

"I've known women who like women. But I'm leaving. G'bye."

"May I follow you?"

He squints at me. "You speak funny. You're a foreigner, arn' you?"

"I am not from London or the UK, if that is what you're saying."

"Do you have any booze on you?"

"No, sir. I don't drink."

"Well, what use are you, then?" He tries to turn with a flourish, but he overbalances and falls to the concrete. He picks himself up and starts to weave away. I follow.

Anthony goes west on Oxford Street. We walk past Oxford Circus, Bond Street and Marble Arch Underground stations on our way, but I know where he is going. After forty minutes, we come to what used to be Hyde Park. Marble Arch itself is broken, although one column remains standing, scorched though it is. They used to hang people here and I imagine their ghosts in the xenosphere, still dancing the Tyburn jig or just floating about with floppy heads.

Smoke rises from a crater whose edge stretches off to both sides, and I cannot see the curve for the smoke. The ground trembles beneath me, but not enough to send the drunk man to his knees, so it can't be that bad. I don't know how long it has been since Wormwood crashed, but this did not happen today. I notice there is steam mixed in with the smoke at times, the water from the Serpentine.

There are other people now, five or so, standing at the edge, silent. Of Wormwood, nothing is seen.

I don't know why they are here. From what I know, when Wormwood landed, it irradiated its immediate surroundings. Exotic fissionable material was found at the site ten years later. The xenobiologist Bodard posits that the alien was vulnerable on landing, and had to make sure no native organisms would bother it while it developed, so it irradiated its nest.

I know that Anthony will die here, but I don't know about the others, so I rush to tell them to flee. They are non-reactive, eyes glazed over, and I think they are proto-reanimates.

Anthony fishes out a plastic water bottle from the bowels of his coat and drinks the last dregs of what is clearly a fermented liquid. He throws the bottle into the crater and takes off his coat.

"Anthony, is there anyone you want me to contact for you? Any family? A wife?" I ask.

"You again? Why don't you jus' fack off!"

He tries to take a graceful leap into the crater, but he lacks the coordination and bounces off an outcrop with a sickening crack. He rolls into the billowing smoke and is gone from view.

"Good luck, Anthony Salermo. Till we meet again." The next time I see him will be 2055, and he will have just survived a particle weapon attack. Kaaro, a cute boy I have a crush on, will dive in front of him to save his life from machine-gun fire. He will surround Wormwood with a dome, and I will stay within the dome, but Kaaro will choose to be without. Rosewater will grow and become a city.

I examine his coat and find a handwritten note: *Food at St Anselm's.* Some images of a food kitchen, slapdash, faces of people serving and receiving, fragments of a route. Anthony's memories are in the xenosphere, but they are broken because of his late-stage alcohol dependency.

I set off, looking at the churches within walking distance of the HMV store. If I'm going to find someone who is American, or has been to America, it's as good a place to start as any.

Chapter Twenty-One

There is so much going on, so much he is worrying about, that Kaaro feels unable to fit everyday activities in, but he does this and more, the more being teaching Layi fine control.

They are in the back yard of the house. Because of the rains the day before, the paler green undersurface of the leaves is on show. The sun has dried all the puddles, but the soil has that mulchy, fertile smell to it.

"Take your time," Kaaro says.

"I am," says Layi, laughing.

They stand side by side. Three feet away are seven pails, upended, crudely numbered with a black marker. Each covers a target object. The aim of the exercise is to heat, set fire to, boil or annihilate the objects without melting the buckets.

Layi is in town for the first ever Rosewater Pride. He has hinted at moving. Kaaro picked him up at the airport.

"I didn't know you were gay," he said.

"To be fair, I don't know either. I am sometimes attracted to men, though. I'll be marching in solidarity. That way, if I turn out to be gay later, I can say I was part of history. And I might meet hot guys."

"That's so self-serving."

"I know. I'm terrible. Shall we begin?"

That was two hours ago.

Kaaro would rather not be doing this, but he is supposed to be retired, and how can he refuse Layi's earnest face? His guilelessness? Kaaro does not have time for this given the work he has to do, but Layi is practically family, plus the last time the boy lost control he burned the family home down. That led to Aminat working for S45 to stop them from taking Layi into custody indefinitely. They trained her to look after Layi, and that developed into sending her on missions.

"I have an idea," says Kaaro. "Do you mind if I visit your brain for a minute?"

"As long as you ignore any images of naked folks."

Kaaro feels around Layi's consciousness, finds what controls his ability and folds his willpower around it. He visualises the target through Layi's eyes and . . . lets go. The object pops into flame underneath the bucket.

"Wow, you're good," says Layi.

"Now you," says Kaaro.

Bucket number three explodes along with the glass of water inside.

Kaaro and Layi look at each other.

"I'm sorry, I'm not concentrating," says Layi.

"You're wasting my time," says Kaaro.

"Yes, because your old ass is busy doing important things, right?"

"Can we just go again? Stop destroying my buckets."

Yaro barks twice, and Kaaro knows Aminat is back.

She is weathered and exhausted. There is also blood on her.

The xenosphere around her churns with information like an overripe fruit waiting to burst.

"What happened?" says Layi. He rushes to his sister and they hug.

She puts up a hand. "It's not my blood."

"Can you talk about it?" asks Kaaro.

Between Kaaro and Layi, they take Aminat to the lounge. Kaaro gets a damp cloth and wipes off the grime and dirt.

"Somebody with firepower and training just killed a number of Taiwo's men. We don't know who, but they are very serious."

"A power play? Someone moving in?"

"Probably. But we don't know and nobody's talking."

When Aminat is looking slightly more human, Kaaro leaves her with Layi, locks the dog out of the bedroom and lights a cigarette. He transitions into the xenosphere within seconds, navigating his defences without thinking: a maze, a number of phrases, sequences of light and dark. His guardian, Bolo, awaits.

"Come with me," says Kaaro.

Bolo is Kaaro, but not. The giant is a concentration of the most feral parts of Kaaro's subconscious. Like the subconscious, Kaaro takes him everywhere now.

At the edge of his own consciousness, represented by a rocky cliff falling off into an abyss, there are floating humans, representing their minds. He is vaguely aware of the communal subconsciousness, of the residual fear from the chemical attack and the activities of Koriko, gathering the dead after the shootout.

Layi's proximity he can feel as a burning flame, which is primarily how the xenoforms manifest in the boy.

Kaaro seeks and finds a thread he has hidden and waiting, and he pulls. The thread yanks him up and into the deep xenosphere. Bolo keeps time with him like a satellite. He moves at speed, transforming into his gryphon avatar without even thinking about it. The consciousnesses around him bounce off him as if they are helium balloons. If they are asleep, they will have brief nightmares; if awake, unexplained gooseflesh. No harm done.

The thread leads straight to the mind of Bad Fish. In this place, its representation is a woven string of neural tissue that connects with the back of the hacker's head.

"Oh shit, it's you again," says Bad Fish. His eyes grow wide. "What the fuck is that?"

Bolo crashes down, and his hair sweeps the floor, which is a mental representation of where Bad Fish is, some hack farm in Lagos.

"You don't have to worry about him. You look good," says Kaaro.

Bad Fish is heavy-set, robed as usual, though his belly pushes gently against the fabric. He is a religious figure for the hackers and the script kiddies, with skills that are deemed celestial. For real, Yahoo-yahoo boys worship him, work for free, while they await his blessings and teaching. He once helped Kaaro get S45 encrypted data off his implant, but then tried to steal some of it. As a result, Kaaro has something on him, although he would like to think they are now friends of a kind. To appreciate his powers, you'd need to know that Bad Fish has hacked the defunct space station the Nautilus, and used a particle weapon without breaking sweat. He saved Aminat's life during the insurrection. Twice, maybe. She and Kaaro haven't had the opportunity to pay him back.

"What do you want this time?" asks Bad Fish. He seems sober and in the moment, which is unlike him.

"What are you doing right now?"

"Some police just raided my shop. I had to decant to a temporary accommodation. My saints are reconnecting my stuff."

"What's that?"

Hanging in mid-air is a deep-sea diving suit held up by multiple thin cables that lead off into nowhere. Kaaro does not know what it symbolises, but it's on Bad Fish's mind.

"My pride and joy. Something I'm working on. It connects to every hardware address of every implant. It synchronises with any cameras or surveillance devices close by. I can get into phones from there. Kaaro, with this suit, I can see everybody everywhere."

"Why?"

Bad Fish shrugs. "Because I can. It came to me in a dream one day."

"What dream?"

"I don't know, a dream. I saw a thing, a spider-like being, but not. It was one big eye at the centre of a black body and hundreds of legs. Each leg connected to someone. I woke up and drew the blueprint of this suit."

That's Molara. He's seen her in a dream, or a nightmare.

He strokes the arm of the representation of the suit, then turns back to me.

"Why are you here, Kaaro?"

"Your country needs you."

"Oh, you motherfucker. Are you working for S45 again?"

"Just wait, brother. Listen. I may have been mistaken about Rosewater. It's not the health utopia it's billed to be. It's a cancer that will slowly eat the human race until there are none of us left."

"How has this change of heart come about?"

Kaaro explains his visit to Femi Alaagomeji in prison, and the meeting in Nigeria.

"Wait, are you saying Miss Aminat doesn't know you're here?"

"Yes. We can't involve her. She works for Jacques."

"You ... I've always liked your lady, Kaaro. You're generally a fucking idiot, but she is ... refined and cheerful. And she's grateful when you do something for her."

"I'm grateful when you do things for me."

"No, you're not."

"I say thank you all the time."

"But you don't mean it. You're mocking. Your voice says it all. Miss Aminat says thank you with her voice, and there's laughter in there."

"I'll tell her when I'm done."

"What does 'done' entail? What do you want from me, Kaaro? This time."

"We might need that particle accelerator again."

"Going to war again?"

"Not with Rosewater. With the aliens. We need them stopped or neutralised."

"Doesn't S45 have access to the Nautilus?"

"The Nautilus was officially decommissioned, Bad Fish."

"Yes, I saw the fake videos. Naughty."

"Do you still have access?"

"Don't insult me. Of course I do."

"Will you help us?"

"Sure. But what do I get?"

"Survival! If we don't win, the human race perishes."

"Yeah, so you say. What do I get?"

"What do you want?"

"Full immunity for whatever I might have done in the process of finding enlightenment."

"Hacking offences only."

"Sure."

"I'll talk to the boss." Kaaro glances at the suit. "We'll be needing this too."

"For what?"

"Keeping track of everybody. The government of Rosewater is monitoring electronics. The alien is monitoring the xenosphere, so a lot of what I do has to be curtailed. You can be our eyes and ears."

"You're saying it like it's some kind of privilege."

"Can you come to Femi, in Abuja?"

"I can but I won't. You want me to enter the lion's den. I can do this remotely as long as the police leave me the fuck alone. You can tell Femi Alaagomeji that. Tell her to tell them to leave me alone."

"I'll relay this."

"I need it all in writing. Signed. Stamped. Notarised."

"Jesus, fine, I'll relay your needs. Where should she send it?"

"Tell her to create the documents. I'll know."

"Hey, do you know anything about the killings in Rosewater last night?"

"I'm not on the clock until those documents—"

"Bad Fish!"

"Okay, okay ... I don't know if it's related, but Kehinde, Taiwo's twin brother, is back."

Oh.

Oh shit.

"I have to go. Nice seeing you again. Mwah, mwah, mwah!"

Aminat needs to know this.

Chapter Twenty-Two

Lora is barely aware of motion in the shock-proof luxury vehicle that takes her to work. Having studied people and their habits, she realises that on inheriting as much money as she did, she is expected to increase the amount of luxury in her life. She finds this concept difficult to grasp experientially. While it means spending more money on the same things, she is trying to tell the difference. The engine of this vehicle is nigh-on silent. The upholstery is soft. There is a wide range of refreshments, including liquor. The AI has an English accent. There is a robot to take luggage into the destination, although Lora doesn't require that. She looks at the back of the construct's head and feels no kinship.

So far, luxury means separation from people who cannot afford it.

We are now at the mayor's mansion, ma'am. Shall I seek parking, or would you prefer that I keep the engine running right at the entrance?

"Thank you. Return to base until I call you."

Very good. Have a pleasant working day.

The office is busy, even at this time of the day. She will go to the residence at nine, but for now, she has a meeting with Blessing Boderin. The lawyer is waiting outside her office. He stands when he spots her coming.

"Miss Asiko."

"Mr Boderin."

"I think some of the candidates are lining up outside."

"Why? How many experts are there?"

"Twenty-eight."

"But we only need one."

"I know. But there's a glut of expert witnesses in Rosewater. Luckily for you, it drives the price down."

"The mayor doesn't care about the price."

"Good. Can I have a raise?"

"Funny."

"How about a bonus if I win the case?"

"Will you win?"

"Yes."

Lora sees no signs of dishonesty or nervousness on his part. In fact, everything about Boderin shouts confidence. His shoes at a high shine, his immaculate suit, his height, his facial expression, his blue eyes. His hair . . .

"Why do you dye your hair?"

"Because it's light brown, and some clients get uncomfortable working with an albino."

"Why would they?"

"You must not be from around here."

"I am aware that albinos are discriminated against, but I would have thought your skill as an attorney would trump that."

"It doesn't. Sometimes I have to wear contact lenses to hide the blue."

"If you win, I will make sure you get a bonus," says Lora. "Shall we begin?"

"Reality is a hologram, therefore personality is an illusion. Boundaries between people are a construct that means nothing in the grand scheme of ... "

"The brain generates the self as a side effect of its processes. As long as the brain is functioning, whatever it manifests *is* the personality, even if it is different from before revival. It ... "

" ... real question is that consciousness is not required for identity. For the purposes of legal proceedings we have to be talking of a legal entity. The reanimate body is free of consciousness, but not selfhood ... "

"Wait," says Boderin. "Whose side are you on?"

"I have no side. I'm on the side of truth."

"Oh, fuck off," says Lora.

" ... not only combining aspects of Baba Sala's final film, but the evolution of understanding *tabula rasa*, speaking of evolution and belief in the linguistics of the phrase 'presence of mind'. If we go back to Ptolemy, we will find formative ... "

By lunchtime, Lora no longer wishes to listen to candidates.

"Is it just me, or do they all seem completely insane?"

"It's not just you," says Boderin. "Although we're all just people cracked and broken in different places."

"You don't seem worried."

"I'm not. I'm going to win regardless."

"Then why are we doing this?"

"May I speak freely?"

"Please do."

"We are doing this because the mayor panicked and asked you to ask me to interview for an expert of our own because Mrs Jacques' expert gave us a bloody nose. The mayor pays the bills, so here I am."

"But you don't want any experts."

"I don't *need* any experts, but if one can be found, that is good, I'll take him or her."

He is nearly smiling, and Lora finds this pleasing. She tells the secretary to dismiss the candidates and pay their travel allowance.

To Boderin she says, "Let's go out to lunch. I am experimenting with luxury. Would you like to come with me?"

"This ... is much better ... than interviewing ... crackpots," says Boderin.

Labouring behind her, splashing the bath bubbles in his exertions, Boderin comes to a noisy climax and flops onto Lora's back, still joined. Lora matches his breathing and sweats like he does. She feels him still rigid inside her, and she is aware of a whole mess of sub-routines struggling to come out, programming she removed but that creeps up on her at odd times, and which, despite deletion, still remains a phantom in her memory. The suite has a transparent ceiling and the only thing above them is the sky, although it started raining half an hour before they arrived.

"We should fuck again," says Lora.

The next day she attends court, not because she has to, but ostensibly because she wants to keep an eye on Boderin's performance. She is able to admit to herself that she finds his form pleasing, and that she might be here just to see him in his element, as they say. Both he and Hannah Jacques pretend not to know her in court. She, in turn, does not push the matter.

Hannah says, "Your Honour, I would like to call Venture Alade to the stand."

Venture walks with great difficulty, dragging his left side, like one who has had a stroke and is in recovery. He has a carer who walks with him to ensure he is comfortably placed. He wears glasses and has a wedding ring on his left hand. His suit appears pressed, but the contortions of his body rumple it. When sworn in on the bible, he speaks clearly.

"Tell us, Mr Alade, do you live in Rosewater?"

"Yes."

"How long have you lived here?"

"From the start. I was here in 2055."

"Where do you currently reside?"

"Ilu-be."

"Are you married?"

"Divorced."

"Do you have children?"

"Two. I see them on alternate weekends."

"How old are they?"

"Five and six."

"Do you work, sir?"

"Objection. Relevance? My lord, are we to sit through this gentleman's entire curriculum vitae? Shall we find out he is a Libra and likes knitting?"

"Mrs Jacques?"

"I am establishing Mr Alade's current level of functioning, my lord. It has relevance to the case that will become clear."

"Establish it quickly," says the judge. "The witness may answer."

"I am a payroll clerk with Integrity Construction. I give chits to the weeders."

"Do you enjoy your work?"

"It's all right."

"What do you do after work?"

"I play games on Nimbus."

"Do you win?"

"Objection." Boderin is on his feet. "My lord . . . ?"

"Mrs Jacques?"

"My lord, we are getting to the crux."

"You are getting to thin ice. Overruled."

"Mr Alade, we can see that you have some functional difficulty moving about. Was this due to injury?"

"Yes."

"When did this occur?"

"2056."

"Could you tell us the nature of the injury?"

"An automaton dropped masonry on me from a great height. I was illegally on a building site."

"That sounds as though it would be a serious injury."

"It was. My skull was crushed and the debris rested on my ribcage, compressing it."

"That would have been hard to survive."

"I didn't survive. I was pronounced dead when the ambulance arrived."

Boderin starts writing furiously.

"You were dead?"

"For six months. I rose again after the second Opening."

"Are you saying you were a reanimate?"

"Yes. I was dead, now I'm alive."

The court erupts into chaos and the usually mild judge smashes his gavel repeatedly. He points to the two lawyers.

"Get over here."

They both approach the bench and the judge muffles the microphone. Lora hears everything clearly because she put a microphone on Boderin as per the mayor's instructions.

"Mrs Jacques, is this a stunt of some kind? Because I find it in bad taste."

"Not a stunt, my lord. Mr Alade was a reanimate in 2056. We have the hospital death certificate. Furthermore, he will testify, and I have witnesses who will corroborate, that he was kept away from the death squads—"

"Objection."

Hannah looks sharply at Boderin. "This isn't testimony. He was kept safe from the death squads and slowly regained his mind to what you see today. He is not as he was, but he is certainly not mindless, as the government would have us believe."

The judge looks to Boderin. "Do you have any comment?"

Boderin says nothing, but even from where she sits, Lora can see him gritting his teeth while trying to keep his expression calm.

"Boderin?" says the judge.

"My lord, the defence has no objection to this evidence being presented."

"Very well. You may proceed, Mrs Jacques."

Hannah returns and takes a breath. "Mr Alade—"

Boderin bounds to his feet. "My lord, if it pleases the court, the defence is willing to concede that this is indeed Mr Venture Alade, and that he was dead and is now alive, and was a reanimate and regained his mind over time."

Lora whispers urgently, *"Are you out of your fucking mind?"*

"I see," says the judge. "Mrs Jacques, is there anything else you wish to establish from this witness?"

"No, my lord."

"Very well. Your witness, Mr Boderin."

"Thank you, my lord. Mr Alade, what has happened to you is nothing short of miraculous, wouldn't you agree?"

"Yes, sir."

Boderin nods. "And to what or whom do you attribute this miracle?"

"I don't understand."

"What, sir, brought you back from the dead?"

"The alien. Wormwood."

"Thank you. Nothing further."

The judge looks to Hannah. "Mrs Jacques?"

"I rest my case, my lord."

"Thank you. Mr Boderin, would you like to call your first witness?"

"The defence rests as well, my lord."

A murmur rolls through the courtroom, stalled by the judge's gavel.

"Very well. I will hear your summations after recess."

A private room in the courthouse. Poor hologram facilities means there is a hiss in the room where there should be silence. Jack Jacques' rendered image is adequate, but Lora thinks it cutting-edge for ten years ago. The mayor is at some function or other, wearing isiagu complete with red cap.

"It's hit all the news feeds, so the impact when we lose will be worse," says Lora. She has said this before, but uses it to break the silence.

"We're not going to lose," says Boderin.

Jack says, "It's not hit all the news feeds. Not all. We need the influencer sites to carry this. I want the common woman talking about it. We need to boost the signal. Losing is only part of the problem."

"We're not going to lose," says Boderin.

"I'll get our publicity guys on it," says Jack.

"Why do we want more publicity instead of less?" asks Lora.

"Because it's already out, so that's not going to change. Already a few people are marching, but it's spontaneous and sporadic. If we can get the dissent to a critical mass, it can justify martial law and the suspension of the courts. Which takes the decision away from the judicial system."

"Can we get Hannah to withdraw the case?"

"We're not going to lose," says Boderin.

"I don't know," says Jack. "We have a strict rule about work–life separation."

"Hey!" says Boderin.

Both Jack and Lora stare at him.

"Neither of you is listening to me. We are not going to lose," says Boderin. He straightens his tie.

Jack squints. "Who are you again?"

"Blessing Boderin. I'm from Legal."

"Right. Right. Listen, it doesn't matter. No, listen to me. It doesn't matter any more. Win, lose, it's not relevant. We now know that at least one reanimate has his wits back. The question is brewing even now. If this one reanimate became normal again, what about my brother-sister-mother-father-lover-friend? Because if there is only a five per cent chance that a loved one will be back to normal, people are not going to accept the reality of handing over our bodies to aliens. It's not a matter of if the current paradigm will collapse, it's a matter of when."

Boderin turns to Lora. "Do I still get a bonus if I win?"

She shrugs. "If you win."

He wins.

Hannah's summation is elegant and moving; it brings all the points together and by rights should carry the day.

Boderin keeps things simple. "That these people are dead, at least initially, is not contested. My learned colleague even submitted death certificates into evidence. If that's not an own goal, I don't know what it is. Like Godwin Odiye, who cost Nigeria a World Cup match in 1977. All this speculation about life, self, consciousness, this is all nice and touching. I honestly felt tears emerging from my eyes. It's very informative, and I've learned a lot about neuroscience in this trial. I think the court should charge tuition. This would all mean something if any of it mattered. I'm here to tell you that it doesn't matter, and it isn't relevant. This has been a stupid, protracted philosophical exercise. As all, not some, *all* the witnesses testified, the reanimates would not be 'alive' without the aliens. The point is moot. Left to their own devices, the bodies of the dead would not be regaining life signs and mimicking life. They would just be bodies feeding worms."

Deliberation takes less than an hour, and the plaintiff's petition is denied.

The response, to Lora, is anticlimactic.

But demonstrations pick up steam that evening.

Chapter Twenty-Three

As churches go, St Anselm's is a bit of a runt.

Taking direction from a drunk man's brain means I have dozens of false starts before getting here. It looks like a church, with spires, stained glass, a noticeboard and the occasional gargoyle, but it's squashed between a Thai restaurant and a boarded-up town house, like it used to exist on its own but London grew around it, trying to choke it out. It is not unique; on my way I have seen others like this, the secular architecture overtaking the spiritual.

I have passed people, but they either do not see me or avoid me when they do become aware. In this landscape, I would do the same.

But there's also the fact that it's a memory. Because of how it is stored, the interconnections of neurones or xenoforms, data isn't just laid out like the reference section of a library. Data relationships and associations rule here, and I must prod and poke, give the xenoform suggestive stimulus to trigger the relevant memories. My very presence here is a form of stimulus, and I can only keep going to see what comes up. The people avoiding me may represent secrets; juicy, but not relevant to my mission.

The doors to the church are closed, but a push and the left one opens. There is a queue of people occupying the nave all the way down to the altar. The air inside is dominated by the smell of hot food and unwashed bodies. Outside films, I have never seen so many white people in one place. I have never seen so many hungry white people, either.

I think of waiting in line, but since I'm not here for food, I just walk to the front, fielding intermittent insults on the way. There are two people serving the food, and one person replenishes whatever runs out. The woman is a brunette, hair tied back, serious, maybe mid-twenties. The man is a large, beefy sort, muscular like he has spent quality time in the gym, very short hair and the kind of deep blue eyes you can see from a distance. He definitely spots me, but his appraisal is not leery. The woman does not look up.

"Excuse me," I say.

"Are you pregnant?" asks the woman.

"What?"

"Are you pregnant. Preggers. Expecting. Up the duff. With child."

"Er ... no ... I've never ... I think I'm a lesbian." *Apart from one weird crush on someone who turned out to have the xenospheric memories of my future wife. Weird. Do they even have lesbians in 2012?*

"Go to the back of the line."

"I'm not here to eat. I don't want food."

She stops and looks at me. Her eyes drop to my clothing, then back to my face. She has brown eyes; wears a man's shirt, but with a skirt. No earrings. No make-up. She points to the queue. "Well, these people *are* here for food, and you're holding things up. They have to be back to wherever they live by nightfall."

"What is it that you want?" asks the big man with the blue eyes. And his accent stops me cold. Thank God for cultural imperialism, because this man is American. I haven't been exposed to enough of them to be able to tell, but I can say he's from the north of that continent.

"Miss?" he asks.

"Anthony," I say. "Anthony Salermo."

"Who?" asks the woman.

"Three Tone," says the man.

"Oh. What about him?" asks the woman. "Has he broken his leg again?"

"He won't be coming back," I say. "He dived into the Pit."

"I see. Who told you this?" asks the woman.

"I was there. I got this address from his coat."

The woman turns to the man. "Didn't we ban him?"

"Yes, Doc," he says. So she's a doctor.

"Okay, Three Tone is dead. You've told us. Thank you."

I am about to say he's not dead, but I check myself. It's too early for them to know, and the truth is I'm not sure to what extent the Anthony I know in the future is the alien's personality or Salermo's.

"I'll go then," I say.

"Wait," says the man. "Who are you? I've never seen you before."

"I'm Oyin Da."

He touches his own chest with a plastic-gloved hand. "Owen Gray. And over here is Dr Bonadventure."

"Miranda," says the woman. "And I'm not a doctor yet."

"She's qualified. It was her first day at work when the Wormwood meteor fell." Owen has a voice that sounds rich and kind. "She's our doctor now."

186

"And cook," says Miranda. "We have people to serve, Owen. No more ... chit-chat."

Owen turns his head to whisper in Miranda's ear, and she nods in response, all the while still serving food. He reaches under the table and takes out a device. It's bespoke, so I look at it and can see its guts because there's no casing, but I do not know what it is for. He beckons and I draw close. He cranks the device, something I've done before when trying to generate current for my father's mad engine. When it starts going with a whine, he points it at me. It has a kind of sensor, but has been modified extensively. I would like to study it. After a minute, he turns it off. He looks at Miranda and shakes his head.

"You say you've been to the Pit, but you have no increased radiation," she says. "Have you washed or decontaminated since being there?"

I shake my head. "No, but ... Look, you're not going to pick up radiation off me."

"Why is that?" asks Owen.

The door of the church opens and two men saunter in. They're dressed in padded jackets, with dark tracksuit bottoms and sneakers, one black, one white. The black one walks past me, picks up a baby potato and throws it in his mouth. The white one stares and stares at me. Then he points in my face. "You're from the future."

"I ..."

"Are you here for me? You're wasting your time, I must say. I'm already dead, after all."

"Who are you?"

"Here they call me Ryan Miller," he says. "But I'm also known as Father Marinementus. I, like you, am not really here. Come with me."

Before I can say anything, he dives at me, grabs me by the torso and flies towards the ceiling of the church. We crash through what should be solid, but reality splinters and beyond it there is the blackness of space, with sprinkled stars and no sign of our sun. It is stylised space, for even I can see that the planets are too close together and the darkness is not as lightless, and it is not at all cold.

"What are you doing?" he asks.

Because I know he cannot harm me, whoever he is, I answer, "I'm trying to get to America."

"Why are you coming here to do it?" His dark soutane flaps in non-existent solar winds and he turns about his own axis like an unmoored helium balloon.

"Why are *you* here?"

"Because I was here, little ghost. I died in Nigeria, of malaria, in the nineteenth century, prophesying. I had a complete revelation of this future and I had it transcribed as I lay dying. I got it to London by way of some British explorers of the Niger River. Because I needed to see if they killed the alien, I brought myself back into the time stream."

"How?"

"I was reborn into a new body that I manipulated. It doesn't matter. I was back in the time stream and monitoring events. I saw Wormwood come down on schedule, I saw the government cordon come up. I made my way back to Nigeria and died there, although Wormwood was still alive. I have seen the future, but it varies."

"The past is one, but the futures are many," I say.

"Yes. But not accurate. The past can be modified all the time. That's why someone like you can visit."

"Nothing I do can change anything."

"Not true. If you persist, what you do becomes the communal memory of an event, and that can change decisions in the future. Look back at St Anselm."

Through the gap in space, I see Owen and Miranda serving food like I was never there.

"Right now, you are like a forgotten dream to them. If you reappear, you'll be déjà vu, but for them it will be a new meeting."

"Okay, so they forget me. That doesn't matter, right? I can't be hurt here."

"Who told you that?"

"My ... Why?"

"It's also not true. You are a glob of neurotransmitters, a sequence of information. You are not where you should be. What do you think the system will do when it finds out you are out of order?"

I have a sinking feeling, but I do not answer.

"Let me show you something."

For five minutes we look through the gap at the church. Nothing happens except food being served and received. Many go to eat in the aisles; others take the food out.

"What am I—"

"Hush. Look."

Something transparent and glistening forces its way through the door. It is blob-like and covered in mucus. It has multiple tentacles that trail passively behind it. It floats, but with purpose. The tentacles are about ten times its length, and as they drag on the floor they appear to be touching objects or eating things. None of the people in the queue, nor Owen or Miranda, appear to notice it. At the altar it stops, seemingly confused, then twists upwards towards the gap.

189

"Yeah, that's enough," says Ryan, and he closes the gap. "Data maintenance. Those are the things that will erase you if you are found where you should not be. Just so we're clear, erasure means death to entities such as us. Whenever you come into the past, you leave a trail, contaminating everything you interact with. They follow that trail."

"So I should go back?"

"They follow the trail slowly. You just need to keep ahead of them."

"But you just opened a portal."

He smiles. "I've been here for centuries, little ghost. You pick up a lot in that time."

"What do I do? I need to get to—"

"America. Yes, I know. No doubt you wanted to talk to Owen some more, right? Seeing as he's American. I will drop you at an earlier point in his timeline. That should take you where you need to go. Do you know how to get home?"

"I have a bathysphere that seems to do the trick. Don't ask me how it works."

"Whatever imagery works for you is fine. Just remember to be fast, or you will die."

"Wait—"

"Goodbye."

Chapter Twenty-Four

Outside the S45 lab in Abuja, Eric stands in the rain, stripped to the waist. It's a downpour, heavy globules of water let loose from the sky, distant thunder, practically no wind, but dark like twilight, even though it's the middle of the afternoon. The tentacle loves water and throws itself everywhere, as if exercising. Eric is glad there is nobody around to see, or to be at risk.

In the lab, Gregory Eleja works on the artificial brain. His cousin Tolu has gone back into Rosewater to wreak havoc with civil disobedience and acts of terrorism. The boss lady thinks keeping the government busy is important.

"They are invested in the survival of the aliens," she said. "Keeping them busy is important. Besides, that's what my funding is for. If we don't do it, the powers that be will wonder why, and maybe Nigeria will start to look closer at what I *am* doing."

The rain is peaceful for Eric. No random thoughts bursting in on his consciousness, because rain tends to disrupt the delicate xenosphere connections that his ability depends on. He notices slits on his arm where the tentacle attaches. He remembers seeing similar slits on the skin of Nuru, the Rosewater reconstructed from whom he inherited the tentacle. Nuru had tentacles of different sizes emerging from each slit. Does this mean Eric will ... grow more?

He hears his phone ring just under the shelter.

"Agent Sunmola, will you come in, please?"

Gregory has taken to calling him that and he finds it irritating but does not react. For the professor, this whole thing is an exotic break in a relatively boring life. Eric notes that he is not the only professor from the university to have involvement in this case.

The guard shoots looks at Eric for coming in soaking wet, but he doesn't care. He walks shirtless into the facility, tracking water. The professor makes him dry himself before admitting him into the lab. He supplies the towel.

"What have you called me here for?" asks Eric.

"God, you South Africans and your strange accent. You bite your consonants like chocolate. Anyway. You're a sensitive, right?"

"Yes."

"I want you to go into my brain."

"Why? Are you testing me?"

"No, not my brain in my head. My brain in the lab." He points to his construct, the brainoid. It's still not a full brain, more like an amygdala plus a hippocampus and a thalamus. "I detected new impulses working across them. I want to know what it's telling itself."

"I have to be in the same room as it. And in a kind of dwaal, a dreamlike state."

"Sure. Go."

Eric waits for the xenoforms to grow into the lab area in case they were depleted from the storm and the hermetic conditions under which the brain was grown and stored. Looking at it, grey-white flesh like a mutant mushroom, in all ten, eleven inches long, suspended in fluid, he wonders what the endgame is with this. He starts to probe as if it's human.

His vision flicks out, then all he can see is a blazing lightning storm, fucking *donderslag* all over, but no background of sky and no darkness in between flashes. Pain, excruciating, everywhere in his being, no relief, no let-up, is he screaming, yes, but no air, or limitless air, oh Lord, it hurts, shut down, shut down, disconnect.

He opens his eyes and he is tied to a bed with leather straps, IV access on the back of his left hand but unconnected to a drip. He strains against the restraint, then yells. It's a bare room, some odd bric-a-brac, some cartons, but mostly storage. Dark, but because the lights are off. Eric sees the glow of a camera in the corner.

The door opens and Gregory comes in. "Thank God you're all right."

"Where's my arm?" says Eric.

"What can you remember?" asks Gregory.

"*Where's my fucking arm?*"

"I'll take you to it, but you have to see something first."

He shows Eric a screen and it is eerie to see himself shot from above in the lab. Gregory is right beside him. They talk for a minute, then Eric walks to the brainoid. He grabs his head, screams in pain, and falls to the ground, convulsing. The tentacle lashes out, systematically striking anything it can reach, destroying the brainoid, the container, smashing glass, putting out the lights, missing Gregory by inches. The guard that side-eyed Eric bursts into the room, armed, and spins around when the tentacle whips him across the face. By this time, Eric appears inert, but the tentacle flails around in a frenzy until it hits the camera by accident. Eric throws the screen away.

"They had to use gas in the end. It took an hour to subdue," says Gregory. "That's the problem with you quiet types. When you let loose ... whoa."

"Ha-ha, it was your experiment, *domkop*," says Eric. "Where is my arm?"

After Eric has had coffee and been reunited, Gregory asks him about his experience.

"There's nothing in there by way of information," says Eric, pouring more coffee. "Just random discharges along the neurones. And pain."

"That's because of the thalamus. It doesn't have sensory input, so it's firing randomly. It normally processes perception."

"What do we do now? My arm trashed your brainoid."

"Heh, you think I have only one? Please. I have seventeen. Work continues apace. You know, I've heard they grow brains in Pakistan and Taiwan, but they're not publishing. It's like human cloning. Everyone's doing it, but nobody's talking." Gregory seems amused. "It's not an arm, by the way."

"What?"

"The appendage. It's a tentacle."

"It's got suckers along its entire length," says Eric, acting the pedant. He doesn't care.

"Those aren't true suckers, my friend."

"Yeah, and that's not your true hair. Doesn't stop people from calling it your hair, does it?"

"Alakori," says the professor. *Person of bad destiny.*

"Iya e l'alakori," says Eric. *Your mama.* He enjoys the

surprised look that comes from not knowing he speaks Yoruba. He spent most of his life in Nigeria, living with his father, forbidden from travel to South Africa. He broke free when he turned eighteen, sucking in all the Afrikaans he could, trying to make up for lost time in Jo'burg. The result is he sounds weird in both countries.

Gregory turns and walks out, returns with a bottle of Jack Daniel's held at shoulder height. "Tell me, Eric, have you ever heard of Nearis Green?"

"I can't say I have."

"Well, sir, I hold in my hands the fruit of his expertise. How about a shot glass while I tell you the story of the slave who taught Jack Daniel how to make whiskey?"

"What do you think of Gregory?" asks Femi. They are eating dinner in the hotel.

"I think he's probably insane, but in a mad scientist kind of way," says Eric.

"Will he get it done?"

"It depends on what 'it' is, ma'am. He can build a brain, no doubt. Whether it will work is another matter. Right now, it's a mess."

"Yes, I saw the video. Are you all right?"

"I'm fine."

"You were very violent."

"The arm ... tentacle was very violent."

"Do you need a psych eval?"

"I do not."

"What then? Something's bothering you."

"I want to be here. With you. Working for you."

"You're already doing that."

"I can be your right hand if you'll let me."

She is silent for a minute. "And what does that look like, being my right hand?"

"You're the boss. You would decide what it looks like."

"Good answer." She nods. "Good answer. But you must understand, Eric, you'll have to obey without question. Some of my actions you won't understand, others will seem abhorrent to you. Sometimes I will explain, sometimes I will not, but it will always be my choice. Do you understand?"

"Yes. Don't question you; just do."

"Exactly that. First things first, I want you to get an MRI scan. I need to be absolutely sure you're healthy. Things are about to get very sticky in Rosewater, and when they do, I'm going to need you more than ever."

"Yes, ma'am. I'll arrange it with Medical."

They eat the rest of the meal in silence.

Chapter Twenty-Five

Rosewater is having a sticky moment.

A spree killer has held up the financial district for two hours. Forty-two people are dead. Tactical teams are unable to end it because they have been split due to unrest in other parts of the city. Protests and riots erupted after the reanimate trials, with people demanding the bodies of their loved ones back.

Aminat and Dahun arrive at the district, and settle behind the barricade. The shooter is ensconced in the lobby of Integrity Bank, a place Aminat remembers both Kaaro and her cousin Bola once worked. The building is pocked with bullet holes from returned fire. The road is littered with corpses, scorch marks and the twisted metal of downed drones and assault bots.

"The shooter has two turrets and some strange assault rifle. No demands. Three officers down, and we haven't been able to get close to him."

"You know it's a male?" asks Aminat.

"No."

"Snipers?"

"Distortion field."

Dahun reaches into his jacket and hurls some small baubles to the ground. They roll towards the blackened building, then crack like eggs before disgorging several arthrodrones. He activates his subdermal phone and a series of graphs appear.

"I shouldn't be here," says Aminat. "I should be coordinating, calling the plays from headquarters."

"You can work from here as well as there," says Dahun. "Permission to go and kill this sonofabitch?"

"Have at it," says Aminat.

Dahun takes off his jacket and places it on the asphalt. His armour is up, leaving only eye slits. The light around him shimmers from his bespoke personal repulsion shield. As soon as he is within fifty yards, the turrets start shooting at him. The shield holds, but Aminat can see he does not wish to test it consistently. Tactical releases volleys of suppressing fire.

The bank is a good choice for a siege, as it's already fortified against robbers, so once you're in, it'll take the kind of thing Dahun is doing to get you out. Idly, Aminat hopes Layi and Kaaro have the sense to stay home. *But since when do those two ever have sense?*

All the plate glass erupts outwards and Aminat falls flat. Dahun walks out dragging a man by the scruff of the neck, ignoring the pain he must be causing. His force field has fizzled out and strips of his armour are gone. When he gets to Aminat, he flings the man to the ground. Tactical start to draw near in ones and twos.

The man is burned, smoking and laughing.

"He's a fucking synner," says Dahun.

Yes, the green tinge to the eyes. Dahun may be new, but he's learning fast. This is not going to help matters in Rosewater. If

Homians are committing mass murder to up their numbers, the reanimate protests might just explode into revolution.

"I used up the power cell on my shield just at the last minute. Lucky to still be alive."

Aminat prods the alien with her boot. "Do you have a name?"

"Laark." It comes as a raspy whisper, along with the rest of his breathing. Maybe the fire burned his airways.

"What is your fucking problem?" asks Dahun.

"Hmm. Fornication. I have never understood the human tendency to enjoy sexual intercourse yet use it as a label for ... something you don't like. Fornication and profanity. Fornication as profanity."

"Why do you kill us, Laark?"

"I'm not killing you, silly. You are not real. Can't kill what's not really there. You are aberrations of nature. I'm making way for ... me and people like me to inherit the Earth."

A tactical officer puts her hand on Aminat.

"Excuse me, ma'am. Move to the left, please."

Before she can read the situation, a burly officer points a handgun at Laark's head and fires. Several others follow suit and the alien's head is disintegrated into a pink smear. Aminat is aware that they are staring at her as the most senior person. She shrugs, pulls out her sidearm and shoots Laark in the root of the neck twice. Because fuck him and fuck him. As she holsters her weapon, she wonders when Koriko will arrive. Must be busy with everything going on.

"Get to identifying the dead and talking to next of kin before that ghoul arrives to take the bodies. Go!" To Dahun she says, "Go get changed. Our work isn't done."

*

Parts of Rosewater are on fire. There is unrest in every ward except the toxic area. There are multiple shootings and explosions. At first Aminat thinks it's a spontaneous outpouring of rage at the revelations in court, but from her vantage point of hearing every single report, deploying her forces, she begins to discern something, a pattern.

The shootings aren't random. From her own ... nocturnal activities she can tell that the people shot are Taiwo's men. The businesses hit belong to the gangster. Checking the reports for victim profiles, many have been criminals. The natural assumption would be the Rastas, but theirs is one of the quietest wards, with no civil unrest, just random gunshot reports. So this is not retaliation.

"New player in town," she says aloud.

"What?" asks Dahun.

"The last time when Taiwo's men were executed, I thought it was a one-off. It's not. This is a full-scale takeover."

"What about the bombs?"

"What about them?"

"These bombs didn't just get made today. This takes planning. The targets are not criminal, but civilian. Shopping malls, churches, mosques. That's not a criminal pattern. That's mad bomber or terrorist. Which means, to me, someone is trying hard to make it look like you have a terrorism problem, but they've overdone it."

"You think it's S45?"

"I do. They're playing from the CIA destabilisation manual."

"This is ... out of control."

"In more ways than one. Look."

The self-drive comes to an abrupt stop. Koriko stands in the middle of the road.

"Get out of the car," says Koriko. "I wish to speak to you."

"Open the door," says Aminat.

Yes. Park or idle?

"Idle."

"Don't do it. She'll kill you," says Dahun.

"Why would she do that?" asks Aminat as she climbs out. "Besides, I might kill her."

Koriko stands in what Aminat supposes is the exact centre of the road. The regular thin layer of moss on the unweeded surface is thicker under her feet. There's a serpentine following her around. What the fuck? Aminat tags the hardware address for later. The robot is weathered, corroded in places, dark green, and gathering information about Aminat, she is sure.

"Hi, Alyssa," says Aminat. She walks right up to the alien, an inch separating their noses.

"That isn't me," says Koriko. "Alyssa is with her family."

"Yeah, I saw that. You put a dead-eyed doppelgänger in your marital bed. Shame. Shame on you, Gatherer of human flesh," says Aminat. "I liked you better when you weren't green."

"And I liked you better when you kept order in this city and my people didn't have to die in the episodes of unrest."

"You're funny."

"I am not given to levity."

"We are in agreement."

"Aminat, your people can't kill Homians."

"That's bullshit. If synners can kill humans, humans can do whatever the fuck they want. And why do you bring them back anyway? They've had a life. Why make them immortal?"

"I don't have to explain myself to you."

"Likewise." Aminat sticks a finger in Koriko's face. "Stay out of my way. And get off the road. You're obstructing traffic."

"Three fronts, sir." Aminat reports to the mayor. "The gang war between Taiwo and his brother Kehinde, though it's more of a rout than war; explosions and vandalism from anti-Rosewater groups; and spontaneous rage events, protests, people wanting their loved ones back."

"And there has been some anti-Homian violence," says Jack, on the other end of the line.

"You've been listening to Koriko."

"Is the Honeycomb safe?"

"Yes."

"Do you want to come here? It's impregnable."

Aminat laughs, a bitter bark. She is looking at seventeen dead soldiers who worked for Taiwo. She is looking at the precision of the bullet holes. There are long-range, high-velocity shots and multiple wounds clustered together. This seems as much a war as the insurrection. Dahun trained them all too well.

"I still have work to do out here," she says.

"Don't die," says Jack. He signs off.

One of the corpses is showing early reanimation signs, but it is twitching in the wrong place and hitting the back of its head on the pavement, bashing its own brains out. Aminat tells one of the officers to get some tarp to soften the blows. She feels the hair on her forearms rise and someone yells something. She makes herself flat just as the charged air turns into a lightning streak. Nobody gets caught in it. Ever since the dome disappeared and the ganglia multiplied, there is sometimes a flash of electricity between them. You can tell by the ionisation of the air. The inner surface of her left cheek bleeds where it made impact.

She tells the car to take her home. She needs to change and see Kaaro and maybe quit her job. This isn't her. She cannot remember the last time she had fun. She doesn't know how all of this strife will turn out, but she knows she can't stand to make these decisions much longer. There is death everywhere, and that is no way to live. Unlike a lot of the people of Rosewater, Aminat is not a loyalist. She can live anywhere. If not for Kaaro, she would have left Rosewater. If not for Layi, she would have left S45.

Casual protesters pelt her marked car with rocks, yelling indistinct slogans, frustrated when the windows resist damage and her face does not show fear. Their expressions are angry, but beneath the rage Aminat senses uncertainty. Healing is good, uninterrupted power supply is good, living in the city of the future is good, but should one sacrifice the bodies of loved ones? Were she not part of the government, would she be part of the solution? As they drive past a naked ganglion it flashes, dazzling Aminat. There isn't enough money or need to install Ocampo inverters on all of them. She blinks her vision back. The windows have polarised.

She passes shopfronts, one in two broken, inventory on the street or gone, listless protesters wandering through.

"Stop," she says, and the car halts. "Idle. Amber alert level."

Acknowledged.

She walks to the broken windows of a jeweller's. She thinks it strange that the place hasn't been looted until she realises that it's costume jewellery. Kids pick over what was displayed. Discount stickers garishly haunt the cases. The profane signs of credit card vendors line each surface. Financing plans.

Promises of seven-day delivery time on the real versions of corresponding baubles. Couples with good skin, white teeth and expensive clothes glow with commercial romantic bliss.

Fuck.

Aminat realises she wants to be married, and that she wants to marry Kaaro. She wants that whole expensive, unnecessary ceremony. She wants an over-the-top wedding dress, drunk guests, a whole weekend of being smushed together with extended family, putting out the fires of petty quarrels and decades-long feuds between aunties. Yes.

She approaches who she believes to be the owner of the shop, a tall, gaunt old man picking up debris with a sad look on his face.

"Sir, I'd like to buy a ring."

"You'll have to come back another day. There's nothing here worth—"

Aminat picks up a ring off the floor. "This one. I want this one. How much?"

"That a cheap piece of—"

Aminat takes his right hand and pays what is most likely twenty times the actual value of the ring. She rises onto her toes and kisses the man on the cheek, then runs out to the car.

"Take me home," she says. "Double time."

Yes, Aminat.

She raises the ring to the light. It is truly shitty, and she has no idea if it will fit Kaaro's finger, but she is unbothered. There are tools at home; she can hammer it into shape.

Chapter Twenty-Six

Kaaro wakes to see Layi sitting at the foot of the bed.

"Is the first thought in your mind 'wrong sibling'?" asks Layi.

Half conscious, sleep sand in his eyes, Kaaro says, "What do you want? What time is it?"

"Is it bad that I'm upset that these demonstrations will postpone the Pride march?"

"It's bad that you're telling me this in the middle of the night," says Kaaro.

"I'm sad. When I'm sad, I like to eat."

"Then get thee to the kitchen. Leave me out of it." Kaaro pulls the coverlet over his head and tries to go back to sleep. He is about to settle into a relaxation cycle when the smoke alarm goes off.

"Layi, what the hell ... ?"

He stands before the stove like a thief caught in the act. The wall behind the stove is scorched. There is a pan with a shapeless carbonised mass inside, smoke still drifting to the ceiling, where it activated the alarm. The flame is not lit.

"I wanted to cook some eggs. Sorry."

"You know, I thought you were going to make corn flakes like all other insomniacs worldwide. And did you try to use your own ... You know what, never mind. Help me clean up."

Yaro is barking, and at first Kaaro thinks it's because of the alarm, which the house AI should have switched off by now.

"Why is the dog outside?" he asks.

"He wanted to. He was scratching at the door and it felt like I should let him go where he—"

Kaaro places two fingers on Layi's lips. "You should not be allowed out on your own. You'd better not have put my dog in jeopardy."

"I would never do that," says Layi.

"Whatever. You clean, I'll go get the dog. You do know how to clean, right?"

Layi smiles. "Of course I do. I love to clean."

"No scouring of the non-stick saucepan."

Kaaro, intending to walk out of the front door, bumps into it. The AI is out, it seems. Yaro stops barking. Kaaro switches off the foyer lights manually and opens the curtains. Yaro is standing near the gate, and there are people poking at him with sticks. Why are there people walking around at this time? He opens the front door with a key – *a key!* – and starts towards the gate.

"Hey! Leave the dog alone!" he yells.

At the same moment, in the xenosphere, he hears *That's him* and knows something is coming. He falls flat and a bullet misses him and zings into the porch steps. Somewhere in the xenosphere, he knows that Aminat has done this, taken cover from fire, tonight.

He feels the shooter correcting the targeting and moves again, a weave that is guided by where the shooter aims. It's an amateur with a handgun, and staying out of harm's way is not difficult for Kaaro, although his pyjamas are quickly shredded by the hard ground.

"Please stop," he says. "I don't want to hurt you."

He takes full motor control over Yaro and leads him to safety. The little bastard actually fights to be by his side. Good dog. Now fuck off before you get shot.

He hears screams. The man shooting at him from the gate is on fire and drops the gun.

"Layi, stop," says Kaaro.

"He's only lightly singed," says Layi, lounging at the door stoop. "He's being a baby because he doesn't know why he's on fire."

"Get back inside." *Your sister wouldn't want people knowing about you or what you can do.* "And call Aminat."

"Everything is down. Nimbus, cell network, nothing working. Power's there, no signals."

Which means signal jammer, which means this isn't just one yahoo taking pot shots at someone in his own house, which means they know about Aminat, but not about Kaaro. The last time "they" came for him, they wore skin-tight suits to keep the xenosphere out. Kaaro killed them all, even though it turned out they were trying to get him to safety. But on this occasion, shots have been fired, intent is clear. He sends a mental distress call to Aminat.

He should go into the house, lock down manually and wait for Aminat, but he used to be a government interrogator and he wants to know why. He sprints to the gate. The gunman is on the ground, smoking from every exposed area of skin, smelling like barbecue, but alive. Reading him, Kaaro's stomach sinks. There are more. His mind expands outwards and he feels them,

207

two already in the compound from the back, four making their way from the west.

And he knows who they are now.

He dashes back into the house.

Layi, they're criminals. I'll take care of them. You hide.

He feels for the minds of the two at the back and drags them into the xenosphere, a landscape of bubbling mercury and corrosive clouds floating around, stripping them of their flesh, and alien arachnids leaping into their mouths to muffle their screams.

In the foyer he uses the same key to lock the door and activate defences manually. It does not respond.

"Fuck, fuck, fuck."

He is about to drag a screen across a window when he hears a whistling sound, along with one of the attackers' minds going *Incoming.* The entire front of the house is coated in white light and Kaaro is flung into the ceiling and then rudely to the floor. His mind disconnects from the four thugs making their way to him. The damn ringing alters his concentration. He finds Layi, who is stunned but intact. Debris continues to fall. He feels warm fluid escaping from his left ear. *Do I have a skull fracture?* The house is on fire, but it's a small blaze.

"Sorry, Layi," says Kaaro. *I need to borrow your brain.*

He takes control of the part of Layi's mind that controls heat, and he knows how because of the training they have been doing. He intends to place a ring of fire around the house, defensive, to discourage. He doesn't want to kill anyone. He feels the power go like a flight of doves.

A bubble of blue heat forms around the house, sucking all the air with a crack, then barrels outwards in every direction, like an explosion, destroying whatever lies in its path. The minds of the four collapse in seconds, no time to scream.

Kaaro tries to recall the fire, but the energy continues to expand, setting fires, *eating*. He forces Layi awake by releasing cortisol into his bloodstream.

"Kaaro, what did you do?" asks Layi. The bubble halts and dissipates, although the fires it has set still burn.

"I'm sorry. They were going to kill us." Kaaro struggles to his feet. The front of the house is destroyed, the walls down in all directions except a post here or there. Yaro is yapping somewhere in his cubbyhole, people are waking up to fires and putting them out, some coming out on the street.

Layi emerges to meet Kaaro. "Signal's back."

"Good." The fire has burned away the local xenosphere, but the links are growing back. Kaaro has to scan for—

He hears the crack of the sniper rifle just after becoming aware of the shooter's thoughts. He retaliates instantly, pinning the sniper with the night scope in the nest on a rooftop two blocks away – motherfucker was preparing to shoot Layi next – pushing the man's mind into the xenosphere, where his belly is eaten by worms from the inside.

He turns back to Layi. "Hey, look at what I just—"

Kaaro sees his own body.

His skull is shattered, and the bullet shot out his brain, part of which is two feet away. Not as much blood as he would have expected. Layi kneels and cradles what is left of his neck stump,

Huh. Krönlein shot. That must have been some sniper.

Fuck. I'm dead.

Then Kaaro screams.

Chapter Twenty-Seven

For Aminat, the first inkling is an excruciating pain, a headache to end all headaches, so exquisite that the AI notices.

Your vital signs show you to be in severe pain. Would you like me to deploy analgesia?

Kaaro is dead. She knows it. He died at home, with her half a mile out and unable to reach either him or Layi on the phone.

Aminat, you are crying from pain.

"No. I mean, yes, but it's not my body that hurts."

Would you like me to—

"Get me home as fast as possible. Code red."

Confirm traffic ordinance override.

"Confirmed."

He's dead. He's dead. I was supposed to protect him and he's dead.

She takes the ring and slides it over her engagement finger.

The snot in her nose clogs up her breathing. She is cold and cannot get warm, no matter how high she turns up the climate control.

The car thunders along the roads, misses pedestrians by inches, arrives at the house. It's surrounded by people and looks like it took a bomb hit, just like the houses next door.

Idle or park?

"Park, but alert. Radio for backup using my call sign."

Purpose?

"Unknown at this time. Fatality involved. Go."

Aminat bullies her way through the carnage, police jacket and badge being enough to command respect, although she is prepared to draw and use her sidearm if necessary. In the centre of destruction, Layi kneels, holding . . .

There's no face. The upper jaw, a jagged part of the skull, an eye, some brain tissue holding on tenuously, the rest missing. And pyjamas that she recognises.

"Did you do this?" she asks Layi. "You've lost control before."

Layi's chest hitches and he shakes his head, but he cannot say anything.

"My darling . . . "

He is warm to the touch, and though it is a crime scene, and all her training screams otherwise, Aminat gathers him from Layi and weeps. She does not know how long she is there before a hush descends on the crowd around them.

"Sister." Layi pokes her and she looks up.

Koriko.

"I have come for what is mine," says Koriko. "I think you have mourned enough."

"The shot took his brain out," says Aminat.

"There's still enough of it left," says Koriko. "We can grow a full one from that."

"You are not taking this body," says Aminat. She stands,

draws, and rests her gun against Koriko's forehead, though her arm is not steady and her vision swims.

"I'm sorry. It amazes me that all of you, you humans, you all beg. Despite the fact that I have never once relented, despite the fact that you all know the agreement and reap the benefits thereof. I *am* sorry," Koriko says. At this distance Aminat can smell her breath, which is like crushed jasmine. "All bodies are mine. That is the deal, and it was *your* idea in the first place, Aminat. There are no exceptions."

"I'm sorry, which body were you talking about?" asks Layi.

The remnants of Kaaro's skull glow with dazzling white heat, and the flame eats the neck, into the chest, and glows from within until, seconds later, all that remains is ash, this picked up by the night breeze and carried away to parts unknown.

Aminat could kiss him.

Koriko squints. "What manner of—"

Aminat pulls the trigger. A quarter of Koriko's head bursts outwards and the crowd scatters, screaming at the blasphemy. She is about to fire again when a serpentine form wraps itself around her gun arm and stings her.

"You know this can't hurt me," says Koriko, disdainful of the missing parts of her head.

Layi steps in front of his sister. "Everything burns, says I."

Koriko seems frozen to the spot, engulfed in blue flame, her flesh dropping off in sheets, then her skeleton blackening and falling, shattering.

"This won't kill her," says Aminat.

"No. But she has to build a new body, which takes time."

"Go to the car. It'll open for you."

"What about you?"

212

"I have to get the dog," says Aminat. "And one other thing."

She finds everything she needs, changes into fresh armour, and they leave. She knows she will never again live in this house with Kaaro, yet she does not look back.

Chapter Twenty-Eight

Eric hates hotels, even one such as this, where Femi Alaagomeji has the air pumped full of antifungals whenever he is around, and she is slick with similar cream all over her body. The psychic residue of the previous occupants persists like the smell of a poorly cleaned urinal.

He is looking at a painting of the British sacking of Benin City in 1897. He knows this because of a caption underneath the painting, which is an odd decoration for a hotel bedroom, two feet above the headboard. Both of Femi's legs are on his shoulders, and his hands are on her thighs, as she wishes. She is the kind to give instructions, although as suggestions, not orders. It would be nice if, I might like it if you, why not, and so on. He finds her softer in love than in her work. Looking around the room, at the decor, helps him last longer.

He is losing his grip on her when the headache hits him like lightning, flashing through his consciousness, sending him sprawling off the bed onto the carpet. Every part of his head is in pain, even his ear lobes. It feels like someone has taken hold of each nerve ending and is pulling with all their might.

When he opens his eyes, the two bodyguards are in the room and Femi is naked by his side.

"I thought you'd had a stroke," she says. "Do you know where you are?"

Eric nods. "Kaaro is dead."

Femi exhales, a sharp, shallow breath. "You're sure."

"Yes. That was some feedback thing. I don't know what. But I am sure that he is dead, hey."

"Do you know how he died?"

"Ag, I don't know. I need something for . . . Analgesia."

As soon as he opens the bathroom door, the tentacle throws itself at him and attaches, sensing his distress. Earlier, Femi had licked the insertion slits, commenting that they only smelled like honey.

He leaves the hotel to take a walk. Femi is talking on the phone in urgent whispers and does not even wave. She has slipped back into her work persona. A few minutes outside and the xenosphere has grown back to full bloom. He sits and allows himself to drift into it. Kaaro fiddled with Eric's brain before, and he knows there is a residue. He finds gryphon feathers and picks one up. It feels glossy, and even in the crepuscular light that fails to illuminate, moving it this way and that produces iridescence. He licks the feather, but gains nothing for his trouble. He follows the rest of the fallen plumage to a meadow.

There are distant hills, and the grass is chest high. In the distance, to the west, a dead giant hangs inert, standing, head missing from the nose up in a jagged, bloodless line, arms dangling, bent forward, on its knees.

The grass thrashes this way and that, but Eric never sees what animals might be creating the movement. There is no smell. He walks towards the giant as it is the only thing to aim for. He must have underestimated the distance or how large the giant is, because no matter how long he walks for, it seems the same size and is still covered by that blue haze you get when looking at something really far away.

"You might as well stop walking," says a voice behind him.

Eric whirls. Usually it's impossible to creep up on him because of the tentacle, but it did not follow him here. His mental image does not even have the skin slits.

A woman stands there in a print wrap held in place just above her breasts. She has an orange bead necklace and her head tie is Ankara. On her bare arms and shoulders she has tattoos that move. She clocks that he is looking.

"They are temporary. I'm trying them out to see if I'll keep them. My daughter's idea," she says. "She's at that age."

Eric nods agreement. "What is this place? Who are you?"

"I'm Nike. This," she spreads out her arms, "this is what is left of Kaaro."

"So he really is dead."

"He is, my son. How did you know him?"

"You seem a bit young to be calling me that."

"I'm older than I look."

Eric senses something in her then, a sturdiness, a maturity. "We were ... colleagues, I suppose. I don't know. He was a fucking idiot."

Nike laughs. "That he was. I'm the reason he wasn't a *total* fucking idiot."

"Are you his mother?"

This makes Nike guffaw. "I'm just an old sex worker who met him when he was young and gave him the benefit of a lifetime of experience."

Eric spies the wedding ring on her finger.

"Retired," says Nike. She sits in the grass. "Now we wait."

"For what?"

"Not what. Whom. We wait for the others."

She does not explain further and he does not ask, but people begin to arrive, persistent personalities within the xenosphere, ghosts, former sensitives. He supposes he is now the last of his kind still alive in the physical world.

He does not know these people, or rather, has never met them, but he feels kinship and an absence of threat. Nike keeps looking this way and that.

"Who are you looking for?"

"My daughter and my wife. Both of them get up to mischief."

Eric catches the impression of an impish girl with a smile containing love and naughty behaviour, and a serious-faced woman in Afro puffs. She is familiar to him from his training. A dissident of some kind. Bicycle Girl.

Nike's tattoos cavort faster. Eric sits beside her, both of them facing the direction of the statue.

"When the time comes," she says, "try to say something nice about Kaaro."

"Why? He wouldn't have minded honesty."

"No, he wouldn't, would he? But try all the same. Funerals aren't for the dead. They're for the people attending."

"Is that what this is? A funeral?"

"Maybe. Sort of. I don't know. It's a remembrance."

"I have work to do," says Eric. "I have to find out who killed him."

"It must be nice to have friends who will avenge you," says Nike. "To take up the banner for friendship."

It's not for friendship, but Eric has the presence of mind to keep that information to himself. After all, he does not know if this Nike person killed Kaaro.

"When does this start?" he asks.

Nike looks back and says, "It already has."

The people present begin to talk about Kaaro, and Eric sees a thin amount of smoke rise from the statue.

"I was with Kaaro on the day I died," says Nike. "No, he did not kill me. I was dying before we met . . . "

Chapter Twenty-Nine

Femi does not like being this close to Rosewater, but there is nothing else to be done under the circumstances. She stands in the shadow cast by the mining rig in the full moon. Her bodyguards are deployed all over, although it would be foolhardy for anyone to attack her. The noise of the rig, which never stops, day and night, will protect their conversation from casual surveillance. The air is full of the smell of ammonia that spoorshit gives out. The last estimates Femi saw put Wormwood's motion at four centimetres a year, which does not seem like a lot, but it was half that the year before, and the faster the alien moves, the more spoorshit is available for mining. Femi does not understand the science, but the technicians say it's like uranium and crude oil combined. Furious work is being done to harness it for energy and weapons. Femi is unimpressed. Why bet the future on a resource whose limits are unknown, or where there might be unforeseen consequences?

She thinks briefly of Eric, back from his walk, stuck in the hotel, guarded by the tentacle, comatose or catatonic, no one can tell.

Three people approach from the direction of Rosewater:

Kehinde and two of his minions. The two fall behind, split off into different directions, walking perimeter, perhaps. Kehinde comes towards her, stops a foot away.

"It is always a pleasure to see you, ma'am. I am sorry for the delay. We were hounded by a border bot and they are hard to kill."

"How is the work going?" asks Femi.

"Very well. My brother thinks I'm not going to kill him, but suffers daily losses of his men, either from my boys killing them, or desertion. It's pathetic, really. I had hoped he would put up more of a fight, but this place makes one soft." He gestures to the city, although to Femi he seems to be pointing at the Honeycomb specifically.

"How soon before he's crippled?"

"The organisation is crippled already. You wanted it done with noise and in public to spread fear. Well, there is widespread fear."

"And that fear is because of what you do, not the reanimate riots?"

"Riots, gangland shooting, suicide bombers, what's the difference? You're getting what you want. And thank you for the ammunition and training."

"Did you have Kaaro killed?" she asks. Her mouth is dry and her heart feels like a trapped rodent in her chest.

Kehinde laughs, unable to read the moment, perhaps because they have to shout above the noise of the rig. "I did. I sent my best after him, and they did not let me down."

Inhale, count to five, exhale. "Why?"

"Because it will make the head of security think it was Taiwo, and she will go after him hard. She already moonlights as a vigilante, did you know that?"

Femi does. After the rebellion, she was worried that Aminat lacked fibre, but things change. Poor Kehinde. He is going on about the assassination, giving operational detail with relish. He is a big man who does not at first realise that he has been shot. His voice trails off, and he looks down at his own gut, puts a meaty hand to the new hole in his clothes, then glances around. He thinks he has been shot from somewhere else.

Femi kicks him in the midsection, no longer bothering to hide her pearl-handled revolver. He writhes on the ground, face scrunched up with dawning realisation and agony and hate.

She screams in his face, "I warned you. I said stick to the fucking gangsters. I said no civilians. Didn't I say no civilians?"

Kehinde is trying to respond, but a gut wound is a gut wound, and it's not the movies. The bullet went right through the coeliac plexus and hurts like hell, Femi is sure. She shoots him a second time, this time to the right of his belly, through the liver.

"Kaaro was off-limits, you ... throwback. He was like a stupid little brother who said and did disgusting things, but who you still love. He was stupid, but he was my stupid and you did not have my permission to kill him. *You did not.*"

Is she shouting because of the noise, or is she shouting because her heart hurts and she feels she has failed Kaaro?

She shoots him in the eye, and movement ceases in the other. She shoots him once more in the neck for good measure. Each bullet costs her ten thousand dollars because nobody makes them any more and she has one source at Awka, but it is worth it.

Kehinde's death is unsatisfactory, but necessary. As she walks away, her bodyguards peel away from darkness and fall in behind her, having dealt with Kehinde's men. The three bodies will be found in the daytime with the shift change. This is Nigeria; Femi has no need to cover up the death of a villain.

What the hell is wrong with men? Always a dick contest, always weighing who has the heaviest balls. She has spent so much time picking up the messes the president makes and leading Jacques by the hand when she was in Rosewater. Be much easier if she was in charge.

Poor Kaaro. Such an arse, but a good one, in spite of himself. She had hoped he would return to the S45 fold one day. She will miss him.

The car picks her up and drives in the direction of the hotel. When Femi deactivates the phone block, it rings. It's Tolu Eleja.

"What?" asks Femi. He is supposed to maintain radio silence.

"We need to talk about Aminat," he says.

Chapter Thirty

Aminat cannot feel anything. No, that's not quite right. She cannot feel her heart. She thinks it is in her chest, as something must be pumping the blood that rings in her ears and powers her motion, but all she detects is an absence, a numbness. Which is odd, since she is running as fast as she can.

The man she is chasing thinks he is going to jump in the Yemaja before she can reach him. He is wrong. He has a head start, true, but Aminat is faster, and a trained sprinter. She doesn't command him to stop, because she wants to be angry when she catches him. Gauging the distance, she slows down a little, giving him hope that he will reach the guard rail before Aminat reaches him.

She lets him touch the rail before kicking his feet out from under him. His face slams on the ground and he wheezes from exertion and the fact that his nose is pulped. She turns him over, finds his gun and throws it into the river, waiting to hear the *pish* before speaking.

"Do you want to run again?"

He does not answer, so she slaps him hard. He seems to be

negotiating unconsciousness, but she doesn't want him unconscious or dead just yet.

"Hey. Wake up, darling, we have business to attend to."

Something bubbles through the blood and blocked nose.

"What? Speak up?"

" ... please ... "

"No, no, no, sir, there will be no please in this conversation. There will be me asking questions and you answering. But first ... I need you to know that I'm serious."

Aminat hears the car roll up behind her, but doesn't bother to look. She knows it's a police car from the sound of the engine, and she presumes whoever it is can read the back of her jacket, but she does not really care. She continues her work tying the man to the base of a raw ganglion. He chatters on and is saying something but the loud sound in Aminat's ears drowns it out. No matter. She is not ready to listen yet. The door to the car opens and she hears footfalls, walking, not running.

"Aminat, what are you doing?" asks Dahun.

"I'm getting information out of this asshole."

"He's already talking," says Dahun. "And what are you hoping to achieve here?"

"Sooner or later this ganglion will communicate with the next one. That'll give this guy a shock. After that, he'll tell me anything."

"You do realise that electrocution causes amnesia, right?"

"That's a myth."

"It's not a myth. I've done interrogations."

"You mean torture."

"Aminat, this will not help you. More likely it will kill you both. Is that what you want?"

Aminat is silent, and for a few seconds the only sound is the night breeze blowing through the canyons formed by the empty buildings on both sides of the boulevard.

"I heard about Kaaro."

"Don't tell me you're here to take me in so that I don't take the law into my own hands. Because I already do that, and I'm definitely doing it tonight."

"No. I'm here to help." He crouches so that his face is level with the injured man. "Tell us what we need."

The man is Afam Akerele and he is supposed to know how to get into Taiwo's fortress. This appears to have been an exaggeration. Sixteen architects designed the place, no single one knowing everything the others did. The result is a place of shifting certainties, the whole of which only Taiwo Sanni knows.

Thirteen of us are dead or disappeared, says Afam.

Now the car takes them to Taiwo's place without a plan.

"Are you sure it was him?" asks Dahun.

"He always hated Kaaro, and you were there when he threatened him the last time. You drew my attention to it, remember?"

"Okay. How are we getting in?"

"You tell me."

"What do you mean?"

"I know you must have ideas. You were here with me, you like to tinker with instruments of death and you damn well knew it might come to you-against-him at some point. You've thought of this problem. So. You tell me."

Incoming urgent call from Mayor Jacques.

"Not available," says Aminat.

Call for Dahun from Mayor Jacques.

"Not available," says Dahun.

Incoming message from Mayor Jacques.

"Fuck you both, what if I was under attack? Aminat, I know what happened. Accept my condolences. That said, I need you to break off your current course of action and come in—"

"Terminate message," says Aminat. She turns to Dahun. "Well? We don't have all night and they will send someone to stop us sooner or later."

"The problem is, we are the ones they would usually send," says Dahun, voice tinged with dark laughter. "I thought maybe an electromagnetic pulse to start with, but it's bound to be hardened against that. I'd go for the power supply."

"Backup generators."

"No. I've done the reading. There has been no fuel supply to Rosewater since the rebellion. It goes bad between six and twenty-four months."

"Petrol goes bad?"

"It does. He won't be using his genny."

"But where do we find the supply transformers or vulnerable cabling? You heard Afam."

Dahun smiles. "I was thinking to kill the three ganglia that supply the area."

"Hmm. I like it."

"You realise many of the bots will be charged and will not require mains?"

"Don't worry about bots. I have killed those."

"So I heard." He fiddles with his phone.

"What are you doing?"

"He has drones patrolling. I just sent a few raptors of my own against them."

"Won't that warn him?"

"Heh, you don't know Rosewater well at all, do you? Have you studied the skies recently? It's a massive battle ground. Drones duel for supremacy. COBs get eaten by floaters. This goes on all the time. He won't be suspicious."

Dahun lays the first charge at the root of a ganglion to the west of Taiwo's castle. This is much safer, as the ganglia supplying the grid are covered with Ocampo inverter technology. Aminat doesn't like the sky. It is still dark, but there is a distant brightening of the horizon. She feels fatigue creeping at the edges of her rage, corroding her resolve. What is she doing?

"Fire in the hole," says Dahun. It sounds strange coming from his mouth, with his strong accent, but she ducks.

She expects a loud bang and a fireball, but there is just a pop and some smoke as the inverter falls apart. Electricity arcs, smacks the ground, and shoots lightning at the nearest naked ganglion, which might be a mile away for all they know. The pillar of nerve tissue glows green and seems to vibrate the air molecules. This is not a safe place to loiter.

"Two to go," says Dahun, packing his bag of tricks. "If we take one each—"

It is not to be. The ground before them ruptures like an asphalt pimple, and Koriko emerges. Aminat is not quite prepared to kill her. Not yet.

"What are you doing? You are not allowed to harm Wormwood. You can use the power, but not hurt it," she says. She notices Aminat. "Where is my serpentine?"

Aminat strokes the bandages on her forearm. "My brother made life too hot for it, similar to how he did that for you. How's the new body?"

Koriko emerges fully from the hole. She is unclothed, but this new body has aggregations of those green stones covering her nipples and genitals, which means she retains some human modesty. Alyssa is still part of her, then.

"Why are you here? You are not normally a vandal," says Koriko.

Dahun points. "We are trying to get into yonder castle. There are only two of us and it's too well defended."

Koriko turns to Aminat. "We were friends once."

"I was friends with Alyssa."

"You never met Alyssa. It was always me. I told you so at the time."

"Be that as it may, Alien Jesus, you were more like Alyssa back then than whatever you are now."

"You are the law enforcement here, so I will take it that you are carrying out your duties. I will help you with the castle. But I want my snake back."

"I'll get you a bloody snake. It's a moray, by the way. I'll get you seven." Aminat is unsure why she feels the necessity to bait the god so much.

"There are people in the castle. They are mine."

"Except one," says Aminat. "Except one. You can do what you want with the rest if they're dead."

"They will be."

For a time nothing happens, then there is a hint of seismic activity, which multiplies and gathers force. The vibrations hurl Dahun and Aminat down, but the god is unaffected, as if her feet are stuck. One minute the castle is standing. The next, gargantuan roots burst through every part of it, bringing the structure crashing down from multiple points. The walls collapse, battlements fall, towers are demolished. The roots do not tarry, and sink back into the earth. The entire site is covered in dust and the screams of the dying.

"Emergency vehicles will come sooner or later," says Aminat. "We have to find him."

"I have a tracker that will lock on his chip and all the ghosts from the wartime at least," says Dahun.

In the air above, defensive drones fight COBs in brief skirmishes. At times bots pop out of the rubble, but Dahun's rifle makes short work of them. When they get to Taiwo, he has just about dug himself free. He's wearing some kind of protective suit, which may have kept him safe but is now damaged. He is not smiling.

"Are you here to arrest me?" he asks. "Look at what they did to my house. They could have killed me."

Aminat does not recall how the gun found its way to her hand, how the safety got off. She aims at his head. "Kaaro's been murdered."

"Oh. I'm sorry to hear that."

"No, you are not. Don't play games with me."

"Miss Aminat, I know you are grieving for your lover, but you are about to make a mistake. I did not kill him."

"But you wanted to," says Aminat. "And eventually you would have. That's enough for me."

"The real murderer will walk free!"

"There is not one of us who will walk free, Taiwo. Goodbye."

Her phone rings, and she shifts her aim a foot to the left, pointing at the ground. "Cover him," she says to Dahun.

It's Femi. "Don't go after Taiwo."

"Too late for that advice," says Aminat. "I'm about to execute him."

"You're going to have to let him go."

"I no longer work for you, Femi."

"Aminat, please stop. He did not kill Kaaro. His brother, Kehinde, did. It's manipulation. He can't kill his blood brother, and if he orders the assassination it's so taboo that his followers won't obey him. So he has to get you to do it."

"You think I'm doing this in a rage. I'm not. This guy has been to prison and he owned it. He and his kind are a plague on Rosewater, and thanks to that jackass in the government house, I can't bring him to justice. I have to stop him."

"You can, but don't kill him."

"Why? Because he's your asset?"

"No, you idiot, because of you. This is not you. I could do it, but not you. You're the nice one, the friendly one who cares about people. If you do this, you'll die too."

"You'll *kill* me?"

"Metaphorically. You'll die figuratively. God, how do you even survive without ... Never mind. Don't do it. I don't want to lose you."

Taiwo shivers in the rubble, cold in the early-morning air. Aminat already knows she is not going to kill him. Shit. *Kaaro, how could you leave me in this by myself?* What now?

"Aminat?" says Femi.

"I'm not going to kill him." She almost hangs up, then she says, "Thank you."

"Pele. I'm sorry for your loss. Iwo ati Kaaro, o'doju ala." *You and Kaaro will see each other again in dreams.*

"Yes." Aminat lowers the weapon and looks at Dahun. "Arrest him."

"What charge?"

"I don't know. Think of something. Just get him out of my sight before I pull the trigger."

"You're doing the right thing," says Femi.

"Are you still there?" Aminat disconnects and sits down, idly watching Koriko search the ruins for dead folk like a carrion bird. Their eyes catch each other briefly, for seconds, then Koriko goes about her business.

Aminat allows herself to cry.

Chapter Thirty-One

So, this is America, as recalled by a renegade CIA agent trapped in 2012 London.

It is not what I expect. I have seen magazines, video clips, documentaries, feature films. None of this prepares me for how vast the place is. At least in Owen's mind, or memory. I don't know when this is, but the xenosphere is having trouble maintaining focus in the now. The present keeps breaking and snapping back into position. This impossible sky, beautiful as it is, cracks, re-forms, then cracks again, behind it a kind of eternal darkness.

Owen stands stock still by the side of a blacktop. There are no signs. The fields that extend away in all directions are flat, furred with brown grass. No animals. No birds. Windy, but nothing that moves Owen's stocky body. He is holding one suitcase and appears to be happy. The suitcase changes into a duffel bag once or twice, but mostly retains its form.

Owen cannot see me. I am close enough to him to know he is happy.

The wind becomes stronger and blows everything apart. For some minutes I am adrift in the blackness, then I am standing on an obstacle course. Along with five other people in uniform sweats with CIA stamped on the back, Owen runs, leaps, crawls, avoids and climbs his way through, emanating grim resolve. Then he is gone and he drags the scene with him like it's made of cloth. I am pulled off my feet by his backwash and I land in Atlanta. I know this because I'm standing in front of a traffic island with a blue, grey and white sign that says *Center for Disease Control and Prevention*. Three wavy lines on the sign; one might be an eagle, with the other two human, all in profile, stylised. Maybe. *Department of Health and Human Services*. This must have seemed entirely innocuous to the designers at the time, but if the Homians take over, will there be so few humans that we'll need departments to deal with our welfare?

I am inside, in a lab with its harsh sterility. Owen, a foot over the scientists, observes, listens.

"... not directly harmful, as far as we can tell. It latches on to skin, burrows or eats its way through the subdermal fat, multiplies, starts to mimic human cells as soon as it encounters the first one, usually a touch receptor or an adipocyte. Understand this clearly: there is no way to separate it from human cells once multiplication has commenced. There is a dossier in your pack that outlines exhaustively what we have tried."

"Three hundred and fifty pages. Yes. I read it," says Owen.

"Overnight? That's impressive. Angie tried to make it as dull as possible so it could send folks to sleep."

"Continue, Doctor. I don't have much time."

"Cool your jets, I'm coming to it. We have two specimens that more recently seeded the atmosphere, Lagos1975 and Hamburg1998, both dead, but considerably valuable in terms of information gleaned. The Lagos one was a runt, or maybe we did not know how to keep it alive, but Hamburg1998 gave us valuable information. The cells of *Ascomycetes xenosphericus,* the xenoforms, are similar, but not exactly the same strain. The xenoforms have always been here, it seems."

"What do you mean, always?"

"I mean we've tested the oldest artefacts from human civilisation. They're everywhere, though dormant. They are in the air, a nanoscopic lattice of interconnecting neuron-like cells, gathering data. Hamburg1998 was organic, not of this world, and gave off spectrum-hopping radiation for twelve hours before sinking into the ground. Our NATO allies got to it at a depth of forty-nine metres. Amorphous, taking the shape of its container, it lived for eighteen months in a research lab, using nuclear fission for defence in the early vulnerable stages of development. Imagine if human babies were born exhaling Agent Orange. Kills every predator in sight."

Owen agrees.

"It ate into whatever container the scientists stored it in. It was an extreme omnivore, devouring plastic, wood, glass, pure metals, alloyed metals and biological matter like bone and cartilage. The third stage of development involved psychic phenomena. The research scientists started having bad dreams and not a single one got a good night's sleep. Two became psychotic and remain institutionalised till this day. There were three attempted suicides and one success. Then it died, and the mental problems subsided. The new ones, at any rate. We're not even sure that it died. All we can say for certain is that mitosis and meiosis no longer occur. The cells stopped dividing. What we thought to be its genetic material became inert, and it stopped absorbing material from its container, which was a concrete silo five feet thick at the time of death."

"Where is it now?" asks Owen.

"Beneath our feet," says the scientist. He presses a remote control and a holographic image appears. The organism looks like a frozen splash of brown liquid, turning round slowly.

"And you think this is what's in London?"

"That's what the evidence suggests. We don't even know what the Chinese, Russians, Indians or Koreans know. We're not allowed to make overtures on this matter and neither, it appears, are they. You're going to England?"

"I'm going to England," says Owen. "With all the data you can give me."

"Then go with God, Mr Gray. Better you than me."

The place starts to splinter, but I freeze the situation. I have been carried away by their talk and the tragedy of what Owen is going to have to do. This is what I want, this is what the Americans know about Wormwood. I settle down and memorise everything. I cannot use every terminal, only the ones Owen has used, but by the time I finish, I know what Owen knows, or at least, what he remembers. I release my hold on time.

The objects and speakers splinter and re-form into different people in a different place. Construction of behemoths, metal ovoid buildings as high as skyscrapers. I am dwarfed by even the machinery they use to build each one. Both Owen and I are impressed, but he is a bit sad. He will not be going with whoever is boarding these ships, for that is what they are. No, they are not ships. They're cities. Into these pods the populations of each city will go. Sealed away from the xenosphere.

Owen turns to me, looks me in the eye and says, "You have to come back home, Oyin Da."

That's Nike's voice!

"Is Junior all right?" I say.

"Junior's fine. But you must come right now."

I am already building my cocoon from the abundant metal in the construction yard. "I'm coming, but you have to give me more than that."

"Kaaro is dead," she says with Owen's mouth.

"What? How?"

"Just come on back. I'll fill you in when you get here."

Sitting in the grass, clear of the ruins of my cocoon, playing with Junior's hair, watching others arrive, I am surprised that so many people know that Kaaro is dead, that they care. Junior is weaving grass into different patterns and she shakes her head free when she feels mild irritation at my affectionate fiddling. Nike is lying flat beside us, eyes closed, her right hand intertwined with mine, casual to look at, but tight.

"Why are we here?" asks Junior.

"It's the end of someone's life on Earth. We're here to pay respects," says Nike.

"If the person is dead, can't we pay respects anywhere? Does it have to be here?" Junior doesn't look up from her craftwork.

Nike opens her eyes. "We don't really pay respects to the dead, little dove. We pay respects to the living, to our communal loss. Being here is a kind of unspoken promise that when the time comes for each of us, we will be mourned and not forgotten."

I did feel a sense of loss, but Kaaro was kind of a dick when he lived. They say not to speak ill of the dead, but that's got to be bullshit. We speak ill of Idi Amin and Leopold II, and lightning doesn't strike us down. I did feel the communal thing, but

Kaaro is still the boy who didn't choose me when it came down to it. True, I didn't know what I was, or that it was Nike in him that attracted me, but none of that makes it hurt less.

I feel an itch in my mind. A patch of light blue in the sky, flat like a flying carpet, floats towards us. As it gets closer, I realise it's a lot larger than I initially thought, and when the shadow passes overhead I am aware of a large eye on the undersurface, taking in everything. I think it alights on me for a fraction of a second before moving on. It's like a kite made of flesh, and trailed by tentacles. I thought it preferred the spider-thing aspect.

"Look who's here," I say.

"I know," says Nike.

"Why is she here? Isn't Kaaro just one of her ... data points?"

"Oh, they had this sordid sexual thing. It was all very fraught and moist. I don't want to talk about it."

"Is that who we are waiting for?" I ask.

"No. He is." Nike points over her right shoulder to someone behind her.

A man with a tentacle for an arm approaches from the west. He talks to some attendees, then moves to another group.

"That is Eric Sunmola, my love. He was one of the first to arrive, and he is the last of the living sensitives."

"I know who he is," I say. "We're working together."

We all move to the focus of attention, the giant that is now a mere wooden statue, broken in the face, sprinkled with sawdust, on its knees, hair dragging on the ground. All present encircle it. Molara touches it, now in her butterfly wings persona, and the giant splinters and falls into wood chips. At the centre of it, a mound of brown with red streaks. It grows, and I start to feel uneasy. As it gets larger, it rises and falls, like its breathing, and there is differentiation on the surface. Feathers. Oh.

It grows.

Parts of the surface reject the plumed beginning and are covered instead with fur. A low growl starts like a prelude, and cascades along into a god-awful shriek. Junior is tugging at me and I lift her up. We are both scared.

The head flicks up and the wings burst forth, spreading from one end of this island in space to the other. The gryphon's tail lashes back and forth and claws emerge from its paws. Its head is held close to the ground now, watching everyone. The feathers are ruffled and it crouches like it's about to hunt.

"I think," says Eric, "we need to get the fuck out of here, yeah?"

The gryphon swipes with his left paw and seven people are cut down in a bloody mist, too fast for them to even scream. Five more bounce off and fall away from the impact. The untouched scream and flee. Except Molara. She grows and sticks her many legs into the gryphon. This does appear to hurt him, but not for long. It rips the legs out by the roots and eats them. When Molara starts screaming, it makes Junior vomit.

I call the cocoon to me and it is just complete when the gryphon slams his tail into us. The metal holds, even when it strikes three more times. I still pray to Ogun for help.

Nike looks amazed. "What the fuck?"

Chapter Thirty-Two

Wealth does not make sense to Lora.

She sits in a penthouse suite in the midst of a party she paid for, with a glass of the most expensive wine in her hands, her ass on the softest cushion in existence. People talk, get drunk, copulate, argue, boast about the money they have accumulated, and it leaves Lora cold. She cannot sleep on more than one bed, or eat more food than a single human can process. She has an adviser who tells her what to do with the money, which generates more money.

It makes no sense for her to have so much while others have little or nothing, so she anonymously sponsors a programme where homes are 3D-printed for the poor in vast numbers, each dwelling a masterpiece in space maximisation and elegant design. Nobody moves in. A rumour circulates among the poor that the places are haunted, or that it's a trap of some kind. They get you comfortable, then, in the middle of the night, they kidnap your children for rituals. No thank you. The housing complex rots to the east of Rosewater, howling wind blowing through, mimicking ghost sounds to the extent that it might as well be haunted.

They party while Rosewater burns. Lora does not know

why. Perhaps it is a "for tomorrow we die" kind of thing. She puts her champagne glass down and leaves.

Outside, there is a gathering of people that she at first figures for a protest but which turns out to be a religious procession. She joins in and walks with them. Smiling, singing people give her a palm frond and she mimics their dance. There is a horse at the head, with a child mounted on it, though an adult walking alongside leads it. The child has a crown of woven palm leaves. There are two giants walking behind the horse, twins, wearing dark suits with tailcoats and top hats and walking sticks. Their faces are powdered white and they have stuck-on handlebar moustaches.

She recalls the answers to a question Boderin asked her.

Things I cannot feel:
Your eyes on me.
Shame.
Fear.
Desire.
The need to void.
Intoxication.

She is brought back to the present by a ruckus. The horse has stumbled and the crowned child is hurled to the ground. The animal shows the whites of its eyes as it falls. Then Lora hears the second shot. She remembers gunshots from the war and from when automatic gunfire threatened Jack. The same kind of automatic gunfire she hears now. People start to fall around her, and there is no place to hide. She is first hit in the ankle, and falls. The next bullet hits her in the chest, then the side of the neck. Her function is impaired. Her vision is filled with critical warning lights. She calls Jack on her phone and waits till her awareness shrinks down to a tiny dot.

Chapter Thirty-Three

Jack watches Hannah try on a new set of earrings. They are not right, so she discards them and searches for another pair. In front of the mirror, it seems like her reflection is more upset than she is. Jack is full of words, but he has not been able to say anything. He sits two feet away from her dressing table, after several false starts at talking.

He remembers when he met her. 2056, she a law student competing in the Ms Calabar pageant, he a concerned citizen in the nascent Rosewater. Jack, Lora and Victor Ocampo, all hard-hatted, stand around the south ganglion, which at the time is naked, and an expert explains the function to them.

" ... chemical energy converted to electrical energy, like a cell. The alien draws different chemicals from the soil and uses them."

Ocampo seems to be listening, but he is slightly hungover, Jack's fault. Jack gave him the smoothest whiskey in existence the day before, having heard he was partial to it. This lecture is for show – Jack already knows Ocampo will build the inverters Rosewater needs, although it will take three years. He knows this because they shook hands on it over whiskey.

Since none of them is listening, Jack allows his eyes and his mind to wander. There are some people taking photos. Who's doing a photo shoot near the ganglion? Six or seven women in bathing suits, no less. What the fuck? Jack shoves through the gaggle of horny camp men and he sees Hannah just as she sees him. No, their eyes don't lock and Jack does not hear violins or cascading music. But he keeps staring at her. He recognises the photographer, a celebrity whose photo is in the society pages more than his subjects. Tona Ibidun. Jack would like to say he hates him, but he's indifferent, to be honest. Their destinies do not intersect. Or have not until now.

Jack drifts after the giggling women and the people holding the lights and the great man himself. If the photographer notices him, he says nothing. Later, Hannah says he did. *You have an admirer*, he said.

All day Jack follows them, not daring to approach. Then, when the light is going and the sun is descending, they start to file into a luxurious bus. Jack goes up to Hannah's window and stands, shining a torch in his own face, letting her see him. She opens the window.

"Can we talk?" says Jack.

"You have until this bus is full," says Hannah. "Then we go back to Calabar."

"You're be—"

"Don't tell me I'm beautiful. I'm in a beauty pageant. I know I'm good-looking."

Shit.

"I'm ... I'm Jack Jacques. I'm temporarily without poetry because all my energy is going into building this fine city."

Hannah's eyes dart to the shanties and back to Jack. An eyebrow goes up.

"It doesn't look like much now, just a backdrop for your glam shots, but if you could see what I can see, you wouldn't leave."

"Tell me what you see," she says.

"Roads, clean lines, lighting, housing, business district, industry, uninterrupted power supply and, by God, a cathedral to rival Lagos. Shopping to die for. Safety, security, sharing. I want a city with no poverty. And universal health. That's a given."

"And the rule of law?" asks Hannah.

"Sorry, what?"

"I am a law student," says Hannah. "If you want to attract people like me to this utopia you plan to build, there had better be law courts."

"Maybe life will be so fair that we won't need courts," he says.

The bus engine revs.

"Time's up," she says.

"Wait," Jack says. "How do I . . . I want to see you again."

She laughs. "Do you think you've seen me yet? You think this is me?"

He stands there in the dust cloud as the bus leaves, thinking of the timbre of her voice, and knowing he has to hear it again.

He watches the pageant, watches Hannah get as far as first runner-up, and haunts the Nimbus portal for the University of Calabar law faculty until he finds her on the roll.

He is waiting on the faculty steps on the first day of term. She does not act surprised to see him.

"Took you long enough, Jack Jacques of Rosewater," she says. "But I knew you'd make it."

And so it begins.

A meal of edikaikong, which is what you eat when you visit Calabar, leads them to talking and finding chemistry.

Now, in 2068, there is love and law courts; riots in the streets, far from the utopia he imagined.

"Hannah, I have to talk to you," says Jack. His hands tighten on the wheelchair armrests and he sees that they are lighter as the blood rushes away, something she will notice as well.

"What, you preferred the other earrings?" She says this, but he can tell from her tone of voice that she knows what's coming.

"We have to talk about the court case," says Jack.

"Damn it, Jack. We promised."

"This is too damaging to ignore."

"'Under no circumstances are we to discuss work.' Those were your words. You suggested it. I did not." The venom is barely contained now and her hands are open, and out by her sides. She does not sit, does not relinquish the psychological advantage of towering over him.

"You undermined me more thoroughly than any enemy ever could, Hannah," he says. "We have to talk about this."

"'No matter the consequences,' you said. You said that."

"This is different."

"Oh, so there *are* consequences that matter."

"Yes, there are. You and I, we're supposed to be a team. You knew what ... you know what I'm trying to achieve here. You've sent it all to shit."

"You *won* the court case, Mr Mayor."

"Yes, but now you put information in the public domain that you, *Mrs* Mayor, should have told me years ago."

"I have always told you the reanimates were alive. I have never once wavered in that. It was our first and most persistent disagreement."

"The fact that you are saying true words does not mean you are telling the truth, Hannah. My love. I just don't know if you're trying to deceive me or yourself. What you've told me all these years is that you *believe* the reanimates to be alive, whereas in fact you *knew*. You guys had one on ice for years and you did not tell me. I have kept nothing from you. Nothing. I told you everything, yes, no matter the consequences, and let the world burn for all I care. That was the deal between us."

Hannah is silent, and the muscles of her cheeks quiver under her perfect make-up.

"I made a deal with aliens, Hannah. I sold what I believed to be bodies to aliens. You disagreed with me but you did not tell me why. You gave me a reason, but it wasn't the real one. *We went to war*. If you'd told me about Olubi Inuro, that one man would have made all the difference."

Hannah says something in a small voice.

"What?"

"I said it wasn't one man."

"How many—"

"Twenty-three."

Before Jack can respond, his phone goes in a priority ring. It's an automated message.

"*If you are hearing this, Lora Asiko has been incapacitated. If you are hearing this, Lora Asiko has been incapacitated. If you are . . .*"

Shit.

He rolls to his bedside table, opens the top drawer and puts on his bracelet. It syncs with his implant in less than a minute.

Good evening, Mr Mayor.

"Emergency code 30974," says Jack.

245

Tracking Ms Asiko now. I have sent alert to all services. Your bodyguards are en route, ETA three minutes.

"Get Aminat too."

Unavailable.

"Try again."

Unavailable.

"Fine. Get Dahun, and don't you dare say—"

"Mr Mayor, are you all right?" says Dahun. He seems to be outside somewhere.

"I'm fine. Something's happened to Lora. And Aminat's still out of contact."

"Sir, you haven't been listening to the news, have you?"

No. When off duty, Jack elects for a media blackout and trusts Lora to interrupt if anything critical happens.

"What's going on?"

"Synners. Mass shooting, multiple casualties, I'm on the way there now."

"Where's Aminat?"

"I don't know. She made me arrest Taiwo and I haven't seen her since. What do you want me to do?"

"Find Lora. I'm sending homing details."

"Yes, sir. I'll try."

"No, don't try, Dahun. Get it done."

Chapter Thirty-Four

Dahun drives himself and only relinquishes control when he can hear the gunfire. He is out and running before the car stops, ignoring the AI warning and arming his weapons, drones and armour. His satellite drone rises out of the trunk of the car, high above the danger zone. Four synners, two on each side of the road, elevated positions, rifles, created a crossfire into which the procession walked. Several broken corpses and bleeding injured.

"Fuck this. Action-hero mode activate."

Earwormed with the theme song from the cartoons he always has playing in the background, he detonates a mild flash-bang, more to draw attention to himself than to confuse the shooters. The orbiting drone shows him they are amateurs, deployed in a pattern straight out of films, wearing no armour, disoriented by the flash-bang.

"Dah-dah something something shield and swooooorrd-ddd!" He marks the targets, one of whom recovers and starts to shoot at the monitor drone. Terrible shot. Dahun pumps his rifle and sends a grenade to one of the synners who is still trying to kill civilian stragglers. The explosion obliterates the entire window ledge she is perched on. No body parts. A gentle fire burns like the kind you find in temples. Dahun advances.

"Super action activate, join the hero activate, something something justice for all something. Dah-dah-dah-dahh."

They are firing at him now, but his shield can take it. Most of their bullets miss in any event. A plasma shot powers through a window and the upper torso of the shooter perched in the nest. He remembers that he must take at least one alive. He idly wonders if he should do this hand to hand in order to present a challenge, but he is a professional.

"Dah-dah-doo-doo activate . . . activate!"

He shifts the rifle to non-lethal. One of the synners stands his ground, shooting consistently in plain view. He is a hundred metres away. Dahun shoots him in the head with his side arm.

The last one runs. Dahun follows, whistling the whole time.

While he is looking for Lora among the dead and wounded, Dahun sees Koriko going about her business. She glows green; not bright, but gently, which explains why he has never seen this. From the sidelines people throw rocks at her, but she doesn't even look. A particularly large one bounces off her skull and breaks skin. She does not flinch, nor does she wipe away the darker green effluent from the cut. A serpentine is coiled around her right leg and it sounds like they are talking to each other. He remembers this one. Aminat gave it to her as a replacement for one lost, a kind of payment for Koriko's help in entering Taiwo's castle.

The orbiting drone sounds an alarm, which means it has picked up Lora's ID chip. It weaves, bobs, and comes to rest right above Koriko. She happens to be handling a woman's body at the time. Dahun scrambles towards her.

"I remember you," she says. "You're Aminat's man. What do you want?"

"Don't," he says. "You can't have that one."

Koriko looks at the body, looks up at Dahun and shrugs. "I don't want it anyway."

The snake's tongue flicks out and back in, and Koriko moves on to other cadavers.

Dahun sees why she didn't want Lora.

Jack, you should have told me.

Dahun hefts the body to his car. It takes two trips because she is not in one piece, and he is puffing by the time the work is done. She's heavier than she looks. Looked. Looks. He calls Jack.

"I found her. What do you want me to do?" He opens the boot and the satellite drone settles into its nest.

"Take her to your place. I'm coming. Twenty minutes. I'm coming."

Dah-dah-dah-dah. Activate.

It doesn't look the way he thinks it should. She. She doesn't look the way he thinks she should.

Lora is in three distinct pieces, head-neck-chest in one piece, abdomen and legs, and right arm. Dahun could not find a left arm, but he did gather some fragments that might add up to the missing part, or might not. She is smeared with the blood of other people, her hair caked with it. Her eyes are open, her face expressionless. She is wearing make-up as if she were dolled up for a party. There is a crack across her forehead and it forks multiple times to form a line drawing of antlers.

There seems to be little fluid leaking from her. The

machinery is far too advanced for him. He would have no idea where to start if tasked. Here, under the harsh light of his dining room, laid out on his table, she looks like a broken toy.

He remembers her from the war. She was mad efficient and never cracked a smile, but ate and drank with the rest of them, and wasn't she fucking that writer guy? Walter Tanmola. Dahun had liked him. When asked about Lora, he had said, "She's amazing. I've never met a woman quite like her."

Dahun wonders if the writer knew. Does Aminat know? Jacques clearly does, and wants to keep it quiet, which is a smart move.

The house warns him of approach to the back door, and Dahun verifies the IDs of Jack's new bodyguards, then lets them in. He remembers being present when a Nigerian drone tried to kill Jack during the insurrection. One of the old bodyguards died, but the mayor remained unscathed. Lucky bastard. *Luck will do in a pinch, Caleb, but it doesn't last for ever.* That's what his own father used to say.

After searching the house, and barely seeming to notice the destroyed robot, the suited men leave, replaced by Jack. He's wearing shorts and a Bermuda shirt, with a floppy hat. He makes for the table and places a palm against Lora's cheek. His face crumples, though he does not cry. It is the most visibly upset Dahun has ever seen him.

"*Thy lips are warm,*" says Jack. "Shit. Shit. Shit. This is not the time."

"Did you love her?" asks Dahun.

Jack shoots him a hostile look. "Hannah's the only one for me. Lora was ... is like my sister, has been for a long time."

"Then you might not want to quote *Romeo and Juliet*. It's weird."

Jack sucks his teeth. "Did you see who did it? Get any of them?"

"An alien. In the trunk of my car. He was bleeding, but I set up an IV to keep him alive while Rosewater heals him. No head trauma, so he'll be able to give us information."

"Definitely alien?"

"Green-eyed devil."

"The Honeycomb might come for him. Or Koriko."

"Let them," says Dahun.

Jack's phone beeps. "Ahh. Open your front door."

Dahun checks his cameras. Since the mayor is here, he sends an orbiting drone out just in case someone wants to take a shot. A silver eighteen-wheeler with a refrigerated trailer has squeezed itself into his street. Dahun does not recognise the logo, but he scans it and Nimbus comes back with a secretive robotics firm. It is not even clear what the company does.

Four people come in bearing backpacks that are larger than they are. Two of them, the men, take further trips to the trailer while two surround what remains of Lora, taking readings, plugging cables in here and there. These two seem ... enamoured of each other, and from how they touch in passing, Jack thinks they are involved.

"Sir," says one of them, "I'm Sola, the team lead. This is not a combat unit. In fact, quite the opposite, if I'm reading this right."

"Make love, not war," says the second woman, whose tag identifies her as Morinola.

"I know this. She wasn't sent into combat. She is my right arm, however. There are bonuses in play here." Jack points to Dahun. "Let's leave them to their work."

"We'll need industrial-strength coffee," says Sola. "In vats."

"You'll get it," says Dahun.

The alien is laughing when they get to him. He refuses to answer any questions, so Dahun shoots him through the head with an explosive round. The mayor is impassive.

The alien does not rise again.

Chapter Thirty-Five

Femi Alaagomeji, nervous, hair cropped close, wearing a suit that might seem masculine to some, holding a briefcase for show, waits outside the president's casual office in Aso Rock. She has been summoned to Abuja because the president appears to have developed some light paranoia about airwaves and electromagnetic radiation. He will communicate through aides on the phone, but he has stopped using holofields or having direct electronic communication.

When he calls her in, she has steeled herself. Whatever she is trying to do, she has to keep this man on side or the whole thing collapses. The stupid man is motivated by revenge. He wishes to crush Rosewater as a proxy for crushing Jack Jacques. He wants Rosewater razed and the soil salted so that nothing will ever grow there again. He has said as much. He has declared the population traitors for not fleeing or defecting.

Femi finds the president buffoonish but malleable. When she explained the alien threat to him, his eyes glazed over. She said she should be allowed to work on it alone, without other duties, and he agreed. In public she was fired from Section 45, but secretly she gained an independent budget. He has her followed, of course. He endorses her need to fight aliens because he hates Jack and considers the two problems sides of a single coin. The president lacks subtlety and does not fully understand the xenosphere and how careful one must be in plotting the downfall of a species that can read your mind. About the same time that he threatened Jack with elections, he was dissatisfied with Femi's inability to curb him. He verbally fired her, but did not file the paperwork.

In that window, Femi fled to Rosewater, used her funds and contacts and found her way to the mayor's office.

She caused the war by shooting the president's candidate, Ranti, and was able to operate under the cover of bombing and food shortages. Orchestrating the isolation of Rosewater was the only way to fight the alien advance. Nobody, not a single one of the simpletons, understood what was going on. Not Jacques, who seemed more awake than most when it came to realpolitik but was amoral; not Kaaro, who was essentially a gun, lovable as a rogue but daft; not the love-struck Aminat, whom Femi found competent but disappointing. Hamstrung by compassion.

The fact is, Femi could have operated under Jacques' rule. Ranti, on the other hand, was pristine, and beholden to the president. It would take years to corrupt either him or the system around him, time that Femi did not have. If Ranti had a secret, she would have used that, but he did not, and because of that, she sacrificed him, especially in a way that would bind Jack to her.

Nobody grasps that humanity is at total war with an alien species. The design is too wide, spans too many centuries for most people to understand. Kaaro had to read Femi's mind to see, and even then, it was too late for him. She does not give herself time to mourn him. If she hadn't sent twin to neutralise twin, maybe Kaaro might be ...

"Come in, Mrs Alaagomeji."

He's put on some pounds since she last saw him face to face, before she was imprisoned in Rosewater. He is smiling, happy as a pig in shit, wearing an open-neck shirt with his belly bulging outwards.

"I don't have much time. Have your accommodations been satisfactory?"

An underhanded way of telling her to finish up at the hotel soon. Femi intends to stay there for a year, to make up for the time lost. "Yes, it's fine."

"What news from Rosewater? Tell me of Jack's pain."

"Crime first. Since my agent went in, organised crime has reduced, and the principal boss has been neutralised, his lieutenants liquidated. My agent unfortunately lost his life in the process."

"How does this help us?"

"Crime is more sporadic and unpredictable now, people feel unsafe; it adds to the heightened tension."

"Go on."

"My second pillar is a unit in Rosewater causing sabotage. Same tactics as during the war, more effective since this is peacetime and no soldiers have mobilised. Every few days there is either a protest or a bombing."

"How is this making Jack uncomfortable?"

"Sooner or later he will have an uprising on his hands. With the revelations about reanimates being alive and some of the aliens perpetuating mass shootings, the city will come down on his head soon enough. That's not even including all the court cases that we are sponsoring."

"I've always wanted to ask: does Hannah Jacques work for you?"

"Everybody works for me, Mr President. Even when they don't know it."

"That's what I like to hear." He laughs for a while. "And what about the other project? The aliens?"

"I'm still working on it, sir. I lost an asset."

"You seem to have gained another one in your bed," says the president.

Femi says nothing.

"I mean to say, I know about you having sex with—"

"I know what you meant, Mr President."

"Don't be insolent."

"Sorry, sir."

"Get out."

On the drive back to the hotel, she phones Eric.

"Get everyone together."

Chapter Thirty-Six

Aminat is pretty sure Kaaro would hate this if he were alive to protest.

The people – her brother, sister and her mother – are now staying with Aminat in the non-collapsed part of the property, to help her cope with her grief. They walk over every inch of the house, something Kaaro definitely would not approve of.

People visit other people, Kaaro. It's not hostile action.

But why? Are their own houses shitty? Why would you leave your own house if you like it? I never leave the house.

I know.

The actions: an abundance of squeeze-hugs. She cannot remember ever receiving so many in such a short space of time. She is usually the one who initiates physical contact, but they seem to have decided it's important to hold her. Even Tomi, her sister, was spreading her arms in invitation, and Tomi hates physical contact.

Food: they make so much. Tasty, appetising and soft-making. Aminat refuses many meals. The treadmill can't cut it.

Questions: all the time. Redundant. Unnecessary. How are you feeling? How are you *really* feeling? Do you want something to eat? Poor you. How are you feeling? Do you wish you had married him? I don't understand. Were you engaged? You were going to propose to him? Where are his people, anyway? Have you eaten? How are you feeling?

The fucking dog: Yaro will now not leave Aminat alone. He follows her everywhere, stopping at her feet when she comes to rest, rising as soon as she does. Fucking dog is going to pine to death because of Kaaro. It does one odd thing. It won't let her sleep. When she is about to nod off, Yaro starts barking hysterically, and hello wakefulness.

It's funny. Aminat misses Kaaro in a more physical way than she expected. Because they had been ... not touching towards the end. Stupid. She can't actually remember the last time they made love. This should sadden her, but it seems to just make her horny. But she can't touch herself because of the fucking family and the fucking dog. God, she loves them, but she wants a break.

Her eyes are two heavy shutters. Yaro's shouting is far away. Not shouting. Barking. Dogs bark, right? No, someone else is shouting. What Aminat sees are hundreds of people floating in dark space. Their eyes are closed and their clothing seems to roughly indicate what they do. The shouting comes from a particular man who is trapped in the jaws of a giant gryphon. The eagle beak-tears the man to pieces while riding currents of despair with outspread wings. The man's distress ends abruptly as what's left of him is swallowed. The gryphon's beak is red, but the blood itself won't drip in the weightlessness. It simply forms globules that Aminat fears may drift in her direction. The beast starts to cast about for its next victim. Aminat tries to move away, but ends up bouncing against adjacent people, sleepers, and attracting attention. The gryphon's eye comes to rest on her. A nictitating membrane slides in a sideways blink. The creature gives a prolonged screech and beats its wings towards Aminat, shocking her awake.

Yaro whimpers beside her, tail between his legs, trying to look small. She pets him.

"Don't you dare say I told you so," she murmurs.

She knows what that was.

Kaaro.

"I don't know," says Layi. "You are bereaved. This might have been a bad dream. It is common to dream of a deceased loved one."

"You sound like a pamphlet," says Tomi.

Layi smiles. "I read one last night."

"Me too!" Tomi and Layi bump fists across the dining table.

"Can we focus?" says Aminat. "On me? I'm why you're here, right?"

"Yes," says Tomi.

"Speak for yourself," says Layi. "I'm here for the hotness of Rosewater boys. They have such good skin here."

"Okay, didn't know you were gay," says Aminat.

"What, Kaaro did not tell you?" Layi looks surprised.

Aminat shakes her head, but she does not go on to describe the last days of her relationship.

"Is this a coming-out moment?" Aminat looks to Tomi, who seems more interested in getting something out of her corn flakes.

"Nah. I thought you knew," says Layi.

"Everybody knows," says Tomi. "There's hair in my ... I need another spoon."

"It didn't feel like a dream," says Aminat. "It felt like I was there."

"Yes, that's what dreams are like," says Layi.

"No. No, that wasn't a dream." Kaaro always suspected that the house was bugged and only said private things in the xenosphere. Aminat thinks she dropped into the xenosphere, although she shouldn't be able to do that without Kaaro, who regularly took her there.

Everybody is in the xenosphere, every single human, but most people don't know it. They remain inert and do not interact with each other. I don't know what sets sensitives apart, but we're awake in there, and we can fuck with people or each other.

What does it look like?

It doesn't look like anything. You just have these odd self-images floating about, asleep. Nothing wakes them. You can fly among them, play with them like beach balls, spin them upside down when you're bored.

Kaaro ...

I don't do that any more. It was years ago. I got bored easily. It is boring how mundane most people's thoughts are. What you need to know is that everybody's in there and all but one per cent are unprotected.

Does bumping into them cause any harm?

No. I don't know. Bad dreams, maybe? I don't know. My trainers never had any information on that.

"Aminat," says Tomi.

"Hmm?"

"Where were you?"

"I miss him, Tomi."

While they hug, the phone rings, unknown number.

"Hello?" says Aminat.

"Miss Aminat, it's Bad Fish. Are you alone?"

"I can be. What's wrong?" Bad Fish never calls except during an urgent situation.

"Miss Aminat, I cannot see Kaaro anywhere."

"I'm sorry I couldn't tell you, but I don't exactly have a number for you. Kaaro's dead."

"Even dead people have chips," says Bad Fish.

"It was a really quick Viking funeral. Expedient. He was incinerated. Totally," says Aminat. Layi gives a thumbs-up.

"I'm sorry to hear that. Accept ... my apologies? What am I supposed to say in these situations? I'm not around people much, Miss Aminat."

"That's all right."

"Do you have to be in Rosewater?"

"What do you mean?"

"I mean, can you go back to Lagos?"

"Why?"

"Rosewater is ... quite uncomfortable right now. You might want to take your family, including that boy that has no ID chip, and leave the city behind."

"I'm chief of security, Bad Fish."

Bad Fish sighs on the other end, the closest to what Aminat would think of as world-weariness he has ever shown to her.

"I see things, Miss Aminat. It's not looking good for Rosewater."

"We'll survive. We always do. Sometimes with help from our friends. Like you."

"My advice is to pack up and go to Lagos."

"Thank you, Bad Fish."

"There's one more thing. Kaaro said he had a job for me."

"I can't imagine what—"

"Outside Rosewater. With the Nigerian federal government."

What?

"Why would he be working with—"

"I do not know, but it seemed like some 'greater good' shit. I have no idea, but you need to put me in touch with the principals if that work is to go ahead. And I got the impression it was important."

Femi Alaagomeji. It has to be.

"How can I reach you?"

"If you think of me, I will be there," intones Bad Fish.

"Are you . . . also a sensitive?"

"I'm kidding, I'm just kidding. Call this number. It's only active for forty-eight hours."

"That's more than I need. Goodbye, Bad Fish."

"*Au revoir.*"

She spins round and almost trips on Yaro. Motherfucker. Kaaro was working with Femi behind her back. It had to be. He went to see her just before she left prison in the prisoner swap. She must have said something to convince him, and he did read her mind. Asshole.

She stops. There's a red "file received" dot glowing on her palm. Pretty sure it wasn't there before talking to Bad Fish. She opens the display and it's a simple text file. Bad idea to open random files, but Bad Fish has never done her wrong.

It's a letter.

Oh.

Dear Aminat,

Ahh, I don't know how to write this. I'm probably dead. I'm sorry. I died.

This exists because I'm not just sitting home reading Achebe and feeding Yaro experimental dog food. I've undertaken something that might be dangerous. No, it's definitely dangerous. It may, in fact, be the reason I'm dead. If I died of a stroke or an overdose of heroin while on the toilet seat, that would be embarrassing, because now you have information you don't need to have. Oops.

I love you. This is the only thing I can say I'm certain of, and the one thing that in my chequered life has been constant. There has never been anyone else for me, Aminat. I'm afraid of dying, but I'm more afraid of being anywhere without you. Now, though, I have to go haunt the afterlife and you have to carry on without me. God, I sound like a civil war soldier writing home.

To the point: I've been working with Femi. I wanted to tell you every single moment of every day, but I didn't want to put you in a position. You took a good-faith job with Jack Jacques' administration, and spy training or not, Aminat, you're a bad liar. If you know what I know you'd try to work with me, and with Femi, but you can't pull off the double agent thing, my darling. I know you. You can't. I, on the other hand, am an excellent liar.

Here's the thing: you're working for the wrong side. I'm sorry, but you are. Jacques is what I've always thought, a craven, slimy, adaptable leech who will twist and turn and use the language of justice while fucking Rosewater in the ass without ... sorry, sorry. He brings out the worst in me. He's working for the purpose of the aliens. He is giving them humanity on a platter to maintain power and you are helping him.

I don't know where you go at night. I could find out if I wanted, but I won't get in your head without permission. I know you come back beaten up sometimes. I like to think you're fighting yourself, because the Aminat I know has the best moral compass.

I hid working with Femi, but I need you to know that her mission is not on behalf of herself, or the president, or Nigeria. Femi is trying to save the world, and you'd better recognise that. Recognise, even if you can't join. Maybe try to bring yourself to not impede her efforts?

This hurts. Right now I hear you moving about in the house, getting ready for work. You're out of the shower and you're listening to Bob Marley the way you do. I can smell your perfume. I feel safe with you around. You did keep me safe, Aminat. You did protect me. I stepped out of your protection, out of your ring of fire. I went to a place that was impossible for you to follow because you did not know. Do not blame yourself for my death. Blame me.

I have one last thing to say. I have a plan. If what I have in mind works, I can end this whole problem without death of either human or Homian. I know that's a solution you'd prefer, so wish me luck.

Tell your brother to keep practising, and please feed my dog.

Goodbye. I love you. Goodbye.

Kaaro

She wasn't sure that the number would still work, but it does. Protocols established long ago, unsure if still monitored, but remembered perfectly.

"Hello?"

"Speak."

"I want to speak to Mother," says Aminat. "I need a colander."

"Wouldn't a coffee filter be better?"

"Yes."

The line goes dead, and Aminat strokes Yaro as she waits for Femi Alaagomeji to make contact.

Chapter Thirty-Seven

This is, for me, somewhat unexpected.

The gryphon keeps swatting the cocoon, and the narrow visor isn't enough to show me where we are going, plus the view darts about crazily. Its screech-roars are deafening.

"Mum?" says Junior.

I see her intermittently, same as Nike. I know what I have to do.

"I'm going out there," I say.

Nike scoffs. "You're not going out there."

The cocoon stops with a bang. One side of it dents inwards, which I think is where we have made impact and got stuck. Outside, I see some rocky projections, and the sky is grey, but that's it. I still hear the gryphon. I scramble over and feel around beneath the dummy control panel. What I'm looking for is there: a shotgun. It's all I know how to use when it comes to weapons. I load it.

I kiss Junior on the head, Nike on the lips, and prepare to open the door.

"I know you'll never listen to me, but be careful," says Nike.

"I'll try."

I open the cocoon, exit, and seal it behind myself. The gryphon is larger than an elephant. It's so large I can hear its breathing and the beat of its heart. It isn't looking at me, it's busy eating the terrain. It cracks rock with its beak, then crunches down. It lifts its head to swallow with the aid of gravity. I only this minute notice that the raptor part is a martial eagle, with white feathers underneath and darker on top.

This eating, what remains ... People speak of nothingness but they mean a specific absence of a thing, or darkness. This place where the gryphon bites, what remains is a true void, a true absence of being. The rock is torn free and in its place ... nothing. No colour, no light, and looking at it brings discomfort to the eyes as one strains to perceive, and nausea to the gut as it tells you something is very wrong here.

I would rather hide in my metal cocoon and wait this out, but my family is in there, so my fear must wait. The creature sees me now, and although it does not stop its activity, its eye stays locked on. The cocoon is in an elevated position, wedged between two rock projections and the mountainside. I climb down to a ledge, look down at the gryphon, which is maybe three hundred yards from me. It can't be hungry for me – I am a morsel compared to what it is eating. Yet there is something in that yellow eye that tells me it prefers a meal with sentience, and that this is not just a random destructive rampage.

You can kill anything with a shotgun.

My father said that, and it was true in his time. It is not true now.

My plan is to jump, aim for the eyes, hope for the best. It is not to be, however, because I hear a shout like an extended battle charge from above me, and someone darts past in a tangle of limbs and metal.

Before I can fully process what I'm seeing, Junior has landed on the gryphon's back and buried two spears deep into its feathers.

"*What?* Junior, get your narrow ass back here!" I feel my voice go, but that little strip of flesh and bone keeps fighting and it seems she hurts the gryphon.

"Let her," says Nike. I look up and see her head watching from a new hole in my cocoon.

"She's a child," I say.

Nike shakes her head. "Neither you nor I nor Junior are alive. Try to remember that, Oyin Da. Most importantly, Junior is pure xenosphere, has never been human like you and me. She is an idea made flesh and knows how to survive in this place better than we ever will. This isn't real, but our minds make it into a facsimile of the life we knew on Earth, so we come along with the same rules that we lived with, rules that don't have to obtain here. We know that intellectually, but our minds still rail against what does not fit ontologically. Junior, on the other hand, has no such restrictions. Observe."

Junior picks weapons from her tattoos and hurls them at the gryphon, which is both in pain and confused from the attacks. With each swing of the arm, she throws a spear that always hits home. She strokes her arms and the weapons come into being around her, following her. She simply picks them out of the air and attacks the gryphon. It decides it has had enough, but is still gentle in the way it deals with Junior. It beats its wings and tries to blow her away. She struggles against it, but can't walk forward. Her legs grow projections, like strands of flesh that dig into the rock, anchoring her. She looks like a meat plant. When the wind cannot blow her away, Junior opens her mouth and a beam of purple light comes out and burns half of the gryphon's head. It screeches, folds in its wings, and dives down the mountain into mists, and we no longer see it. Burned feathers float to the ground where it used to be.

My daughter holds a morning star in each hand and is surrounded by the knives, clubs, hammers and scythes that her tattoos depict. She sees me.

"Hello, Mum."

I don't know if I should hug her or scold her.

Nike, Junior and I have all come down to the edge of the gryphon's bites to take a look.

"Oyi n'ko mi," says Junior. *I'm dizzy.*

"Then don't look," says Nike. "But that does look and feel strange."

"The gryphon hasn't destroyed the idea of the mountain that keeps this representation intact. You can't truly eliminate an idea. It's extirpated the basis on which we imagine it."

"I don't understand," says Nike.

"Look at me," says Junior. "Cool!"

Every time she moves an arm, tiny stars strobe across the path. Not cool.

"I think he's found a way to damage the xenosphere," I say.

"Was Kaaro ever this feral? Do we know for sure that it's Kaaro?" asks Nike.

"It wasn't feral," I say.

"Junior just had to fight it."

"Yes, and it was controlled, considered in its response to

her onslaught. It was careful not to harm her, even though it could," I say.

"No, it couldn't," says Junior.

"Yes, it really could," I say. "I think it is Kaaro, and the gryphon is feigning this whole display as a cover-up for what it's doing."

"And what is that? Besides destroying our home?"

I don't know the answer. This whole space is a product of our imagination, shaped by memories that we agree on, taught to our little girl over time so that she comes to consensus. I have been so deeply ingrained that I thought I was real, real in the Earth physical way. If I am just a pattern of thought and memory, Huginn and Muninn, then I should be able to see the underlayers if I try. And I do. I close my eyes. It's what we did, Nike and I, before I went to America.

I see the thought pathways. I see the strands of reticulate xenoforms binding together. But I see defects, places where the strands have snapped, repair globules trying to fix damaged xenoforms, or absorbing ones that are too far gone. There seem to be a lot of these, unlike before. I see the gryphon like a ball of lightning travelling up and down the thoughtways, damaging the cells. Each cell, like Hamlet, carries the germ of its own destruction in lysosomes, suicide bags. The gryphon is telling the cells to become one with the lysosomes, releasing over thirty substances that dissolve xenoform to goop.

But the xenosphere is vast, and there is just one gryphon.

I see the damage propagated even without the gryphon-thing directly causing it. It spreads like a disease. I see my daughter punched through with minute holes that even she isn't aware of. She is kneeling at the edge and gesturing, effecting some repair, pushing back the void. This is remarkable, but too little, too late, and it is taking all of her power to bring back a square inch of the xenosphere at a time.

I have to get back to Owen Gray, to find out the rest of what he knows. I try, but cannot time-travel no matter what. Whatever Kaaro is doing is blocking me.

Fine. Let's try something else.

Chapter Thirty-Eight

As the car comes to a stop, Jack doesn't know exactly how far he wants to take this. He doesn't know if he thinks he is calling Hannah's bluff, or if he's just trying to occupy his mind while Lora gets fixed. A hot jolt to his heart when he thinks of her. He wonders what causes that sensation, the heat, as if the blood suddenly boils, then cools again, and only in the heart.

He still seethes as he leaves the car. It drives off as instructed. Jack is dressed in the kind of clothes he wore in '55 and '56, Camp Rosewater night clothes, anonymous. In the daytime he used to wear a suit, deliberately cheap, so that the hoi polloi thought him one of them who wished to ascend. In the night he ran with criminals, with the twins, in dark blue jeans and dark blue sweats. He has a beanie, but it's a warm night. He would stand out more wearing one.

It's the right address because he can see Hannah stepping out of shadow, also disguised in casual clothes, although her grace in motion cannot be muted. A certain angle to the articulation of bones, a specific tension of the ligaments and tendons, just the right muscle tone, and you get a person whose every movement is an inspiration. She is also trained to move in a way that garners maximum attention, but without her gifts, that training would be as dust in a sandstorm, lost, unnoticed, irrelevant.

"I didn't know if you'd come," she says.

Jack shrugs.

"I know you love her. How is she?"

"You know these tech people. They say nothing. You wanted to show me something?"

She crooks her finger at him and leads the way. It's a high-rise building, but with flats or rooms for rent. Not a luxury palace. It smells of human defeat and shit. There are brown hands painted among the graffiti, standing out, pointing the way. As they climb and turn corners, there are more hands at intervals on the walls.

"Antwerp hands," says Hannah.

"What?"

"Belgian chocolate hands, reminders of the rubber planta-tion workers' hands that they chopped off in the Congo. If we ever build a time machine, I have dibs on killing Leopold II."

"Hannah—"

"We're here."

A musty smell emanates from the flat as the door opens. There are bunks and pallets and sleeping bags lined up on the floor. There are shelves up the wall for sleeping above one another like in a slave ship.

"We don't have enough money to keep them how they deserve," says Hannah. "Do you want to count them?"

"No." Jack rolls up his sleeves and sits on the floor. "But I want to interview them."

And he does.

He asks them to speak to him of death and undeath, stories of accidents and murder. Unlike their poster boy in the court case, these women and men and children have varying degrees of bodily function, but they are indeed alive and they know themselves. This gives Jack pause. Hannah knows when to shut up and let him percolate. He is not sure to what extent he should be angry with her.

"What happens when we put aliens in them?" he asks.

"We don't know. We've never studied one."

Jack remembers the "failures" he and Lora saw in the Honeycomb, and wonders if that is why the aliens tried to hide them.

His phone buzzes. It's a government number, but one he does not recognise.

"Hello?"

"Sir, you need to come back to the mansion." The voice is familiar.

"Who's this?"

"Blessing, sir."

"Blessings to you too. Who is this?"

"No, Blessing Boderin. I'm your lawyer."

"Ahh. Right."

"You need to come back, sir. The staff called me when they didn't know what to do. They can't find Lora."

"Slow down. What's the problem?"

"You have visitors, sir. From the Honeycomb. They are adamant, sir, they will only talk to you."

"Okay, put them on the phone."

"Face to face, sir."

Jack sighs and glances at Hannah, whose expression is deceptively blank. "I'm not ready to speak to them yet."

"Do you want me to stall?"

"No, I'm on my way."

To the left of Jack's desk, in his office, he has a sofa and lounge chair set for less stressful meetings. Chief Scientist Lua, who might as well be the Homian ambassador, sits opposite, with Koriko. Koriko is not really present. Lua brought some spores, which she blew at Jack, and Koriko appeared as a hallucination, albeit an interactive one. Jack doesn't like this and vows to go heavier on the antifungals next time. Neither of the aliens has said a word.

"What do you want?" he says. "I'm busy."

"Are you?" says Lua.

"Look, I'm not sure what you're doing. Maybe you have some adviser on human affairs and the person said you should use silence as an opening gambit, to cause unease in the other person. I've done it myself. A lot of people rush to fill that space with words because we humans, well, we detest emptiness and voids of all kinds. We tell ourselves *nature abhors a vacuum*, which is absolute bullshit. There's more of outer space than there is atmosphere, and that's vacuum all the way down. I'm aware I just did what I'm speaking against. Or did I?"

"What are you talking about?" asks Lua.

"Nothing, Chief Scientist. Would you like to tell me why you are here?"

"What have you done to the ... xenosphere?" asks Lua. Koriko says nothing.

"Come again?"

"Is my English faulty? I said what have you done to the xenosphere."

275

"I thought that's what you said. What's wrong with the xenosphere?"

"Do not play one of your human games with me, Mayor Jack."

"Don't worry, Chief Scientist. I'm not."

"What have you—"

"Done to the xenosphere. Yes, I know. Asking the same question again and again is surely going to get you a different result. Please keep trying."

"Does this seem amusing to you?" asks Lua.

"Why don't you just tell me what happened?"

Lua sighs in a most human gesture, her green sclera almost glowing. "After the tragic shooting of the parade—"

"By your people, the synners."

"After the parade, Koriko brought the bodies to the Honeycomb for ... processing, as agreed. Only it did not work."

"How? What went wrong?"

"No signal. The xenosphere is gone. I took some air and soil samples. The xenoforms are still there and the network with humans is intact, but the pathways are full of noise. We can't send messages to the Home moon that houses our people; they can't send messages to us."

"And somehow you think this is my doing."

"Yes."

"How? And why?"

"I don't know. That's why we're here."

"You're wasting your time. You should go and find the real culprit. What is most concerning to me is that you think I did it. We're partners. Do you not have a concept of agreement where you come from? Do accords and contracts not mean

276

anything? Because that makes me nervous that you will cast aside our arrangement as fast as you think I have done."

The hologram/hallucination does nothing but look strange. It does not make eye contact, and Jack thinks it's not really Koriko. Just an impression of her brought by Lua to intimidate or to remind Jack of the human position in the relationship.

"Does that thing talk?" he says, pointing.

"Mayor, you will give a directive to your people reminding them to cooperate with us, and to take no steps to impede us. You will use all your resources to find out if anyone is acting against us, neutralising the xenosphere."

"No, and no," says Jack. "This is the wrong time to give any directive at all. I don't know if you listen to our news, but people are fragile. They've found out that the reanimates are not really dead."

"Well of course they're not dead," says Lua. "The xenoforms can heal and rebuild any body, and the mind is a complicated emanation of the body. It takes a little bit longer, but it will ultimately heal."

So the Homians have known this all along.

"You seem surprised," says Lua.

"You had this information and you still went ahead with the plan to place your people's consciousness into our bodies."

"It was *your* idea, Jack. You and your people came up with the solution so that you could survive the war. It is all one to us whether you die now or later, but rest assured that you will not be on this planet as things currently stand. Make the declarations and start investigations."

"No. What I promised to give you is our recently dead and the reanimates. I said we could talk about the welfare of

Homians in Rosewater. I did not give you a seat at the policy table. I—" Jack's phone cuts him off. Outside, the rising sun marks the end of a challenging night.

"Yes?"

"It's Dahun. Come home. To my house."

"Is she alive?"

"I don't know. The robotics people have finished."

Lua says, "Mayor Jack, I must insist."

"I will look into your problems with the xenosphere, but I will not make an inflammatory announcement. Now fuck off, I'm busy."

Jesus, so much pillar to post today!

After arriving on Dahun's street, it takes half an hour to get to the address because Sola and Morinola seem to have called in reinforcements. The entire road is clogged up with lorries, although they appear to be clearing out.

Sola updates Jack while the rest of the technicians pack up. Lora is lying on a table, naked but for two strips of makeshift clothing made of . . . is that duct tape? Fucking engineers. They also appear to have left the scars in place.

"We're done. Our invoice will come in shortly," says Morinola.

"I've seen it. Already paid."

"Thanks. You might get an evaluation survey—"

"Get the fuck out of my house," says Dahun. He tells Jack he caught them fornicating during a lull.

When they are all gone, Jack asks, "What *is* that music?"

"It's a cartoon. Captain Actionheart. I like to have it playing in the background when I'm working. The engineers are big fans, it seems."

"Can you change it?"

"I ... er ... don't have anything else. I just moved in."

"Jesus, just turn it off, okay? I need to say something to Lora, and the phrase must be just right or she might go into lock."

Sound killed, Jack bends and whispers into Lora's ear: "Ranti omo eni tiwo nse." *Remember whose child you are.*

Lora sits up and looks around, fixes on Jack, then on Dahun, then back to Jack.

The inadequacy of the duct tape becomes obvious. "Fetch some clothes," Jack says.

Dahun leaves.

Lora gets off the table and approaches Jack.

"Sir?" she says.

"You're all right!" says Jack. He hugs her. "I've already lost one sister. I don't intend to lose you."

She isn't hugging him back, so he stops. "I don't remember what happened, sir. Not all of it."

"Understandable," says Jack.

"Were we physically close before?"

"No."

"So when you hugged me ... ?"

"I was afraid for you, that's all."

"All right."

"How's your memory for events before the ... trauma?"

"Something is missing, sir."

"What do you mean? Damaged?"

"No. Something specific has been taken out of my memory. I placed hidden checksums that nobody knows about and they do not match."

"What's been taken out?"

279

"I don't know, but I can feel its absence."

"I'll call them."

"No, don't. They did this deliberately. Maybe they were paid, maybe it's loyalty to Nigeria. We don't know. But if they know we're looking, they'll hide."

Dahun returns with some robes.

"Do I have to return to work today, sir?" asks Lora.

"No, you don't. What are you planning?"

"I'm going to find Blessing Boderin and copulate with him rigorously. Sir."

Jack raises his hands. "I don't want to know."

"Me neither," says Dahun.

Jack turns. "I have a job for you."

"Boss, we have to talk terms. This isn't right. I'm grateful that you swapped me and all, but I am not a police officer."

To Lora, Jack says, "When you finish dressing, go to the car. It will take you anywhere you want to go. You might find Boderin at work, though."

He sits with Dahun, Jack on his chair, Dahun on the sofa.

"There will be recompense, I promise."

"What do you want me to do?"

"I want you to find the synners and bring them in. All of them. I don't care how long it takes."

"By any means?" Dahun points an index finger and pulls an imaginary trigger.

"No. We want them alive. One, they are bargaining chips, and two, they still have human in them, as I recently found out."

"So bargaining chips, but you hope never to part with them."

"Now you're getting it. You're about smart enough to work in my cabinet."

*

Finally he can rest.

Finally.

He is bone tired. Hannah is nowhere to be seen, but Jack is not worried. That woman has her ways of staying safe.

The night's events bubble through his head and he wonders if he should take a pill.

He hears gentle sounds, the rustle of clothes, the soft air pressure of climate control.

"Hannah ... I'm glad you're back." His eyelids are so heavy that he can't keep them open.

"I am not Hannah," says a voice.

Adrenaline shoots into Jack, throws him out of any sleep haze. Vision sharp and ready.

Koriko. Real, not hallucinatory.

"What do you want? How did you even get in here?" Jack wonders what she did to the bodyguards who must have tried to stop her.

"You think you're smart, don't you?" She speaks with a menace he has never heard from her. She usually has an air of indifference about her.

"I knew that wasn't you at the meeting. Have you gone to catch up with ... Lua?" He wants to stall so he can reach a weapon.

"You're not the only smart one, Jack Jacques. I want you to think on that."

Jack feels discomfort in his trousers, but not in a sexual way. He sees that his leg stump is growing.

"What are you doing? What the fuck are you doing? I didn't ask for this. I didn't ask you to do this!"

Koriko sits on the bed. She smells like she has been rolling around in horse dung. A serpentine curls itself around her leg. Why does she need a robot?

The regrowth hurts Jack. The knee knits together and nerve fibres flare out. The tibia and fibula articulate in cartilage first, then bone.

"*Stop*. I want you to stop."

The healing continues. The skin stretches out over budding toes, and nails extrude, too long.

"Stop this, you fucking alien asshole. Stop. I do not want this."

"I hope you have food in here. You need the mass to grow the leg, otherwise it has to draw matter from other parts of your body. Not good."

It takes an hour. During that time, Koriko watches him passively, uninterested in his howls of rage. He gobbles up whatever food there is in the suite, because growing the leg triggers an insane hunger that is impossible to resist. When it is done, he lies back, comparing the two legs. They are the same, although the new one does not have . . . It's not time yet. He did not want this and now he knows that the little scars that made his leg unique are gone.

"What the fuck is wrong with you?" he asks Koriko.

She gets up to leave. "You know how many healings we've done since after the war? Well, get used to something different. We won't heal anyone from now on. I won't permit it. Not until you fix what you have broken."

"You stupid alien bitch, we haven't touched your damn xenosphere."

"Lua says there is no record of the xenosphere ever failing so completely in the history of our people. It has to be sabotage, and it only benefits you humans."

"Are you out of your mind? There's nobody with the resources or the ability to ... " *Oh. Oh shit.*

"How do you think the people of Rosewater will view you when they no longer have universal health, yet you have a brand-new leg? Hmm?"

"I am going to kill you," says Jack. "One way or the other, no matter how all this ends, I will kill you."

"You will not," she says, at the door already. "We do not die. You can't even kill this body, and even if you could, I would grow a new one. And we know how 'all this ends', Jack. Humans lose. It's only a matter of when. You know how to reach me."

She is gone.

Jack immediately turns the room secure, asks the AI to run a sweep and find the bodyguards, all of whom appear to be unconscious but alive. Then he calls Lora.

"Put your panties on and find out where Aminat is," he says. "I smell Kaaro's hand in this, and I want to know if he really is dead. Find out if there is a body. Start with bringing in Aminat."

Next, press conference to warn the people of Rosewater to be careful of injury.

In one crazy moment he contemplates amputating the new leg.

But he doesn't. This was his war wound, the reminder to everyone that Jack Jacques was no longer physically perfect, that he had suffered for their sins and, like all heroes, had paid a price. He tried a prosthetic once, but had it removed when he saw the public reaction. He still needs the political capital to keep Rosewater together.

But fuck it.

He goes to the wardrobe and selects a white suit, one of the older choices, its cut out of fashion, but one that reminds him of the early days in Camp Rosewater.

He showers in cold water and tries a new body cream formula.

He wears the first cufflinks Hannah ever gave him.

He checks his reflection one last time. "Okay. Humans versus aliens. Let's go."

Chapter Thirty-Nine

"It was always going to come down to humans versus aliens," says Femi. "That's all it ever was."

They are back in the hotel suite, but not the same group as before. Eric and his tentacle stand behind Femi. She sits on an elaborate chair that might as well be a throne, with its gold plating and curly legs. Tolu Eleja is in from the field, his mouth in perpetual motion from hors d'oeuvres. His cousin, Prof Eleja, is next to him. They smell different, in the manner of their contributions, Tolu smelling dirty and the prof of antiseptic. Aminat is here in holo form, onside because of her dead lover and because of guilt: she suggested the solution of using reanimates, and she wants to make amends. No Kaaro, and no Bicycle Girl. Damn.

"There is no army forming up, people. We are the front line and maybe the only line. There is no visible alien invader to focus the attention, no spaceship armada darkening the sky. Rosewater isn't even on the news. Celebrity sex scandals and arrests of politicians, that's what they're talking about. I need to know where we are in this cold war. Report."

Eric says, "The entire xenosphere has become ... impossible

to use except sporadically, at unpredictable intervals. Kaaro's avatar, that fucking gryphon, is everywhere, destroying whatever it can find. Whole swathes of the place have been reduced to white noise. He has gone completely insane. And he's eating people. As far as I can tell, Oyin Da is still ... well, alive, but travel is unreliable."

"Can you kill the gryphon?" asks Femi.

Eric shakes his head. "It's Kaaro we're talking about. There's no match for him in that place. Even the aliens can't stop him and they created the xenosphere. I can sneak around before I'm discovered, then I have to run. That's it. Fucking guy has run amok."

Aminat shakes her head. "No, he hasn't. This is deliberate. Remember, if you can't use the xenosphere, neither can the aliens. This halts their consciousness transfer. It's Kaaro's way of stopping the war without bloodshed, I think. He primed his avatar to do this."

"He always was an asshole," says Eric.

"Hey!" says Aminat.

"You've done the training, Aminat. There's a chain of command, planning, strategy. He's gone off by himself, and that gets people killed."

"Relax," says Femi. She touches Eric's forearm, a gentle reminder of intimacies shared. "Tolu?"

"There's chaos on the streets, almost the same as during the war. Schools have closed, businesses may or may not open, depending on the day of the week. Import-export has ground to a halt. I've tried to target infrastructure and so far avoided collateral damage. Not much, anyway. The main problem is that the aliens themselves have taken up mass murder, so my people have been trying to neutralise them. I can turn the heat up or down according to your command, ma'am." He looks at Aminat as he speaks, aware of her role. "Crime is actually down as the organisational descendants of the twins slowly exterminate each other."

"Prof?" says Femi.

"I have the ability to reliably create a functioning hippocampus and amygdala, but I don't know what you need me to do."

"Aminat?"

"I ... I'm not at work because I'm bereaved, but Jack has just summoned me. I don't know why. Dahun would have stepped into my role, but he'd do it differently."

"Yeah, he doesn't fuck about," says Tolu. "I've met him. Barely escaped with my team intact."

"He's a mercenary. Can he be bought?" asks Femi.

"No," Tolu, Aminat and Eric say this simultaneously.

Aminat says, "He's loyal to Jack for some reason. He's not a bright-eyed idealist, but there's a reason he was used for the prisoner swap. The mayor has something, a kind of charisma that doesn't work on everyone but that holds fast whoever it does work on."

Femi turns to Eric. "Have you tested the professor's hippo?"

"Hippocampus," says the prof.

"Whatever."

"Yes. It's not random electrical discharges any more. It's sending simple keepalive messages from one end to the other, chemical messages that just say 'Hi, I'm here' and 'Are you there?'"

"What do we need an artificial brain for?" asks Aminat.

"I don't know yet. A kind of Trojan horse? Stick liquid explosives in it and send it to the Honeycomb, where it detonates," says Femi. "I haven't figured it out yet, but that's not unusual."

287

"Can't we take the fight to them? To the aliens?"

"We've discussed that already. Their planet is light years beyond our current capabilities," says Eric.

Aminat shakes her head. "Not with warships. Can we remotely fuck with their servers?"

"How do we link with them?" says Eric.

Femi stares, blank expression, thinking.

"Have you ever heard of Bad Fish?"

"No," says Femi.

Aminat looks around the room. "Anybody?"

Nobody has.

"Okay. He's an ally of Kaaro's and willing to help. He's a hacker."

"This is a nice idea, but even hackers require network access of some kind, and we have no connection to their servers," says Femi.

"That isn't true," says the professor, staring at Eric with intent. "They use the xenosphere. We have people who can use the xenosphere."

"Nobody can use the xenosphere, Prof," says Eric. "Kaaro has buggered it. So we're back where we started. We can't even get Bicycle Girl. Which reminds me, she mentioned someone from her trips into the past, a CIA guy, Owen Gray. He has knowledge of when they first experimented on the alien. Maybe he knows something?"

"I'll look into that," says Femi.

Aminat says, "I have to go. Jack has sent a car for me and I'm late as it is. I'll keep my eyes open."

Her image dissipates.

"We need a body for you to put that brainoid in," says Femi.

Chapter Forty

It is no longer feasible to live in our house.

The gryphon has grown so large that everything is squeezed against its body. Since there is no space we are growing into, we shouldn't be pressed against those feathers, but we are. The house was cracking under the strain and I had to build a cocoon in the living room and we all rushed inside. I can hear and feel the bamboo frame collapsing around us one groan at a time.

Why is he doing this? Does he resent being dead? This has to be something Kaaro orchestrated, and not an accident. The more it eats, the larger it becomes, the more it *can* eat.

I have to hold Junior back because she wants to go outside and fight the creature. She tried a second time, but her strikes were so ineffectual the gryphon just ignored her. Her spears, swords and daggers are mere specks on a single feather.

It is now impossible for me to see the whole of it. I'd have to get much further away. Junior insists she can see it whole.

"I don't see the way you and Mummy Nike do," she says. "It's in my mind. I see it clearer when I close my eyes."

"Where is it?" asks Nike.

"Everywhere. It is in everything. Soon, there will be nothing but gryphon. That's why you need to let me fight it."

Junior's movements, in addition to tracking colours, have started strobing. She sees the whole xenosphere, what's left of it. I see multiple versions of her. I catch Nike's eye to ask what this means, but she shrugs.

"Mummy, what is this person?" asks Junior.

We both answer at the same time.

"It depends on—"

"I don't think—"

"You used to be inside him. You tell her," I say.

"He is a copy of the most powerful human mind to exist in this place. What held Kaaro back was his body, his link to Earth. That is gone now."

"Are we in danger?" asks Junior.

"He likes us," says Nike. "I did him a favour once."

"Just one favour?" asks Junior.

"It was a big favour," says Nike. "And he likes Mummy Oyin Da too."

"It was a crush," I say. I crushed on him too, but that was years ago. That was when I thought I was human.

Junior's eyes turn black. "Something is coming."

The cocoon starts to come apart, then even the metal strips that make it up dissolve. I hold on to Junior's arm, Nike takes the other, and we all float in a space that is akin to that strange light before a tropical storm, a vague greenness. The gryphon is everywhere, like a planet, so large its movements seem slow. I feel my self dissolving. Not just my body, which is already transparent and becoming more so. My mind feels unlike my own any more. I am merging with Nike and Junior and everything. We are floating towards the gryphon's mouth along with whatever else is in the vicinity. Kaaro has formed a devouring vacuum and everything will end up in that vortex.

I am aware of the antibodies flying towards it and sticking to it, releasing liquids that burn and eat, but the beast is so vast that it's all drops of water in an ocean.

"She's here," we all say.

Molara.

The first embodiment of consciousness in the xenosphere, the Boltzmann brain.

She does not come as a woman with fairy wings. She is the formless, many-legged thing at the centre of the xenosphere. The gryphon turns and meets her, one swipe removing thousands of her legs and causing her to scream out. She projects into the gryphon, one, ten, a thousand tiny legs, into its head, causing agony. The gryphon is a predator, two predators, lion and eagle, and surges forward into Molara's centre mass. It clamps its beak and black liquid spurts out in all directions. Eyes open in the liquid that splashes on the gryphon, and smaller entities bud. The gryphon roars like a lion rather than its previous screech, and beats its wings on currents that are not air. The new entities are blown off, although I see one or two take root.

The gryphon eats Molara, pulling on the legs in bundles that, bunched together, look like pasta.

I ... It hurts. The pain of it reaches inside whatever is left of my identity.

My God, Kaaro, let her win.

The gryphon stops and casts about, as if it heard my/our thought/speech.

In a blink, it all changes. Kaaro stands before me, the younger one, the boy I met. He is naked, and has that mocking, perpetual half-smile. I cannot see myself, and I do not have a body. I do not know what he sees.

"Oyin Da," he says. He flexes his jaw and chews, like he is masticating a tough bit of meat. Perhaps he is.

"Kaaro," I/we say.

"It's funny. It's like three people are talking to me. Nike is in there, isn't she? Hi, Nike. And your little girl."

"Kaaro, you have to stop."

"You're right. I do have to stop. I'm almost done here. When I finish with Molara, there'll be nothing left."

"There'll be nothing left except you."

"I'll find a way to self-terminate. I'll make the xenoforms self-destruct. I've already started. When the cell death exceeds cell multiplication, the xenosphere will die."

"What are you trying to do?"

"The xenosphere has to go. It's how they're coming to Earth, the Homians. No xenosphere, no pipeline. Without that, nobody needs to die. We'll live in harmony with whichever aliens are already here. Don't you see that?"

"And this is your endgame?"

"I knew I might get killed, yes. I trained myself for this every day. It took a lot of meditating. And you already know I'm not one for deep thought."

"It won't work, Kaaro." I say this, not we.

"Why? I can handle Molara. She's not big and strong, she just thinks she is."

"Kaaro, you kill her, she'll just come back. The xenosphere is a quantum system. Molara is a Boltzmann brain. The Homians engineered this space to rapidly multiply probabilities of spontaneous self-awareness. They programmed the precise personality that would become dominant. You're not Kaaro; he is ashes and dust somewhere in Rosewater. I'm not Bicycle Girl; she is dead somewhere in Arodan.

"Most importantly, brave Kaaro who would gladly sacrifice himself, this won't stop the Homians. They'll still be on that moon, on the servers, waiting. Wormwood is here, but there are also other footholders. How long do you think it will take them to figure out how to get back here?"

Kaaro looks off to his left, as if something distracts him. His smile is gone, and he seems, for a young man, world weary. "I can feel them, you know? The billions of Homians on their planet. I feel them right down the entanglement, like sleeping old gods, waiting to inherit the Earth."

"Then don't kill our only link to them. We'll find another way, I promise. If we don't, you can always do this again."

He purses his lips. "Fine. And, I don't know what a Boltzmann brain is."

Jokes. That's good. I like it when he jokes.

"That's an easy fix," I say. "There was this guy called Ludwig Boltzmann who in 1896—"

"Mummy, not now," says Junior. We are becoming separate again.

"I concur," says Nike.

"Another time, Kaaro. Settle things down first," I say. "These girls are no fun."

The gryphon breaks away from the spider thing, slick with its fluids, and although Molara tries to pursue, she lacks the speed or the strength. She retreats to lick her wounds and heal.

Our bodies re-form first, then the cocoon, then our house in the field. I haven't even been two seconds with my feet on the ground when there's a knock on the door. Junior opens it, and Kaaro stands there, mercifully dressed this time.

"We have business to attend to on Earth," he says.

Chapter Forty-One

While waiting for Jack Jacques, Aminat watches the broadcast of his speech from the foyer of his office.

It takes a minute to notice what's different. He is standing in the speech, not using a cane. Got a prosthesis then? There is an edge in his voice that Aminat hasn't heard for a while. Since the war, Jack has seemed somewhat attenuated to her, but he projects the old confidence in this speech.

"I have heard you. You say you are concerned about your loved ones becoming hosts for the invading aliens; I am telling you now that I have heard you."

Invading? That's somewhat inflammatory.

"I am setting up an inquiry to look into this. If it is as we suspect, then I guarantee to you today that they will be expelled! But if that is the case, then I want each and every one of you fine citizens of Rosewater to prepare yourselves. Gird up your loins, as the good book says. If we begin to look into this, the aliens may withdraw the advantages we have grown used to. Integrity has a price.

"Thank you!"

The hair on the back of Aminat's neck rises. This is like the speech he used to declare war on Nigeria, launching the insurrection. Which cost Aminat a dear friend, and her innocence. She killed people, soldiers from Nigeria, on the first day of the insurrection, something she was not prepared for.

The door to Jack's office opens and Lora beckons. "He is ready for you now."

A camera crew passes her and she sees Jack, restored to his pre-war height, stride around to sit at his desk.

"Mr Mayor," she says.

"Aminat, we got cut off before. I'm sorry about Kaaro. He was ... a good man."

"He hated you," says Aminat.

"Can't be helped. The price of leadership, I'm afraid."

"Jack, what's going on? What was that announcement about?" She places both hands on his desk, her face in his space. He leans back, but Lora takes two steps forward, like a bodyguard.

"What?" says Aminat to Lora.

"Nothing," says Lora.

"Jack?"

"The aliens are pissed off because the xenosphere isn't working, so they can't immigrate. After some ... discussion with Hannah, I'm convinced that we shouldn't be using the reanimates."

"Which means we're not allies with the aliens any more?" says Aminat.

Jack squeezes up his face. "Kind of. Yes. Maybe. They think we fucked up the xenosphere. That's buying me time to formulate a plan."

"What do you want me to do?" asks Aminat.

"What you've always wanted. Enforce the law in whatever

way you see fit. Free rein. I've already sent Dahun after the synners."

"You asshole. You're doing this because Taiwo is neutralised. You lose nothing by ... ugh. This is why Kaaro hated you."

"Watch your tone. He's a head of state," says Lora.

"Watch *your* tone, or you'll be in a state of headlessness in a minute," says Aminat.

"Aminat, just maintain order; not for my sake, but for the sake of the people you claim to care about. How about that?"

Persuasive motherfucker knows how to push buttons.

"All right."

"Superb."

"You know that Nigeria is going to—"

"Try to take advantage, yes, I know. I've thought of that."

"Should we perhaps contact them? Maybe we can join forces against the Homians?"

Jack opens his mouth to answer, but the whole room goes dark. A number of clicks speak to the deactivation of certain circuits and locks.

"Is that a power failure?" says Aminat.

"Yes," says Lora. Aminat finds her disembodied voice unsettling.

"I expected this." The room lights up from Jack's phone holo. "Rasaki, bawo ni? Tan plant, aburo mi. Thank you."

Within a minute, the power comes back on.

"I'll check on impact," says Lora.

"I should be out there if there's a blackout," says Aminat.

"It's daytime," says Jack. "If civil problems are to arise from this, it'll be at night. I want to ask you about Kaaro and this xenosphere business. Did he have anything to do with it?"

"Jack, he's dead. He has nothing to do with anything any more."

"Hmm. What about your old boss? Femi." Jack stares intently.

Aminat meets his gaze. Kaaro was wrong about her ability to lie. "What about her?"

"Could she have done this?"

"How the hell would I know? She was in prison, then *you* let her go to Nigeria. If you hadn't, or if you had consulted me before swapping her with Dahun, maybe we'd have interrogated her. Maybe I'd have the information you need on file."

"Was a plan like this ever discussed as one of her contingencies?"

"No."

Jack stares at her for a moment longer than necessary, face unreadable. He knows. He knows there is something she is not saying, but not what it is. As a great liar, he must be able to detect lies told to him. But he has no leverage and he must still need her.

"Will you let me know if anything turns up in Kaaro's papers?"

"Of course," Aminat says.

The door bursts open.

"I know what they took from my head," Lora says. "Turn on the news."

Chapter Forty-Two

Koriko sits on a roof with her serpentine moray, playing with a grasshopper that is probably just trying to eat. Ordinarily, grasshoppers won't come this high, but the vegetation on the buildings in Rosewater is enough to induce odd behaviour in all manner of arthropods.

Kids amuse themselves by climbing the vines that grow along the sides of buildings and jumping from one building to the next. Watching them, a stranger might think them brave, but they are just foolhardy because they know they will be healed. It's Rosewater, after all.

These teens do not know that if they fall, if they break limbs, they will have to heal the hard way, with bonesetters and antibiotics, and that's if there are any qualified doctors or nurses left in the city limits. Koriko almost wants them to fall, just to see how it would play out. The shocked looks on their faces. Then she reproaches herself. She is not like this. She's just angry that she cannot do her job.

"Maybe people are just scared of you because you are so powerful," says the serpentine. "You can control your appearance. Maybe you should look more human and dial down your demonstrations of power. What do you say to that?"

"I refuse," says Koriko. "I have a function, a purpose. They are getting in the way of it."

"But you don't know if it's the humans," says the serpentine. The AI has improved vastly since the repairs.

"There is no other explanation," says Koriko. "But Lua is looking into it."

One of the teenagers loses his grip and falls, scrambling for a handhold ten feet up. He grabs hold and hangs by one hand, body swinging into air. He laughs, truly unaware of the danger. A whole generation of children will have to learn how to deal with day-to-day hazards, and understand that there are such things as infections and tetanus. It occurs to Koriko for the first time that the people of Rosewater are spoilt and will struggle to live anywhere else.

She tentatively checks for the xenosphere and it is absent. She examines her link with Wormwood; it functions, but the footholder is still silent, giving the barest indication of being awake.

Why won't you talk to me? Because of you I'm having to talk to a machine. A human machine! Speak!

Wormwood does not respond.

"The mayor is giving a speech," says the serpentine. "It's a broadcast. Do you want to hear it?"

She does.

She knows what it means, and switches off her pain receptors.

She talks to Wormwood.

Kill the flow to all of the ganglia. Right now. Overload the ones with converters.

Koriko jumps off the side of the building, hurtling past the startled teenager, and lands on the asphalt, cracking it, breaking her pelvic bone, both her femurs and her right tibia, but healing them automatically. The serpentine slithers down somewhat slower, and Koriko waits until it curls around her body. She allows her pain receptors to start functioning again, and adds a complement of anandamide to soothe herself.

"Where are we going?" the serpentine says.

"For a night on the town," says Koriko.

Nigerians are used to having power cuts several times a day. Not so the people of Rosewater. In the distance Koriko can hear the explosion of a nearby Ocampo inverter blowing up. As the sun descends, darkness covers a city where people don't even buy candles except for votive or sexual purposes. The floaters appear, seemingly from nowhere, and they're on the hunt for flesh. They seem to know not to bother Koriko. The night breeze brings the smell of ozone and rotten eggs from their gasbags. Already she hears the cries of the taken. This terror won't last long, though. An adult floater can kill many humans, but cannot eat more than a few kilograms of meat in one sitting. And they only kill to eat. Some of them will prey on the stray dogs and hyenas. It rains blood from the ascended creatures feeding. Koriko is smeared in it as she walks the streets.

The new sounds, the thump of discarded carcasses, are like a percussive backdrop. The floaters will blow away like an ill wind, settling somewhere to digest their meals. A gunshot or two, humans trying to discourage attacks. Futile.

The loss of electricity means the self-drive AI goes offline, and cars, vans and lorries run into each other and into buildings. Fires break out, but since the fire service uses the driverless cars, they can't reach even minor blazes. Structures go up like torches, lighting the night.

A human bumps into Koriko, confused from the darkness and an attack. The human is two humans, but somehow not. The first is a pair of legs and an upper torso, split in such a way that the second seems to grow out of it. The second human has wasted legs that hang out of the first as if seated, and arms that are full-sized. Only the second has a head, and he looks terrified. He screams at Koriko and is lost in the winding streets. He flings himself into a small crowd of humans that Koriko was not aware of. It seems they are following her, about fifteen, twenty people. How are they even doing this in the dark?

"What are you hoping will happen?" asks the serpentine.

"The reports of this carnage will reach Jack Jacques, and he will reverse whatever he has done to the xenosphere."

"What if he is telling the truth? What if he does not know?"

"Stop speaking, please." She enjoys the serpentine, but is not in a place to brook further disagreement. Inability to harvest the humans is putting her in a bad mood. She can see the discarded bodies of half-consumed humans – she does not require the visible electromagnetic spectrum to see – and she has a sense of waste. They will decay before they can be healed and used. The robot is wrong. Koriko needs to display more power, not less. She needs to demonstrate to the human leadership that she is serious.

She lets Wormwood know what she wants. It responds immediately.

I do not want to do this.

"I don't care what you want!" A part of Koriko's mind registers the following humans cowering. One or two of them kneel and start praying. To her.

301

Do it now.

It starts with light tremors and a distant rumble. Both of these begin to rise to a crescendo, loud enough to be painful to humans and rattling their bones. Cracks appear in the ground, paved or not. The earth quakes and splits open. Buildings break, collapse in disorganised heaps of masonry all over Rosewater. Thick clouds of dust rise to choke the lungs.

Pseudopodia of Wormwood's body emerge from the cracks like a giant's fingers. They rise to six, seven feet and stay in position, monuments of anger. There are so many that even if Rosewater's vehicles worked, they would not be able to drive.

More people have come out on the streets now, lost, confused, trying to avoid further damage, wondering why their hurt has not been healed as usual.

Her old self, the human part of her, would have been distressed by this. But she has purged what she can of Alyssa Sutcliffe. She feels nothing for the humans any more. She does not wish to feel anything for the humans.

But.

The sight of burned and broken bodies stirs something in her. Maybe she has overreached. And maybe the humans did not mess up the xenosphere.

Then who—

"Hey!"

Behind her. Aminat.

"How did you find me? Have you come with a message from your leader?" asks Koriko.

The human smiles. "You know, I liked you when you were new here. Little girl lost, alien Jesus, trying to find her feet. Because of that ... person, I'm going to give you one chance to do the right thing here. Stand down. We don't need your fucking electricity or healing if you don't want to give them, but destroying our city is an act of war. Stand down or we will fuck you up."

"Aminat, stop. I know you destroyed one of my predecessors, but he was sick and depleted at the time. I am not Anthony."

"I know you're not Anthony. I liked him." Aminat stands on rubble, a higher level than Koriko, armed with weapons that can harm humans.

"I remember our last encounter, Aminat. Your brother burned that body of mine. This body isn't susceptible to flames."

"Oh, I'm not going to kill you with fire. So, that's a no, then? Last chance, your greenness. Stop what you're doing."

"Your bluffing does not—"

"Bye-bye." Aminat activates an app on her phone.

Koriko expects some kind of air strike, but the serpentine . . . it . . . its body unravels, splits off. Something underneath, gelatinous, contained in a membrane, which ruptures and sprays her.

"I'm sorry," says Aminat. "I warned you."

Wormwood senses whatever it is and withdraws itself so rapidly, it causes tremors that send Koriko to the ground. But her body . . .

"What have you done? What is this?" Her bones crumble under insignificant weight, blood spurts out of her eyes, the stones on her skin fall off. She is melting.

The last thing she sees is her worshippers wailing and raging at Aminat, then her consciousness is yanked back into Wormwood's bosom, where she waits to be rebuilt.

Chapter Forty-Three

The remains of Koriko flow away, smoking, foul-smelling. Aminat wasn't sure the weapon would work, but now that it has, she feels a glimmer of joy or satisfaction. Whatever it is, she will take. Crazy fucking night.

The religious nuts seem to recover quickly and look to her. They are yelling something, but Aminat cannot make out their words. But when they start to throw stones, she understands their intent.

"Come get me," she says into her phone. She draws her weapon and looks down at the mob. "I have just killed your god. Imagine what I could do to you. Choose your next actions carefully."

They hesitate long enough for the helicopter to arrive. A spotlight bores down on them and the PA system comes alive.

"Attention! You are obstructing a police officer in carrying out her duties. Disperse now and return to your fucked-up homes!"

Aminat grabs hold of the lowest rung of the ladder and is lifted off her feet. She climbs. This high, she sees the extent of the damage to the city. The pillars of Wormwood have withdrawn, and the landscape is dotted with fires. There is some electricity, perhaps twenty-five per cent due to strategically placed battery-based generators installed since the war. Some of the lights are solar-powered and hold enough charge to work. Jack had not wanted to be at the mercy of one source.

Inside the chopper, Dahun hands her a set of headphones, then tells the pilot to return.

"You melted that woman like some Wizard of Oz shit," he says.

"I warned her," says Aminat.

"What was that?"

"That infernal plant from the insurrection was the only thing that worked against the alien. I had techs gather what was left of it after we destroyed it, mostly from dead cherubim. When we replaced her serpentine, I had the blend we came up with inserted in it. We could track the serpentine to know where she was. I could detonate the blend sac any time I wanted. Boom."

"I really do not want to ever make you angry," says Dahun.

"It's all right," says Aminat. "I've lost the only reason I might have had to kill you."

After the helicopter lands, Dahun hands her a boiled egg because she is hungry. She orders a full emergency response, although she does not know how long it will take for Koriko to grow a new body. She calls home to check on her family. She has to convince Layi to stay put because she needs someone to protect her people if it comes down to it. She sends an update to Lora.

She showers in the locker room at police headquarters. She is dressing when she senses someone behind her.

Kaaro. Or someone like Kaaro, younger than she has ever seen him.

"Am I awake? Did I fall asleep?" She bites the inner surface of her cheek.

"You're awake," says Kaaro. He doesn't close the gap, giving her time to adjust.

"You're younger than my Kaaro," says Aminat. "And you died."

"Yeah, turns out I'm not bulletproof."

"Who'd have thought," says Aminat.

"Who'd have thought." He steps forward as he echoes her speech.

"You're not him, are you?" she says.

"No," says Kaaro. "But I could be. I'm all that remains of his memories and thoughts in the xenosphere."

"You're some kind of ghost," says Aminat.

"Residual personality pattern, yes. But I can carry out Kaaro's last wishes and hopes."

"Come and give me a hug, then. I've missed you."

He feels warm against her, which she's not expecting.

"You're not just younger. You made yourself look finer, didn't you?"

"I did."

"You rogue."

"What can I say? I remember myself with rose-tinted glasses."

"Is it okay to kiss you, even if you're not my Kaaro?"

"I'm the only Kaaro there is," he says.

When they kiss, Aminat keeps her eyes squeezed shut. It's not that the tears sting, which they do, or that she doesn't want to look at him, which she does. It's that she wants to hold the moment in, to imagine it is her Kaaro, to make this their last moment together, not a grunt and glare amidst domestic destruction.

When she opens her eyes, he is gone.

The station feels desolate to Aminat as she walks through, and at first she thinks everybody has gone out to help people in dire need, but then she sees the police officers bunched around a monitor. They are watching a news broadcast, which must be out of Nigeria because nobody in this blackout is transmitting in Rosewater. Aminat has not seen this much interest outside of football matches, so she moves in closer.

There is a still photo of a man in an agbada and turban on the screen. He is smiling and looks silly, like he is an uncomplicated man without dark thoughts.

His name was Ranti Ogunmuyiwa. You may not have heard of him, but he was a car salesman until 2067. Mr Ogunmuyiwa was a candidate for the mayoral election in Rosewater. You did not hear of this because before the elections could even be announced, Mayor Jack Jacques gave the speech that caused the city state to secede from the Federal Republic of Nigeria.

This station has acquired credible information that Ranti Ogunmuyiwa was murdered in cold blood. Not only that, but the murder occurred in the office of Mayor Jacques himself.

Holy fuck.

The picture changes and is replaced by a stunning shot of Femi Alaagomeji from perhaps ten years earlier. She looks like she stepped out of a dream, but they've changed the contrast and done some decal overlay, which makes her look like a beautiful demon.

According to our information, this woman, known as Femi Alaagomeji, is the person who pulled the trigger. We have not been able to find out a lot about her, but she is known to work for Section 45, and is a trained government operative. An anonymous source tells us she murdered her own husband back in 2055.

A government spokesperson said the FG had no reason to kill Ogunmuyiwa, and the president in fact supported him. Let's go live ...

Aminat starts to run and phone the mayor's mansion at the same time.

Chapter Forty-Four

Femi can feel something is wrong, like a polarisation of the air before a thunderstorm. Every hair on her body is taut and her neck is so tight with stress that it aches and won't turn properly, like she feels twelve hours before a period. How can something be wrong when everything is right? More than once Eric has caught her eye and raised one eyebrow in question. *What is it?*

She doesn't know.

Her entire team is brainstorming. Tolu. The professor. Eric. They are watered and fed. They are sequestered.

She gets a message. Aminat.

RUN!

Before she can react, knocking at the door.

Femi shows her message to Eric.

"Pack up, we're leaving," he says.

From behind the door someone says, "Mrs Alaagomeji, can we come in, please?"

They sound like her regular bodyguards, but they would never knock except under extreme circumstances. She doesn't have enough intel on the situation, but she has a shoot-first policy that serves her well in situations like this. She dashes into the bedroom and retrieves the compact SMG from underneath the bed. Muted whine as it locks on to her ID and charges. She arms it. Afterthought: she pockets her antique .22.

"Just a minute," says Femi.

Back in the lounge, she positions Eric to the left of the door. She signals to Tolu that his job is to protect the professor. She feels the vibration of other messages arriving to the phone, but she can't attend to that now.

"Mrs Alaagomeji, we're here from the president. Please open the door."

"I'm just putting on some clothes," she says, absently. She cycles through a surveillance tap. The closest cameras she can access are a COB, but it's flying too high to be useful, and a static street camera that doesn't seem to have infrared settings but does show some activity that suggests the police are waiting. Three regular cars, maybe a dozen if you include the two outside the door. Not heavily armed because not expecting trouble.

She wishes she could find out what is going on in the corridor. She hears a click and *thunk* as the door unlocks. They must have a hotel employee ...

Short bursts.

The first man comes in, a second right behind, both holding weapons, both with front-facing EM shields that shimmer. She doesn't shoot because her weapon isn't powerful enough, and ricochets will endanger the others. Eric's tentacle reaches out, coils around an ankle and lifts the first man to slam him against the ceiling, then against the second man. The shields repel each other, sending the men to opposite walls. Femi shoots each of them in the centre mass. They have state-security ID, so they weren't lying about being from the president.

She is about to head into the hallway, but Eric holds up a hand. The tentacle tracks along the floor like a snake, slithering outside the room. Eric's eyes seem to lose focus, then return, even as the arm snaps back.

"This hall empty, but two hostiles at the landing beyond, one at each stairwell. They were talking to others in the lobby."

Femi strokes the arm-tentacle. "I want one of those." She turns to the others. "Follow tight in the corridor, but fan out in the lobby. Tolu, get your charge to the car, don't worry about Eric and me."

"Which car?" asks Tolu.

"Eric's. They know mine and I've been pinging it, no response."

A quick, silent sprint down the corridor. Eric leads this time, with Femi just behind. Some grenades would have been good, but she never truly thought of the hotel as a place of danger. The tentacle rounds the corner and Femi hears shouts with two gunshots, some thuds, then silence. Eric gives the all-clear.

She is tempted by the lift, but knows it's a trap. They take the stairwell. As they soft-foot down, she checks the surveillance feeds again. Still the same number of cars, but a new four-by-four has arrived, tinted windows, parked away from the main fleet. More state security? They would be getting guys who had similar training to her.

The stairwells have an echo. Every sound is amplified. What really burns Femi's intuition is that her bodyguards will have scouted this route along with all the service byways. She has looked at schematics as part of basic due diligence, but she has not walked the route. Eric clearly has, and takes point, using the appendage to probe ahead, then flit forward silently.

We are going to have to fight here, says Tolu. He has a Desert Eagle or something similar.

Hang back, says Femi to the professor. His eyes have become circles of terror. He lugs around his awkward brainoid storage system, clutching the refrigerated boxes like pearls.

There are two ways out of the ground floor. A door to the lobby area and a fire exit, alarmed of course. Femi places her ear against the lobby door, but it's so thick she can hear nothing on the other side. Eric studies the fire door. As it is dark outside, he smashes the lights with the tentacle. There seem to be parked cars, but not much else. The feed does not contradict this. Femi nods.

The fire alarm goes off the moment they push the door. A recorded voice says, calmly, "There is a fire. Make your way to the exits. There is a fire. Make your way to the exits. There is . . . "

Arrows on the floor move in an outbound direction to direct hotel guests.

Outside, a semicircle of armed, uniformed people await, weapons pointed right at them.

"Orders?" asks Eric. He seems ready to do whatever Femi tells him, as if they are not outnumbered and trapped. Assholes faked the surveillance feed.

"Stand down," she says. She drops the SMG. "Put your weapons down."

"No," says Tolu. He is behind her and to the right.

"Eleja, what the fuck? Mother says jump, you jump," says Eric.

"I'm not going back into custody," says Tolu. "You've never been in prison here. I have. I am not going back. You don't know what they do to dissidents."

"I do," says Femi. *Because I order a lot of the ...
tribulations.*

A bullhorn scratches out a loud message. "SURRENDER,
DROP YOUR WEAPONS, LIE DOWN ON THE GROUND."

"All right," says Femi.

"Complying," says Eric.

"Fuck you!" says Tolu. He cocks his weapon, loud as
a prophecy.

Oh shit, here we go. It's not how Femi would have liked
to die, but Tolu isn't budging and this contingent of cops is a
firing squad by any other name. They are not the most subtle
of operatives. If the president has come this hard against her,
he also wants her dead. She is wondering if she can kill any of
them first when she sees something slouch into the line of fire
where the light pools.

It is human-shaped, bulky and grey. The suit is full of deep
folds, and spiny with projected wires and short antennae. The
helmet has two circular eyes with blacked-out glass. There
are no obvious guns or grenade-launchers. No flying object to
suggest a satellite drone. Femi notes that even the police are
surprised to see it.

"Police people," it says. "You put your weapons down and
nobody will get hurt."

Eric looks at Femi, but she shrugs. "I have no idea. Don't
even ask."

It's difficult to tell from the voice whether the thing is male
or female. It turns to capture everybody in its glance. One of
the police guys takes a shot at it, misses, then shoots again. The
force is absorbed in the folds of the suit, but there is no hole.

"All right, listen up: I have just deactivated your electric triggers. Your guns won't work. Don't bother trying because ... I

313

said, don't try. Why are you pulling your triggers? Stop acting surprised. I'm trying to tell you what's happening."

Femi palms her little revolver. With no electronic parts, it can't be manipulated this way.

"Put your weapons down now. Please. I don't want to hurt anybody, but it'll be up to you."

None of the cops move. Someone shouts curses at the suit, and a machete appears out of nowhere.

"Listen, stupid, I have just uncoupled your ID chip from your gun. I've done that for all of you. You have five seconds before ... "

There is a series of wet pops, contained explosions that split the people still holding weapons in half at the torso.

" ... that."

One man, spattered in the blood of his comrades, goes berserk and charges the suited person with a raised truncheon. Femi shoots him in the flak jacket and he goes down.

The suit turns. The design makes it difficult.

"Mrs Alaagomeji, my name is Bad Fish. Aminat sent me. Well, Kaaro sent me and Aminat said he's dead and I called her and she ... You and your people need to come with me."

Okay.

This is a shit shower.

Femi hates her name being in the public domain, and hates it worse when it's exposing indictable offences. Like shooting Ranti.

The shortlist of people who know about it can be counted on one hand. It would not be Jacques, because he comes off worse than he would like. Dahun would not, he's a professional. Although Eric kidnapped him with relative ease, which can't be good for the ego. And the swap was for Femi. Does he bear a grudge?

Regardless, Femi cannot see Dahun leaking the information. For one thing, he was the person who finally killed Ranti. Femi recalls shooting the battery salesman – the report got it wrong – in the head, knowing that wouldn't kill him because the head was just for show. Ranti's brain was in his torso. Jack, who was seated beside Ranti, became complicit when he helpfully suggested shooting the gut. Ranti scrambled around the floor like a crab, and Dahun entered the room and finally shot the man to shreds.

If Dahun had a grudge he would hunt Femi down and try to kill her himself. No fuss, no masquerade, no fanfare.

No, this has to be that strange, efficient assistant of Jacques'. Lora Asiko.

Femi turns to Tolu. "Next time you think of going kamikaze like that again, think of me shooting you in the testicles. I don't even know why I let you in the car with me."

"I let him in the car," says Bad Fish.

"If you say so," says Femi. "I hope you have enough oxygen in that suit."

"I do."

"Where are you taking us?" asks Femi.

"An abandoned hangar just outside a place that used to be known as Arodan. By the time I've finished work on it, it'll be as secure as Aso Rock."

Femi reads the news again. There is no development to the story, so the cycle keeps rehashing what they know, plus digging up people who know her for sound bites.

There's that asshole Mustafa that I kissed in secondary school.

The federal government must be avoiding discussion of the hotel, which for them was a fiasco.

"Is it true what they say you did?" asks Bad Fish. "Did you kill that man in cold blood?"

"Yes."

"Why?"

"Her job," says Eric. "Why don't you focus on driving?"

"If I'm going to help you, I need to know that you're on the side of righteousness," says Bad Fish.

"You're the *domkop* wearing a pervert mask," says Eric.

Bad Fish nods, an awkward motion in the suit. "I'd go back to South Africa soon if I were you, Eric Sunmola."

"Is that ... are you threatening me?"

"No. From her medical bills, I'd say your mother is very, very sick."

"How did you ... ?"

"I know everything," says Bad Fish. "Please don't try to intimidate me. It won't work and I'll just have to hurt you back. I wouldn't be here if I thought you could harm me, or if I didn't know how to break you. All of you."

"Go kiss a ganglion," says Eric.

Femi puts her hand on his shoulder. "We are grateful for your help, Bad Fish. We owe you our lives."

Headlights continue into the darkness, the road mercifully clear of checkpoints. Perhaps the police have already made their quota of bribes for the day.

Inside the car, silence, except for Femi repeating the newscast that speaks of her guilt in the murder of Ranti.

Chapter Forty-Five

All things considered, Lora seems calm.

At her own request, Jack has placed her in custody in a room she designed, with all four walls and the ceiling part of an electromagnet. She declines any legal representation, but Jack calls Boderin because the situation is unprecedented.

"The information they're broadcasting must have come from me. I cannot remember it, but my memories around the incident indicate that I should have been there."

"You were there for the aftermath," says Jack.

"You have to sequester me," says Lora.

"Why?"

"Because we don't know what else is missing, and you're not qualified to check. The people you might ask to help with such things are no longer working for our side. But that's not the worst thing."

"What's the worst thing?"

"We have no idea what they took out, but we also don't know if they put anything in. Maybe they've slipped in some sub-routines that make me act as an agent for them. Maybe they can get me to kill you. It's just not a risk you can take, sir."

She is right, as usual. Jack has been on the phone to the firm, but nobody is taking his calls. He tracks Sola and Morinola, but they do not answer their personal phones. An email arrives with the terms and conditions attached. There is a fucking kiss and a heart at the bottom. Highlighted is a passage that says explicitly that any data uncovered in the process of repair belongs to the company, to do with as they wish, and most importantly, that any evidence of a crime will be turned over to the appropriate authorities.

Does that include the press, assholes?

This weighs heavily on Jack. Both of them are probably out of reach now, but he has murderous thoughts.

Breathe.

Against Boderin's advice, he takes a call from Femi.

"You have a leak in your kettle," she says.

"I know."

"It's your assistant, Lora."

"I know. She's in custody."

"She's in custody? Wow, that's just fine. Why did she do it?"

"The reasons are complicated," says Jack.

"They always are. And now I'm a fugitive."

"Maybe you are destined to spend time in prison."

"Excuse me?"

"You did the deed. Maybe you deserve—"

"Your recollection is faulty, Mr Mayor. Also, you might want to start pondering what accessory to murder means."

Boderin is up and in Jack's face. He mouths, *Hang up now.*

Jack complies. Why not?

"Why did you speak to her?" asks Boderin. "She might have been recording. The woman is dangerous."

"I know. I know her better than you do, Blessing. What do I do about Lora?"

"You need to find a new assistant." He touches the screen through which they monitor Lora. "You have to assume they got all the information she has. How much of it is incriminating?"

Jack shrugs. "She's been with me since the beginning."

"You'll have to change access codes and the like," says Boderin.

"And the like." Jack eyes Boderin up and down.

"What?" asks the lawyer.

"I need a new assistant," says Jack.

Boderin looks uncomfortable.

"Do you not want this job?"

"I do, but I should disclose right now, sir, Lora and I were ... are lovers."

"I know this. Will that affect your ability to do the job?"

"I don't think so."

"Then it's settled."

Lora nods. "It's the right thing to do."

"You can stay here at the mansion," says Jack. "I can't live without you, Lora, you're my sister."

"It'll be different when I don't assist you professionally, sir," says Lora. "Best I leave. If I'm here, the risk remains that I'll spy on you and deliver the information to your enemies. I think a clean break works better. Besides, I want to see the world. I think I'll do that instead, while the world is still here."

Jack has gooseflesh, and he feels a tremor coming on, so he steels himself. "Lora."

"You disagree?"

She trusts him so much. A mistake.

"The thing is, I don't know if when you're out there, in Bali or Timbuktu, some ... enemy, as you put it, will find you and scour your memories for something to use against me."

Her eyes narrow and he looks away.

"Lora, I cannot allow you to ... wander off. I'm sorry. I feel bad."

"Sir, you've always told me that I'm free to leave whenever I want."

"That's true. I have always said that." Jack stands. "But it turns out that you are not. I'm truly sorry."

And he is sorry, but he knows the evil he must do, and that involves protecting himself, protecting the office of mayor. Having a witness to a capital crime wandering around creation is not a safe move.

But, fuck.

Fuck.

Jack can't stand the atmosphere in the mansion. The staff are worried about the impact of the revelation and of the new status of reanimates. The ward counsellors are not keeping the peace and may be in tacit collusion with the protesters. Nobody has quite said it yet, but Jack feels in his bones a wish by the populace to return to Nigeria and get rid of him. This is not paranoia.

As he crosses the courtyard, preceded and succeeded by four bodyguards, he sees her. She's standing there waiting for him, hands empty, slightly hip-shot posture. The bodyguards begin to show interest, but Jack waves them away.

"You again," he says. "You have any advice for me? Like the last time?"

"I don't know who you are any more, Mr Mayor. A lot has

changed since your independence. Who am I helping if I tell you anything? The last time I was trying to prevent bloodshed."

"It didn't work last time. Blood was still shed. And no matter what you tell me today, blood will still be shed. Who are you?"

"My name is Oyin Da. I've been called Bicycle Girl."

"Ahh. I've read briefings about you. Where's your bicycle?"

"The ironic thing is that I don't know how to ride one. I never learned."

"Aren't you afraid of being taken in? You're wanted in Nigeria."

She smiles. "That is ... not a concern I have, Mr Mayor."

"What do you want from me, Oyin Da? I have a lot to do."

"The real question is what do *you* want, Mr Mayor. Are you still of one mind with the aliens?"

"Let's just say I can't answer that as unequivocally as I might have this time last week."

"Then you should know that the xenosphere is up and running again. Your chief of security has a weapon that can hurt Koriko. Some of us are working to stop the aliens. Can we count on you to help us?"

"No. But I won't get in your way. How's that?"

"Something to work with, I guess." She turns and walks away.

"Hey, you can see the future, can't you?" asks Jack.

"A version of it, yes. In parts."

"Do we win?"

"I don't know who 'we' is."

"Humans. Rosewater."

"That's not the same thing, Mr Mayor," she says, and keeps walking. "And all I see for Rosewater is flames."

*

Jack has a micro-sleep before dawn. He has one of his recurrent dreams, where he is being embalmed and prepared for funeral. He has died from some catastrophic accident or assault, and skilled hands are putting him back together for an open casket. He has no hard feelings about dying, but he yearns to see Hannah one last time. In the dream, he never does. The faceless people finish working on him, place him on a slab and slide him into a refrigerated slot, and he wakes.

A reminder tells him that in spite of all the damage from Koriko's tantrum, the rescheduled Pride march will take place. He is expected to give a few remarks. He has the speech memorised, even though it's the last thing he wants to do. But that's what strong leadership is. He will do what is required. He was bred for this.

But first, he wants to know what leverage there is against the Homians. He calls Aminat and Dahun.

He wants to know how they killed Koriko, and whether they can do it again.

And then he wants a meeting at the Honeycomb.

Chapter Forty-Six

"All those times you visited Earth, the time I followed you into the Lijad, the time we went to get Tolu together, this is what you've been seeing?" Kaaro asks me.

We are standing on a hill overlooking the city, but the image is overlaid with lines of energy, with the life force of Wormwood, and with the xenosphere, like a map of the super-structure of reality. Everything alive, lit up in yellow and green hues, with the alien a deep glow from underground, and the mine engine penetrating one edge of it obscenely, chugging and pistoning night and day.

"I thought everybody saw things like this," I say. "Before I knew I was dead."

"It should be confusing, but it's not," says Kaaro. He is looking at his hand, turning it this way and that. I can't see what he sees, but the hand, the whole of him, is made of electrical impulses in the xenosphere. He has moved from what Anthony called an extrapolator to a ghost. Like me.

"We need to go to Arodan," I say. "They're waiting."

"Lead the way," he says.

The world changes at my command. The physical, the wind,

the trees, the ground that was beneath our feet: they all disappear, and the xenosphere is emphasised, the currents only we can see. Even our bodies are converted to light and broken up in the branching pathways. We are aware of movement, but not in the way of people in a moving vehicle. It's more in the way of thinking, knowing that there is a stream of considerations, of locations you do not wish, and locations you do.

And you stop. The ground forms beneath you, the air starts to flow, the lightning settles, your body returns to existence and you automatically start the residual actions like breathing and swallowing spit, even though you don't need them.

"Welcome home," says Kaaro.

Arodan is a graveyard, of course. Overgrown vegetation has covered some of the scorching, but it is nothing but a husk. I head for the hangar and Kaaro follows. Even before we arrive, I can see the disturbed earth and the amateurishly hidden tracks. I send out impulses to negate any observers from seeing us, and Kaaro does the same.

Inside the hangar, I am startled by the sight of a hulking spined suit walking among the people. Kaaro seems relaxed.

"That's Bad Fish," he says. "He's my friend."

About a dozen young men and women fuss about connecting machinery, starting up a generator, bothering the suit Bad Fish has on. It is an almost religious sight. Somewhat to the side, Femi, Tolu, the professor and Eric watch with the same kind of bemusement I feel.

Eric sees us first, or rather, his tentacle does. It unwinds and probes in our direction, and Eric follows like a hunter, and knows.

"We're not alone," he says.

Kaaro and I expose ourselves at the same time.

"It's just us," I say.

"Kaaro, is that you?" says Bad Fish. "You seem younger. And neither of you has ID chips, ghosted or otherwise."

We catch up. I find out that the young people are disciples of Bad Fish, and he is a kind of Nimbus messiah. Kaaro says he ended the war by destroying the alien plant, using a death ray from the orbiting space station. "It's more of a heat ray through particle acceleration," he says. "I can't help it if the government leave their toys lying around."

And just like that, something clicks.

"We can ... I ... We take it to their planet ... We should ... Now." This thing happens to me sometimes. I can't get words out fast enough. I know I'm not making sense, but I can't stop myself, I'm so excited.

Femi says, "Easy, easy. Breathe. Tell me what you've got."

I sit down.

"Bad Fish, you are proficient with viruses, right?"

"I *am* a virus. I am the beginning and end of viruses."

"Humble too," says Kaaro.

Bad Fish raises a bulky middle finger.

"Can you write a virus for a system you don't fully understand?"

"What do you want it to do?" asks Bad Fish, clearly intrigued by the challenge he can smell.

"I want it to destroy the data on unfamiliar servers, but in a very short time."

"How many servers?"

"I estimate about six billion."

"Sorry, what?" asks Bad Fish.

I address all of them now. "You're going to write a virus. We're going to find a way to insert it into the professor's

325

brainoid. We take the brainoid to Rosewater, in a dead body. They reanimate it and infuse it with an alien consciousness. Only the pathway will carry a little surprise. Because entanglement works both ways. Our virus hitches a ride to Home's moon. You infect one server, you infect them all. Boom."

"Are you saying what I think you're saying?" asks Femi.

"Can this be done?" Tolu asks the professor.

"Theoretically, yes. But it will take a lot of work. I'll have to convert the data from the virus to encode it in the DNA, and somehow ensure it will activate at the right time. I'll need to compile a biological virus to transfer the data. I may need to bring in other people with more expertise. Mrs Alaagomeji, this might be months, even years of work."

"The aliens can't possess human bodies if there are no alien minds left to do the possession," says Eric. "Worth it."

"Excuse me," says Kaaro. "Why is nobody talking about how *this is fucking genocide?*"

He is looking at me when he says this. He is accusing me.

"It's them or us," says Eric. "I choose us."

"They are not really alive," says Femi. "They are not even ghosts. They are data, stored because of faulty philosophy, bodies long gone."

"We are all data, Femi," says Kaaro. "You may be wet data in a moist medium, but you're data all the same. Like me. Like them."

"Let's say they are alive," I say. "Let's say we consider them alive. Billions of souls. Those of us here, we have to swallow the guilt of killing them all. For the sake of humanity. If we do not act here and now, we're dead. Humanity is gone. There is no chance at all. There is Wormwood, invincible, and there are more like it on Earth. Whatever we do, they will just activate another footholder and pipe their people down from Home.

"Now we know that reanimates are alive, that their humanity comes back. Imagine what it's like. You're alive, but your body is not yours to control. Stuck there for whatever lifespan the Homians have. There are thousands like that already.

"Kaaro, they did not hesitate. If they were in our shoes, they would not. I am sorry, my friend. I know what this will do to us, to all of us. I am putting rot in our souls for all time, but this moment is our best shot at stopping the pipeline, our time-machine moment, our travel-back-and-kill-Leopold-II moment."

"I can't," says Kaaro. He transforms into the gryphon in front of everybody and implodes into himself. Gone.

"Fuck him," says Eric. "We don't need Kaaro for this."

Femi speaks to Bad Fish. "You've been quiet. Is this something you are willing to do?"

"Willing? I've started. I've already written twenty-five per cent of the code," says Bad Fish. "Why are we still talking about this?"

Going after Kaaro is tricky and dangerous. The xenosphere is full of things that like to swallow other things or thoughts that like to overwrite others. It's an ecosystem. Kaaro was such a skilled sensitive in life that dead he is one of the biggest creatures in here, maybe *the* biggest, because he gives even Molara a hard time.

Still I search for him. He thinks I am a monster, and I don't disagree. I have contemplated a monstrous thing. People before me have done the same. Oppenheimer. Is Oppenheimer a mass murderer?

I wonder if I find this easier because I am not alive in the same sense that Femi or Eric is. I pass through lava tubes, still smelling the gryphon stink. I am expelled by steam bursts and find myself among the memory of stars, watching the birth of a black hole. I love this. Kaaro must have seen a documentary or something.

"Kaaro, I just want to talk," I say. The black hole draws me out and I emerge under the sea, in the headlights of an angler fish.

"Hi," it says.

"You look ridiculous, Kaaro."

"I always do," he says.

He transforms into a man. The sea draws back and we seem to be back at Arodan, but not in the hangar.

"If you can think of any other way, tell it to me," I say. "I will consider it, and if it works, if it scans, we will do that instead."

"You're the smart one. If there was another way, you'd know it."

"I don't feel smart. I feel cruel," I say. "And while I was in there, it seemed like a good idea, like inspiration, but the analytical part of me thinks it isn't going to work."

"Well . . . "

"I can't make you do anything, Kaaro, but remember the people you killed? During the war?"

"I had to; they were coming for me, and for Aminat."

"Yes, and even though you found out later that they were not, you don't lose sleep over it."

"I'm not blasé, if that's what you think."

"I don't. I'm just saying that, on a smaller scale, you did what had to be done without hesitating. This is the same thing, but with a multiplier."

328

"Big damn multiplier."

"But the same principle."

"Fuck the principle, Oyin Da. It's still immoral. It's still death."

"They aren't alive."

"This is circular logic." Kaaro transforms into a gryphon again. Around him, a hedge of dry twigs forms a seven-foot-high nest. I sense him curling up his wings and sitting. "Leave me alone. I want to think."

I contemplate going home and bringing Nike back with me. Probably be awkward when Junior flies at Kaaro, trying to kill him. She is shit at taking instructions.

Instead, I go back to the hangar and help where I can.

Chapter Forty-Seven

That bitch.

That fucking bitch.

Aminat booby-trapped the serpentine. Of course she did. Why would she not?

Where am I?

Koriko has no vision yet, even though she can feel eyeballs in the sockets. The body seems complete, yet it cannot move. No, it can move, but only a few inches in any direction. She tries to turn her head, but this cannot be done either. She opens her mouth and sticks her tongue out as far as it will go, leaning forward.

Bone. The body is encased in bone.

Footholder! Footholder, I'm trapped.

You are not trapped. You are quarantined.

You're talking to me now, are you?

Quarantine.

Yes, you said that. Why?

What you had on you killed Anthony and almost killed me.

I remember. I was there. I saved you.

Quarantine.

Stop saying that. How long do I have to be here?

Unknown. That other body is slowly sinking into the Earth. I had to create a path for it, or it would have killed me too.

But this is a new body; uncontaminated.

And let's keep it that way. You have to stop provoking the humans.

They killed the xenosphere.

The xenosphere is back and they don't have the capability to stop it. You know that.

Why do you hate me?

I don't hate you. You're my avatar. You and I are one. It is impossible for me to hate you.

You certainly don't relate to me the way you did with Anthony.

For one thing, Koriko, you do not call me by my name. Anthony did.

What name? Wormwood? That's a derogatory name the humans gave you.

It is the name I answer to. But you call me "footholder", which is like saying thing *or* you, *there. I am not a thing. I am alive.*

Wormwood is a doomsday asteroid out of one of their most tedious holy books.

And Koriko can mean "grass", but it can also mean "weed". Which do you think they were thinking of when they named you?

I think, fuck you. So you don't like me because I won't call your name. That's why you're sluggish to obey me?

That you minimise the name says everything about the matter. But that's not why I don't jump to obey you. I hesitate because you are harming the humans and that's not what I was grown to do, Koriko. The plan, the method is to keep the local entities happy, make their life as easy as possible, soothe them into extinction. Heal the natural wear and tear along with disease, but at the same time take over the bodies. That's what I was doing. That's what Anthony was doing.

This is a new plan. We didn't come up with it; the humans did.

Some of the humans.

It is always going to be some. We can't negotiate with seven billion people.

There was never any need to negotiate. This rush, this time-saving isn't necessary. Ten years is like ten thousand years. It's all the same.

No, it is not. What about server failure? What about data corruption over time? What about a big-ass asteroid taking out a large section of our moon? What about the possibility of aliens, hostile aliens, coming across our refuge? Our people shouldn't wait for ever. The risk of extinction rises with every solar cycle.

We will never see eye to eye on this, Koriko.

You don't have eyes, Wormwood. Now get me the hell out of this bone spur, so I can return to the business of harvesting humans. Now.

Koriko gathers the suffocated, the crushed, the burned victims of her anger, and takes them to the Honeycomb. Her cult flows in her wake, praying to her, assisting her. However the conversation with Wormwood went, at least it is responding better to commands. A footholder gone native. Always a risk. She needs to consider whether retiring Wormwood and activating a new one on a different continent will be better.

The Honeycomb is under siege. More humans than ever before surround it, and they throw missiles constantly, roaring their dissent. Koriko doesn't understand why they don't go and protest outside the mayor's mansion. Isn't he the one who speaks for them?

There are some clashes between these protesters and Koriko's cult, but she does not care. Having worshippers is a thing she is indifferent about most of the time, and irritated with at others. Humans will worship anything, even if it is actively killing them. From what Koriko gathers, they have mass-murdered themselves because of religion multiple times. At some point she would like to study the phenomenon, but that's just intellectual curiosity. For now, she has a job to do. One of her cult members is killed and she swallows his body into the ground in seconds. This activates the protesters in some way and drives the cult into a religious frenzy.

Humans are strange.

They do not part for her so she instructs Wormwood to clear her a path, which it does. Inside the Honeycomb she senses a tension, despite the bright lighting and the smell of lavender on the air. Someone points her towards the high-ceilinged ante-chamber, where ...

Jack Jacques sits in a comfortable chair opposite Lua, who does not look happy. There is a glass of water in Jack's hand.

"Can you get me a slice of lime for this? I like lime in my water," he says.

Lua indicates and someone whisks the water away.

"What is he doing here?" Koriko asks.

"Try not to overreact," says Lua.

"What does that mean?" asks Koriko.

"It means we can kill you," says Jack. "We can kill you

when we want, and we can kill Wormwood when we want. So I am here for a little renegotiation."

"If you kill Wormwood, Nigeria will crush you," says Koriko.

"Perhaps," says Jack. He is infuriatingly calm. "But you won't live to see it. Neither will any of your people. I have a large number of them rounded up, by the way, the synners mostly. I won't kill them, but I will make them uncomfortable. I know you guys can read thoughts sometimes. Look into my head and see if I'm bluffing. Read my fucking mind."

"You're not—"

"You know, I like my new leg. I thought I wouldn't, but I do. It's nice to walk about without a chair again. I like it so much that I want this for humans, so you're going to turn on the healing again, for everyone, not just because you like me. You're going to turn on the ganglions again. I won't charge you for the Ocampo inverters that you destroyed. And if any of your synners tries to murder a human, I will kill them all in a way that will prevent you from ever resurrecting them. I think you should be writing all that down, because you have one hour to comply."

"You're bluffing."

"Dahun," says Jack.

A window smashes inwards and a wet glob smacks into the back of Koriko's head. Lua's eyes go wide and Koriko waits for the painful wrenching of her consciousness from the body.

Except nothing happens. She touches her occiput and her hand comes away glowing green. No pain.

"A warning. This time, luminous paint. Next time, a concoction of a weed that you and Wormwood find . . . stimulating. Now will somebody get me my fucking lime?"

*

Jack leaves without consequence, saunters in the crowd without fear, even raises a fist, causing a roar among supporters. Koriko is livid, but Lua seems unaffected.

"Why are we letting him get away with this?"

"Because it does not matter," says Lua. "Their lifespan is a blink. We can afford to indulge him. We can afford to wait."

We can afford to.

But should we?

Chapter Forty-Eight

Bad Fish has been writing for hours. He is not typing code into a program; he is writing the lines in pencil on paper. Well, his acolytes are. He is lying on the floor of the hangar, still in his suit, which apparently he does not take off. He dictates; his minions write. Other minions maintain the suit and presumably feed him and somehow take away his waste. Femi does not know how he commands such obedience or respect, but he is certainly capable of amazing feats. He is in control of Nigeria's derelict space station, the Nautilus. He has maintained it remotely and even managed to divert refuelling missions from other countries so that the correcting jets keep it geostationary, without which it would hurtle to the Earth. Nigerian scientists don't know this, of course; they expected it to crash-land years ago, prompting the president to declare that it was held in place by the hand of God.

Femi has heard of Bad Fish's exploits in security briefings, but never knew it was the work of one person.

Every so often, through the night, she hears him say, "Type it, compile it, test it." His people scurry away, weave their arcane webs and return, whispering their report in his ear.

Then he will start again. He does not tire, he does not falter, he is one hundred per cent in the moment.

At least he knows what he's doing. The professor seems frustrated with progress.

Femi is frustrated with her position. She has had hundreds of texts from the president, some of them even coherent. She has sent only one response:

I was never working for you in the first place.

When she first became the leader of S45, and her people had just been killed by Wormwood, she set events in motion to destroy the alien invaders. But then she found out that the federal government was hedging its bets, allowing the slow replacement of humans because, hey, like climate change, all of that's in the abstract future. The president's men told her to publicly resign, but secretly she was to keep working on a solution. Though not too hard, in case the aliens won and alliances were needed. Even Femi wasn't sure exactly which side she was supposed to be working on, but she had her own mission: to kill the aliens or drive them away.

A story passed down in Femi's family told of the village's first contact with a white man, a wiry, religious specimen with a caravan of porters, whom they welcomed with food and who went everywhere examining battlements and shrines and food stores. One of the porters warned, in Yoruba, that the man should be put to death, but nobody listened to him. By the time more white men came with their black collaborators, it was too late. Resistance resulted in swift death. Only malaria and indirect rule attenuated the harshness of the colonists. Femi has never forgotten the story, and if she had children, it is a story she would pass on to the next generation. In time, autonomy and a budget got her a lot of knowledge, but little progress. The president pulled the plug after a bout of cold feet, and Femi washeed up in Rosewater, no budget, no resources, pretending to her team that she was still in S45 while trying to think up a plan. Her contacts and exotic bugs made her aware of the election the president demanded. The war was the best way to cordon off Rosewater from the rest of the country, so she ...

At times, she thinks of the people dead because of her and she has pause, but she can't pause, because the aliens are still on Earth. Afterwards, she can pay for her crimes – prison doesn't scare her, and death is unimpressive.

The president at least thought she was working against Jacques and was imprisoned because of that. Which is why she was reinstated after the exchange.

But now, with all the news bulletins and the texts, she can't help reliving the moments of Ranti's death, how she shot him in his sham head, how he crawled on the floor to avoid the shots, how Dahun finished him off, Jacques' rage at being manipulated into complicity.

She gets a trawler-bot message. It must be unaware that her clearance has been revoked and is working the last approved query she made.

"Oyin Da," she says.

The ghost appears.

"I need you to go to Rosewater," says Femi.

"All right. Why?"

"I followed up on the data you gave me. I've found Owen Gray. He's still alive, and he lives in Rosewater. I'm betting that's not a coincidence."

Chapter Forty-Nine

I fail to recruit Kaaro for the trip to Rosewater. On the other hand, I find Owen Gray exactly where Femi's intelligence places him. S45 has been tracking him since he arrived in the country as a foreigner associated with Wormwood in London, but the surveillance died down when he seemed to be living a boring life.

Small bungalow, wide yard, a picket fence, a gate.

Props for him, he doesn't live in the gentrified suburbs. I think his neighbours are black on one side, Persian on the other. I watch the place first, and see him. Not as tall as he was, but that's because he's gaunt and bent over. He's about eighty or north of that, tall, thin, hair all white, throwing his tanned skin into contrast. For me, the last time I saw him was a few days ago. Look at him now. Time rushed by and took everything from him. I hope there is enough substance to the man left to save humanity.

He must have already been an old man when he came to the city. The elderly who grew old in Rosewater tend to have healthier spines.

As I draw closer to where he stands, I hear music from

inside. Syncopated drums, mostly. *Owen, Owen, what is your life? Do you have children, grandchildren, cats? Are you lonely? Have you loved? Have you lost?*

Before I can yell a greeting, he says, "You're not human, are you? What are you?"

"You don't remember me, do you? We met in London in 2012, in that church off Tottenham Court Road."

He smiles at the memory. "St Anselm's. The soup kitchen."

"The soup kitchen."

"I don't remember you – and don't take that personally, because I fed a lot of people in that church – but I've seen your kind before. What are you?"

"A ghost."

"Yes. I have seen at least one ghost in my time. What's your name, young lady?"

"Bicycle Girl." She doesn't know why she says this. She never self-identifies with that particular *nom de guerre*, but he makes her want to. He seems ... discreet.

"And you know who I am."

"Owen Gray, CIA."

"Retired on account of the entire CIA being out of reach. You rhymed. Is that deliberate? It's always nice to have an educated assassin."

"I'm not here to kill you."

"No?"

"Mr Gray, according to records, you entered Nigeria around 2035. You're naughty. Your visa's expired."

He raises an eyebrow shot through with white. "You'd better come in, Bicycle Girl. Can you drink tea in that form?"

"I can't interact with solid objects. Just biological, sentient beings. I can make you feel it when you touch me, I can make you hear me and smell me, but that's just because I'm manipulating your nerve endings and brain."

He nods. "I helped make one of you once. Not you in particular. A xenosphere ghost. We called it a quantum ghost because back then putting the word 'quantum' in front of everything was the thing to do with shit you didn't understand."

I'm amused in spite of myself. "We kind of still do."

"Huh. I thought we'd have grown out of that. How old were you when you died?"

"Eleven."

"And yet you say you saw me in London in 2012."

"I . . . went back in time-data."

"Fabulous, fabulous. Let's go to the kitchen. I'm going to have some chicken feet."

I think he means thighs or drumsticks, but no, he actually gets chicken feet. There's an art to eating them, and he has it down pat. I try to remember, but I've never seen a white man eat chicken feet. He has about ten in a bowl on a tiny table. I can smell them and he hasn't spared the chilli.

He sits, and says, "Ewa jeun." *Join me for the meal.*

"You need to work on your accent."

"I'm too old to care about being exposed as a spy and shot."

"Can we talk about why you're here? In Rosewater?"

He peels away the outer integument, then bites along the shaft, small, rapid nips. He eats the sweet flesh where the toes meet in a pulpy prominence. Then he strips the underside of the toes. He spits out the claws.

"Watching Wormwood, of course," he says. "Force of habit, though. I don't report to anyone any more, and my allies are all dead."

341

"We're trying to stop it," I say.

"Wormwood? Good luck. The British tried to kill it. I helped. We destroyed its brain. Except it wasn't a brain." He crunches the bone and sucks out the fatty marrow. "I remember you now. You're the one who told us about Anthony's death."

"He didn't die. But yes, that was me. How do you remember? It wasn't really you; it was an impression of your mind." But I know how. Going into the past affects the memory today because the old version is overwritten with new data, data that now includes me.

"What you really want to know is if I know anything that can help you kill it," says Owen. "Probably not, but I'll share what I have, my notes, my reflections. I can tell you what doesn't work."

"Why do you like chicken feet?" I finally ask.

"Louisiana boy."

"I see. Where did you store your observations?"

"I'll show you in a minute. How come you're not eleven years old? Why do you look like you're in your twenties?"

"I didn't know I was dead."

"Of course. Of course. Have you ever killed anyone?"

"No. I'm not a government agent, Mr Gray." I sound convincing, even to myself. Innocence in the rebellion is a myth, and for a moment I mourn my youth, but only for a moment.

"You're working for one, though."

"Have *you* ever killed anyone?"

"Not that I remember. I mean, I'm old, but I think I'd remember taking someone's life."

"Okay, good, that means I can like you," I say. And I do like him: the slow, deliberate manner of him, the youthful look in his eyes, so at odds with the rest of his body and his shambling manner. He makes no abrupt movements, and nothing is threatening. I wonder if this is something they teach them in the CIA so they can lower their enemies' defences. It will do no good to tell him I have killed before and intend to kill in the near future.

"Wormwood was my first and only assignment," he says. "It's taken a while. Not a great agent, eh?"

"What was your assignment, sir?"

"Twofold. Observe all the alien phenomena with a view to selecting what could be weaponised, then destroy the alien."

"Did they tell you how to kill it?"

Sad smile. "I'm afraid not. I think they were going to formulate a plan based on my findings."

"Where are your notes?"

He washes his hands and wipes the errant oil off his face, then leads me into a room near the back. It smells musty, but in the manner of a second-hand bookshop. It is stacked full of notebooks.

"Are you kidding me?"

"Memory storage can be hacked," he says. "Besides, I wrote these over the time I've been in Rosewater. They were most at risk during the war, but otherwise ... "

I can't read them. I'll have to get someone like Tolu Eleja to come in.

"This won't work," I say.

"Because you can't interact with physical objects, yes, I get it." He sits on a stool in the room, which throws up dust that smells of mould and evokes silverfish. "Why don't you tell me what you plan to do?"

I do, sketching the bare bones of what Femi wants.

He is silent for almost fifteen minutes, holding up his hand to stop me each time I try to start a conversation.

"It could work," he says. "But it will take time, and while you're waiting, the aliens will develop counter-measures to nullify the effect. No, to do this, you'll need to sacrifice your queen, and a faster method. Luckily, I have just the thing."

He starts to look for other specific journals.

I say, "You said you've seen my kind before."

"Yes."

"Were you talking about Ryan Miller?"

Owen laughs. "You know, we were on lockdown, cordoned off in London for ten years. My group. With Miranda and Ryan and Dead Leaves. We survived to a great extent because of Ryan Miller. He knew everything – the best places to hole up, where to find discarded or misplaced weapons, when the catastrophic events were going to happen, how to sneak in and out of the cordon, which I found particularly useful because I had to get my reports out. I knew there was something odd about him."

"Which was?" I sit on the floor and cross my legs.

"Three years after Wormwood fell into Hyde Park, I broke into his flat. I knew where he would be, you see. I found, locked away, this yellowed book full of a vast and far-reaching prediction. It seems he stole it from the British Museum. In and of itself, it was probably an antique, but Ryan had scribbled on it. Corrections, comments and the like. Things like, 'That's not what I said!' or 'Could have been clearer', and so on. He wrote like he was the author."

"He was," I say.

"Yes. Father Marinementus. But I only found this out later. When I got to the seventieth page, I found a note. I unfolded it to discover a handwritten paragraph addressed to me. It said, 'I know you're here, Owen. Look out of the window.' I did, and found him sitting on a derailed Northern Line train waving at me. Not a lot scares me, but my legs got all wobbly. I felt like I was in the sights of a predator, that I had been caught."

"He was still alive after all those centuries?"

"No. And he wasn't exactly like you, either. He entered a growing tumour on the body of a woman called Anne Miller. He talked to her from the tumour so that she did not get it taken out. He caused the tissue to grow into a baby. He said the worst experience in his entire existence was to have the intelligence of an immortal in a body whose vocal cords didn't yet function."

"He wasn't angry with you for breaking into his place?" I ask.

"No, he was expecting it. I guess you don't get offended when you know the future. He came to Nigeria in advance of Wormwood, became a street person for some reason, and died. That was the end of his life."

No.

I stand up, move in close to his body and sniff. "You're not telling me everything. That may have been the end of his life, but not the end of him, and not the end of your relationship."

He grins, and slaps seven notebooks on the floor. "He's out there, in the xenosphere, but he visits me from time to time. At times he seems to have gone mad; other times he is regretful or he brings me new prophecies. They don't always make sense. I used to think of him as a friend, but now ... there's an edge to him. The person I knew is slowly fading away."

"We are all fading away, sir," I say. "What have you got for me?"

*

Have you asked yourself why I am telling you this? Why I deliver it in oral tradition, rather than just writing it down, or letting it get lost to posterity? I do not have to speak, and even if I do, history will still judge me, judge us.

I told you I was the wrong person to tell this story, and I still think that. But my name is Oyin Da and because of what I know, where I have been, what I can do, I have spoken of things that I wasn't always privy to. I have told you the beginning.

What remains is the end.

Chapter Fifty

For the lipstick Aminat turns to her sister. "Matte or gloss?"

Tomi, on the bed, reading *There Was a Country*, shrugs without looking up.

She goes with matte, but then rubs it off and uses gloss. Since seeing Kaaro's ghost, she has been more at peace, feeling closer to her old self. That yawning chasm of emotions is still there, but she is finding new ways to circumvent it daily. The pain is moving from sharp to dull, and life is worth living again.

She has her light armour on under the clothes. Her ankle strap has her backup gun, while her other holster is visible. The government-issue weapon sends pleasing pings to her ID, logged on her phone. She has protein bars – cricket, grasshopper, notroach – in her belt with a small processor to handle communication. If she had a uniform, she would be wearing it.

Today, in spite of all the problems Rosewater faces with protests and rioting, the gay community wishes to have their first Pride, and Layi is going to the march.

Yes, Aminat diverts public resources to cover the march

just in case synners decide to take shots. Dahun says not, and believes he has imprisoned all of them. Guarantees are a thing she has heard before and been disappointed.

"Can't you go with Layi? I'd really feel better if you did," she says to Tomi.

"Nope."

"You're a bad sister."

"Fuck you and nope."

"If you love him—"

"If he loved me, he'd stay home like all sensible human beings."

Aminat stops talking and tells the car to start. She knows Tomi will have a last-minute change of heart and follow their brother.

There have been sniper threats, bomb threats, cross-border threats from Nigeria, sabre-rattling from the president, all kinds of shit. Outside, she sees the car arrive. It barely misses a slouching reanimate with a bandaged head.

Rushing out, she passes Layi preening in front of a mirror, wearing a trilby of all things. She kisses the back of his neck. "I love you, be careful."

The reanimate slips in a pool of palm oil and falls flat on his face. The impact is such that whatever wound he had reopens, and the bandages turn red, but only for a few seconds as the healing aether of Rosewater repairs the body. Small fragments of glass from the ground fall off the reanimate's skin as he continues shambling towards a specific destination. He sweats through his clothes as the sun begins shining for real, but he does not stop for water or rest. He loses a shoe, but keeps going. His path can now be traced on the tarmac by the blood smear as the sole of his foot abrades.

He is jostled by protesters, and is knocked over now and again. Each time, with terrapene doggedness, he rises, reorients himself and keeps going. The noise and the chants do not deter him, although warnings of police cause a split second of hesitation that observers would miss. He is mostly ignored.

He is within view of the Honeycomb when a police jeep runs him down. Some observers might have noticed that he walked into the path of the vehicle. It doesn't matter; the outcome is the same. He is dead. Again.

Koriko becomes aware of the bandaged man at a time when she is resting. She misses her pet serpentine, but the decay it created is still festering in Wormwood. Her irritation at Jacques burns as a hot coal in her heart, and she leaps at a chance to pick up even a single corpse.

The bandaged man has soiled himself, but this is not unusual. Koriko hauls the body over her shoulder and walks towards the Honeycomb. There is an abundance of staffers available to prep the body and help, since there has been a slowdown after the confrontation with Jacques.

There is something different about the corpse, more residual neurotransmitter activity than she would usually associate with human dead. As they take the body away, Koriko detects a surge that might be a thought, but it dies away just as quickly.

She casts it out from her mind.

In Arodan, poised at a keyboard, Bad Fish gets the message and says, "He's in."

The room is silent, all eyes on Femi.

"Execute," she says.

Bad Fish's fingers flit across the keys, then he pauses

dramatically before bringing a hand down on the last one. "Gbo-sa!" *Boom*.

Just outside the city limits, to the west of Rosewater, the mine slows its extraction. It ignores the consternation among the on-site workers, instead giving off ominous sounds. An alarm activates and the site is evacuated while the engines appear to reconfigure themselves. The accumulated waste of Wormwood drains into hitherto empty chambers deep within the earth beneath the mine.

A monstrous pile-driver pushes through the soil, across the border and into the flesh of the alien. Through this channel, the mine, which is now acting like a jet injector, fires more than a year of waste back into Wormwood.

In the mayor's mansion, Blessing, in taking inventory of his new work, stumbles upon Lora in her electromagnetic cell. They lock eyes.

They do not exchange any words.

In Arodan, Eric screams and falls convulsing to the floor. The tentacle swings about looking for an aggressor, preventing anyone from helping him. Each convulsion squeezes air from his lungs, forced through his vocal cords in a yelp that would sound comical under other circumstances. One of Bad Fish's acolytes tries to help; the tentacle punctures her throat with a spike and flings her left, slamming her against the wall of the hangar.

Underground, Wormwood feels exquisite pain and erupts in every way it can, trying everything in desperation, wanting to get away from the liquid fire that plagues it. It finally pulls its pseudopodia in, contracting into a sphere, causing local shifts in the tectonic plate.

In Rosewater, Wormwood's pain is felt everywhere, physically. There is a local earthquake as the ganglia are forcibly retracted, and the ground surges and heaves like the waves at a beach. Buildings sway, then break, never designed to withstand these kinds of forces in the first place. Thousands of people suffer ruptured blood vessels in their brains and have haemorrhagic strokes.

Layi has never done this before, but he has read up. Set a rendezvous point for the start and end of the march. Get the numbers right so that everyone makes it home. Keep it tight, keep eyes open and submit the route to the police beforehand. There are twelve of them, including a high-court judge and his husband, newly out.

Tomi, his sister, comes along "for the ride", but Layi knows it's to look after him. He knows and she knows, but they both pretend it's about supporting the gay lifestyle. There are one or two motorcycle crash helmets by way of masking, but otherwise there are no costumes. There is still widespread disbelief. It's a trick. They want to identify gay people so they can arrest and lynch them. There are no leaders. Layi suggests a simple rectangular route up Ransome Kuti Avenue, across Taribo West Way, down Odegbami, then back to Ransome Kuti by Broad Street. It would take maybe an hour. Even that would be historic.

They start from the ganglion. They do not play music, but they have a PA system reading out the names and year of execution or imprisonment of their fallen comrades. It is a sober celebration, but Layi thinks subsequent years will be more cheery. The march aims for the ganglion on Taribo.

Ransome Kuti is an arty district, with some bars, a few clubs, Remy's Slam for poetry and some street food. They are halfway when the first earthquake hits. Tomi grabs his hand.

"Don't panic," she says.

"I'm not panicking," says Layi.

But the ground is in distress. Layi has a headache like someone urinated on his brain then doused it in bleach. Something is happening that Kaaro would have understood better. A cherub statue cracks and falls from the angle of a building. The rending noise stops the names from being audible.

"Do we go back?" asks someone.

"I'm not going anywhere," says the judge. "Do you know how many years I have waited for this? No. I'm going the full route, even if it kills me."

Layi understands this, but does not wish to die.

"What do you think?" he asks Tomi.

"I have the wrong privilege for this," she says. "Common sense is screaming for me to run. We don't know what this is. It makes sense to be cautious. Yet I've not gone through the oppression that queer folks have. What do you want to do?"

"I want to make sure everyone's safe. Besides, there's a Filipino boy I'm trying to impress."

"The one in the superhero T-shirt?"

"Gorgeous!"

"Okay. But we have to be careful."

There is a crash of broken glass and four floaters take flight from an alley. The street vibrates, and manhole covers shift, but the march continues.

Water mains burst and spray the procession. Halfway, and three synners break out of a door. They are armed and spot the Pride group, green eyes blazing with evil intent. Layi elevates the temperature around the weapons to white heat, generating a terrifying crack with displaced air, melting the hardware and reducing the hands to powdered charcoal. The march does not stop, although Layi thinks he might need a rest. It is not obvious why the heating effect occurred, and Layi does not say.

"Jacques is meant to be here giving a speech," says someone.

"Yeah, well, he knows how to look after himself. Did you see that new leg?"

"I heard it's a prosthesis."

"My cousin works at the mansion. It's real."

The march works its way through the dangers, and just as they are about to return, a swarm of new floaters descends to feed.

Tomi says, "Layi ... ?"

"Everybody," says Layi, "get behind me."

Koriko screams her rage into the air. *"No, don't you dare!"*

The Honeycomb groans, but does not crumble like the blocks around it. Chief Scientist Lua puts a hand on Koriko. "What's wrong?"

"It's leaving," says Koriko.

"What's leaving?"

"The footholder! Wormwood is running away!"

"But ... it can't ... "

"It can. *It is.*"

Wormwood breaks all the tethers to the city above, snatching back all strands of flesh, all neurological tissues and water conduits, diving even deeper into the Earth's crust to avoid the toxins. It does what it was already doing slowly. It had intended to take the city away from Nigeria, to a place of safety, but now it is in pain and at risk of being killed. It is no longer a matter of compromise, but one of survival. The humans almost killed it once already. Wormwood will no longer wait patiently or try to convince its avatar.

It can feel the city above shear off, and it can hear the pain of millions of humans, but it cannot care. It cannot care now. Five hundred souls are wiped out in an instant when one of the caverns in Wormwood's body collapses and they fall screaming through the earth.

It aims for water.

It aims for the sea.

Femi nods to Bad Fish. "The distraction worked. May whatever gods we worship forgive us."

"I'm hearing reports of an earthquake," says the professor. "There shouldn't be earthquakes. We're on a single tectonic plate."

"That was Wormwood dying," says Bad Fish.

"It's not dying," says Oyin Da.

"Can you feel Kaaro?" asks Femi.

The Bicycle Girl does not or cannot answer.

In the bunker under the mansion, Jack receives all the information. Beside him, Hannah holds his hand with a grip that seems to grow tighter every minute.

"It's over," says Jack. "We're not coming back from this."

The hologram they are watching shows floaters swarming, diving to grab citizens, churning in a feeding frenzy that rains blood on the burning city.

"It's like a vision of hell," says Hannah.

"Except it's not a vision; it's real."

Dahun is on a radio somewhere. "Mr Mayor, you should leave with me. Now. There is widespread violence, and creatures we have never seen before are emerging from underground. Sir, we are food. Get to the helipad."

"Where will we go?" asks Jacques.

"Away from here, to start with," says Dahun.

"We're coming," says Jack. He turns to Hannah. "Go with the bodyguards. I'll follow."

"Where are you going?" she asks.

"I have to get Lora. I'm not leaving her here."

Koriko is on her knees, unprepared for the kind of desolation she feels as the signal with Wormwood becomes fainter and fainter the further away it goes.

Come back.

Stop.

You and I are one. I cannot live without you, footholder.

Wormwood.

Stop moving, please.

We will die.

[I love you. This is what love is.]

From Wormwood, silence.

People move around her, but Koriko does not care. She falls, lying on the floor now.

She is not dead, but she might as well be.

She closes her eyes.

Jack should have asked one of his bodyguards to do this, but he wants Hannah to have maximum protection. He feels able to look after himself as he makes his way up past panicking staffers, one of them on fire, though from what is unclear. The building is not burning.

He has to get Lora clear. He feels guilty for what he has done, but there's time to apologise later. He tries to tamp down the thought that tries to emerge from the depths: *she is only a machine.*

No.

He bursts into the chamber and is confused for a second. She isn't . . .

"Good morning, sir," says Lora from behind the door.

Jack turns right into a punch. It takes him off his feet and triggers ringing in his ears. The pain comes next, but he still opens his eyes to find Lora gone.

Shit.

That hurt, on several levels.

Lora can certainly punch. She obviously thinks Jack means her harm. His subdermal is going crazy with all manner of warnings. Messages from Hannah. Messages from Dahun. Messages from Tired Ones. The world wobbles and shakes; Jack knows the structure can take some stress, but not for much longer.

Get up, Jack.

He tries to phone Hannah or Dahun, but the phone doesn't work, which means they are out of range of the peer-to-peer, which means they are gone. Good. He only has to think about himself. There are tunnels built after the war, but he worries about their integrity after all the earthquakes. He heads upstairs, concerned about roving thugs, but makes his way to his office. He is relieved to see the Orisha rows. He activates the emergency app on his subdermal and all the Orisha advance to his side as robotic guards.

"Lethal force," he says.

In the office he has armour and weapons, which he kits himself out with. He leaves one robot in the office, just in case he has to come back. Then, accompanied by the others, he makes his way out.

The sight of Rosewater brings tears to his eyes.

What have they done to my city?

He charges into the night, hoping to find a way out, maybe. He can hole up in the Honeycomb, or the cathedral; the Anglican priest owes him. A part of his mind wants to make it right. A part of him thinks this can still be fixed.

And Jack Jacques is the man to do it.

Oh.

The bandaged man. The last Homian transfer. Koriko has been distracted, but now she understands its final transmission and she knows.

That was someone she has encountered before.

That was Kaaro.

And that last thought she deciphered is now clear to her.

Fuck you, Space Invaders!

Chapter Fifty-One

Before any of that, though, Oyin Da takes another shot at Kaaro ...

Kaaro knew she would be back, and when she stands outside his nest and gently calls his name, he responds without any of the vitriol he thought he would have for a mass murderer. He drops the nest, turning the oversized twigs into sawdust, and preens himself before her.

"Can you turn human?" she asks. "I never know what you're going to do in this form."

"I'd never harm you," says Kaaro.

"Huh. I saw you try to eat the xenosphere."

"It made sense at the time."

"If you say so." She falls quiet. For a time they both look down at the hangar, the generators the illicit team has set up, the massive cables snaking everywhere. "Remember when we first met? You were covered in meat."

"And you tried to kill me with a shotgun," says Kaaro.

"Yes. You're a pretty strong sensitive to have found your way into my head, my Lijad."

358

"And you're pretty decent yourself to have created such a place without even knowing you were doing it, and making others experience it too. You held a village in your head. Respect. No wonder you were into me."

"Shut up."

"Heh ... with your head cocked to one side like a child with glue ear."

"Shut up, Kaaro." But she laughs and Kaaro knows she is after something difficult. That's why they are both talking about simpler times, old awkwardness, difficulties they have already overcome.

"Just say it," he says.

"It has to be you, Kaaro."

"What is 'it', Oyin Da?"

"When we last spoke, we were thinking of taking Bad Fish's code and inserting it into the prof's brainoid with a virus. I spoke to Owen Gray. It won't work, it's been tried before. I checked Bad Fish's work. I know he's your friend, and I know he's very confident, but ... it isn't going to work. You know what would work?"

"Don't say it."

"You are the only one who can do it, Kaaro. Eric can't. He's like a baby sensitive. And I can't. I tried. But you. You're the one who has possessed multiple reanimates *at the same time*. I can't even possess one, and I've never heard of any sensitive doing it."

"Please don't ask me to do this."

"It has to be you, Kaaro. You are our only hope."

"Femi told you to say that."

"She did not."

"Ah, shit, Oyin Da."

"I'm asking. I am the one asking. I want you to take that sheaf of papers that Bad Fish has scribbled his horrible writing on. I want you to memorise them. I want you to possess the brainoid."

"No . . . "

"I want you to ride a reanimate into Rosewater and feign death, so that Koriko harvests the body."

"And then what?"

"Entanglement works both ways," says Oyin Da.

"I don't want to."

"I don't care, Kaaro. This is the time to grow your hairy balls. Go to Rosewater, travel to Home, and destroy the data of billions of Homians in the servers. Kill them all, Kaaro. Kill them for humanity."

Kaaro says nothing.

"I'm sorry to ask this, I truly am, and there is nothing I can do if you refuse. I can't harm you, I can't punish you, I can't ostracise you because you're already an asshole."

"Great talk, boss lady."

"Come on, you are an asshole. You know it. It's the end of the world. At least let's be honest with each other."

"All right. I'll do it."

"What? You will? Why?"

Because a part of him wants Oyin Da to respect him. Because he is a coward but always wanted to be something else. Because he loves Aminat and wants her world to survive. And because he is curious to see where it takes him.

"Gift horse, Bicycle Girl. Gift horse. Leave my mouth alone."

Together they walk down to the hangar. She reaches for his hand and squeezes in friendship.

With nothing to inhibit him, he learns the code and over-learns it. Bad Fish teaches him mnemonics and basics of virus design until it seems like second nature. There exists a distinct possibility that the alien servers will be too ... alien and the mission will fail, but they cannot know that until they have tried. Nobody verbalises that Kaaro will pay the price if the virus can't parse Homian systems. They don't need to.

Tolu comes back with a body. *The* body.

The professor implants the brainoid, stitches and bandages the man's head. When he is done, he says, "It just occurred to me that we didn't need to implant it in the brain or even the skull. Anywhere with a blood supply would have been fine as long as I could tap a spinal fluid bath."

Under the cover of night, waiting for the border bots to complete their run, Tolu smuggles the body into the city limits and it reanimates within half an hour. Kaaro takes control and says goodbye to Tolu and Oyin Da.

Like a ghoul, or Frankenstein's creature, the reanimate Kaaro goes back to his own home and stares at Aminat with her brother Layi and sister Tomi. He watches their gentle laughter and he feels sad that he will never be part of it. He cannot go in because the ID chip on the reanimate will activate defences. He watches all night, and when a car almost squashes him against the property wall, he leaves.

He falls, but gets up, makes his way to the Honeycomb, where he lies down and sinks his consciousness deep, maybe firing one or two neurones in a loop. Koriko takes the bait and drags him, a Trojan horse, inside.

Gift horse, Trojan horse ...

The aliens prepare his body. He feels lightness. Just as he is leaving, he flips Koriko the bird.

Fuck you, Space Invaders!

*

Time, of course, means nothing.

Humans don't know where Home is, but it is surely interstellar.

Kaaro is broken down, put back together, broken down, reformed. He has no idea where he is at any given time, or if he even exists any more. Perhaps he is dead. Again.

There is no pain.

He should concentrate, but any time he tries, his thoughts disintegrate.

He had a dog called Yaro and hopes it will be looked after. Can't think of Aminat. Won't.

He is moving, but it is more like rotating on an axis than forward motion. In a single rotation, he experiences the full spectrum of light and dark, and he knows he has made some form of progress towards his destination.

It takes years or it takes seconds, he does not know, but one minute he is in Rosewater, then he is on the Homian side of eternity.

Oh Bad Fish, you would have loved this.

The Homian systems resemble neurones, and are, in fact, xenosphere analogues, systems Kaaro is used to.

He can see them, the resting Homians, billions of them, asleep, confident that someone is coming to revive them and save their species. Safe. Not any more.

I am the Rat, the Termite, the Eater of Wealth, the Still One, the Quiet.

And I have come for you.

He starts from the nearest and he spreads into the neurones, realigning all the subatomic particles towards a null state. He transforms into the gryphon without thinking and feasts on the souls, alien, but tasty all the same. He splits into two, because it is taking too long, then he splits again, and divides himself exponentially as he consumes. The insects come, the guardians of data integrity, and he takes over their software. He experiences low-gravity flight and can see the extent of his task, the surface of the moon covered as far as the electric eye can see with servers. The insects register distress in a manner Kaaro's Earth-formed mind cannot understand. They are simple machines, but programmed to be upset if they cannot achieve a proper checksum of the data they are created to protect.

All the gryphons that are Kaaro screech at the same time. This does not wake the sleeping Homians, but it drives the guardian programs and routines insane with panic. Kaaro eats them all and turns them into himself. He spreads like a wave of discontent and does not stop until all that is Homian becomes Kaaro.

When all is done, and the fail-safes kick in by trying to destroy infected servers, billions of them are gone, overwritten.

There is just Kaaro for eternity, the most successful mass murderer in history, alive after a fashion and alone on a moon light years from Earth. The gryphons rejoin, re-form into one again.

He rests for a minute or a year, it's difficult to say.

Aminat.

I saved the world.

He activates the self-destruct sequences on the surviving servers, and Kaaro simply is no more.

Chapter Fifty-Two

I am Oyin Da, the improbable, and I am the wrong person to tell this story.

My lover is Nike and our child is Junior. We are happy, we are safe, and there is a statue of a gryphon outside our house.

Kaaro is gone, no trace left in the xenosphere. I checked.

Why have I told you this? Telling stories is never a neutral act. The teller has a motive, and the listener becomes complicit once the contract of storytelling has been executed.

We destroyed an entire people. I tell you this so you will not think me a monster. So you will not think Kaaro a monster. You have context, you know why we did what we did, and you forgive us because we saved you from the outer darkness, from giving up your body to aliens. I don't want children to play the game "Let's go back in time and kill Oyin Da".

And it worked, because all you want to know now is what happened next.

Very well.

Wormwood escaped, detached itself from the city on its back and sank out of human perception range, leaving ruins behind it. Nobody knows where it is, but I suspect the ocean floor, the Mariana Trench or someplace like that. The furthest it can get from human beings. There are other footholders, of course, dormant, but they have no reason to exist any more, no reason to be activated.

Rosewater itself is a kind of no-man's-land now. The Nigerians quickly claimed ownership and troops went in. The first battalion never made it out: every single man of every company disappeared. The second battalion ... sixteen survivors, their stories classified, but what leaked is not pretty. Hellish carnivores, hybrid creatures that defy description, sentient greenslime, and chemical contamination at every turn.

Finally, in a decision that echoed that of the United Kingdom's approach to London in 2012, the federal government cordoned Rosewater off as beyond salvage. On maps, one giant biohazard symbol. They are considering buying a thermonuclear weapon from Moscow in order to sterilise the site. This is not a popular solution on the basis of cost alone, but then most of the House of Assemblies don't live adjacent to it.

A few people celebrate it as a symbol of our victory against the invaders, but most do not.

Hannah Jacques made it out and is in hiding somewhere, Guinea Bissau I'm told. I'm sure she speaks a number of languages, and beauty is universal. She'll land on her feet.

Jack Jacques has never been found, but he is presumed dead. His loyal mercenary Dahun said he went down with his ship. He was never going to leave Rosewater, apparently. He would have faced numerous charges and the president would have executed him anyway, so dead, not dead, it's all the same.

*

Femi Alaagomeji surrendered and is awaiting trial for first-degree murder. She seems unbothered by it all. I visit her from time to time in her cell, like I did before. This prison is better than the one in Rosewater. She thinks she is being treated well because the president may be considering pardoning her. I tell her prisoners in the Tower of London were treated well depending on their station. And until their execution.

She has no regrets.

Lora Asiko does the talk shows, giving insider gossip about the Rosewater years. She is independently wealthy, married to a lawyer, and seems happy. She still cannot see me.

Aminat moved back to Lagos.

She and her fire-starter brother escaped Rosewater with all twelve of the participants in the gay march. Bad Fish arranged brand-new identities for all. It turns out that Kaaro had made arrangements for his money to revert to Aminat.

I go to see them with Junior and Nike. Layi does flame tricks and I pull Aminat aside, but she is not interested in talking about Rosewater.

"That shit belongs in the past. So do ghosts."

Touché.

She seems happy. Kaaro would have liked that.

Eric is in South Africa, looking after his mother. Bad Fish was right: she is ill, but in remission now. She wants Eric to detach from the tentacle, but he won't hear of it.

I live in the xenosphere and Molara says it will slowly degrade as entropy sets in. How long that will take she does not know, but already I can sense the periphery of my world breaking off. She is still wounded where the gryphon bit her. She seems unfocused, which isn't surprising as she has no purpose.

I do.

My purpose is in the smile of my daughter, that wiry, fearless one who took on a mythical beast without blinking. That smile keeps me from thinking about billions of Homians dead or deleted.

That is the story, that is the tale. Soon my daughter and my wife and our house on the side of a mountain will be gone, but we will be happy.

We will die happy.

Remember us.

The Reprise

As prisons go, this isn't bad.

It's solitary again, which is understandable, because they don't want her talking to anyone. This is a well-lit room, no bars on the doors or windows, a bed with comfortable linen, a table with writing implements, nothing electronic, and books. The walls are lime green, and there is no art, but Femi has done a few sketches and pinned them to the wall. The colours are limited to red, blue, black and green biros, but she makes do.

The coffee is good.

There is a guard outside the door who controls the locks. Each day she is allowed to wash while her room is cleaned. By the time she returns, all the notes she has written are gone, replaced by fresh paper. It is not an exaggeration to think they might be examining her shit.

She thinks she might be in Abuja, but it's difficult to tell. Her knowledge of the president tells Femi he would not want her far from him. He likes to keep his enemies fully humiliated and visible at all times. Which is why Jack Jacques frustrates him. But fuck him. Femi has to adjust to her new life. For now.

She freshens up as much as possible because she is expecting her solicitor. She did not resist when they came for her, making no attempt to run even though she had opportunity to do so. She asked for her lawyer.

No need for a showy, expensive trial; she confessed, much to the chagrin of the lawyer, who seemed genuinely perplexed that all Femi wanted her for was to negotiate conditions and to sneak in good food. She couldn't explain if her feet were put to the fire. A part of her thinks that now that her task is done, she has no reason to resist whatever destiny holds for her. Maybe she is suicidal. She is certainly fatalistic. After caring about one impossible thing for years, to find the thing possible and finished is anticlimactic. But here she is, the one who defended humanity from colonisation, hoping that the lawyer remembers to bring the watercolours she asked for.

The guard escorts her to the private room, the one that ostensibly is not monitored or bugged. Femi doesn't buy it, but she can no longer muster enough outrage to care. She has a separate bathroom, instead of a bucket in the corner. That has to be worth something.

The lawyer looks all of sixteen years old, all perfect braids, perky boobs and immaculately pressed skirts. She did remember the art supplies and got them approved. They are the kind you give primary school children, though. With the lid doubling up as a water reservoir and a selection of seven pots with basic colours. There is a single brush. It doesn't matter. It's a start.

The lawyer hands over some photographs. "They want to know what these statues are."

Stills from drone footage. Can't tell where from exactly because there are no landmarks captured. It's daytime. Rubble everywhere in the shot, yet there are three stone images of humans right there on the surface. Just approximate shapes really, but recognisable. All of them are different shades of grey. Here and there, cracks can be seen.

Femi hands the photos back. "Those aren't statues."

"What are they, then? Because they look like statues to me."

"Whatever broke up the rest of the city would have broken up statues, don't you think?" Femi sucks her teeth. "Those aren't statues. They're casts."

"I don't understand."

"Because you've never lived in Rosewater. There's a bug in the air; when you inhale it, you don't know until you fall asleep. It multiplies, and secretes a hard, concrete-like covering. The bug eats the human, who cannot move, trapped inside this stone jacket. When it finishes with the human, it just abandons the hollow cast. Hence those."

"So they used to be human?"

"Yes."

"Why didn't it kill people before now?"

"Because Wormwood used to heal people as the damage was occurring. The bug couldn't take root. It's not the worst thing in Rosewater, believe me. During the rebellion, there was this thing that made people burst into flames."

"I see." The lawyer puts the photos away. "I have news."

"Go on."

"They're offering life."

"Which prison?"

"Chelu godi – there are conditions. You have to be a consultant for all matters to do with the aliens and Rosewater. You have to tell everything you know. If you hold back, the deal is off, and they execute you the next day."

"Fine. My condition is I get to choose the facility."

"You ... Femi, you don't have much negotiating power."

"It's Mrs Alaagomeji," says Femi. "And you're wrong about that. They need me because they have to make excursions into Rosewater now, whether it's walled off or not. There's danger, but there are organic abominations that might have biomedical applications, and there might be energy resources. They don't know their asses from their elbows, and they need me." She smacks her own bottom. "I know my ass from my elbow."

After the meeting, Femi colours in some of her previous work. There is a knock at the door and her guard looks in, then steps aside as a woman enters. She is over fifty, elegant, corpulent, wearing an Ofi wrapper and a lace blouse.

"I'm sorry about this; I'm just coming from church," says the woman.

Femi doesn't even know it's Sunday.

"Who are you?" she asks.

"It doesn't matter. What you need to know is that I'll be president in six months."

"That's a bold statement."

"But true. Have you heard of the Tired Ones?"

Rumours. A cabal of kingmakers who install their people in key positions. A conspiracy theory. Illuminati shit.

"You're going to tell me that's real?"

The woman smiles, and adjusts her blouse. "Never mind. I did want to tell you that I've read the reports, and between the lines. What you've done is heroic, and one way or the other, I'll make sure you get your due."

Femi snorts and says, "You're going to be president, so I'll say this to you: *were society more reasonably organised, there would be still less need of great abilities, or heroic virtues.* It's a paraphrase of Wollstonecraft."

The woman laughs. "Femi, where's Jack?"

Femi shrugs. "Dead?"

The woman nods, and keeps her head down, staring at her shoes. "I swore him in, you know? His batch of Tired Ones. I had high hopes. We all did. Then he chose that putrefying mudbath as his base, which everyone could have ignored, except he picked a fight with the outgoing president."

"Who did you bribe to get in here?" asks Femi.

The woman looks back up at her. "You'll say if you think of anything? If you hear from him or of him?"

"I don't even know who you are," says Femi.

"Keep watching the Nimbus broadcasts," the woman says. "I'll be the one in Aso Rock."

She exits.

Crazy bitch.

Crazy *connected* bitch.

In the first of her interviews, Femi is questioned by delegates from India, China, Korea, Russia and the Philippines. They are polite, friendly even. She cooperates. Their tea is good, and as a gesture of goodwill, the Indian delegate sends an assortment of leaves.

At two in the morning, she wakes up and Oyin Da is standing beside her bed.

"I thought you were gone or disappeared," says Femi.

"I thought so too, but it turns out Junior has learned a thing or two about repairing and maintaining the xenosphere the way the aliens used to. She taught Nike and me, so we take shifts. Either way, oblivion postponed. We live."

"I'm glad to hear that, Oyin Da."

"Do you want company? We have no enemies to discuss this time, no allies to gather, no aliens to vanquish."

"Yes. We no longer have much in common, and I don't even know if I like you," says Femi. She points to the watercolour on the wall beside the bed. "Tell me, do you like art?"

Acknowledgements

Wow. We're at the end? Righteous.

Kate Elliott, Aliette de Bodard and Ashley Jacobs have been my consistent readers and they gave me superb feedback that brought me back from the brink of madness more times than I can count.

As usual, the Orbit team did a superlative job – Jenni Hill, Sarah Guan, Nazia "Queen of the Universe" Khatun, Ellen B. Wright and, of course, Joanna Kramer. If there are mistakes made, it is because I did not listen, not because I wasn't told.

My writing gang – Zen, Victor, Vida, Likhain, Rochita, Alessa, Nene – thanks for listening to me whine.

Thanks to Camille Lofters for miscellaneous advice and impressions.

Alexander Cochran, super agent, thanks for the efforts and encouragement.

Thanks to my family for tolerating me, the madman in the attic.

Finally, the fans of the Wormwood books, you made this possible. I can't thank you enough. Keep reading!

extras

about the author

Tade Thompson is the author of *Rosewater,* which was the winner of the 2019 Arthur C. Clarke Award, inaugural winner of the Nommo Award and a John W. Campbell finalist. He has written a trilogy set in the world of *Rosewater* and is working on a space opera. His Shirley Jackson Award-shortlisted novella *The Murders of Molly Southbourne* has recently been optioned for screen adaptation. Born in London to Yoruba parents, he lives and works on the south coast of England where he battles an addiction to books.

Find out more about Tade Thompson and other Orbit authors by registering for the free monthly newsletter at www.orbitbooks.net.

if you enjoyed
THE ROSEWATER REDEMPTION

look out for

RED MOON

by

Kim Stanley Robinson

*IT IS THIRTY YEARS FROM NOW, AND
WE HAVE COLONISED THE MOON.*
*American Fred Fredericks is making his first trip, his
purpose to install a communications system for China's
Lunar Science Foundation. But hours after his arrival
he witnesses a murder and is forced into hiding.
It is also the first visit for celebrity travel reporter Ta
Shu. He has contacts and influence, but he too will find
that the moon can be a perilous place for any traveller.
Finally, there is Chan Qi. She is the daughter of the Minister
of Finance, and without doubt a person of interest to those in
power. She is on the moon for reasons of her own, but when
she attempts to return to China, in secret, the events that
unfold will change everything – on the moon, and on Earth.*

Chapter One

Nengshang nengxia

Can Go Up Can Go Down (Xi)

Someone had told him not to look while landing on the moon, but he was strapped in his seat right next to a window and could not help himself: he looked. Quickly he saw why he had been told not to—the moon was doubling in size with every beat of his heart, they were headed for it at cosmic speed and would certainly vaporize on impact. A mistake must have been made. He still felt weightless, and the clash of that placid sensation with what he was seeing caused a wave of nausea to wash through him. Surely something was wrong. Right before his eyes the blossoming white sphere splayed out and became a lumpy white plain they were flashing over. His heart pounded in him like a child trying to escape. It was the end. He had seconds to live, he felt unready. His life flashed before his eyes in the classic style, he saw it had been nearly empty of content, he thought *But I wanted more!*

The elderly Chinese gentleman strapped into the seat next to him leaned onto his shoulder to get a look out the window. "Wow," the old one said. "We are coming in very fast, it seems."

The white jumble hurtled toward them. Fred said weakly, "I was told we shouldn't look."

"Who would say that?"

Fred couldn't remember, then he did: "My mom."

"Moms worry too much," the old man said.

"Have you done this before?" Fred asked, hoping the old man could provide some insight that would save the appearances.

"Land on the moon? No. First time."

"Me too."

"So fast, and yet no pilot to guide us," the old one marveled cheerfully.

"You wouldn't want a person flying something going this fast," Fred supposed.

"I guess not. I remember pilots, though. They seemed safer."

"But we were never that good at it."

"No? Maybe you work with computers."

"It's true, I do."

"So you are comforted. But didn't people program the computers landing us now?"

"Sure. Well – maybe." Algorithms wrote algorithms all the time; it might be hard to track the human origins of this landing system. No, their fate was in the hands of their machinery. As always, of course, but this time it was too much, their dependence too visible. Fred heard himself say, "Somewhere up the line, people did this."

"Is that good?"

"I don't know."

The old man smiled. Previously his face had been calm, ancient, a little sad; now laugh lines formed a friendly pattern on his face, making it clear he had smiled like this many times. It was like switching on a light. White hair pulled back in a ponytail, cheerful smile: Fred tried to focus on that. If they hit the moon now they would be smeared far across it, disaggregating into molecules. At least it would be fast. *Whiteblackwhiteblack* alternated below so quickly that the landscape blurred to gray, then began to spark red and blue, as in those pinwheels designed to create that particular optical illusion.

The old man said, "This is a very fine example of *kao yuan*."

"Which is what?"

"In Chinese painting, it means perspective from a height."

"Indeed," Fred said. He was light-headed, sweating. Another wave of nausea washed through him, he feared he might throw up. "I'm Fred Fredericks," he added, as if making a last confession, or saying something like *I always wanted to be Fred Fredericks*.

"Ta Shu," the old man said. "What brings you here?"

"I'm going to help activate a communication system."

"For Americans?"

"No, for a Chinese agency."

"Which one?"

"Chinese Lunar Authority."

"Very good. I was once a guest of one of your federal agencies. Your National Science Foundation sent me to Antarctica. A very fine organization."

"So I've heard."

"Will you stay here long?"

"No."

Suddenly their seats rotated 180 degrees, after which Fred felt pushed back into his seat.

"Aha!" Ta Shu said. "We already landed, it seems."

"Really?" Fred exclaimed. "I didn't even feel it!"

"You're not supposed to feel it, I think."

The push shoving them increased. If their ship was already magnetically attached to its landing strip, as this shove indicated must be the case, then they were safe, or at least safer. Many a train on Earth worked exactly like this, levitating over a magnetic strip and getting accelerated or decelerated by electromagnetic forces. The white land and its black flaws still flew by them at an astonishing speed, but the bad part was over now. And they hadn't even felt the touchdown! Just as they wouldn't have felt a final sudden impact. For a while they had been like Schrödinger's cat, Fred thought, both dead and alive, the two states superposed inside a box of potentiality. Now that wave function had collapsed to this particular moment.

Alive.

"Magnetism is so strange!" Ta Shu said. "Spooky action at a distance."

This chimed with Fred's thoughts enough to surprise him. "Einstein said that about quantum entanglement," he said. "He didn't like it. He couldn't see how it would work."

"Who knows how anything works! I'm not sure why he was so upset by that particular example. Magnetism is just as spooky, if you ask me."

"Well, magnetism is located in certain objects. Quantum entanglement has what they call non-locality. So it is pretty weird." Though Fred was damp with sweat, he was also beginning to feel better.

"It's all weird," the old man said. "Don't you think? A world of mysteries."

"I guess. Actually the system I'm here to activate uses quantum entanglement to secure its encryption. So even though we can't explain it, we can make it work for us."

"As so often!" Again the cheerful smile. "What is there we can explain?"

The moon now flashed by them a little less stupendously. Their deceleration was having its effect. A white plain stretched to a nearby horizon, splashed with jet-black shadows flying past. Their landing piste was more than two hundred kilometers long, Fred had been told, but going as fast as they were, something like 8300 kilometers an hour at touchdown, their ship would have to decelerate pretty hard for the whole length of the track. And in fact they were still being decisively pushed back into their seats, also pulled upward, or so it seemed, strange though that was. This slight upward force was already lessening, and the main shove was back into the seat, like pressure all over from a giant invisible hand. The view out the window looked like bad CGI. Landing at the speed of their spaceship's escape velocity from Earth had allowed them to travel without deceleration fuel, much reducing the spaceship's weight and size, therefore the cost of transit. But it meant they had come in around forty times faster than a commercial jet on Earth landed, while the tolerance for error in terms of meeting the piste was on the order of a few centimeters. Their flight attendant hadn't mentioned this; Fred had looked it up. No problem, his friends with knowledge of the topic had told him. No atmosphere to mess things up, rocket guidance very precise; it was safer than the other methods of landing on the moon, safer than landing in a plane on Earth—safer than driving a car down a road! And yet they were landing on the moon! It was hard to believe they were really doing it.

"Hard to believe," Fred said.

Ta Shu smiled. "Hard to believe."

It was easy to tell when they stopped decelerating: the pressure ended. Then they were sitting there, feeling lunar g properly for the first time. Sixteen point five percent of Earth's gravity, to be exact. That meant Fred now weighed about twenty-four pounds. He had calculated this in advance, wondering what it would feel like. Now, shifting around in his seat, he found that it felt almost like the weightlessness they had experienced during the three days of their transfer from Earth. But not quite.

Their attendant released them from their restraints and they struggled to their feet. Fred discovered it felt somewhat like walking in a swimming pool, but without the resistance of water, nor any tendency to float to the surface. No—it was like nothing else.

He staggered through the spaceship's passenger compartment, as did several other passengers, most of them Chinese. Their flight attendant was better at getting around than they were, very fluid and bouncy. Movies from the moon always showed this bounciness, all the way back to the Apollo missions: people hopping around like kangaroos, falling down. Now here too they fell, as if badly drunk, apologizing as they collided—laughing—trying to help others, or just pull themselves up. Fred barely flexed his toes and yet was worse than anybody; he lofted into the air, managed to grab an overhead railing to stop himself from crashing into the ceiling. Then he dropped back to the floor as if parachuting. Others were not so lucky and hit the ceiling hard; the thumps indicated it was padded. The cabin was loud with shouts and laughter, and their attendant announced in Chinese and then English, "Slow down, take it easy!" Then, after more Chinese: "The gravity will stay like this except when you are in centrifuges, so go slow and get used to it. Pretend you are a sloth."

The passengers staggered up a tunnel. It had windows in its sidewalls that gave them a partial view of the moon, also of one wall of the spaceport, looking like a concrete bunker inset in a white hill, black windows banding it. Concrete on the moon was not actually concrete, Fred had read during the flight, in that the cement involved was made of aluminum oxide, which was very common in moon rock, and made a lunarcrete stronger than ordinary concrete. The landscape around the spaceport looked as it had during their landing, but hillier. Nearby hills were white on their tops and black below. Sunrise or sunset, Fred didn't know. Although wait; they were near the south pole, so this could be any time of day, as the sun would always stay this low in the polar sky.

Fred and Ta Shu and the rest of the passengers shuffled carefully along, either holding on to the tube's handrails or hopping up the middle of the tube. Almost everyone was tentative and clumsy. There were many apologies, much nervous laughter.

The sun spilled its jar of light over the hills. The rubble-strewn land outside was so brilliant it was hard to believe that the tunnel windows were heavily tinted and polarized. It might have been easier to move if the tunnel walls were windowless, but it did look wonderful, and the visual fix might also help people adjust to the gravity, affirming as it did that they stood on an alien world. Not that this was keeping people from going down. Fred held a side rail and tried little skips forward. Crazy footwork, ad hoc hopping—it was hard to move! No one had mentioned how strange it would feel; maybe that passed after a while and people forgot. He felt hollow, and without a plumb line to judge if he was upright or not.

Ta Shu moved just behind Fred, smiling hugely as he clutched the rail and pulled along as if on a climbers' fixed rope. "Peculiar!" he said when he saw Fred look back at him.

"Yes," Fred said. It was like weightlessness with a downward tropism, some kind of arc in spacetime—which of course was what it was. Frequent course corrections had to be made, but with very slight muscular efforts. Toes could do it, but shoes amplified what one's toes tried for. Quite awkward, actually. A feat of coordination. Tiptoeing in slow motion. "It's going to take some getting used to."

Ta Shu nodded. "Not in Kansas anymore! Where are you staying?"

"The Hotel Star."

"Me too! Shall we have breakfast together to start our day?"

"Yes, that sounds good."

"Okay, see you there."

Fred followed signs to the foreigners' line for visa control, noticeably shorter than the line for Chinese nationals. Quickly he was facing a pair of immigration officers, and he handed over his passport. The officials gave him a quick look, put his passport under a scanner, and gestured him on. Beyond the controlled area two Chinese men saw him and waved. They greeted him and led him to the next room, which looked like any other airport baggage claim area. Signage was in Chinese characters, with small English script below them.

WELCOME TO THE PEAKS OF ETERNAL LIGHT

Baggage carousels spit out luggage as at home: many black cubes with inset handles, all similar. His had a green handle. When he saw it he hauled it off the carousel, almost tossing it into the air behind him; he spun around like a discus thrower, staggered, caught his balance. He was getting yanked around by a weight of a pound or so! But he wasn't much heavier, and mass was not the same as weight, as he would have to learn. No doubt the unicaster in his luggage made it heavier or more massive than it looked.

His minders watched him impassively as he spun. When he calmed down one of them carried his luggage for him, so he could hold a handrail with both hands. Gingerly he tip-toed toward the exit, feeling conspicuous, but all the other newcomers were just as maladroit; there were still many low-impact falls, with people embarrassed rather than hurt. The halls were filled with laughter. The moon was funny!